Knock 'Em Dead

Books by Rhonda Pollero

KNOCK 'EM DEAD

KNOCK OFF

Published by Kensington Publishing Corporation

Knock 'Em Dead

Rhonda Pollero

KENSINGTON BOOKS
http://www.kensingtonbooks.com

KENSINGTON BOOKS are published by

Kensington Publishing Corp.
119 West 40th Street
New York, NY 10018

All Kensington titles, imprints, and distributed lines are available at special quantity discounts for bulk purchases for sales promotion, premiums, fund-raising, educational, or institutional use.

Special book excerpts or customized printings can also be created to fit specific needs. For details, write or phone the office of the Kensington Special Sales Manager, Attn: Special Sales Department, Kensington Publishing Corp., 119 West 40th Street, New York, NY 10018. Phone: 1-800-221-2647.

Kensington and the K logo Reg. U.S. Pat. & TM Off.

ISBN-13: 978-0-7582-1560-4
ISBN-10: 0-7582-1560-6

First Kensington Books Hardcover Printing: March 2008
First Kensington Books Mass-Market Paperback Printing: July 2009

10   9   8   7   6   5   4   3   2   1

Printed in the United States of America

Acknowledgments

Thanks to the wonderful staff and management of Barton's Jewelers for sharing their knowledge and letting me try on so many stunning pieces.

With much thanks to Donald O. Harrison, Raymond James Investments, for his crash course on all things high finance.

Special thanks to Kathleen Pickering for sharing her ring with me. I still think the research would have been more detailed if you'd just put me out of my misery and give it to me.

As it turns out, there is something a guy can't live without.

One

I was having an erotic dream about a seriously hot guy with blue eyes, and black hair—*not* Liam McGarrity, a so-wrong-for-me man who can turn me into a quivering pile of hormones with a single glance—and definitely not my perfect-in-every-way boyfriend, Patrick, when the knocking started. It was loud and insistent.

Some impatient someone wanted my attention at this ungodly hour of—I slitted bleary eyes at the bedside clock—five-twenty A freaking M. On a Sunday, no less. This better be good.

I groaned heavily, missing my thousand-thread-count sheets even before I'd tossed them aside. Patrick was just back in town, so I was dressed in a cotton tee and matching boxers. No sense wasting the good stuff when I'd spent the previous evening watching the *What Not to Wear* marathon I'd been storing up on my new DVR. A gadget I'd only been able to afford after Visa upped my credit limit.

Bam. Bam. Bam.

"I'm coming, damn it!" Three-quarters asleep, I pulled on my robe and started out of the bedroom, stubbing my toe against the bed frame in the process while whoever the idiot was at my door kept right on knocking. Like I hadn't heard the first ninety-nine knocks. Me and all my neighbors.

I winced, hopped, and cursed, not necessarily in that order. The banging on my front door became more urgent. In the few seconds it took me to hobble through my darkened apartment, flipping light switches along the way, I mentally ran through some possibilities.

Could be Sam, my upstairs neighbor and friend. Soon to be former friend if he was the one on the other side of the door.

Patrick was a more remote possibility. He flew cargo for FedEx and often arrived and/or departed at off hours. But we were two years into our relationship and he knew me well enough to know I wouldn't appreciate an early morning drop-in. Not when I'm at my most visually vulnerable, pre-shower, -hair, and -makeup.

Definitely not my mother. Even if she needed me urgently, she'd send a messenger before she'd break protocol. She doesn't even use the telephone other than during the socially acceptable hours of 10:00 AM to 10:00 PM.

I got up on tiptoes to peer through the peephole. Though the figure was silhouetted by backlighting from the parking area, I recognized my friend Jane Spencer instantly.

Fumbling with the safety chain and flipping the dead bolt's lever, I yanked open the door so fast that Jane's balled fist caught me square in the center of the forehead.

I stumbled backward, my head now throbbing along with my toe. "Jesus, Jane! What the f—"

"*Ohgodohgodohgod,*" she babbled, closing the door and gripping me by the shoulders as I teetered.

I'd met Jane at the gym almost six years ago. Though we were total strangers, we'd agreed to pretend to be friends in order to take advantage of the gym's two-for-one special. I don't like to think of it as a scam so much as the broadest interpretation of the term *friend*.

My friendship with Jane quickly became a reality and we get together whenever possible. My attendance at the gym is spotty at best. Jane, on the other hand, works out religiously, hence the reason her accidental blow had me seeing stars.

"I'm okay," I lied, shrugging off her hold. Moderately pissed, but okay. Then my vision cleared and I looked at her. Really looked at her.

Her dark brown eyes were red, puffy, and filled with a kind of abject terror I'd never seen in my calm, reasonable, rational friend. Though she looked a lot like one of the Pussycat Dolls, Jane was an accountant and investment broker. A geek in sex kitten clothing.

She was covered in deep crimson blood.

Wet deep crimson blood.

It was matted in her hair and soaked through the right side of her thigh-skimming, aqua La Perla negligee. The streaks of partially dried blood continued down the side of one leg to her bare foot.

My brain dealt with the blood first. Why she was outside, in the middle of the night, in her nightie, could wait for later. "What happened? Did you have an accident?"

Jane's fingers trembled as they snagged in the crusting blood in her hair.

I followed her as she walked stiffly into my living room, leaving single-footed, reddish brown marks on my tile and carpet as she moved, her hands hugging her bare, blood-streaked arms.

"He's dead. There was so much blood . . ."

My initial hope that maybe she'd picked up some run-over animal or something evaporated. "He who?"

"Paolo. He's dead. Oh God, worse than dead."

Paolo? The name didn't register. Nor did the concept of worse than dead. It's one of those absolutes, like being pregnant. You definitively are or you aren't.

"Back up," I insisted, gently lowering her to the sofa. I grabbed the pashmina throw draped over the back of the couch and wrapped it around her shoulders. Taking her hands in mine, I knelt in front of her. "Take a deep breath and start from the beginning."

She swallowed audibly and nodded. "Paolo was my date. You know, from that meet a rich guy introduction service Liv represents?"

Sure I remembered it. Olivia Garrett, one of our mutual friends who owns an event planning company, had been hired by a very exclusive, very expensive dating service to create "fairy-tale fantasy dates" for available men and women of means. Liv had persuaded the owners to waive the whopping five grand membership fee for Becky and Jane.

Becky Jameson and I work together at a law firm in West Palm Beach. She's an attorney in the contracts department, while I'm a few rungs down on the professional ladder. I'm an estates and trusts paralegal.

Because of Patrick, I was blissfully exempt from the free-bie. Jane was willing to give it a try. Becky was not. If I remember correctly, her exact words were, "I'd become a celibate lesbian before I'd go out on a buy-a-guy date."

Back to dead Paolo. "So he was your date and . . . ?"

"Heart Association Fund-Raiser at the Breakers. Cocktails after. Then he drove me home. He had chilled champagne waiting in the limo and by the time we got to my place I was feeling pretty good. So I invited him up for some coffee and we, um, you know. At least I think we *you knowed*."

"You don't remember?" God, sex with Patrick was methodical, but at least it was memorable.

"We must have," Jane decided with a small shake of her head. "Why else would I be wearing my get lucky lingerie?"

Good point. "And then?"

"I woke up and there was bloo—"

"You fell asleep?"

"Apparently," Jane snapped. "I know, total breach of first

sex etiquette, but I must have had more to drink than I realized and the guy was gorgeous. Anyway, he was on one side with his back to me. I thought he'd breached too, and was fast asleep, so I shook his shoulder."

I felt her shiver before she yanked her hands free of mine.

"He was ice cold, and then I went to move closer to him when I felt the wet sheets."

"Gorgeous and incontinent. Interesting combination."

Jane glared at me. "I tossed back the covers and there was blood everywhere. It was exactly like that producer guy in *The Godfather* who wakes up with the horse head in his bed.

"I think I crawled over him or maybe it was around him and I see this big knife in his chest. I pulled it out, rolled him over, and was about to feel for a pulse when I just happened to glance down and see . . ."

Jane looked like she wanted to vomit. Her skin bleached white and her eyes squeezed shut for a second.

"And saw what?"

"It was gone."

"What was gone?"

"*It*," Jane repeated succinctly.

"*It* it?" I felt disgust churn in my stomach along with serious confusion. "So what? The police showed up, took your statement, and then just let you leave? Dressed like that?"

"I didn't call them."

I practically leapt to my feet. "*What?*"

"Everything was so bloody and I'd just touched a dead guy. I was terrified and not exactly thinking straight. It isn't like I've ever awakened and found a man with his privates cut off in my bed before. Plus, I didn't know if the killer was still in my apartment so I just grabbed my keys and jumped out the window."

I blinked. "You live on the second floor."

"The jump wasn't bad. The landing was a bit of a bitch. So what do I do?"

"We call the police and then we call Becky." I reached for the phone, changing the order of the calls in my mind.

Becky answered in a groggy, guttural voice. "Hello."

I don't think I stopped to breathe as I quickly told her the tale of Jane's date culminating in the discovery of Dickless Paolo.

She mumbled a few curses, then said, "Call the police and stay put. I'll be there in thirty minutes."

"Okay."

"Finley?"

"Yeah?"

"I don't want either one of you to say a word to the cops until I get there. Understand?"

"Not a word." I glanced over at Jane, who was now curled into the fetal position at one end of my sofa. I had a feeling the cops would expect more than a "no comment" when they got their first glimpse at Jane. "Do we tell them our names?"

"Name, address, age, occupations, all fine."

"Jane is covered in blood. I'll get her cleaned up and she can—"

"No. No shower, no change of clothes. Nothing to compromise the forensics any more than they've already been compromised. Why didn't she call the police?"

"She wanted out of her apartment."

"Then she should have driven to the sheriff's office." I heard Becky's frustrated sigh. "Why didn't she think?"

"How am I supposed to know?" Cupping my hand over the mouthpiece, I whispered, "She's totally freaked out. Stop lecturing me and get over here."

I'm not sure if I said good-bye to Becky or not before calling the cops. Only that a few seconds later a calm, monotone voice came on the line. "Nine-one-nine. What is your emergency?"

I shot a quick glance over at Jane's huddled form on my sofa. "I, um, well . . . I need to report a . . . a, um, bloody friend."

"Do you need an ambulance, Ms. Tanner?"

"How'd you know my name?" I pushed a strand of my disheveled hair off my forehead. "Forget that. What I mean is, my friend was in some sort of . . . See, she had this date and it didn't go well."

"Ma'am, what *specifically* is your emergency?"

"Specifically? I think I need to report a murder."

"Who has been murdered, ma'am?"

"Paolo."

"Is that a first or last name?"

I rolled my eyes. What difference did it make? Was she going to send help or carve the freaking headstone? Jane was pretty useless, so I gave what limited information I had, including Jane's address so someone could check on Paolo.

"I've alerted the sheriff's office. Please stay on the line with me until help arrives."

I did as she asked, though it felt weird holding the receiver to my ear when we weren't talking to each other. Maybe 9-1-1 should invest in Muzak or something. Anyway, it seemed like days passed before I heard sirens and then the screech of tires. I hung up, opened my door, and counted no fewer than a dozen sheriff's cars careening into the parking lot in front of my apartment. In a matter of seconds, several of the officers leapt from their cruisers and crouched behind their squad cars, guns trained in my direction. Then I was blinded when they turned their mounted spotlights on me.

Through a megaphone or radio or whatever, a disembodied male voice boomed through the predawn quiet. "Lace your fingers and place your hands behind your head. Get on your knees. Slowly."

"But I'm—"

"Now!"

Squinting against the harsh light, I dutifully followed instructions. My pissed-off meter went into the red zone. The cement was rough, painfully digging into my bare knees. As if it wasn't humiliating enough to be assuming a position I'd only seen on episodes of *Cops*, I heard my neighbors whispering as they began stepping out of their apartments to investigate.

Jane came up behind me.

"Hold your position, Ms. Tanner," the male voice instructed. This time his tone was compassionate as he spoke to Jane. "Let us subdue the suspect before—"

I rolled my sightless eyes. "I'm not the suspect and she's not Finley Tanner. I am. I'm the one that called you." *Morons*.

Oh, and like I wasn't already mired in Suckville, a photographer's camera flash strobed where the cops had busily set up neon-yellow crime scene tape to cordon off my parking lot.

Getting the police to understand that I wasn't an imminent threat to society was a lot like trying to bathe a cat. But eventually, I was allowed to put my arms down and get to my feet. Much to the disappointment of my neighbors. My complex is a pretty laid-back place, so the commotion was a really big, if personally mortifying, thing.

Finally, two plainclothes detectives stepped forward, escorting Jane and me, with two uniformed officers trailing us inside my apartment. The female detective directed a motion with her head to the deputies. Leaving me helpless and annoyed as the officers dispersed, one went into my kitchen, while another strode toward my bedroom. "Where are they going?" I asked.

Ignoring my question, the female detective instructed Jane and me to sit on the sofa. She was African-American, with skin the color of a caramel latte. She wore utilitarian navy blue slacks and a plain white cotton blouse. No jewelry, unless you counted the silver-toned grommets on her sensible shoes. Or the gold badge clipped at her waist. I didn't.

The male detective came over to me and caught me by the elbow. There wasn't anything the least bit chivalrous about the gesture. Using my right arm like a rudder, he quickly got me to my feet and escorted me into the bedroom, pushing the door just shy of completely closed.

The detective stood next to my dresser, stiff and devoid of expression. He reminded me of the guards outside Buckingham Palace. Not that I've ever been to see the queen, but it is on my list of things to do and places to go.

Reading the gold nameplate above the badge dangling out of his right shirt pocket, I locked eyes with the detective. I didn't even attempt to soften the contempt in my tone. "Detective Graves, Jane's in shock or something. Maybe you should—"

"EMS will check her out," he said. He asked me for identification, then reached into his back pocket. He pulled out a small memo pad and took a nub of a pencil from inside the spiral binding. I grabbed my purse off the nightstand and pulled my license from my wallet.

My thoughts were fractured, racing in every direction. Jane, Paolo, blood, and the inappropriate memory of finding the pink Chanel wallet at the outlet mall. So what if the clasp was broken? It wasn't like I passed my wallet around, so my secret was safe. No one, not even my closest friends, knew that I'd been reduced to buying factory seconds. But I couldn't think about that now. Jane's predicament was far more pressing than my tenuous financial situation.

He dispensed with the standard questions—name, age, etc.—all while comparing the answers to my driver's license. "Please tell me your version of tonight's events."

"Version?"

"Yes, ma'am," he answered, pencil poised. "Approximately what time did Miss Spencer arrive?"

"Before I had a chance to make coffee," I said. I wasn't trying to be snotty, I just couldn't help myself. The detective had coffee breath and it didn't seem fair that he'd gotten his while I was expected to provide lucid answers without an ounce of caffeine in my system.

His single, bushy unibrow pinched between his chocolate-colored eyes. He was also African-American, but unlike his partner's, his complexion was very dark. He either worked out religiously or had a serious steroid problem. His neck wasn't a neck so much as a thick stump. His biceps and over-sized chest strained against the fabric of his blue oxford shirt. And his tie was at least five seasons out of date and knotted wrong. The thinner black-and-gray-striped strip hung pathetically about two inches below the front flap. In fact, now that I had an opportunity to look at him, I realized he'd worked out so much that his body no longer fit conventional clothing. The waistband on his slacks bunched beneath his cinched belt. Because of the bulk of his thighs and calves, the seams on his khaki slacks were stressed almost to their breaking point.

While some women find muscle-bound men attractive, my brain goes in only one direction. If a guy's lats make it impossible to lower his arms completely to his sides like a normal person, how does said guy aim to pee?

"The time?" he prompted.

"Five-twenty."

"You noted the *exact* time?"

"Cursed it, actually." I glanced through the slit in the door, trying to catch a glimpse of Jane. I couldn't hear her conversation with Detective Sensible Shoes, but every so often the muffled sound of Jane hiccuping wafted into my room. "She's really distraught, Detective. I know she needs medical attention."

"She'll get it," he said. "Now, if we could get back to your statement?"

Raking my fingers through my hair, I was about to give him the abbreviated version. Screw Becky's advice. In fact, screw Becky, she should have been here by now.

The radio clipped to his belt crackled, and then an almost unintelligible voice said, "One-eight-seven confirmed at 636 Heritage Way South."

Graves grabbed the radio, depressed a button, and asked for more details. "Hispanic, approximately five-ten. According to his wallet, the vic is Paolo Martinez. Palm Beach address. The ME hasn't gotten here yet, but COD is definitely multiple stab wounds and . . . uh . . . mutilation."

"Mutilation?" Graves asked. For the first time real interest seemed to kick in.

"Yeah," the voice on the radio answered. Like Jane, he seemed to have a difficult time describing the injury. "There's been an, well, um, a—"

"For Chrissake," I cut in, my hands slapping against my sides. "The killer cut Paolo's penis off."

"Yeah," Radio Voice agreed. "What she said."

"Signs of a struggle?"

"Negative. We've been unable to locate the missing, uh, er—"

I glared at Graves. Why was it so hard for men to say the word yet so easy for them to adjust it in public whenever the mood struck? Amazing. "Penis."

"Yeah. We haven't found it."

"Keep looking," Graves said.

I thought about that assignment, repulsed as I imagined how it must feel to be the one assigned to find the penis.

Graves asked me all sorts of pointless questions. Did I know Paolo?

No.

Was the deceased Jane's boyfriend?

Heck no.

Would I characterize Jane as a violent person?

Hell no.

Graves seemed frustrated by me, my answers, or both. He left me under the watchful eyes of the uniformed officer as he slipped into the living room. Balancing on the edge of the bed, I leaned to the right, hoping I might be able to catch bits and pieces of the huddled conversation between the detectives.

Silently, I tried to send Becky an urgent telepathic message to move her ass. Especially when I saw the vacant look in Jane's eyes. Hearing a knock at my front door, relief washed over me, but it was short-lived. Instead of Becky, two paramedics lumbered in, carrying what looked like large red tackle boxes.

I stood, only to have my progress blocked by Officer Useless. "Keep your seat, ma'am."

Kiss my seat, and don't call me ma'am. "I don't understand your problem," I muttered.

"Standard procedure," he said, as if that explained the whole divide and conquer thing they had going on.

"She's a dear friend who's suffered a terrible trauma. I'd simply like to offer some moral support."

"I can't let you do that, ma'am."

I swear, if he "ma'amed" me one more time Paolo wouldn't be the only one in Palm Beach County missing a body part.

The EMS guys checked Jane for injuries, flashed penlights in her eyes, and then declared her injury-free.

"Like hell," I yelled loud enough so the group in the other room could hear me. "Look at her, she's obviously in shock."

"This will be a lot easier on everyone if you calm down, Ms. Tanner," the officer insisted.

"Why the hell should I?" I asked emphatically, standing up and tugging at the edges of my robe.

The officer opened his mouth to say something just as Detectives Steadman and Graves slapped handcuffs on Jane.

"Have you all lost your minds?" I demanded as I pushed past my official babysitter. "Why are you handcuffing her? At best she's a witness and at worst, an almost-victim."

"Stand back," Graves warned in a very official tone.

"But!" I started to argue, then realized I had nothing convincing to say beyond "Vacant-expression Jane is my friend and I know for a fact she would never de-penis a guy."

My phone rang then and I was torn between answering it and a strong urge to muscle my way through the throng of cops to save my glassy-eyed friend as she was being led toward the door. Counting paramedics, there were six of them and only one of me, so I went for the phone.

"Yes?" I snapped into the receiver.

"The whole parking lot is cordoned off. They won't let me past the police line."

I added this bit of information to my growing list of irritations. "Hey, Kojak," I called to Graves, who had one hand on Jane's bound wrists and a brown paper sack in the other. He glanced in my direction as his latex-gloved minion was depositing my pashmina into an evidence bag. "We're being denied our right to counsel."

"You and Ms. Spencer will be afforded an opportunity to make a call from the station," he replied blandly.

Me? What had I done? What had Jane done? *Shit.* "Our attorney is right outside. Her name is Rebecca Jameson and I happen to know she has every right to be present during arrest and questioning."

Both he and his partner gave me that "you're a real pain in the ass" look. Not that I cared. I just wanted Becky here to put an end to the idiotic notion that Jane was in any way responsible for Paolo's death.

Graves made a call on his radio and within a matter of seconds, Becky was rushing through the door. In the forty-seven minutes since I'd made the frantic call to her, Becky had obviously been busy.

I was a scrunchie and a bad shoulder tattoo away from looking like a skanky warehouse shopper. Jane was a zombie, a barely conscious, bloody, La Perla–clad mess. Becky, however, looked polished and professional.

Her red hair was twirled into a loose knot, secured by a couple of lacquered chopsticks in the same shade of coral as her blouse and wedge sandals. With her cream jersey skirt, she had the perfect casual business look of a no-nonsense attorney. I'd berate her later for taking the time to accessorize and applying a full complement of makeup, but for right now, I was just glad she was here.

I'd known Becky since our freshman year of college, so I recognized the look of horror that flashed briefly across her face when she saw bloody Jane cuffed and surrounded by sheriff's deputies.

She introduced herself, conveniently leaving out the part about being a contracts attorney who hadn't seen the inside of a courtroom since her moot court assignment when she was a third-year law student. "Who is in charge here?"

"That would be me," Detective Steadman said, stepping out of the small group. She didn't offer Becky her hand. "I'm the lead on the case and this is my partner, Detective Graves."

Graves nodded, then walked out on my patio when his cell phone rang. His part of the conversation consisted of a series of grunts—lots of "umms" and "uh-huhs" and "reallys?"

"Do something," I mouthed to Becky.

"Unless you have cause to hold Miss Spencer, I want the handcuffs removed now."

"That isn't an option," Steadman said without inflection.

"Why not?"

"Miss Spencer is under arrest on suspicion of murder."

Suddenly my babysitter twisted my hands behind my back and slapped handcuffs tightly around my wrists. "Ow!"

Steadman's expression didn't so much as flicker. "And I'm taking Miss Tanner in as well."

"For what?" I practically screamed.

"Accomplice, material witness, assaulting an officer after she was told to stay in the bedroom. Take your pick," Graves said, his dark eyes flashing something that looked annoyingly like pleasure.

Steadman turned to Becky and added, "You have thirty seconds to vacate these premises. Based on evidence found at Miss Spencer's home and the blood trail here, I'm designating this apartment a secondary crime scene."

*A good lawyer seeks justice; a great lawyer
gets you the hell out of jail.*

Two

On the plus side, even in boxer shorts, a matching cami with demi robe, and my pink rubber beach flip-flops, I was better dressed than the half dozen prostitutes chained to the railing along the front edge of the bench. Most of the pros looked pretty haggard, except for the statuesque brunette seated next to me.

I thought about offering some free advice concerning a career change, but figured it wasn't my place. Looking down at her gigantic, scuffed leather Kate Spade shoes, I wondered if I was the one in the wrong line of work.

She noticed that I wasn't handcuffed to the bench at the same time I noticed she had an Adam's apple. I almost blurted out "You're a man" but then I figured he/she already knew that.

What the hell was taking them so long? It was well after nine o'clock. I'd been sitting on the hard bench for what felt like hours. My butt was numb. My temper was not.

The desk sergeant, after some serious threatening of a civil suit on Becky's part, agreed to remove the handcuffs. It was progress. Jane's plight trumped mine, so I hadn't seen Becky or Jane since they'd been sucked into the "Authorized Personnel" area.

Across from the booking bench—a term I'd learned about twenty minutes ago—was a long wall. It was scuffed and desperately in need of a fresh coat of paint. There were large plate-glass windows that allowed me to see out into the public waiting area. Though I couldn't hear it, I could see a grainy picture flickering from the television mounted high up on corner brackets.

I winced when footage of Jane and me doing the perp walk out of my apartment played for the umpteenth time. Hopefully no one I knew was up this early on a Sunday morning to see the humiliating images. The way my luck was running, that didn't seem like a realistic expectation.

I was sure Margaret Ford, the office receptionist and self-appointed thorn in my side, was probably gleeful seeing me on the early morning news. She'd be doing a happy dance between the traffic update from Captain Jodi, hottie helicopter pilot, and pet picks (viewer-supplied photos of everything from snakes to schnauzers), as the local station had aired the footage of Jane and me in handcuffs.

It caused an instant knot to form in the pit of my stomach. I was still on moderately shaky ground with the ultraconservative law firm of Dane, Lieberman and Zarnowski, my employers and the providers of that great thing called my paycheck. As an estates and trusts paralegal, I was expendable. Especially to Maudlin Margaret and her band of jealous secretaries—um, administrative assistants.

A few months back, I'd almost been killed trying to solve a series of murders related to an estate I'd been assigned. My direct supervisor is Vain Victor Dane, managing senior partner and king of the buffed and manicured nails.

Because she'd been there for twenty-five years, Margaret considers it part of her job description to rat me out at every opportunity. My guess is that she had Vain Dane's home number on speed dial by now. Or maybe she'd gotten so excited that she'd driven to his posh Palm Beach waterfront digs to deliver the news in person.

Vain Dane had been furious over my actions during the Hall investigation, so I knew for a fact he wasn't going to be thrilled with the news that I was again on the wrong side of the law. Particularly if he was being spoon-fed selective and unflattering facts by Margaret.

Bitch.

The passive-aggressive relationship I shared with Margaret started about ten minutes after I was hired. She didn't like that my salary exceeded hers. Forget that I actually have a degree and she doesn't. In Margaretland, all that matters is seniority.

Margaret and the Mediocre Maidens—her posse from the file room—call me FAT behind my back. Sometimes she doesn't even bother waiting until my back's turned. It has nothing to do with my size, either. I'm a respectable size 4. The nickname comes from my initials—*F*-inley *A*-nderson *T*-anner. May sound like a classic DAR name, but in truth, it's a family name. Names, actually.

Forever ago, my mother had an incredible voice and was at the beginning of a promising career with the Metropolitan Opera. Her career was derailed when nodules were found on her throat and the resulting surgery weakened her voice. Apparently, during her brief career at the Met, she'd been sleeping her way through the tech guys when she discovered she was pregnant. I should fault her for not practicing birth control, but that would mean I wouldn't exist, so I can't really go there. Based on simple math, she narrowed the potential fathers down to two, Steven Finley or Jeff Anderson.

But by the time I came along, both men were long gone— and as far as I know, neither of them knows about me to this day. Maybe I should suffer some sort of identity crisis or daddy abandonment issues, but I'm relatively normal—thanks to Jonathan Tanner. I was eighteen months old when he married my mother. Thirteen when I found out he wasn't my biological father. Mom does enjoy keeping her dramatic little secrets. By then it didn't matter. Jonathan was my father in every way even though we didn't share DNA. He loved me, which is more than I can say for my mother.

He died when I was seventeen. Since then, my mother has devoted her life to serial marriage. It's worked out pretty well for her, too. Between divorce settlements and death benefits, she's got enough money to support her search to find hubby number six in fine style. Though she never admitted it—especially to me—I'm not sure she can really love another man after Jonathan.

No doubt she'd already seen the morning news. It wouldn't dawn on her to come to my aid. Hell, she'll personalize it so that by the time we actually do talk, she'll have found a way to make the horrifying ordeal of finding my friend soaked in blood and hours in police custody some intentional and diabolical choice on my part to humiliate her. She's probably already on the phone to her travel agent and/or shrink.

I checked the clock on the wall behind the desk sergeant. Who, by the way, was sipping coffee from a foam cup. The last time I'd been awake for almost five hours without a hit of caffeine, I was in the womb.

While I was sympathetic to Jane's predicament, I knew she hadn't maimed and killed Paolo or anyone else. "What the hell is taking so long?" I grumbled. Again.

He/she patted my leg, saying, "What'sa matter, honey? Got someplace to be?"

"Logged in to eBay," I replied benignly as I inched my leg away from his/hers.

He/she looked at me as if I'd just uttered the atomic number for barium. "Is that your outcall service?" He/she lowered her voice. "What percentage do they take?"

"Outcall? No. EBay is an auction site. There's a Betsey Johnson dress in my size—worn once—and I was hoping to get in at the last second." Was I really sharing my clandestine shopping habits with a transvestite-for-hire? Apparently I was. Talk about a Fellini moment.

"Ooh. You're pretty enough. If you ever want a job, you just head on down to Riviera Beach and ask for Raylene."

Mouth dry, I nodded and stared at the floor. The good part was I doubted the he/she would out my bidding on a used dress thing to my friends. It wasn't as if I was frugal—far from it. That's the problem. Well, part of the problem.

My mother, in what she liked to call a character-building exercise, stopped subsidizing the very free shopping habits I had learned at her feet. It was her control-freak countermove to my decision not to go to law school. So, for the last seven years, I've been forced underground, into the scary but affordable world of knockoffs and online auctions. I'm pretty good at it now. By finding a decent dry cleaner that can remove almost anything and learning the archaic skill of sewing, I've beaten the master at her own game.

And believe me, Cassidy Presley Tanner Halpern Rossi Browning Johnstone is a formidable foe. If you're me. If you happen to be my perfect sister Lisa, the pediatric oncologist engaged to the blue-blood surgeon, planning the fall wedding of the century, you're golden. Truth be told, I do like my sister, even if we have drifted apart over the years. We just don't have anything in common.

Right now, I actually feel sorry for her. Between the iron-willed snobbery of David Huntington St. John IV's family and the society-pleasing whims of my mother, Lisa is having the wedding she never dreamed of.

She'll be wearing a custom Vera Wang and a St. John diamond-encrusted tiara that some descendant of the family brought over on the *Nina*, the *Pinta*, or the *Who-Gives-a-Shit*. Or maybe it was the *Mayflower*. Me? I'd be in diamond-encrusted heaven. Lisa? She's more the hospital scrubs and Jesus sandals type. She doesn't just wear Birkenstocks, she actually likes them. At any rate, seven hundred guests will be gathering in three short months at the St. John estate in Buckhead for the event of the season.

It'll be the first time Lisa's worn heels since she abandoned stilettos for a stethoscope.

Like I had any room to mock my sister's footwear. I'd just been offered a job by a ho.

"Miss Tanner?"

I was well past the point of preserving dignity. Leaping off the bench, I hurried past the come-hither scent of coffee to where Detective Steadman waited on the opposite side of a swinging gate.

The hinges squeaked loudly as she held it open and jerked her head in the direction of Interrogation Room One. The slap of my flip-flops echoed, drowning out the various telephone conversations and clicks of fingers entering information into computers. Even with the smell of too-strong, hours-old coffee, the place stunk of sweat and desperation.

She pushed open the interrogation room door and motioned me inside. The quiet click of the door shutting us in was unnerving. I was a little surprised, and a lot nervous, because Becky wasn't in the room. "Where's my attorney?" I asked as I scraped the metal chair away from the table and took a seat.

"She's with Miss Spencer."

"Doing?"

"Miss Spencer is being processed. I need your statement," she said in a no-nonsense tone as she pressed the Record button on a small tape recorder set on the table between us.

I reminded myself that I was an innocent bystander, but my heart was racing, and my clasped palms started getting clammy. "Shouldn't I wait for Becky?"

"Your call, but she could be a while."

"If you're going to arrest me—"

"I don't have grounds to arrest you at this point, Miss Tanner. I simply need you to tell me what happened, beginning with Miss Spencer arriving at your apartment. The statement will be typed, and you'll have an opportunity to read it and make any corrections before signing it. However, for your protection, I need to read you your rights. You have the right to remain silent. You have the right to an attorney. You have . . ."

My mind drifted as she enumerated each of my rights. I knew them by heart. I've watched enough episodes of *Law & Order* to know them at least as well as she did. I wanted her to move along so Jane and I could go home. Too bad I didn't have a constitutional right to tell the officer she was totally wrong about Jane.

When she finished, I said, "I already told Detective Graves everything I know."

She gave a dismissive little nod. "Miss Spencer arrived at your apartment at approximately five-thirty this morning?"

"Five-twenty," I smugly corrected her. The air conditioner kicked on, sending a low hum and rush of musty, cool air into the room. Tightening the belt on my demi-robe, I spent the better part of twenty-five minutes recounting the wee hours of the morning. That should have been it, but it wasn't.

"How well did Miss Spencer know the victim?"

"If this is going to take a while, may I have some coffee?" I knew by the smell that the coffee here would be thick and disgusting. I wanted it anyway. Caffeine was caffeine and because of the air conditioner, I was nipple-poking freezing.

The detective rose, pressed a button on a grimy intercom before barking a request for coffee, then retook her seat at the table. I was absently tracing the gouges in the laminated Formica tabletop that spelled out A-S-S-H-O-L-E, silently agreeing with the sentiment as Steadman's black eyes narrowed in my direction.

She was a daunting-looking woman. Tall, lean, and athletic. She had man hands and she bit her nails. I'd bet my Christmas bonus—the same one I've spent three times already and it's only July—that she's never had a manicure.

Then the door opened and some mousy underling brought in a Styrofoam cup. I'd been given the nectar of the gods. The fact that it was bitter, stale, and eating away at the cup was immaterial. It was coffee and it was mine.

"How well did Miss Spencer know Mr. Martinez?"

I met the woman's level gaze, wondering where she was going with that question since I'd already told Graves and anyone else who'd listen that Jane and Paolo were virtual strangers. Didn't they talk to one another? "I told you, she didn't know him at all."

"But she took him home with her?"

"Yes." Was the detective judging Jane? "The last I heard, depending on your religion, that's a sin but hardly illegal."

"Is she in the habit of taking men home on the first date?"

I swallowed a healthy amount of coffee. I didn't feel comfortable answering questions. I knew with every fiber of my being that Jane could not have killed anyone, so I didn't want to risk saying anything that might get her in more trouble. *Like there's more trouble than being arrested for murder?* "Jane isn't in the habit of dating. Period."

"Why is that?"

An image of my boyfriend, Patrick Lachey, popped into my head. He was kind, sweet, dependable, completely non-needy, thoughtful, and, on paper at least, the perfect man for me. He's a pilot. Blond, blue-eyed, and genetically perfect. His salary is good, with decent growth potential. In the two years we've been dating, he's never been anything other than an ideal boyfriend. He's everything I should want in a man.

His image slowly morphed into Liam McGarrity. He was a P.I. who sometimes did work for my firm and had helped me out on the Hall investigation. And he was trouble. I shouldn't even be thinking about Liam. A—I have Patrick. B—I hardly know the guy. C—He's still got something going on with his ex-wife, Ashley. D—Did I mention he's over six muscular feet of trouble? He's the kind of guy who makes you crazy. He has the most incredible blue-gray eyes that make you think you can fix him by falling in love with him. Well, I'm not that stupid.

At least not since I met Patrick. Yeah, yeah, my pre-Patrick dating history kinda sucks—I'm usually the first to fall for a loser and the last one to find out that the said loser is a real jerk. But Liam, I saw him coming. That crooked smile, dark hair, and those piercing eyes weren't going to reel me in. My date-a-lost-cause days are over. Probably.

The detective cleared her throat. "Tough question? I asked why your friend isn't 'in the habit of dating.' "

I felt my shoulders tighten in response to her sarcastic tone and the annoying air quotes, so it took extra effort to answer calmly, "The pool of decent guys out there is pretty shallow."

"What can you tell me about . . ." She paused, flipping through her memo pad. "Fantasy Dates?"

"It's an introduction service."

"Is that a euphemism for escort service?"

"Do Jane and I look like hookers to you?"

Slowly, Detective Steadman glanced down at my attire. I felt my cheeks burn, partly from embarrassment but mainly from annoyance. "You're the one who dragged me out of my home in my pj's."

"You were being . . . *uncooperative*."

"Handcuffs bring out my temper." I finished my coffee and held out the empty cup in a silent request for more. It was summarily ignored. Since she had me by the thong, I figured the sooner I answered Steadman's questions, the sooner I could leave. "Fantasy Dates is an exclusive introduction service. Apparently clients fill out applications, go through rigorous background checks, including financials, pay a membership fee, and then they're paired up with other eligible singles of means."

"What's the membership fee?"

"Five thousand."

"Dollars?" she asked, one badly-in-need-of-waxing eyebrow arched.

No, rupees. "Yes. I told you it was exclusive."

"Miss Spencer is an accountant?"

"And an investment broker," I added, sounding ridiculously defensive despite my best efforts to play nice.

"How did she swing the membership fee?"

"Olivia Garrett is a mutual friend of ours. She owns Concierge Plus. Liv plans parties and events. Fantasy Dates is one of her clients."

"What does she do for them?"

"When you fill out the application to join Fantasy Dates, you list your interests, favorite vacation spot, favorite wines, favorite restaurants, plays, that sort of thing."

"And Olivia Garrett does what, exactly?"

"She looks at the people's lists and then makes all the arrangements. You should probably ask her, but last week she told me one of the couples had both listed French cooking classes as an interest. Money was no object, so Liv booked them into the Ritz Escoffier Cooking School in Paris for a week."

"That sounds pricey."

I shrugged. "I'm sure it was. But that's the point. These people are accustomed to luxury and they can afford it."

"And Miss Spencer can afford it?"

I shook my head. "Liv asked the owners to comp Jane and Rebecca Jameson memberships."

"Miss Spencer's attorney is also a member of this service?"

"No. Becky declined. And last night was Jane's first date."

"So she was looking for a rich man?"

"No, she's holding out for a poor, smelly homeless guy with no ambition and a big heart."

Steadman almost smiled. Almost. "Did Miss Spencer tell you anything about her evening with the victim?"

The woman was getting on my nerves. "Jane, my friend, was bloody and babbling and scared."

"So what did she say?"

"That she and Paolo went to a charity thing, had some champagne, went back to her place, possibly had sex, then she fell asleep." When I saw Steadman's expression perk up, I realized I probably should have left the sex part out.

"Possibly had sex?" She gave an indelicate snort. "Did she tell you how someone can 'possibly' have sex?"

"Dom."

"Excuse me?"

"Dom Perignon. Apparently they had a little too much to drink in the limo."

"Does Miss Spencer often drink too much and have blackouts?"

Uneasiness settled in the pit of my stomach. "I didn't say that she had a blackout. I just said that she and her date had a little more to drink than she's accustomed to and they weren't driving, so unless there's a new law against dating while intoxicated—FYI, if there is, you're going to need a much bigger police force—neither Jane nor her date did anything wrong."

"If that were true, Mr. Martinez would still be breathing, now, wouldn't he?"

Whoever said money can't buy happiness was both poor and wrong.

Three

Liv was waiting for me outside the police station. "What are you doing here?" I squinted against the harsh sunlight as I looked beyond her. "Where are Becky and Jane?"

"Hold that question," Liv said pointedly. The area was full of people to-ing and fro-ing. And staring. We made quite a pair. She started walking and I fell into step as she shifted several pieces of crisp paper from one hand to the other, then moved her fabulous tortoise Coach sunglasses from securing her pale brown hair down to shield her stunning violet eyes. Not tacky contact-lens violet—my original assumption—but genetically perfect, exotic violet. Liv is probably one of the most beautiful women I've ever seen. The kind you want to hate on sight, but truth be told, she's so nice you just can't help but like her.

It was a struggle for me to keep up with her long strides. Liv is five-seven to my five-three; plus, she's got on killer Anne Klein sandals, adding three and a half inches to her statuesque frame. Her casual couture sundress and spanking new Coach signature soft duffel made me feel even more self-conscious as my flip-flops slapped and echoed along the stone walkway.

I quelled the urge to smack the two lowlifes giving me the once-over as they shuffled past. As if I didn't know I was out in public in my robe probably looking a lot like something a dog chewed on and spit out.

"Becky called." With her thumb, Liv clicked the silver keypad to open the doors of her champagne-colored Mercedes. "She needs you to notarize this."

She passed the pages to me as she rounded the back of the Mercedes.

I flipped through the papers as I slid into the passenger seat. The tan leather burned the back of my thighs and the air inside the car was hot and thick. I left my door open until Liv got in and turned on the engine. I suffered the blast of super-heated air knowing cool was coming. "Why do you need a financial power of attorney?"

"They're charging Jane with voluntary manslaughter," Liv said in a frustrated rush, adjusting her air vent. "Can you believe it? Our Jane?" She glanced my way. "What's the difference between manslaughter and murder?"

I blinked and opened the glove compartment, hunting around until I found the extra pair of sunglasses I knew Liv always kept on hand. She was more than just a fashionable business owner.

"Intent and/or premeditation," I answered. "And no, I can't believe it. Jane couldn't have killed Paolo. Not even in the heat of passion, no pun intended. The charge doesn't make sense, unless they're planning on upping it to murder after they gather all the evidence."

"Oh, speaking of evidence, they're also charging her with littering."

"Excuse me?" I said, turning to look at Liv's profile as she started the car. Another blast of hot air whooshed out of the vents, then immediately began to cool the interior.

"Littering," Liv repeated, jamming the car into gear. "Someone in the state attorney's office decided they'd include that because they still haven't found the penis."

Placing the pages on my lap, I pressed my fingers into my temples. Insufficient caffeine and knowing my dear friend was under arrest were making my head throb. "So why the power of attorney for Jane's assets?"

"She needs a good criminal lawyer and Becky said bail might be as high as a hundred thousand dollars."

I felt my stomach plummet. "Jane has that kind of money?" The mental image of my friend in some dank, nasty holding cell gave me a shiver. She must be scared out of her mind. Anyone with half a brain would be under the circumstances. She was my friend, I loved her, and knew she wasn't guilty of anything other than poor judgment in taking a strange man home with her. I fumbled with the seat belt. Jane wouldn't hurt a fly. Especially one with a zipper.

"Not enough, but she's got some savings and a credit line. When the bank opens in the morning, I'm going to get her cash and pull every penny possible out of Concierge Plus." Liv leaned over and cranked up the air as she glanced over her shoulder, then pulled out in the inch or so of space left between the two beaten and mangled pickups parallel parked in front and in back of her. Damn, she was good.

"Can you do that?" I asked over the sound of the pickup honking behind us, as if Liv would care that she'd cut the guy off. In Palm Beach, she who has the best car wins. "I mean, not Jane's money, the POA covers that. But Concierge Plus? You've got a partner and I'm sure Jean-Claude won't let you bleed all the operating capital."

Liv shot me a quick look. "Forget him. I'll deal with Jean-Claude. Becky gave me a list of lawyers' names and said either you or one of the bigwigs at Dane-Lieberman should contact them. It's the last page."

Like I had the clout to get any of the senior partners to do my bidding on a Sunday afternoon. I hurriedly checked the attorneys listed and whistled. "These are heavy hitters." I flicked my fingernail at one name. "This guy gets fifty grand up front. Why can't Becky represent Jane?"

"I asked the same thing. She said she's a contracts attorney and unless Jane and Paolo agreed, in writing, that he'd be breathing and have all his body parts at the end of the date, she doesn't feel qualified to do it."

Valid argument. If you're having a heart attack, you don't go to a pediatrician.

Liv's cell phone gave a muted chime from inside her purse. I started to reach into the back footwell to retrieve her bag when she yelled, "Don't!"

"Why?"

"Go ahead and check the ID. Unless it's Becky, let it go to voice mail. I've already blown off calls from nervous clients. Not to mention two from Shaylyn and Zack." I glanced at the blue LED as the phone vibrated against my palm. I recognized the 561 local area code and read out the telephone number.

Liv muttered a curse. "Ignore them."

"Them?"

"Shaylyn Kidwell and Zack Davis."

"Who are?"

"The owners of Fantasy Dates. I'm guessing they need to fire me before they sue me."

"They can't sue you," I said, trying—and failing—to sound positive. "Okay, anyone can sue anyone, but suing and winning are two different things. Besides, *you* should sue *them*. They're the ones who hooked Jane up with a guy who had a serious enemy. Serious enough to slice off his genitals."

Liv shook her head as she shivered. "And took the penis. What kind of nut job—sorry, poor word choice—would do that?"

"Someone either seriously disturbed in general, or someone who had a real issue with Paolo."

Liv stopped at the traffic light a block from my apartment

complex. "Great. Nothing like knowing there's a deranged, penis-lobbing psycho roaming the streets with Paolo's privates in his pocket."

The light changed and we drove forward. A remnant of torn yellow crime scene tape dangled from one of the trees at the entrance to the parking lot. It was a grim reminder of the morning's events, but at least it provided a momentary distraction from the scenario Liv had described.

She pulled into a spot two cars down from my leased BMW but left the engine idling. "So, you'll notarize that stuff and find an attorney? Becky said the arraignment would be sometime tomorrow morning and that we all needed to be there."

"Tomorrow?" I cried, slumping deeper against the seat. "Crap, I forgot. Judges don't sit on Sundays. No judge, no bail hearing."

"Poor Jane," Liv sighed heavily.

"We can't think about that now. We'll keep busy getting everything squared away." A very, very selfish thought ran through my mind. I was out of vacation days, so I'd have to find a creative way of getting out of work tomorrow. Screw it. I'd think of something. "My notary seal is at the office. I've got to shower first. And I'll find a lawyer, but usually they want something that resembles a retainer before they set foot inside the courthouse."

"I'm assuming you're tapped out?"

The best I could muster was a guilt-ridden shrug. "Personally? Yes. Flat broke, sorry."

"Can you ask Patrick to front you some cash?" Liv asked. "Unless you've already started easing into the breakup."

I ripped the borrowed sunglasses off my face as my eyes narrowed in her direction. "Excuse me?"

"Becky *might* have made reference to the possibility that you were considering making a, er, change."

I felt a flash of anger and betrayal. "Obviously Becky

missed the part of that conversation where I specifically asked her not to say anything to the rest of you."

"Minor slip," Liv insisted, flicking her hand so the collection of chunky bracelets on her wrist jingled. "Last week at lunch I brought up the Gagliano Labor Day party I'm doing. It will be one of the hottest parties of the summer, so I mentioned I might be able to swing invitations for all of us, including Patrick. All Becky said was I should check with you before I had anything engraved with his name on it."

"Nice," I groaned.

"So?" Liv asked, shifting in her seat as she pushed her glasses on top of her head. "Are you?"

"Probably not." I felt a rush of fear. What was I thinking? Patrick was perfect. So what if the sex was getting routine and boring? "No," I said more forcefully, not sure which one of us I was trying to convince.

I could tell by Liv's expression that she wasn't buying any of it. Since the best defense is a strong offense, I smiled sweetly and asked, "Speaking of boyfriends, how is Garage Boy?"

My friend let out a haughty little scoff. "He serves his purpose, thank you very much. Unlike perpetually traveling Patrick, he's always available."

I reached for the door handle. "Of course he is, he doesn't have a job and he still lives with his parents."

"His apartment has a separate entrance."

"Right. Put *that* in the win column."

I started out of the car when Liv grabbed my forearm. "This will all work out, right? Jane can't be tried and convicted, can she?"

I turned back and we hugged. I didn't have an answer, at least not one I could offer with any degree of certainty.

"I'm going over to Jane's to get bank statements and Becky told me to put together some clothes for the arraignment. She's going to stay with Jane for as long as possible."

That was good. That meant Jane would be in the counsel room instead of dumped into the general population at the county jail. Of course, I also knew that they wouldn't let Becky spend the night, so at some point Jane was going to be on her own.

I knew a thing or two about county lockup. During the Hall case, a part of my investigation resulted in a B&E charge. I'd spent four very creepy hours in a holding cell until Becky came to my rescue. Well, not just Becky. Liam had played a part as well. He'd not only gotten the garage owner and his friends on the police force to drop the charges, he'd also retrieved my impounded car. And ragged me. For some unknown reason, I still had the Monopoly Get out of Jail Free card he'd given me tucked into my wallet. I don't know why I hang on to it, especially since he'd scrawled a mocking note on the back. I didn't want to dwell too deeply on my motives. Liam was not an option. But Jesus, Mary, and Joseph, he was hot.

The sound of Liv's voice yanked me back to reality. "I'll call you in a couple of hours for a progress report, okay? Unless you find a lawyer before then. If so, we'll talk sooner."

I nodded. "I'm on it."

The first thing I noticed when I stepped from the car was the querying eyes peering out from several of the neighboring condos. The second thing was the layer of grimy black fingerprint dust on my doorknob. Great. I'd probably be cited by the condo association for failure to maintain the exterior of my unit. Or worse, they could ask me to vacate. Stretching on tiptoes to reach up behind the light fixture above the door, I retrieved the emergency key I kept taped to the back. Turned out to be a wasted effort. The door wasn't locked. I added that to my growing list of things to be pissed about.

My mood didn't improve much when I opened the door only to be greeted by the smudged, bloody outlines of Jane's footprints. Footprint, I mentally corrected. As if it mattered. In my mind's eye, I could see the crime scene techs photographing the stains, their L-shaped rulers marking the size and context of the evidence.

I shivered as the reality continued to set in. My apartment was a crime scene. But I didn't have the time to dwell on it. I needed to shower and dress so I could get to the office to notarize the POA and try to find a criminal attorney for Jane. I said a silent prayer that none of the Dane-Lieberman employees—specifically one of the partners—would be in the office. It was rare, but not unheard of, for one of them to drop in on a Sunday.

Apparently the blood evidence wasn't the only focus of the crime scene people. The pashmina I'd draped around Jane was gone. And I could tell my things had been moved. The picture of Patrick and me on vacation in the Bahamas last year wasn't in its usual place on top of my entertainment center.

As I put it back where it belonged, I fleetingly recalled the trip. Even though we'd gone on lots of weekend getaways, I'd kinda thought that particular Bahamas trip might lead to a proposal. That was thirteen months ago and I guess I might have said yes before he'd even finished asking the question. Now I wasn't so sure. Which made no sense.

I decided my vacillation was a result of the unpleasant combination of insufficient caffeine and lack of sleep. I couldn't do anything about the sleep deprivation or my possible Patrick issues, so I started a pot of Kenyan coffee. Instantly, my apartment filled with the tantalizing aroma as the dark, rich coffee dripped into the carafe of my brand-new DeLonghi coffeemaker. Okay, so "my" was a stretch. Technically, about ninety percent of it belonged to Visa, but I was making the minimum monthly payments. It, and the DVR, were anticipation-of-my-Christmas-bonus purchases. Now I felt more than a little guilty for maxing out my credit cards.

I'd feel like a better friend if I could contribute financially to freeing Jane. I wished I had more than eleven dollars and sixteen cents in my pitiful savings account. Hell, even selling everything I owned, I in all likelihood couldn't help with the retainer a criminal attorney would demand. Mainly because I owned very little. I'm in debt up to my hairline. My car is leased, my condo is rented, and I basically live paycheck to paycheck.

It was a depressing thought that a twenty-nine-year-old woman couldn't splurge on a really good attorney when she needed one. Luckily I was distracted by a knock at the door. It was my neighbor Sam. I adore him and we have a lot in common. We've both spent our adult lives hunting for the perfect man.

Sam's expression was all scrunched with concern as he dramatically threw his arms around me and gave me a tight squeeze.

"Thank God you're okay. I've been worried sick since I watched them put you in the back of the squad car. What on earth happened?"

I poured coffee for the two of us; then Sam followed me into my bedroom and sat on my bed while I turned on the shower and went to my closet to decide what to wear. I gave Sam a brief version of the events while I inventoried possibilities. Guilt hit me square in the chest. Here I was worried about my clothing options when Jane was undoubtedly wearing an ugly county-issue orange jumpsuit. "I'm a horrible person."

"We know that," Sam called from the bedroom. "So, did you see any hot guys in jail?"

"*You're* a horrible person, too." Grabbing a gauzy white cotton skirt, I paired it with pink and lime-green tank tops I could layer. On my way between closet and bathroom, I shot Sam a nasty look. "Hot guys? You trolling for felons now? Just for the record, I wasn't in jail, just interviewed."

"So why the handcuffs?"

I walked into the bathroom, leaving the door ajar as I stripped off my clothes and shoved them in the overflowing laundry basket. I considered tossing the boxers and the cami and I will, eventually. They'd forever be known as my jail jammies. Not very conducive to a good night's sleep.

I showered quickly, washing my hair and accepting that I didn't have time to properly blow-dry or flatiron it. Subjugating my vanity to help Jane was a no-brainer. With one towel securely twisted around my hair and another tucked around my still damp body, I did the magical "MAC face in five minutes" thing. I had enough of a tan—I know, bronze now, pay later—to forgo foundation, so I simply swiped a pinky peach blush on my cheeks and lids. A little mascara and some translucent rose gloss on my lips and I was set. In record time, I completed the transformation from pj-clad prison bitch to blond-haired, blue-eyed, cultured, casual, drop-by-the-office weekender chick.

After squeezing as much water as possible out of my shoulder-length hair, I ran a wide-tooth comb through it. A single spritz of Lulu Guinness perfume at my throat and I was done.

Sam, a consummate neat freak and talented interior decorator, had been busy. In the short time I'd left him alone, he'd refilled my coffee mug, made the bed, rearranged the symmetry of the items on my dresser, and draped a scarf over the bedside lamp. Oh, and the three throw pillows I'd just bought were nowhere in sight.

"I hate when you do that," I said, completely comfortable wearing a towel in his presence. I knew full well that if Sam ever saw me naked, he'd critique my body and suggest various plastic surgeries. Well-intentioned, of course. Just like his need to redecorate my room. He was into visual perfection and he'd probably find my body was on par with my decorating skills. Like I don't already know that I'm entering the danger zone.

Things are starting to droop and sag. Thanks in large part to my addiction to Lucky Charms. At least I'm a purist—I eat them straight from the box and delude myself into believing I'm saving calories by nixing the milk. But, as usual, I digress.

"Those pillows were all wrong. Much too large. They overwhelmed the bed and the lime green was more yellow than the lime in your bedspread." Sam laid on the bed, lacing his fingers behind his head, his eyes fixed—critically, I'm sure—on the ceiling fan.

I grabbed panties from my dresser—my irritation renewed when I realized someone had rifled through my undie drawer—and stepped into my walk-in closet and began dressing. That accomplished, I twisted my damp hair up to prevent it from soaking a big wet spot on my tops. I didn't have a hope in hell of it drying while I made phone calls.

When I returned to the bedroom, Sam was still contemplating my fan. "You know, there's a great lighting place in Boynton Beach." He waved his hands around in small circles. "I'm seeing something bolder than that fan. Something with a little color that would anchor the room." He looked over at me. "How is it you can have such impeccable taste in clothing and yet your home, your personal sanctuary, looks like a cross between yard sale and college dorm?"

This too was an ongoing lament. There was nothing soothing about having the same conversation over and over again with Sam. Very Groundhog Day–ish. "It's a work in progress. Where are my pillows?"

"Under the bed next to that ugly Christmas wreath you insist on displaying for two weeks every December even though the ribbon desperately needs to be replaced."

"My friend is in serious trouble. Do you think you could save your Extreme Apartment Makeover for another time?"

Sam had the good sense to look ashamed as he pushed off my bed. "What can I do?"

"Have any cash?"

"I've got an emergency hundred in my wallet."

Sam had only recently struck out on his own, and while

his decorating business was growing, I knew he was pouring all his money into the new venture.

He checked the diamond Bulova watch that was a gift from the cute brunette he'd dated last year. "I can swing by the ATM and see how much I have in my checking account. Will that help?"

"Everything will help," I said, placing a kiss on his cheek. "The more I can borrow from friends means the less I have to beg from my mother."

"You aren't!" he exclaimed, clearly horrified.

"No choice. A criminal attorney is going to cost a small fortune and I want to make absolutely sure we have enough money to bail her out in the morning."

"But you told me you'd gnaw off your tongue before you'd ask the Wicked Witch of the East for money. What about your sister?"

"See, this should tell you precisely how desperate I am. I can't ask Lisa. I still owe her for the loan she gave me in April."

Sam followed me through the living room to the kitchen. My ground-floor apartment was small, but the walk-out patio made it seem larger. Percentage-wise, I was much more likely to be robbed living on the ground floor, but I'd decided the patio was worth the risk. An eight-year-old could jimmy the lock on the sliding glass doors. An accomplished and/ or determined thief would probably just do a smash and grab.

The message light was flashing on my machine. My body tensed with impending dread as I gulped the rest of the coffee. Sam must have sensed my fear because he said, "You knew she'd call. Your arrest was on the morning news like every fifteen minutes. Plus, she was doing drive-bys."

My head whipped around. "What?"

"Well, either it was your mother or there's another woman driving a white Rolls-Royce with a nasty little Yorkie in one of those pet seats. She was very stealthy, though. She circled the parking lot a few times wearing big, dark sunglasses with a scarf tied on to obscure a lot of her face. Very Jackie O, dodging paparazzi."

"Great."

"Oh, and Patrick called."

"How do you know that?"

"You assigned a unique ring tone for him on your cell. I heard it when I came down earlier to see if you were back. I'm off to hit the bank. I'll call you from there."

"Thanks. Call my cell, okay? I've got to go to the office."

"Will do."

Yes, I'm a wuss. Instead of checking the messages on my home phone, I dug into the white, slightly irregular Dooney & Burke–logo purse I'd gotten on my last clandestine run to the Vero Beach Outlets. Unless you really looked, you didn't notice that one tan handle was a little shorter than the other. Thanks to that small manufacturing defect, I'd scored the purse for under one-fifty, a major D&B discount.

Scrolling through the missed calls on my cell, I discovered that Patrick had called five times in the past three hours. I smiled halfheartedly. If he really, really loved me, he would have shown up at the police station, right? Maybe not. Patrick was very considerate about my personal space. Besides, I hadn't called him. Did that mean that I didn't really, really love him? Had I wasted the last two years on a relationship with no future?

Patrick had all the qualities I was looking for in a man. All save for one. The initial physical spark had kind of fizzled. But I'd read in *Cosmo* that that was pretty normal. Something about greedy lust being replaced by comfort and security the longer two people were together. That was probably it. I was comfortable with Patrick and God knew he treated me well. But secretly, I longed for passion with a capital P, underlined in red and italicized. I couldn't remember the last time I'd felt the tingle of excitement in the pit of my stomach. Or anywhere else for that matter.

Well, that was a lie. I do remember it.

It happened a couple of months ago when Liam McGarrity walked into my office and shook my hand for the first time. Zing.

I closed my eyes briefly and dismissed all thoughts of Liam. Sucking in a deep breath, I pressed the Redial button. Patrick picked up on the second ring.

"Fin, honey, I've been worried."

He sounded so sincere that I felt more like a creep for replaying the Liam moment in my head. My guilt was so palpable that I was certain I was sending out a telepathic confession that bounced from cell tower to cell tower.

"I'm fine."

"You can't be fine," he insisted. "I saw the footage. What happened?"

I told him the sordid tale, finishing with, "So I've got a tight window to raise some cash."

"I can help with the cash," Patrick offered without hesitation, tugging at my heart. "I can get my hands on three, maybe four grand by tomorrow. Just tell me you won't do anything wacko like doing your own little investigation. Yes, you had some measure of success on that Hall thing, but you also nearly got yourself killed in the process. You're Finley Tanner, not Jessica Fletcher."

Three or four grand.

He didn't ask me to promise about the investigating thing, so I didn't feel bad about not doing so. But I crossed my fingers behind my back just in case the promise was implied despite my nonanswer. Those gods could be tricky.

Three or four grand. Three or four grand. I kept repeating that over and over. I needed the money more than I needed to comment on the dismissive way I'd taken his remark. Besides, he was right. I had gotten in way over my head in the Hall thing and had almost been killed. Patrick was just expressing concern for my safety, not diminishing me. That was my mother's domain. We agreed that I'd call him as soon as I knew the who and how much.

"Are you sure you don't want me to come over?"

"Thanks, no, I've got a lot of calls to make and I've got some stuff to do at the office." Investigating? Until that moment it hadn't even dawned on me that I could look into a few things. I knew the details of the date and I had a key to Jane's place. Wouldn't hurt to gather some preliminary information for the as-yet-secured attorney and might just give me some leverage in the hiring process.

"Fin?" Patrick prompted.

"Sorry. No, thanks. I'm fine and I know you just got back last night. How was your trip?"

"Uneventful. I got you presents."

"Thank you. Do I get a hint?" Patrick always brought me thoughtful gifts from the cities he visited for work.

"Sex on the beach."

"Ah, peach schnapps, vodka, cranberry juice, orange juice, and pineapple juice?"

"Not the cocktail," he said, his voice tinged with amusement. "Think black and red."

"A sunburned zebra?"

"Lousy guesses, Fin. You're slipping. I can swing by FedEx and get them to cash a check. I'll bring you the money and then take you out for dinner. You can probably use the diversion."

He was so sweet. How could I even think of dumping him? How stupid would that be?

After thanking him and agreeing to dinner at seven o'clock, I paused for a minute to steel myself before I called my mother. Every muscle in my body tensed as I punched her number and waited for the connection. Three rings, four rings; then her machine picked up.

"I apologize but I'm unavailable right now. Please leave a message at the tone."

Beep.

"Uh, Mom, it's Finley. I guess you saw the news this morning and, well, I need—"

Click.

"Finley Anderson Tanner," my mother cut in, using the tone a parent uses on an errant four-year-old. I had various visceral reactions to the various disapproving tones my mother used on me. This one crawled down my back like a particularly nasty black spider. I was going to have to buck up. I was going to have to beg the spider for a hefty chunk of change.

She'd probably do more than crawl up and down my back. Knowing my mother, she'd want her pound of flesh. Which was mixing metaphors, but that was my mother. A mixed bag of unpleasant metaphors.

"You were screening?" I practically choked.

"Of course. Do you have any idea how many of my friends were tuned to Channel 5? My phone has been ringing nonstop. You can't imagine how distressing this morning has been."

"My morning wasn't all that great either." I winced. Now was so not the time for sarcasm. Unfortunately, my mother had a unique ability to bring out the worst in me. Which under normal circumstances was okay, since I brought out the worst in her. I figure that makes it pretty much of a wash. But today was a long way from normal.

"What have you gotten yourself into now? And what on earth were you wearing? Your hair wasn't even combed. You looked absolutely dreadful."

"I was caught a little off guard." A *little* off guard? I admired my own subtlety.

"Without a brush or a proper negligee? What happened to the satin lilac one I gave you for your birthday?"

It's in the top of my closet with the other lilac things you insist on buying me even though I look like an autopsy photo in lilac. "It's so . . . *lovely* I save it for special occasions."

"I think an arrest would qualify as a special occasion. What happens if the St. Johns get wind of this? The wedding is ninety-one days away and now is not the time to upset them."

"I won't tell them if you don't."

"Do not get flippant with me. I've already had to cancel the Junior League luncheon today because of your antics. What *were* you thinking, Finley! How could you become involved in the murder and mutilation of a man?"

Like the murder and mutilation of a woman would have been okay? "I'm not involved," I said, striving for an even tone. "My friend Jane is."

"Then you need a better caliber of friends." I could just imagine her tattooed eyebrows trying to squeeze through the Botox into a frown. "I think you should do everything possible to extricate yourself from this mess expediently."

Ease into it. "It will all go away as soon as Jane is cleared. You remember Jane. You liked her."

"That was before she was accused of cutting off a man's . . . his . . ."

"Penis?" God, why were those two syllables so difficult for people to say? "At any rate, once Jane has a proper attorney, she'll be released on bail and I'm sure she'll be cleared in no time."

"For everyone's sake, I hope that's true."

"I'm glad you feel that way." I took a deep breath. "An attorney and bail are expensive and I don't have any cash. I'm not saying I need money right now, but just in case, will you help me?"

There was a deadly silence that didn't bode well. My mother won the battle; I cracked after sixty seconds. "I wouldn't ask but Jane is a dear friend and you just said that the best possible course of action was to get this over with quickly."

"I don't recall offering to pay for it. Really, Finley. You're almost thirty years old and you don't have any money saved?"

"It's on my to-do list." I grimaced while a neon sign flashed "Wrong Answer" in my head.

"That's your problem. The minute I got into the musicians' union, I signed up for the pension plan. Your sister, who is nearly five years your junior, has a 401(k) *and* an IRA. Granted, my pension is small, but at least I understood the value of saving and of maximizing my earning potential. You've chosen to be a secretary."

She said it as if "secretary" and "serial killer" were synonymous. I badly wanted to say, "Never mind, forget I asked," but my pride wasn't going to help get Jane a good attorney. "I'm a para—" *Don't go there.* "Mom, will you help me if it comes to that?"

"How much?"

"I don't know. Maybe nothing, maybe a lot. Or, whatever you're comfortable with."

"How do you plan to repay this money? *If* I decide to help you."

I felt a small flicker of hope. She hadn't said yes but she hadn't said no either. "I'll, um, make monthly payments."

"Are you willing to sign a note?"

Absolutely. So long as it says, "Screw you for making me grovel," in big, bold letters. "Whatever you want."

"I'll speak to my financial adviser and call you back."

"I'm in a bit of a time crunch here."

"Do you want the money or not, Finley?"

That big black spider was now crawling up my ass, but I managed to say politely, "Thank you for your generosity."

"You're welcome."

"Any chance your divorce lawyer has an in with any of these criminal attorneys?" I read off the list provided by Becky.

Her industrial-strength Botox must be fighting the good

fight against the weight of her attempted frowns today. "So you want me to have my attorney vet these names for you as well? Am I going to do everything?"

No, just two things. And I'll be paying for them for the rest of my natural life. "I would appreciate any help. As I said, time is an issue."

"You work for a gaggle of lawyers. They can't help you?"

"My firm doesn't do criminal stuff."

"It isn't your firm, Finley. You're an employee."

The spider was eating my liver. Slowly, I repeated myself in my most humble tone. "The firm I work for doesn't do criminal work."

"I won't make any promises, but I'll see what I can do."

I thanked her and hung up feeling like I'd gone all fifteen rounds in a prize fight. And lost. Deep down she was a good person. It was just hard to remember that fact when she wrapped everything in a blanket of disapproval.

With funding in the works, I needed to get to the office and touch base with Liv. I called Concierge Plus and got a busy signal. Which was weird since I knew they had four phone lines, so I tried her cell.

"I've got my loan officer on hold, he's crunching numbers to see how much I can pull out of the company and my house. I've got the Mercedes dealer on another line, trying to negotiate a decent buy-back price for my car. I've got concerned clients calling for reassurance and five more messages from Shaylyn Kidwell and Zack Davis."

"Sorry."

"Forget them, we've got to focus on Jane."

I told her that both Patrick and Sam were willing to contribute money to the cause. Then I sucked in a deep breath, let it out, and said, "My mother will probably come through with some money." My call waiting signal beeped, cutting Liv's words into undecipherable syllables. I ignored the incoming call. "Say that again."

"You called your mother? Finley, are you sure that's a good idea?"

"She's got it and—" The call waiting cut me off again. "Don't worry about it."

"Got it. We should—"

"I'd better take this," I said apologetically. "It might be Patrick or Sam."

"We'll touch base soon," Liv said. "Bye."

I tapped the Flash button to switch calls and practically growled into the phone. "Yes? What?"

"I'm guessing by your tone that handcuffs don't agree with you."

Liam's deep voice resonated through my entire body. "You saw the news?"

"Everyone saw the news. Nice robe, by the way."

"Did you call to mock me or do you have a point?"

"I called to offer my services."

That stunned me stupid but I recovered nicely. "That's fabulous. Really. Jane didn't do it."

"I don't really care whether she did or not."

"Then why are you offering to help?"

"I'm a sucker for a challenge. But you already know that."

It would help my composure if I wasn't picturing him gloriously naked in my mind. He had that kind of voice that dripped with sensuality without the slightest effort on his part. While I didn't want or need a distraction, a P.I. would be a great addition to the Free Jane Team.

"Finley? You there?"

"Yeah, I was just . . ." I stopped talking and started shuffling papers around on the countertop. He didn't have to know the papers were takeout menus. "Thank you. Can you meet me at my office? I'll fill you in on the details and then we can decide on the best plan of attack." *Something, please, God, more appropriate than my overwhelming desire to jump your bones.* The image of his gloriously naked body was burned into my brain.

"Sure, whatever you need."

Sex. Lots of sex. "This is really nice of you."

"And it gets better."

Naked. Naked. Naked. *Stop it!* "How?"

"Because Jane's a friend of yours, I'm even willing to cut my fee in half."

Prick. Prick. Prick.

Sex is good; spontaneous sex is even better.

Four

Sam met me at the coffee shop off Clematis Street a couple blocks from my office. Not only did I get a Café Vanilla, slushy frappuccino out of it, he also handed me five hundred dollars in a crisp white envelope. As a token of my gratitude, I bought him a Chai Tea. The gesture was definitely laced in irony since I'd just spent basically my entire savings on the two drinks. I consoled myself by focusing on Sam's donation instead of berating my piss-poor ability to manage money.

We parted ways at the street corner with our usual European-style, both cheek kisses. While I wasn't totally comfy with it, the European beat the hell out of the country club air kisses I'd grown up with.

Okay, confession time. Not wanting to risk being caught at the office on a weekend, I'd parked at City Place just in case anyone other than maybe the janitorial staff was at Dane-Lieberman. Tucking the power of attorney under my arm, I freed my hand in order to push the strap on my slightly irregular purse higher on my bare shoulder.

It was hot. Then again, it was July and the streets were crowded with people rushing to make the matinee performance at the Kravis Center. Who knew so many people would be in such a hurry to see John Davidson?

I tried to use what little shade was available. Not because I don't worship the sun; I do. I was simply trying to avoid unwanted tan lines from forming during my ten-minute walk.

As soon as I turned the corner to the six-story building occupied entirely by the firm, my stomach clenched. Ellen Lieberman's beige Volvo was in the parking lot. Normally, I'd simply dismiss that since she had no life outside the office and often spent her dateless weekends writing and reviewing mind-numbing contracts. I almost envied Ellen—somehow she'd managed to put her hormones on hibernate. Either that or she had the estrogen level of a postmenopausal corpse.

No, the Volvo wasn't the reason acid was burning through the lining of my stomach. It was spotting the H3 Hummer taking up two spaces across from the sensible silver Neon.

The banana-colored H3 Hummer was the newer, smaller model Vain Dane claimed he purchased as some sort of concession to gas prices. Right, like the sixteen miles per gallon it gets is a huge savings over the thirteen miles per gallon he was getting in the black urban assault vehicle the banana had replaced. Who needs a Hummer in South Florida anyway? The closest thing we have to a hill is Mount Dora, which isn't a mountain or hill so much as a tourist haven just north of Orlando. There are some cute shops there, and most visitors walk away with a sticker that reads I CLIMBED MOUNT DORA firmly affixed to their bumper.

The silver Neon belonged to Margaret.

Shit, shit, and triple shit. Any hope I had of making a covert trip to my office was history. Fleetingly, I considered shimmying up the drain spout to my second-floor office. But I'm not a great shimmier. My last attempt at climbing an obstacle had resulted in a nasty bite courtesy of Boo-Boo the guard dog. So I had no option other than to waltz in the front door, head held high, palms sweating profusely. Margaret was an annoyance but having two of the active senior partners in the building bordered on terrifying. It made me long for the days when sweet old Thomas Zarnowski ran the firm. Not only did he hire me right out of college, he actually liked me. He was semiretired now, and sorely missed. At least by me. Especially after he'd crowned Vain Dane as his successor.

I knew even before I reached for the double doors with the firm's name etched in posh gold lettering that Margaret would be at her post like some freaking God-Country-Corps Marine. The only difference being, Margaret didn't have an M16. At least I didn't think she did.

As expected, she was seated behind the freshly polished, crescent-shaped reception desk. In one of her frumpy suits, no less. Margaret obviously maintained her rigid if god-awful standards regarding workplace attire, even on a Sunday. The only difference between workweek Margaret and weekend Margaret was the ever-present Bluetooth absent from its usual place plugged into her right ear.

Her dull brown eyes followed me like hate-filled tractor beams as I crossed the lobby. To her credit, she made a weak attempt at a compassionate smile. "On instruction of the partners, I've been calling your home and your cell for hours."

Then you must know I've been dodging those calls. "Sorry, it's been a . . . crazy morning and I must have forgotten to turn on my cell." I reached into my purse and switched the phone to vibrate. The last thing I needed was for it to ring while I was lying like a rug. "Yep. Turned off."

Margaret went for the elaborate intercom panel as she lifted the receiver. "I'll let them know you've arrived."

I bet you will. "Could you give me five minutes?" I asked.

Margaret was about to refuse when I did an exaggerated little foot-to-foot dance and lifted my coffee higher in the air.

"I really need to hit the powder room first."

"Five minutes," she grudgingly agreed.

I felt her light-saber eyes shredding me all the way to the elevator. Tucking one earpiece of my can't-tell-the-difference-unless-you're-up-close faux Gucci sunglasses in the front of my layered T, I pressed the button and listened to the slight buzz as the compartment climbed the two floors. The arrival *ding* of the elevator echoed loudly in the deserted space. The scent of furniture polish, deodorizer, and industrial cleaner greeted me as I exited to the left.

The layout of my floor is a lot like a rat's maze. The center area is a complicated labyrinth of open cubicles. The twenty or so workstations are for interns and other support staff. When the office is in full swing, the vast area is a noisy, distracting place to work. I know. My first desk at Dane-Lieberman was a postage-stamp, single-drawered built-in desk in the third cubby to the right. No privacy, no personal adornments, and absolutely no opportunities to linger over long lunches.

Eventually, I'd earned a private office. After solving the Hall case, I'd gotten a decent upgrade. Not only did I have a shiny new nameplate mounted next to my door, but I had a bigger window and a better view. Okay, so it overlooked the parking lot, but hey, it was a step up from the air conditioners outside my old office.

Out of habit, I turned on the coffeepot I kept on the credenza behind my veneered desk as soon as I sat down. My notary stamp and seal were in the top drawer. I got them and retrieved the power of attorney from my purse. It took just a few strokes of a pen, a little pressure on the stamp, and a pinch of the metal seal-embossing tool and the document was ready for Liv to present it at the bank.

I'd used four and a half of my allotted five minutes. I considered taking a roady of coffee but thought better of it. I didn't want anything in my slightly shaky hands. Especially not coffee when I was wearing a white skirt.

I breathed deeply and evenly, something I'd learned in the only yoga class I'd managed to attend even though I'd paid for a full year of sessions. Apparently a single class wasn't enough to convince your heart to stop pounding against your rib cage when summoned to meet with your bosses in the executive offices on the top floor.

Crap, I should have brought a pad. Vain Dane got off on people taking notes. It must have made him feel powerful.

Which he was since his ultraconservative butt had the power to fire me.

Walking past the pin-neat, unoccupied desk of Dane's executive secretary, I slowly went down the corridor toward the impressively carved mahogany door to Dane's office. Catching a whiff of Burberry cologne was slightly soothing. The signature scent reminded me of Jonathan Tanner. Even though he'd been gone for more than a decade, I missed him every time I smelled that cologne.

The door was ajar, but I knocked and waited to be granted entrance.

"Come," Dane's voice boomed from inside.

Victor Dane's office was very posh, very masculine, and very, very self-congratulatory. The walls were lined with various diplomas, awards, and community service acknowledgments. The custom shelving held professionally framed photographs of Vain Dane with various celebrities, politicians, and dignitaries, including a nearly twenty-year-old photo of Dane dancing with the Princess of Wales at the Palm Beach Polo Club.

Dane was seated at the edge of his desk, arms folded, expression hard. Ellen Lieberman was seated in one of the leather chairs opposite Dane. She seemed more relaxed and while she wasn't overtly friendly, I didn't get the angry vibe from her that was practically dripping from Dane's body language.

The wall behind Dane's desk wasn't a wall. It was a floor-to-ceiling window with breathtaking views of the intracoastal Palm Beach proper and the Atlantic Ocean in the distance.

The silence dragged on so long that I contemplated throwing

myself through said window. Not a good plan since Jane needed my help and I knew the glass was impact-resistant and hurricane-proof, so my 107-pound body would just bounce off.

Dane reached behind him, grabbed the phone, and pressed the button. "Margaret, thank you. You can go."

To hell, I added mentally.

If Dane was the picture of coiffed and polished, Ellen was his exact opposite. He was dressed in casual but expertly tailored navy blue slacks, a gunmetal-gray golf shirt, and navy blue Bruno Magli loafers.

Conversely, Ellen looked like she was on her way to an audition to play a bulimic, red-haired version of Cass Elliot. Some sort of shapeless dress made from a bright paisley print hung from her slight shoulders. If she had a waist, it was lost inside the yards of fabric. Her naturally curly hair, complete with ignored gray streaks, was secured with a black velvet barrette at the nape of her pale neck. Black was apparently part of her accessory scheme. The straps of her sports bra were black, as were the black Oasis sandals. I knew the shoes cost almost a hundred bucks; I just couldn't understand why anyone would pay that kind of money for something so intentionally unflattering. Well, yes, I did. They were practical and functional. Just like Ellen.

"Sit," Dane said as he strode around to his thronelike chair and took his seat.

I did as instructed and ignored my nerves begging me to ask for a fake bacon treat in recognition of my obedience. Dane didn't care for, nor did he share, my sense of humor or my irreverence. He was kinda like my mother, only with testicles.

Running his palm over his artificially darkened hair, for a split second the sunlight glinted off his overly buffed nails. The prisms of light arced across the ceiling, disappearing as soon as he laced his fingers and rested them on his desk.

My heart rate picked up again. I'd seen this posture before. He'd assumed the same position just before he'd suspended me, without pay, for a month.

"I'm sorry about this morning," I said.

"I'm sure you are," Dane agreed, his tone tinged with annoyance. "Which is why we're having this meeting."

I glanced over at mute Ellen. To my surprise, there was a touch of compassion in her green eyes. Thank God. Her feminism could have kicked in and maybe she'd be my ally. Now I was sorry I'd mentally berated her shoes.

"Ellen and I have discussed your situation at length and have made some decisions that directly concern you."

"I didn't do anything," I insisted, hating that my words came out so wimpy and whiny. "My dear friend came to me for help and then the whole situation kind of snowballed out of control."

"We know," Ellen said. "I've spoken with Becky several times today."

"But," Dane injected quickly, "that doesn't mean that we aren't going to set some parameters."

That sounded a lot like new rules for me. Ones I wasn't going to like. "O-okay."

Ellen crossed one unshaven leg over the other. "I made some calls at Becky's request," she began. "Jason Quinn is willing to meet with you at five at his Boca Raton office."

I blinked. Jason Quinn was an über-lawyer. And his services came at an über-price. "Thank you. He's very expensive."

"Becky led me to believe that you and several other friends of the accused would be able to raise the necessary funds." One of Ellen's red brows arched questioningly. "Is there a problem?"

Accused? Hearing Jane slapped with that moniker riled my temper. I shook my head. "No. I'm on it."

"You understand that you have to limit your involvement in this case, right?" Dane asked me.

"That might be hard. The police have already taken my statement."

"I'm not talking about that. I'm simply reminding you that as an employee, you can't use the resources of this firm for your own purposes."

"I wasn't planning on using anything," I said over the angry lump in my throat. "I've been focused on raising bail and finding Jane an attorney."

"Ellen has arranged for you to meet with one of the best criminal lawyers in South Florida. And just so we're clear, that was a favor to Becky Jameson and it will be the end of your participation in any defense mounted by the accused."

"Jane and I are friends," I explained, trying not to clench my jaw. "I'm not going to turn my back on her when she's eyeball deep in sh—trouble."

"That's not what we're saying," Ellen injected. "We're simply telling you that in exchange for the introduction to Jason Quinn, we'll need your word that you won't go off half-cocked like you did the last time."

"I solved the case."

"Yes," Dane acknowledged, though he looked as if he'd choked on the syllable. "But you also placed yourself in great danger and garnered a lot of press for this firm. Negative press. That isn't how we do things around here, Finley. This firm exists entirely on reputation. I won't have it impugned because you do crazy things like you did this morning."

"*I* didn't drag me off in handcuffs." I could practically feel my blood boiling in my veins.

"The way I understand it, you wouldn't have been handcuffed at all had you not shoved that deputy, then been mouthy and argumentative with the detectives," Dane said. "So I will repeat. After the arraignment, the only person from this office authorized to involve herself in this case is Rebecca Jameson."

"Because?"

"She's a lawyer," Dane answered, as if that explained all the great unknowns in the universe.

I got to my feet. "Are you telling me I can't visit my friend? Support her through this?"

Ellen just sat there. Dane shook his head. "Becky said it was important for you to attend the arraignment tomorrow, so I'm giving you the day off."

"Thank you." *I think*.

"After that, I want your word that you will cooperate fully with the police and the attorneys. Other than that, I don't want to see your name in the paper or your face on the news. Clear?"

"Crystal." With my spine stiff, I pivoted on the ball of my Cindy Says sandals and started to leave.

"Finley?" Dane said.

"Yes?" I half turned to glance back in his direction.

"One misstep and I will fire you. No suspensions this time."

And no compassion either. I took some of my frustration out on the elevator button, punching the Down arrow with my knuckle. It didn't help and now my finger hurt.

I glanced down at my watch and frowned. It was a little after two and all I really wanted to do was hit the closest bar and get drunk. Not an option, since I had to call Liv, check on Jane, drive to Boca to meet *the* Jason Quinn, and then meet Patrick for dinner. Since getting drunk wasn't feasible, I did the girlie thing and started to cry while I was still in the elevator. Not *cry* cry, more like sniff as my eyes welled with tears. Tears of anger, frustration, sleep deprivation, and an overwhelming sense of impotence.

I brushed the tears off my cheeks on my way back to my office. Margaret was gone and I knew from hearing the tail end of the conversation between Ellen and Dane as I was leaving that they were on their way out, but still, I didn't want to walk the halls weeping like an unprofessional loser.

I had one foot in the door when I spotted Patrick placing

a vase of white roses in the center of my desk. With my emotions still raw, I was definitely glad to see him. He turned and flashed me that perfect smile, and I rushed forward into the haven of his embrace. It felt good to be held.

Patrick brushed the hair off my forehead, then tenderly cupped my face in his hands. Our eyes met before he lowered his mouth to mine.

The kiss was soft and gentle. But I didn't want soft and gentle. My day had seriously sucked and I'd earned a few minutes of wild lust.

After practically jerking Patrick around, I hopped up on my desk and pulled him into the cradle of my thighs. I expected him to get hard immediately; after all, it had been weeks since we'd last been together. When it didn't happen immediately, I locked my arms around his neck and thrust my tongue hungrily into his mouth.

My skin warmed. Patrick didn't. His fingers gripped my forearms but he neither pushed me away nor pulled me closer. "Fin," he said against my mouth. "This isn't the best place for this."

I swallowed a groan. Once, just this once I wanted him to get off script and have some quick, spontaneous sex with me. "No one's here," I assured him as I made teasing circles with my fingernails up and down his back. Then I slipped my hand between us and stroked him through the fabric of his cargo shorts. The parachute-thin material and my determination made it impossible for him to do anything but respond.

Okay, so it wasn't rip-your-clothes-off passion, but Patrick got with the program and began nuzzling my neck, nibbling and kissing his way down the side of my throat to my collarbone.

I sucked in an excited breath when his teeth tugged the straps of my tops off my shoulder. At the same time, his hand slipped up and tested the weight of my breast.

My fingers weaved into his hair, pressing him to me as heat poured into my belly, feeding my sense of urgency. A small moan gurgled in my throat when his thumb flicked across my erect nipple. With incredible one-handed dexterity, I managed to free the button at his waistband and had the pull of his zipper between my thumb and forefinger when I heard a sound.

Patrick leapt away from me before my I-need-sex-saturated brain could even process the sound. He stumbled into one of my office chairs, leaving me to face the man framed in my doorway.

Liam McGarrity was wearing jeans, a faded cotton island-print shirt, and an unapologetic grin. "Sorry, didn't mean to interrupt your, er, thing."

Before I got off the desk with what little dignity I had left, I straightened my clothes and waged a fruitless battle against the heated blush beginning to sear my cheeks and throat. It wasn't until I put my feet on the floor that I realized one of my three-inch wedges had come off, leaving me no option but to hobble over to my chair like Quasimodo on his way to ring the bell.

The urge to dive under my desk was tempting but impractical. The amusement in Liam's eyes didn't do much to improve my mood. I fluffed my hair with my fingers in a futile effort to look less like I'd just been caught in the act. Well, the lead-up to the act.

Liam sauntered over to Patrick and extended his hand. "We met at the hospital."

The two of them shook hands as Patrick stood. His button was still undone but his erection was history.

"Yeah, right. You're the investigator?"

"That's me," Liam replied, still gripping Patrick's hand. "How was New York?"

I was starting to feel invisible, since the two of them hadn't so much as glanced in my direction. "Patrick flies international, not domestic."

Liam shrugged. "Sorry. My mistake."

"Not a problem," Patrick said, his cheeks slightly flushed.

He fished his car keys out of his pocket as he turned in my direction. "I've got to hit American Eagle Outfitters before they close."

My mind went blank and it must have shown on my face.

"The hiking trip?"

"Right." I nodded. Then my body tensed. "You can't leave in the morning. Jane's arraignme—"

Patrick held up his hand and offered a warm smile. "I've already switched my flight to six PM. I'll be there for you and the girls."

The fact that he called us "girls" rankled for about thirty seconds. The realization that he still planned to go on his vacation was just damned irritating. Especially since Liam was just standing there, thumbs hooked in his belt loops, obviously enjoying his role as a fly on my wall.

Patrick came to my desk and leaned over the roses to kiss my cheek. "Oh yeah. I almost forgot." He reached into his back pocket and handed me a stack of bills.

"Thank you."

"I could only get three," he said.

"That'll help," I assured him. "We'll pay you back."

He tapped the tip of my nose. "Don't worry about that now. We still on for dinner?"

"I've got a meeting in Boca at five."

"Not a problem. Just call if you're running late."

It was really hard to stay mad at Patrick when he'd just handed me three thousand dollars, delivered roses, changed his flight, and happily took off any time pressure I might feel about our dinner.

Conversely, it was a piece of cake to transfer my pissed-off mood to Liam. "What are you doing here?" I demanded as he folded his large frame into one of my chairs.

"You told me to meet you here, remember?"

Oh, crap. "It slipped my mind."

"I guessed as much when I walked in and your boyfriend

had you bent over your desk. Those must be some magic roses."

I pulled one from the vase and breathed in the fresh, clean scent. It was better than focusing on the fact that Liam smelled of soap and masculinity. Obviously my endorphins were still pumping. Either that or a few hours sharing a bench with prostitutes had turned me into a slut.

"How's the wife?" I asked, slapping a sarcastic smile on my face.

"Ex-wife, and she's great. Her salon opens next week."

"How nice for her."

He shot me that famous, lopsided, toe-curling grin. "Don't you like Ashley? She's a decent person and she likes you."

If she's such a freaking saint, why'd you divorce her? Why are you still sleeping with her? Why do I give a flying fig? "I hardly know her. Can we talk about Jane's case now?"

"Your meeting."

I got coffee for both of us, then did a thorough recap of the case. "So, I got to thinking, maybe Jane and Paolo were drugged. What if the killer slipped something in their drinks? That would explain why she doesn't remember if they had sex or not. And why she fell asleep. *And* how the killer could slip in, kill Paolo without a struggle, then slip out unnoticed."

"Interesting theory."

My mood brightened. "So, will you help me?"

"No."

My jubilee faded. "No?"

Liam shook his head, causing a lock of his jet-black hair to fall haphazardly across his tanned forehead.

"Why not?"

"I took a job from a new client an hour ago."

"But you called me this morning. You said you'd help."

"At a reduced fee. Sorry, sweetheart, but I got a better offer."

"From who?"

"Ellen Lieberman."

"Doing what? Following some insurance-defrauding plaintiff all over town?"

"Nope."

"Doing background checks on corporate clients?"

"Nope."

My blood pressure was soaring. "Walking her dog?"

Liam chuckled softly. It was a deep, resonant sound that seeped straight into my cells. "Nope."

I grabbed my purse. I was tired of playing games with him and said as much. "Go be Ellen's flunky. I don't care what you've got to do. I've got to get to Boca."

"So do I."

"Because?"

"That's my job."

I froze. "What?"

"Lieberman hired me to keep you out of trouble."

My eyes narrowed. "Since when does she care if I'm in trouble?"

"I didn't get the impression she does, but Becky got to her. Lieberman insisted on a guarantee."

"Like?"

Liam stroked the half day's stubble on his chin. "Like you can't investigate the murder."

"Not going to happen."

"I didn't think so."

"Then why take the job?"

"I told you, I like challenges."

You can either learn from your mistakes or just
repeat them over and over and over.

Five

Like my apartment, Liam's car is a work in progress. And like my apartment, I didn't see any progress. His 1964 Mustang had grayish putty along the driver's side, and the rust spots on the hood had faded to sun-bleached blue. The *pièce de résistance* was the duct tape holding the side mirror in place.

"Go ahead, get it out of your system," he said.

"What?" I asked innocently.

"I can tell you're dying to say something bitchy about my car."

Liam had an unnerving ability to read my thoughts. Scary. Frequently *I* didn't want to be in my own mind. And I sure didn't want Liam peeking inside when my thoughts of him were erotic, bordering on carnal.

Time to redirect my thinking. "Nothing to say. Your car speaks for itself. Besides, I'm more worried about impressing Jason Quinn."

"No," he countered. "You want to *hire* Quinn. Making your car a poor choice. You should consider taking mine."

My BMW was, if I did say so myself, a thing of leased beauty. I wouldn't trust his to get me to the grocery store. "Why?"

"Yours is all wrong for this sort of meeting. It implies that you have financial resources. Which we both know you don't."

My back stiffened at the accurate but unflattering summary of my money situation. "How do you know I don't have money?"

His square-tipped fingers splayed at the center of my back as he steered me in the direction of his dilapidated excuse for transportation. The strength and heat of his touch penetrated both layers of cotton, stirring an unwelcomed warmth in my belly. Much as I wanted to, I couldn't very well blame this involuntary reaction on the lingering effects of my almost-sex with Patrick.

Liam opened the passenger door for me. It creaked loudly, then made a crunching sound as if the door might drop from the hinges at any second. "Where are you taking me?"

"To get your car."

"It's parked near—"

"Macy's," he finished as he got behind the wheel, key hovering just above the dashboard ignition. "Very frugal, and probably a first, to choose metered parking. Must have been quite a sacrifice for a valet girl like you."

"You're making me sound like I'm one step away from eating government peanut butter." Not all that far from the truth, but I wouldn't tell him that. "I'm not desperate."

"Is that why your boyfriend slipped you cash? I'm guessing three or four Gs based on the size of the wad. Then there's the thin bank envelope in your purse, probably a smaller donation from another friend. Your notary stamp was on your desk, so someone else—I'm thinking Jane, since she's the one who's indisposed at the moment—gave you power of attorney to drain her accounts before the arraignment in the morning. All adds up to the classic profile of a compulsive shopper. Maybe you should think about a twelve-step program."

"What are you? My babysitter *and* my financial adviser? Besides, you're wrong about Jane giving me her power of attorney." The rest of his assessment was pretty dead-on, so I clung to the one detail that proved Liam McGarrity was fallible. "It's illegal to notarize anything when the notary benefits from the document."

"Whatever."

He started the engine. Or more precisely, it took three attempts and a lot of mechanical grinding sounds before the car sputtered reluctantly to life. The roar of the engine was deafening and the pitiful excuse for air-conditioning did little more than circulate the stifling air.

When Liam rolled down his window, I did the same. Not that it made much of a difference. Sweat glued my back to the torn leather seat and I felt perspiration begin to trickle down my cleavage. I tasted exhaust soon after he'd pulled into traffic.

Liam seemed immune to the heat. At least that was my impression when I flashed a quick glance in his direction. Okay, only part of my impression. An unimportant part. My brain detoured to the danger zone as I mutely admired his profile.

He wasn't the *GQ* polished type that normally popped up on my radar. Strike one was his clothing. His jeans were faded and fraying at the seams and the edges of a small tear just above his left knee. But the mold of the soft fabric flattered his really impressive thigh muscles. Strike two was the shirt. I'm not fond of island prints, unless it's Tommy Bahama, which this wasn't. But the white background and palm tree motif did complement his complexion. Well, they would have if he'd bothered to stand a little closer to his razor. Strike three should have been the scruffy, Colin Farrellesque hint of a beard, but it was too sexy to warrant a strike.

My other third strike option was his black hair. Not the

color; that suited the seriously tall, dark, handsome thing he had going on. It was more about the fact that his over-the-collar hair desperately needed a trim and was completely devoid of product. What man didn't use product these days?

Not classically handsome Liam, with his slightly crooked nose. My guess is it's been broken. Maybe more than once.

I had to stop obsessing over him. It wasn't healthy. And it wasn't fair to Patrick. Though my interest in Patrick seemed to be slipping on an almost hourly basis. I blamed Liam for that. It was easier and more convenient than confronting my growing ambivalence toward a man who'd been a good, supportive, kindhearted, thoughtful, and decent boyfriend for two years.

All I really knew about Liam was that he was still boffing his ex and he used to be a cop. Deciding I had no desire to discuss his sex life, I asked, "Why'd you leave the police force?"

"It was time."

Exasperated, I shook my head as I let out a slightly frustrated breath. "Because?"

"It was time," he repeated as he pulled alongside my car. "Enjoy your trip to Boca."

"You aren't coming with me?"

He shook his head, then leaned across me to open the door. In the process his forearm brushed against my breasts and I had to press my lips shut to keep from letting out a gasp.

"Nope. The partners gave the green light for you to meet with the attorney."

"But aren't you getting paid to keep an eye on me?"

"Not until you start screwing up. If you take the turnpike, there's a Starbucks in the service plaza just north of Boynton Beach." He checked the Breitling Chronograph watch on his tanned wrist. "Gotta go. I have a thing. We'll touch base soon."

Liam was famous for his "things." While I didn't have any

proof, I was fairly sure "thing" was synonymous with hooking up with his not-so-ex. The expression irritated me so much that I was tempted to slam the door on his prized Mustang. I would have too, except that my attention was diverted to the yellow parking ticket tucked under my windshield wiper.

"Later," he called as his trash heap of a car spewed bluish smoke while he drove away.

"You have got to be kidding me!" I groused loudly as I grabbed the ticket and discovered I now owed the City of West Palm Beach fifty-three dollars because I hadn't put enough money in the freaking meter.

Fuming in silence, I stuffed the ticket in my purse, got in my car, and headed south on I-95 to Okeechobee, then cut over to the turnpike. Because it was a toll road, traffic and construction weren't a problem. I had a vague idea where Quinn's office was, but just to be on the safe side, as I slowed to go through the SunPass lane at the tollbooth, I pulled my cell phone out and adeptly called up the navigation software, queried the exact street address, then selected VOICE COMMANDS. Hitting the SPEAKER feature, I laid the phone on the passenger seat, knowing it would guide me to my destination.

A new toy always boosts my spirits and this was the first time I'd used the get-me-there feature on the new phone. Well, new to me. I picked it up on eBay for a fraction of the retail price. Though it had a small scratch where the QWERTY keyboard tucked away, that was the only visible imperfection. One of the tech support guys at my office switched out the SIM card and loaded lots of fun things for me—all gratis.

Yes, I knew he'd wanted more than a polite thank-you for his troubles, but that was his delusion. I never said I'd trade sexual favors for cell phone setup.

I'd gone less than fifteen miles when I veered off into the service plaza. My stomach was growling reminders that I had yet to eat. I smiled as I headed inside the building, remembering something Jane had said a few weeks back when we'd gone to John G's in Lake Worth for Sunday brunch and an afternoon at the beach.

"Finley," she'd begun, her brows pinched in a frown as she watched the server place a plate of biscuits in front of me. Her plate was a large assortment of fresh fruit with a side of fat-free yogurt. "The body should be treated like a temple, not a drive-through."

My smile faded. I was still having a hard time reconciling the fact that Jane was in serious trouble. Plus, I couldn't get the image of her covered in blood out of my mind.

The service plaza was an odd collection of fast food joints, tourist information stations, souvenir stands, vending machines, and large, basically clean bathrooms. I hit the ladies' room first, washed my hands, and reapplied lip gloss. My hair had seen better days, but all in all, I was presentable.

I was also running low on cash. So low that I had to settle for a Tall Coffee of the Week. Slipping the hot sleeve over the white cup, I wandered past rows and rows of local attraction brochures. The offerings from the Orlando area didn't intrigue me nearly as much as the color tri-fold map of Sawgrass Mills Mall. Three hundred fifty name-brand outlet stores all under one alligator-shaped roof. It was a bargain hunter's mecca, one I couldn't indulge given the dire circumstances of my friend. Not to mention the near capacity balances on my credit cards.

Digging into the bottom of my purse, I foraged around. I had exactly two dollars and eleven cents in change. Enough for a medium-sized bag of peanut M&M's. Protein. That was healthy. Chocolate covering, well, that was just necessary.

Once I was back in the car, I was directed onto the turnpike by the pleasant British accent belonging to the computer-generated navigational assistant. Boca is one of the hot spots in Palm Beach County. Like every place else in the state, the city was a mix of posh communities, old-style Florida homes, and compact trailer parks. Though in recent years, thanks in large part to hurricanes, many of the aluminum mansions had blown away, opening up small tracts of land to developers. The new construction didn't include trailer parks, or anything even remotely resembling affordable housing. Every sign I passed as I weaved my way through downtown Boca advertised preconstruction prices between the mid five hundreds to in excess of a million dollars.

The rent on my thirteen-hundred-a-month apartment was a virtual bargain.

Even without the aid of the Daisy the Direction Giver, I spotted Quinn's satellite office from two blocks away. It was all glass and shaped like a skinny pyramid. There was some sort of wash over the glass, making the building reflect the golden rays of the sun.

I found a parking spot around the corner from the office—not metered—put my cell back in my purse, and headed up to meet the great Jason Quinn.

The door was locked, so I tried the button set in a bronze faceplate just to the left of the door. Simultaneously, a buzzer sounded and I heard a click. Moving quickly, I stepped inside. If I thought the exterior of the building was impressive, it paled in comparison to the lobby. A two-story fountain centered the space, surrounded by a colorful assortment of fragrant tropical plants and flowers. I looked up, counting no fewer than eight floors, all with walkways overlooking the fountain.

Interesting abstract artwork lined the walls, adding color and brightness to what might have been a harsh, austere walk. Some of the stuff was dimensional metal, but most was oil on canvas and I'd bet my—hell, I was pretty much out of things to bet—I'd just have to settle for guessing that they were originals.

A directory hung between the elevator banks and though Quinn's name wasn't listed, I figured the top floor would be a safe guess. I called for the elevator, heard the din of the motor and pulleys, and then watched as the numbers ticked off in descending order.

I popped a breath mint into my mouth. I didn't want coffee or chocolate breath and I hoped the peppermint might stave off the acid starting to accumulate in the pit of my stomach.

When the elevator doors slid open on the third floor, I started out and found Jason Quinn waiting for me. Startled, I think I let out a little yelp before slapping my brightest smile on my face.

The woody, ambery smell of Aquarama by Follio Di Aquarama filled the small compartment. It wasn't one of my favorite men's fragrances, but it suited the man standing in front of me. He looked like a high-priced lawyer, from the top of his lacquered, graying hair to the tips of his tasseled Santoni loafers. Quinn was doing the monochromatic thing, a stone-colored silk short-sleeved shirt and tan pleated pants. Before he even said hello, I'd deduced that he'd had some plastic surgery; eye-lift and maybe a mini face-lift. He was also sporting a spray-on tan that in my opinion was a tad too orange to pass for the real thing.

"Let's go up to my office," he suggested.

Though his demeanor was pleasant enough, I was not sensing a good vibe. He didn't bother with chitchat, nor did he even remotely resemble the affable man who spent a good deal of time doing commentary and/or spin on CrimeTV. I didn't like him. But I needed him.

Following in the vapor trail of his cologne, I was ushered into his office, er, shrine. It made Vain Dane's digs seem subtle. The office was like twice the size of my apartment, with sweeping views of Lake Wyman and Mizner Park. Every piece of furniture was large, which made sense given that Quinn was at least six-five. According to the professionally framed photographs scattered around the room, I learned that in addition to being number one in his graduating class from Harvard Law and a Rhodes Scholar, he'd spent his undergraduate years as a star basketball forward at Duke.

Like Vain Dane, he had a decent amount of "me and the celebrity" photos as well as laminated and mounted covers featuring him in *Newsweek* and *Forbes*. Just in case a potential client was still on the fence, Quinn had framed a half dozen news clippings from his most famous trial wins.

"Thank you for seeing me on a Sunday," I said as I primly sat on the edge of one of three chairs facing his ultramodern, chrome, and technology-embracing desk. The prim part wasn't my way of playing the coy damsel in distress. Nope. It was the only way short me could sit in the huge chair without my feet dangling above the floor. Quinn had obviously ordered the furniture with only his comfort in mind.

"I was a little surprised when Ellen called," he said as he took his seat. "I haven't talked to her since she interned for me years ago."

"Really?" I'd never thought about Ellen having a life before Dane-Lieberman. I'd always kind of pictured her emerging from some kind of pod, hairy and fully grown.

"Well, we do see each other at the occasional Bar Association function."

When he blinked I realized he was wearing blue contact lenses over brown eyes. Vain Quinn. Nope. It didn't have the same ring to it. "I don't want to take up too much of your time, so I guess I should start with the basics."

"Fine."

"Jane Spencer is being arraigned sometime tomorrow morning."

"Hang on," he said, his fingers adeptly moving over a Lucite keyboard.

From my vantage point, I couldn't see much of the paper-thin, state-of-the-art flat-panel screen.

"She's scheduled to appear before Judge Benjamin Faulkner at ten-thirty."

"Okay. Good to know."

"It isn't a secret. I use CourtAccess software. It makes things easier since I have cases in several counties." He leaned back in his chair.

"Anyway, Jane did not kill Mr. Martinez."

"Irrelevant," Quinn remarked. "It's never about guilt or innocence, Ms. Tanner. It's about evidence and proof."

Thanks for that sound bite. "Well, she needs a good criminal attorney and you are the best in the state."

He smiled. It was a sly, kinda slimy expression that made the hairs at the back of my neck stand on end.

"True, but that aside," he said, "I'm afraid I can't help you."

My hopes and my heart nose-dived. "If it's about your fee"—I paused and opened my purse—"I can give you a small retainer today and more when the banks open."

"It isn't about the fee, though I wouldn't have taken the case on that basis alone."

"Then why?" I heard my voice and it sounded like a desperate plea. Because that's exactly what it was.

He reached around and retrieved a folded white sheet of paper that he passed to me. "Consider yourself served."

Opening it, I stared down at the page as if it were written in Farsi. "I don't understand."

"I've been retained by the Halls. I'll be deposing you next month."

He got to his feet as casually and calmly as if he'd just handed me a gift basket instead of a legal document requiring me to appear at some stupid deposition. "I wish you luck finding representation for Ms. Spencer. And thanks for saving me the trouble of having to send a process server up your way."

The numbness was fading by the time I left the building. My body was practically shaking, I was so pissed at that arrogant, self-important asshole.

It was incredible to think that a little over twelve hours ago, I'd been tucked in my comfy bed, having an explicit dream. And in the brief span of time between then and now, I'd been handcuffed; dragged to a police station in my pj's; bonded with a transvestite prostitute; been interrogated; hit up all my friends for cash; been berated by my mother and my boss; got caught almost having sex in my office; been mocked by Liam; had my car ticketed; and now become the owner of my very own summons.

After making an illegal U-turn—what were the chances of me getting two tickets in the same day? Huge. I checked my rearview mirror and expelled the breath I hadn't even known I'd been holding. I was reaching for my cell when it rang. It was Liv.

"Hi," I said, knowing full well my attempt at sounding positive had failed miserably.

"Bad news?"

"A lot."

"Damn. Me, too. You go first."

I switched to hands-free and told Liv I still hadn't found an attorney. Worse yet, because Ellen had made it sound like it was a lock, I'd pinned all my hopes on Quinn. Meaning I hadn't even called the other names on the list. "But," I said, "on the plus side, I've collected thirty-five hundred dollars. What's your bad news?"

"Jane's finances are a disaster."

"How can that be? She's a freaking accountant."

"No," Liv countered. "She's a freaking financial planner. She has about seven grand in liquid assets. Almost everything else is tied up in long-term investments, muni-bonds, T-bills—"

"In English, please?"

"According to a banker friend of mine, it will take at least a week, maybe longer, to turn those things into cash."

"The arraignment is at ten-thirty tomorrow morning," I told her, feeling panic surge though my system.

"It gets worse."

Impossible. "How?"

"I've got eleven major events between now and Labor Day."

"More English, Liv?"

"I pay the vendors out of my operating account, then replenish it when the clients pay me. I get a deposit, but I don't get the bulk of the payment until the day of the event. So bottom line, the best I can scrape together before the hearing is about five thousand." There was just the smallest quiver in Liv's voice. She was on the verge of tears.

So was I. "So it's almost six PM and between the four of us, we've got less than fifteen thousand dollars and no one to represent Jane."

"Pretty much."

"I'll call the Bank-O-Mom. I can't make any promises, you know how she is. Then I'll go back to my place and see if I can get in touch with any of the other lawyers on the list."

"No. You focus on the money. Becky and I can work on the attorney thing."

"Isn't she with Jane?"

"Only until seven. I talked to her about an hour ago."

"How's Jane holding up?"

"Becky says good, considering. She still can't remember much about last night after getting into the limo."

That fact was gnawing at me in the worst way. "I need the name of the limo company Paolo and Jane used last night."

"Drive Right. We use them all the time."

"Do you always use the same driver?"

"No. Just whoever's available."

"Give me the address."

"Why?" Liv asked.

"I might have a theory."

"Finley," Liv warned. "What are you up to?"

"Nothing." *Yet.* "I'll talk to you as soon as I have news."

After I'd finished talking to Liv, I called my mother but didn't get an answer. I cursed her for not answering the phone, then cursed her again just because I could.

Wanting and needing to hear a friendly voice, I called Patrick.

"You sound down," he said after hearing my pitiful greeting.

"I'm not really up for going out to dinner. Is that okay?"

"How about I bring dinner to you? I'll grab some moo shu from China Delight."

Again guilt washed over me. Breaking up with Patrick would be just plain stupid. No more vacillating. I would definitely put more effort into this relationship. "That sounds great. I should be home in about forty-five minutes."

"I'll be waiting. I'll bring your gifts and I'll even throw in a foot massage. How does that sound?"

"Heavenly."

"See you soon, Fin. Try not to worry. This will work itself out."

"Thanks, I needed to hear that."

"I'll tell you again when I see you. Bye."

"Bye."

I tried my mother a few more times during the uneventful drive to my apartment; still nothing. Not even when I announced it was me just in case she was still screening.

As promised, Patrick was waiting by the door, his arms loaded with takeout, two small gift bags dangled from one wrist. One was black, the other red. He kissed me softly, then waited while I unlocked the door. There was a distinct odor of citrus cleaner with an undertone of bleach. Looking at the door handle and then the floor, I knew immediately that Sam had come down and scrubbed away the blood and the fingerprint dust. What a sweetheart.

"This place is spotless," Patrick commented as he laid the food containers out on the countertop. "Did you get a maid or something?"

"Or something," I mumbled as I kicked off my shoes and rolled my head around on my shoulders, trying to loosen the knotted muscles at my neck.

"Poor Fin," Patrick said as he came up behind me to knead the tension. "You've had a helluva lousy day. Maybe presents will make you feel better?"

I didn't think so, but I smiled all the same. The black bag held a teeny, tiny thong bikini from a shop in Rio de Janeiro.

I smiled, wondering what local beach I could wear it to and *not* get arrested for indecent exposure.

"Thank you." I kissed him. Twice. The second time I gently nibbled his bottom lip until I heard a satisfying, guttural groan spill from his open mouth. I slowly flicked open the buttons of his shirt, feeling his heart racing as I flattened my palms against the hardness of his chest.

"You have another present," he said, a hitch in his voice.

"So do you," I replied, placing my mouth against his heated skin. I drew his nipple into my mouth, teasing it with my tongue as I felt Patrick reach down and cup my tush, pulling me closer so that his erection pressed against my stomach.

I went a little wild and I'm not sure why. Maybe I needed to prove to myself that we were still capable of passion. Maybe I just wanted to feel something other than sadness and despair over Jane's predicament. Or maybe—and I hated myself for the nanosecond I considered the possibility—I wanted to indulge my fantasies about Liam.

It didn't matter. I just started yanking Patrick's clothes off, tossing them on the floor while doing my best to kiss him senseless. I reached for his hand, gently tugging him in the direction of the sofa. He didn't budge. Instead, he lifted me up and carried me to the bed.

My passion ebbed a bit; it might have been fun to do something just a little bit different. We always had sex in a bed—mine or his. Just when I was going to suggest a change of location, Patrick stripped off my tops and teased my nipple to a hard pebble. His lips burned a path down my throat and over my breasts while his fingers slipped inside the waistband of my skirt. Location didn't matter anymore.

The knock on my door did.

In a flash, I went from aroused to concerned. Scrambling over Patrick, I grabbed my robe and knotted the belt. "It could be Becky or Liv," I said as I checked out his lean, toned body. "Or my mother."

Hearing the "m" word had an interesting effect on Patrick.

It was like taking a pin to an inflated balloon. His erection shriveled and his eyes registered genuine fear.

"Just stay in here," I said, kissing his furrowed brow.

I opened the door and found Liam McGarrity on my doorstep holding a large paper sack. One dark brow arched as his eyes lazily roamed from my mussed hair to my bare feet. Slowly, a broad smile curved his mouth. "Am I interrupting something?"

"No."

He looked past the threshold and then back at me. "Either I interrupted you and the pilot or some strange man left his clothes all over your living room."

"Do you have a point to make?"

"Always. I brought you something," Liam said, his tone laced with the same amusement I saw flash in his eyes.

Irritation inched up my spine. "A brown paper bag from Publix?"

"A brown paper bag from Publix *with* the champagne bottle and glasses from the limo Paolo and Jane used last night. I'll have it tested for drugs and/or prints."

"That's great! I was planning on doing that tomorrow."

"I figured as much. So, that's the good news."

"There's bad news?"

He nodded. "I talked to a friend at the crime lab."

"And?"

"The knife they recovered from the scene came from Jane's kitchen."

"That's bad, right?"

His expression turned solemn. "Very bad."

The best things in life are free; the better things require a promissory note.

Six

I faked it. *Sleepless in Seattle* deli scene faked it. I should have felt bad, but in the bright light of a new and important day, me feeling guilty wasn't on the top of my list. Nor was reflecting on why I'd been unable to respond to Patrick. No, that would mean admitting that Liam's interruption had an effect on my sex life and I so wasn't going there.

Patrick left around midnight, none the wiser. Amazing how easy it is to fool a guy into thinking you've had a mind-blowing orgasm. Anyway, he still had some packing odds and ends to handle for his hiking trip before he came with me to the courthouse. We agreed it would look good if he was all decked out in full pilot uniform for the arraignment. Uniforms impress people. Hopefully, it would impress the judge enough to drop the absurd charges completely or at least consider releasing Jane ROR. If anyone deserved to be released on her own recognizance, it was Jane.

Maybe I could blame my lack of sexual spark on worry over one of my best friends in the world? But then I felt worse, knowing that, orgasm or no orgasm, I'd been home in my own bed while Jane had slept in a cell.

As I wandered into the kitchen, I noticed Patrick's second gift, the one in the red bag, lying forgotten on the counter. While I did love a good gift, my first priority was and is coffee, so I started a pot before I looked at what he'd brought me.

My eyesight hadn't yet reached full focus ability, so it took a minute for me to realize that Patrick's present wasn't the only thing I'd neglected last night. My answering machine was flashing an insistent red light. I hit the speaker button, then dialed the speed code to access my messages before reaching for my always-at-the-ready, oversized pink coffee mug. While the machine voice told me I had one message, I bypassed the carafe and shoved my mug under the spigot to catch the first thick stream of a strong arabica blend.

My whole body stiffened as the shrill, stern sound of my mother's clipped voice filled my apartment. "A courier will deliver a cashier's check and a promissory note to that woman who greets people at your office by nine. Please execute and properly notarize the document and return it to me via express mail. Oh, and I've canceled our brunch reservations for Sunday."

Hallelujah!

"Instead, I've made a reservation at Willoughby Country Club in Stuart. It was the only place I could think of where I won't run the risk of bumping into my friends. Sunday at eleven o'clock. Do try to be punctual."

Halle-shit!

Beep. "To save this message in the archives, press—" I smacked the delete option.

"How much is the loan?" I asked the now-silent phone. Jeez, leave it to my mother to give me specific instructions on the Mandatory Brunch and completely blow past the amount of the check. It was tauntingly cruel. It was so like my mother.

My morning plans needed some rearranging. Since I'd been given the day off, sans pay I'm sure, I was supposed to meet Becky and Liv at Tommasso's Deli at nine-thirty. Patrick would hook up with us at the courthouse. Now I needed to up my departure time by at least thirty minutes so I could get the check, sign my financial life away, and hit the bank.

So much for a leisurely start to the day. I had just enough time for two very quick cups of coffee before I had to be in the shower. As I poured refill number one, I remembered the unopened gift bag.

I could and probably should wait until Patrick was here to watch me open it. But that would mean waiting two full weeks, until he returned from his guys-only, Outward Bound–ish hiking trip. I'm not that patient. As Liam has often pointed out. Usually punctuating the remark with that cocky, sensual half smile.

I gave myself a little mental slap. No Liam thoughts allowed. Specifically no remotely carnal ones. None. I am strong. I know better. I can control myself.

Liar, liar, pants on fire.

The red gift bag was calling me. Being an accomplished gift recipient, I knew from the weight and size of the bag it wasn't clothing. Not heavy enough. Nor was it jewelry. Too bulky. It was featherlight and stuffed to the top with slightly crumpled tissue. A small gold sticker with three indecipherable letters pressed into the foil topped the professionally arranged tissue. Slipping my thumbnail underneath to break the seal, I carefully lifted the whole wad of tissue from the bag.

Peeling the layers like an onion, not that I've peeled all that many onions, I eventually uncovered an absolutely stunning blown glass ornament. I sighed and smiled all at the same time. How incredible was Patrick? Once, in passing, I'd mentioned I might want to put up an actual Christmas tree this year but I'd never gotten around to buying ornaments. Now I was holding a lovely, six-and-a-quarter-inch-tall likeness of a Brazilian beach babe. She was holding a large pink shopping bag, dressed in funky, fun accessories. A little tag hanging from the top hook of the ornament explained that she was hand-painted by an artisan and hand-molded in the tradition of the Murano sculptors in Italy.

Thanks to Patrick's generosity while in Rio, I had my very first holiday ornament and a killer new bikini. I tried Patrick's number but didn't get an answer. He could be doing his morning run or might be in the shower, which was exactly where I needed to be. The shower, not running. I don't run. I stroll.

Following a quick shower, I dried my hair and applied makeup. Now I had to make an important decision. What to wear? Conservative, I decided, homing in on the Ann Taylor outlet section of my closet. While I wasn't crazy about the dark cinnabar color of the pebble crepe, flounce hem, sleeveless dress, and matching cropped jacket, it screamed *subdued professional*. To quiet the screaming, I paired it with the Haircalf d'Orsay pumps in zebra print I'd picked up at Burdines's, now Macy's, semiannual sale. Even on sale, I couldn't swing the matching bag, leaving me no choice but to go with my tried but true Gucci Croro black tote.

While high on cold medicine last winter, I'd purchased a silvertone link and pearl necklace and matching earrings from the Home Shopping Network and figured now was as good a time as any to give them a test drive. I've never worn silver-tone, and wasn't exactly sure what it meant, beyond not real silver. Hopefully, the stuff wouldn't turn my neck green.

Switching things from my purse to my tote, I made myself a roady of coffee, wrote Sam a quick thank-you note for cleaning my place and stuck it under his door, then headed to Dane-Lieberman.

On the way, I tried Becky's cell, but it went directly to voice mail. Same with Liv. Where were they?

A few minutes after nine, I was parked in front of my office. Leaving my jacket in the car since the temperature was already topping eighty-five, I grabbed my tote and went inside. Margaret was at her post, Bluetooth in place, hair teased and sprayed into a helmet shape. I wondered if she looked this disapproving and nasty at home, or if she just saved her scowly face for work. But wait . . .

Either my mind was playing tricks on me or she was actually smiling. No trick, she was definitely grinning. Not a "gee, I'm happy to see you" grin, more of a "you're going to hate this and I get to watch" grin.

As soon as she lifted the express mail envelope, I saw it had been opened. I didn't bother to hide my contempt for the nosy bitch. "You opened it? When it was sent to me?"

"It wasn't," Margaret said, her eyes practically shimmering with delight when I narrowed my gaze on her. "It was addressed to me with instructions to have your signature witnessed and notarized before giving you the check."

It felt like steam was shooting out of my ears as my whole body heated with a blend of intense anger and utter humiliation. Of all people, why did my mother have to make Margaret the go-between?

"I'll buzz Mary Beth," Margaret said.

While waiting for the peppy litigation paralegal to come down from her third-floor office, I sensed movement in the doorway that led to the foyer vending machines. Ahh, I should have known. Three or four of the homely, miserable twits from the file room were taking turns peeking around the corner. Obviously Margaret had sent out an alert. "Come one, come all! F.A.T.'s mother won't give her a loan without making her sign a note!"

Yesterday hadn't been a great day and today wasn't looking a whole lot better. Unless you were Margaret or one of the file room flunkies, all of whom seemed to be delighting in this awkward moment. I really, really wanted to turn around and yell, "Bite me!" I considered the rabies shot *that* would necessitate and kept my mouth shut. My jaw ached from gritting my teeth.

I'd known when I'd asked my mother for a loan that she'd get her pound of flesh. Until this morning, I hadn't realized the depth of her need for control coupled with her nastiness. I should have known. There's no free lunch with my mother.

This thing with Jane had clearly clouded my normally sharp mother radar.

Mary Beth, notary stamp and seal in hand, virtually danced out of the elevator. She was smart, kind, more organized than the Dewey decimal system, and more into entertaining than Martha Stewart. Mary Beth was so kind, in fact, that she'd accepted all my lame excuses for declining to attend her home parties with a bright smile, sometimes even apologizing for planning them on dates I was unavailable.

She was our office's version of head cheerleader, baking birthday cakes, sending sympathy cards, and often bringing in home-baked goods to share. She was a crafty woman, too, not in a snarky way, but literally. Give the woman a hot glue gun, a little time, and a lot of glue sticks, she could probably construct a scale version of the Eiffel Tower out of pretzel rods.

"Hi, Finley," she said in a chipper voice I could only achieve under the influence of a triple-shot espresso drink.

"Hi. Sorry to take you away from your desk."

"Not a problem," Mary Beth said. "Just happy to help."

"I don't want to keep you." When I turned to take the envelope from Margaret, I realized it was too late. A single typed page dangled from her fingers. Where, I wondered, annoyed, was the freaking check?

Snatching the paper, I skimmed the terms, swallowing the groan bubbling up in my throat. My mother, my flesh and blood, was charging me 17.9 percent interest. One-tenth of a point below the usury limits allowed in the state of Florida. Obviously she didn't feel any compulsion to offer a daughter discount.

I signed where indicated, then fumed as Margaret took her time scribbling her name and address in as a witness. Always efficient, Mary Beth quickly notarized the note and wished me well at the arraignment.

Mary Beth squeezed my shoulder. "I'm sure things will work out for your friend. Let me know if there's anything I can do for her or for you."

Can you crochet the real killer before ten-thirty? "Thanks." Turning to Margaret, I asked for an express envelope and label.

"Sorry," she said, though the inflection in her tone and the glint in her eyes told me she was anything but. "This isn't firm business, so I can't allow you to use the Dane-Lieberman account."

"Whatever," I grumbled, mentally giving her and the file chicks the finger as I took the loan-shark-worthy promissory note and the check and bolted from the lobby. I stopped at the drop box outside the office, got an envelope, a blank air bill, and the last laugh. I knew the Dane-Lieberman account number by heart and since the accounting department handled the monthly bill, Margaret wouldn't ever know I'd bested her. Besides, I was content to view the twenty-something-dollar charge partial payment for my unpaid leave day.

Before I reached my car, I got my first look at the check and nearly fell to the ground. I had a dozen reasons to loathe the woman and twenty-five thousand reasons to like her, for a few seconds. I'd been hoping for ten, praying for fifteen, but never even dreamed she'd lend me this much. Or that in accordance with the terms of the note, the repayment would nearly double the amount of the loan. I'd worry about that later.

As I stopped for traffic lights on my way to the bank, I sealed the note in the envelope and filled out the air bill, sorely tempted to address it to Mommy Dearest.

Be nice, I told myself firmly. Mommy Dearest or not,

she'd come through when I really needed her to. I had to give her props for that.

Though Tommasso's wasn't far, I wanted to stop at the bank for two reasons. First, I wanted to know if I needed to do anything with the cashier's check before turning it over to a bail bondsman. No. And second, I knew the assistant manager well enough to ask her the favor of seeing that my express envelope went out with the first pickup.

I'd forgotten to put a thank-you note inside the envelope. That would cost me. I'd also neglected to put on a watch, stupid since I have several nice ones. Nice, but not my fantasy watch. That would be a pink-oyster-faced Rolex with a diamond bezel. Buying one retail was my first choice, but hardly realistic. I couldn't even swing one on the aftermarket. However, being a resourceful and adept Internet auction person, I was building my own. To date, I've acquired three links, the face, and a screw-down crown. EBay is a beautiful place. Not only can I score slightly used clothing, but someday I'll have everything I need to make my Rolex dreams come true.

Without a watch, I had no choice but to check the time on my cell phone display. Not only was I running ten minutes late, a small icon on the screen indicated I had a new text message. Hopefully it was Liv or Becky telling me they'd found an attorney. I drove the three-quarters of a mile back to Banyan Street, found a parking spot, and just to be safe, overfed the meter.

During my block-and-a-half walk to the deli, I pulled up the message.

Hi Fin. Last night was great.

For you maybe. The thought just popped into my head, making me feel small and mean. Which just showed how freaking unworthy I was to have such a terrific guy care about me.

Sorry, can't make the arraignment. The later
flight was canceled so I had to take the earlier
one. Give Jane my best and tell her I've got my
fingers crossed for her. I'll call you from
Arizona. Patrick.

I texted back Have a safe trip. The second I hit SEND, I
wondered if I should have added something like Love, Fin.
No, that didn't feel right. Maybe Hugs, Fin. No, I wasn't
twelve. Ah, screw it. I'd already let my mother, Margaret,
and the File Flunkies annoy me; I wouldn't add Patrick to
that list. I'm not usually so filled with hate, I'm just scared
and worried about Jane. Besides, Patrick had been planning
this trip forever and it wasn't like Jane was his close friend.
Sure, we all socialize, but Patrick's only role in the arraignment would have been to offer me moral support. I had
Becky and Liv for that and he knew it.

The smell of garlic and onion bagels mingled with the
scent of freshly brewed coffee. Tommasso's was a casual
place that catered to the downtown work crowd. Most of the
patrons got orders to go, so it was easy to spot Becky and
Liv at their table near the back of the narrow restaurant.
They had a cup of steamy coffee waiting for me.

Walking past food cases that displayed everything from
cured meats to cheese Danish, I was relieved when I read the
relaxed, happy expression on Liv's face. Hopefully the attorney issue had been solved or, at the very least, there was
hope on the horizon.

Like me, Becky and Liv had opted for classic attire.
Becky's coral suit was tailored and paired with a cream silk
blouse. Her leaning-toward-red auburn hair was pinned up,
held in place with an amber clip that matched her hair, and
she had simple gold hoops in her ears.

Liv's cotton dress was white with small, periwinkle polka
dots and she'd tied a periwinkle sweater around her shoulders. Her updated take on the preppy look was a simple

ponytail coupled with a thin gold choker and gold stud earrings.

I pulled out a chair, sat down, and gulped a hefty sip of
coffee. "We look like we belong in a 1950s sitcom."

Liv smoothed her sleek, shiny brown hair with a well-
manicured hand. "Where are we on ready cash?"

I told them about the mother loan, intentionally leaving
out the terms. "What about a lawyer?" I asked.

Liv grinned, her exotically stunning features bordering on
luminescent. "All taken care of. He's meeting with Jane as
we speak."

"Who is it?"

"Clark Taggert."

I groaned. "He's like a hundred years old. That was the
best the two of you could do?"

"*We* didn't do it," Becky said. "She did. I tried to tell her
he isn't up to it. He's CRS."

"CRS?" Liv asked.

"Can't remember shit," Becky and I said in unison.

I took a deep breath and tried to look on the bright side.
"He does have a decent reputation."

"Did," Becky clarified. "He's been semiretired for years."

"He's free." Liv's voice was tinged with irritation.

"How?" I asked.

"Shaylyn and Zack."

I sat back against the metal frame of the vinyl chair. "The
owners of Fantasy Dates are paying for Jane's attorney?"

Liv's irritation morphed into guarded enthusiasm. "That's
why they were calling me all day yesterday. They feel horrible about what happened to Paolo and they want to see that
his killer is brought to justice."

My bullshit-o-meter beeped. "But they don't know Jane,
so why would they fund her defense? We love her and know
she didn't do it. They don't, so why would they assume she
isn't guilty?"

"They know *me*," Liv replied. "I vouched for Jane and

that was good enough for them. I think it's a generous offer and Becky thinks it might look good to the judge. Having the owners of the dating service who hooked Jane up with Paolo supporting Jane can't hurt. Especially when they believe Jane is innocent. Hopefully that and our united front will convince Judge Faulkner to set reasonable bail."

"A bondsman will require ten percent of the bail. I can cover anything up to two hundred fifty thousand."

Becky's eyes grew wide. "Your mother?"

I nodded.

"And then what? You sell a body part to cover the debt?"

Because she loves me, and knows my mother issues, Liv sent me a sympathetic glance and shook her head. "I've already been to the bank. It'll take a few days, maybe a week, but I've already started the ball rolling on liquidating Jane's assets. We can probably repay your mom with that."

I hated to admit it, but I felt a huge weight lift off my shoulders. While I was happy to take one for the team, owing my mother money gave her a lot of power over me. Power I knew from experience she'd lord over me at every possible opportunity.

"We might need that money to hire a real attorney," Becky commented as she brought a paper cup to her lips. "I think we should keep looking."

"Can you do that? I mean, does the court let you change attorneys in the middle of a trial?"

"Yes," Becky answered as she turned and met my gaze. "But hopefully it won't get that far. My paralegal is going to take emergency leave starting tomorrow."

I tried to connect switching lawyers with Becky's paralegal and failed. "What's wrong with Denise?"

"Nothing," Becky said, her mouth curved into a sly smile. "But with Denise out, I'll need to borrow a paralegal from another department. Of course, I'll need someone who won't mind spending a lot of time on the road. I'm in the middle of negotiations with a company whose corporate office is in South County."

Ah. I smiled. "Smart."

"I don't get it," Liv said.

"Estates and trusts are pretty slow right now," I explained. "It's off-season. Fewer people around to die. I've only got four active estates open. So I'd be available to help Becky."

"Help her what?"

"If I'm out of the office, I might accidentally run into someone with information that could help Jane."

Liv's gaze bounced from me to Becky, then back to me. "I thought Dane said he'd fire you if you got involved."

"What Vain Dane doesn't know can't hurt me. Besides, I'll have help."

"Who?" Liv asked.

"Liam," Becky said. I could almost hear the swoon in her voice.

"The hot P.I. guy?"

I nodded.

"Am I a good friend, or what?" Becky asked.

"Liam is annoying," I said. *Like McDreamy is annoying,* a small voice taunted inside my head. I took another sip of coffee and told it to shut up. Like the TV character, Liam was married. Maybe the divorce was final, but any man who hung around his ex-wife as much as Liam did was still committed. As good as married was a Do Not Pass Go sign.

Besides. I had Patrick.

"Yes, but he'll get you off the fence."

I glared at Becky. "I'm not on the fence." *Liar, liar.*

"Are too," she shot back. "Put us all out of our misery and make a clean break from Patrick. It's time."

"He's a good guy," I defended. The defense of my position on Patrick was knee-jerk. He was everything a fantastic boyfriend should be. *He* isn't the problem. I am.

"Yawn," Becky said. "Face it, Finley, you're bored. Cripe,

I'm bored and he's not even my boyfriend. Your problem is you can't bring yourself to come right out and tell him it's over."

I was practically squirming in my seat. "How did this conversation go from Jane's in jail to Patrick and me?"

"I can fix you and Patrick. Jane's situation is a lot harder," Becky said.

"She's right."

I tossed Liv a nasty look. "I'm not taking dating advice from either of you. Becky's last date was with a guy who took her to see *Men in Black II* on opening night. And you're using an unemployed homeless guy for sex."

Becky rested her elbows on the worn wooden tabletop, then laced her fingers. "Finley, all you have to do is tell Patrick it's over. You know? The old 'it's not you, it's me' kinda thing?"

I vehemently shook my head. "He's the perfect guy for me."

"Right," Becky agreed sarcastically. "If you want to spend the rest of your life in a coma."

"Don't we need to get to court?" I asked. I didn't want to have this conversation. Self-analysis could wait for later.

We opted to drive separately to the courthouse on North Olive Street. I was the only one with the day off, so it was decided I would handle posting the bond and then taking Jane home once she was released.

I arrived to find a half dozen satellite trucks flanking the building. Great. I hadn't given any thought to the idea that Jane's case might attract media attention. Of course it would. The salacious details of a woman charged with killing and de-penising a rich guy was bound to pique a lot of interest. It isn't like Palm Beach County is a hotbed of criminal activity. Sure, there's the occasional murder and we do have minor problems with gangs and drugs. For the most part, journalists working the crime beat have to content themselves with reporting on drunk drivers, dog attacks, and domestic disputes.

I parked and met up with my friends. Sandwiched between Becky and Liv, I managed to make it to the breezeway separating the criminal and civil divisions before I heard someone identify me as the woman arrested with Jane. We had to hurry to avoid the sudden rush of photographers and videographers.

Once inside, we passed through the metal detectors, then consulted the directory. Arraignments were scheduled in Courtroom Number Two.

Unlike full-blown trials, arraignments are almost always quick and handled by newbie assistant state attorneys fresh out of law school. But the minute I stepped into the austere courtroom, I knew this was going to be different. First of all, the gallery was filled to near capacity. Normally only public defenders and defense attorneys occupied the hard wooden benches that lined either side of the long aisle facing the banister that separated the spectators from the counsel tables and the elevated bench.

I recognized several of the attendees. The cute new guy from Channel 12 was seated in the third row, a pad resting in his lap. All the other local affiliates were represented, dressed in camera-friendly attire. I'm fairly sure the more casually dressed men and women scattered around were from various print media. Obviously a de-penised dead guy was hot news.

As if we were wedding guests required to declare our allegiance, Liv, Becky, and I slipped into place on a bench on the defense side of the courtroom. Though I heard the hum of the air conditioner and a large ceiling fan circulated overhead, I was sweating. Bullets. I kept my eyes on the door in the left front of the room, waiting anxiously for Jane to enter. I didn't see Taggert, so I assumed he was with her in the holding area down in the first-floor level of the courthouse.

The room smelled of coffee and breath mints. I noticed

the seasoned veterans of the crime beat had smuggled water into the room, ignoring the large signs prohibiting gum, beverages, food, and cell phones. My cell was still set on vibrate, so I figured I was safe. Water would be nice; my throat felt as if it had been stuffed with cotton.

Liv was to my right, Becky was on the aisle. I think that was intentional. She'd clerked for Faulkner and was probably hoping he'd recognize her and go easy on Jane. I was, too. I wanted this to be over.

On the wall behind the judge's large black leather chair was the circular seal of the state of Florida, and above that a large, slow-moving clock. The chair was flanked on either side by flags—one U.S., the other the official, if potentially offensive, Florida state flag. At least staring at it gave me something to focus on as my toe drummed nervously against the carpeted floor.

My state flag was slightly politically incorrect because of the diagonal red bars set against a white background that was a tad reminiscent of the Confederate flag. The State Seal was repeated in the center, featuring a Seminole woman scattering flowers, a steamboat, a palmetto tree, and a brilliant sunshine. I didn't get the steamboat, or why the Seminole woman had flowers. It would probably make more sense for the seal to have a picture of the space shuttle, a hanging chad, a big RV, and Mickey Mouse ears.

My silly mental redesign of the seal stopped when the room hushed to complete silence. Turning, I saw Allison Brent walking toward the prosecutor's table. She wasn't alone; Detectives Graves and Steadman were with her, and involuntarily, I shrank back in my seat. My heart wasn't beating, it was racing.

"What's wrong?" Liv whispered against my ear.

"Brent is a senior staff attorney."

Liv leaned closer, her shoulder pressed against mine. "Aren't there supposed to be two lawyers? One for the defense, too? Where's Taggert"

I kept my eyes on Brent as she placed a slender accordion folder on the counsel table and went into a huddle with the two detectives. She was smart, petite, with cropped, wash-and-go red hair and perfect skin. She was well-respected by peers and adversaries alike and generally adored by juries. In her nearly twenty-year career as a prosecutor, she'd never lost a case.

"Taggert's probably with Jane. But I'm freaked because the state doesn't usually send in a heavy hitter for an arraignment. Maybe she just wants press exposure. I hear she's going to run for state attorney next year."

A low buzz worked its way around the room when the door opened and Jane was escorted into the room by two deputies. My chest constricted when I saw the dark circles under her terror-filled eyes as the handcuffs were removed.

She shot us all a pathetic look and a weak smile before her hands gripped the empty chair at the table. Her long hair hung limply to her slumped shoulders. I desperately wanted to rush over and give her a hug, but I knew the rules. And, with Graves and Steadman in the room, I didn't dare violate the no-touching one.

"She looks horrible and it's all my fault," Liv whispered.

"She spent the night in jail," I reminded my friend, patting the back of her hand.

"No," Liv insisted. "I brought her one of my dresses."

Though I was battling tears, I did a brief catalog of Jane's attire. I'd never seen her look so . . . so . . . subdued. "She looks fine," I said, hoping Liv would feel better.

"It wasn't like I had a lot of choices. It was either my stuff or hers and Becky said it would be better if Jane didn't walk in here looking like a pale version of Beyoncé."

Okay, that remark lifted my spirits slightly. Liv was right; Jane's personal style was pretty sexy, not exactly the best impression when you're facing a judge and charged with a crime that includes cutting off the sex organ of the victim.

Clark Taggert, Esq., took his place next to Jane. He was

tall, white-haired, and unkempt. Kinda like an elderly, chubby version of Matlock minus the seersucker suit. In his heyday, which I think was before I was born, he'd been a fierce advocate. He'd successfully defended lots of high-profile defendants and did a bunch of pro bono work as well. But that was then. Now, if the rumors were true, he was almost seventy and in the early stages of senile dementia. Hardly confidence-inspiring. Especially when I watched him fumble to open the latches of his own briefcase.

Leaning across Liv, I poked Becky's leg and asked, "Are you sure you can't do this?"

She shrugged her shoulders. "Maybe I should."

"No," Liv insisted. "You already said Jane needs a trial lawyer and you're not one."

"When I said that, I meant one who could remember his own name," Becky snapped.

Liv ignored the dig. "Okay, so maybe he's not the best choice but he's all we've got for now. Once Jane's released, we can find someone else to handle the case from here on out."

A stiff, no-nonsense-looking bailiff came out and ordered us all to stand. Good thing too, since the sound of shuffling feet drowned out my cell phone that was supposed to be off as it started to chime an incoming text. I forgot to switch that feature to vibrate. Liv, Becky, and a few other people around me heard it and hurled chastising glances at me. Discreetly, I fished the thing out of my tote, saw I had a new text message, then powered it off. Probably Patrick checking in during connecting flights or something.

A second later, Judge Faulkner, one of the most highly regarded jurists in the county, entered, his black robe billowing as he strode quickly to his perch. Even though he was well past my acceptable dating age range—he's in his fifties—he was pretty hot, in a judicial kinda way. He had dark hair and light eyes, and for a second, I felt as if I was seeing and admiring an age-progression version of Liam.

The bailiff announced the case name and number, then handed a small folder to the judge. Faulkner was all business, settling the room before turning his attention to Assistant State Attorney Brent. "Proceed."

Brent spent several minutes describing the crime, including her assertion that Jane was the perpetrator of said crime. "I'll be presenting to the grand jury shortly. Until then, the state asks that the defendant be held without bond."

I stopped breathing for a second, then gulped air. "What?" I asked, loudly enough to earn me a stern glare from the judge.

Taggert lumbered to his feet. "If I may, Your Honor?"

Faulkner nodded.

"Miss Spencer is a model citizen and an active, productive member of the community." He spoke slowly with a North Florida drawl. "She hasn't so much as had a parking ticket."

Brent leapt to her feet. "That's a serious misstatement of facts," she said as she pulled some papers from her folder and waved them around. "Miss Spencer has a criminal record."

I gasped. Hell, everyone gasped except for Jane, Steadman, and Graves.

Jane? *My* Jane had a criminal record? Bullshit.

The bailiff retrieved the papers from Brent and delivered them to the judge. His eyes narrowed and he glared over at Taggert. "Show this to Mr. Taggert," he instructed the bailiff. Several seconds passed; then he prompted, "Well?"

"Your Honor, I was unaware of this," Taggert said slowly. "And since the charges were dropped, it shouldn't be relevant to these proceedings."

"Not relevant?" Faulkner's voice thundered loudly around the room.

Every reporter in the place had pen, pencil, or laptop at the ready. Me? I just had a boulder-sized lump in the pit of my stomach.

"No, sir," Taggert said after consulting the document he'd been given by the prosecutor. "The charge was filed more than a decade ago and dismissed by the court in South Carolina."

Brent shook her head. "Dismissal or not, those charges clearly demonstrate a predisposition to violence on the part of the defendant."

The judge stroked his cleanly shaven chin, then nodded. "I have to agree, Mr. Taggert. Based on the heinous nature of this crime and the fact that your client was previously charged with a similar crime, bail is denied."

Similar crime? What was similar to stabbing and maiming besides, well, besides more stabbing and maiming?

His gavel fell along with any hopes I had that this whole thing would be over soon.

Those that can, do; those who can't, wing it.

Seven

Immediately after the adjournment, Becky jumped up, flashed her Bar Association card, and then followed Taggert and Jane into the restricted section of the courthouse.

Brent and the detectives left next. Steadman paused in the aisle next to my bench long enough to acknowledge me. Maybe it wasn't an acknowledgment so much as it was to make sure I knew they'd won the first round. I had to give her that one even though I was still shell-shocked by the bomb dropped so effectively by the prosecutor.

The press corps swarmed out of the room like Africanized killer bees preparing to mount an attack. I winced just imagining the headlines the revelation about Jane's past could generate.

Then Liv and I were alone. I didn't know about Liv, but I was feeling a little numb. Here I'd thought the biggest hurdles facing the Free Jane Team were securing representation and raising sufficient funds to post bail. *Was I ever wrong!* I cared enough about my friend not to care about that past, only in how it impacted her present situation. Things were going from bad to worse.

"So what now?" Liv asked, a slight tremor in her voice.

I shrugged, then tucked my hair behind my ears as I reached for my phone. It wasn't that I was dying to read the text message, I just needed something to do besides sit on a hard bench trying to process the fact that Jane had a secret past. Correction, *criminal* secret past.

"I don't know," I answered, powering on my phone and pulling up the text.

> The cops have something on Jane.
> Something big. Looking into it. Liam

Talk about a classic too-little, too-late heads-up. But I could hardly blame him. I'd known Jane for years and never once had she so much as dropped a hint that there'd been trouble in her past.

Trouble? That was the mother of all understatements. But I knew from experience that a charge didn't necessarily mean guilt. Hell, I'd been charged with a B&E. Technically, I was guilty of breaking and entering at the time, but it wasn't as if it was step one in a life of crime. It had been a necessary and integral part of the Hall investigation. The charges against me were dropped. The charges against Jane had been dismissed, so it was highly probable that Brent had used damning information just to prevail on the bail motion. Smart move. Annoying. Terrifying, but *really smart*.

It was hard to know if Liam's text message required a reply. There hasn't been an update from Emily Post on texting etiquette.

"Patrick?" Liv asked.

"Liam."

"Maybe he can find out what Jane did," she said, her spirits clearly lifted.

"Apparently he's already aware there's a . . . problem."

"Call him back!"

"Okay." I stood up. For some reason I needed to pace as I mustered the will to dial his number. I told myself it was because I was afraid of the possibility he'd already uncovered the mysterious "fact" and I wasn't sure I could handle any more bad news. I'd already had my allotment for the day.

As I waited for him to pick up, I saw that Liv had pulled her cell from her purse and was also making a call. Probably to her office. None of us had seen this coming. The plan had been for Liv and Becky to leave right after the arraignment, so she was probably making scheduling adjustments with Jean-Claude.

"McGarrity."

"I got your message." *And now I have a tingle in the pit of my stomach just hearing the sound of your voice.*

"Still working on getting the details," Liam said. "They're being pretty tight-lipped around here. Anything on your end?"

"Something happened about a decade ago."

"Something? Can you be more specific?"

"Maybe after Jane talks to Becky and Taggert." I gave him a quick recap of what Brent had said to convince Judge Faulkner that Jane was a menace to society.

"Taggert?" Liam repeated.

The way he said the name told me everything I needed to know about his opinion of the once brilliant attorney.

"What happened to Quinn? I thought he was going to represent Jane."

I remembered the summons back at my apartment and suffered a surge of renewed indignation. Not wanting to share the awkward outcome of my meeting, I simply said, "It didn't work out. But whatever happened with Jane happened when she was in college."

"How do you know that?"

"Because I can do simple math. Ten years ago, Jane was working on her undergrad degree."

"Where'd she go to school?"

"College of Charleston. I need you to go to South Carolina ASAP. Do . . . whatever it is you do and get as much information as possible so—"

"Can't," he interrupted.

"If this is about your job to babysit me so I don't go off and do my own investigation, this certainly qualifies."

"I understand that. I'll consider going in the morning."

"Sooner is better. Once we have the facts, Taggert can file a Motion to Reconsider on the remand."

"First, you'd better wrap your brain around the possibility that the facts might not work in your favor."

"Won't happen. The charges were dismissed, so they must have been baseless."

I could almost see him smirking at my flawed logic. Charges were dismissed for a lot of reasons, including the pitiful reality that a victim could decide not to cooperate with the prosecution. No victim, no case.

"Look," he began, his deep voice calm, bordering on soothing. "I know Jane is your friend, but you need a little perspective and objectivity."

So much for soothing. "And you need to get your fanny on the next plane to Charleston."

"Can't. I've got a . . ."

Don't say it!

"Thing."

"I hope your *thing* has something to do with the fingerprints on the champagne bottle and the glasses from the limo service."

"Nope. Won't get those results for at least a day or two. You seem to be forgetting, Lieberman is paying me, so she's the one calling the shots. She didn't hire me to fly up to Charleston."

"Yeah?" I shot back, so furious I was seeing red. "Well, neither am I." The problem with a cell phone is you just don't get the same feeling of satisfaction pushing the picture of a little red phone that you get slamming a receiver onto a cradle.

After taking a few deep breaths to restore equanimity, I turned to Liv, who was just finishing her own call.

"Zack and Shaylyn want to meet at noon at Concierge Plus."

"Fine. You go on ahead. I'm gonna wait for Becky. We need to know what they've got on Jane."

Becky's throat and cheeks were flushed red when she finally emerged. I knew that look. Becky was seriously pissed.

"Well?" I prompted as I fell into step with her and exited the courtroom.

Becky was silent until we reached the elevators. "She lied."

My stomach sank faster than the elevator compartment. "She killed Paolo?"

"No, she lied to Taggert. He specifically asked her if there was anything in her past that he should know about before the arraignment."

"So he wasn't being inept?"

"Far from it. He's so mad he's threatening to get himself excused from the case."

"Isn't that what we wanted?"

Becky sighed audibly. "I'm not so sure anymore. Taggert is older than dirt and maybe he is a little slow on the uptake, but he's forgotten more criminal law than most people ever bother to learn."

"Then we keep him?"

"For now. But just to be on the safe side, Taggert and I agreed to officially add me as co-counsel."

"Thank God."

"Well, don't toss all your eggs in that basket. I'm not going to be much help on trial strategy, but at least it puts you and me under the umbrella of attorney-client privilege."

"How?"

"Jane is now my client, even if I'm only peripherally involved. You're a paralegal who, starting tomorrow, will be working under my direct supervision. So that makes her your client as well."

"Good thinking."

"Not my idea. Taggert's. From what I saw today, the guy is competent. He spent almost two hours with Jane before the hearing and hit all the high notes. Jane screwed herself."

I had to ask again. "But she didn't kill Paolo, right?"

"Of course not. She was stupid for lying but she isn't a killer."

There was something calming in her quick and fervent reply. I told her about the meeting with Zack and Shaylyn. "We should head over there."

"I can't. Ellen and I have a conference call at eleven-thirty," Becky said, clearly torn. "You'll have to be my eyes and ears." She stopped suddenly, retrieving three xeroxed pages from her purse. "Here's the copy of DD5 from when Jane was arrested and a copy of the Order of Dismissal. Not much to go on, but it's a start."

"Wait, didn't Jane give you details once Brent outed her?"

"No. She's hiding something and I sure as hell don't know what it is."

"Should I talk to her?"

Becky shook her head. "We need Liam to go interview the victim, the roommate, the public defender who handled her case. Anyone he can find. Fast. The sooner we have proof that Brent was just posturing and there's nothing to the South Carolina thing, Taggert thinks he can get Jane released on bond. God, I wish I could blow Ellen off, but she's being great covering for me. For us."

I didn't want to add to Becky's worries by telling her Liam wasn't available. Nor did I want to risk sending my blood pressure sky high knowing he was doing another "thing."

Especially since I had a decent hunch that these recurring "things" were with not-really-the-former Mrs. Liam McGarrity. Friends with benefits was an almost acceptable thing; boffing your ex-spouse was just creepy.

Patrick called from Arizona as I prepared to drive over the bridge. Over the bridge isn't just a way to cross the stretch of the intracoastal separating West Palm Beach from Palm Beach proper. It's also a euphemism for the dividing line between the Have-a-Lots and the Have-Everythings.

"Fin, honey, I'm so sorry. What can I do?"

"Nothing. It'll get straightened out."

"What did Jane do when she was in college?"

I breathed in the scent of briny air laced with diesel fuel from the marina at the west end of the bridge as I waited for the light to change. "She stabbed someone."

"You're kidding."

"I wish," I admitted. "All we've got is a partial police report and the dismissal. Actually, I only have the first page of the DD5. It doesn't even list the victim's name."

"DD5?"

"The report police officers type when they make an arrest."

"So, what does Jane have to say?"

"I wasn't in the room, but apparently Jane is claiming it was all some sort of misunderstanding. She wouldn't really talk about it."

"Wow," he said.

His comment was drowned out by an airport announcement that baggage from the inbound flight from Palm Beach International, connecting through Pittsburgh, was now on carousel number four.

"Not a very direct flight," I remarked. Probably even more frustrating to a pilot accustomed to pointing his plane toward a destination and going direct. "I never can understand why a commercial airline would fly you so far north when your ultimate destination is so far west."

"It wasn't a problem," he said. "Is there anything I can do for you? Anything?"

That was the problem with our relationship. Patrick was perfect. He always did and said exactly the right thing. Unfortunately—small of me, I know—I was starting to find his perfection annoyingly . . . predictable. Just once I'd like him *not* to be so blasted . . . *nice*. Not that I wanted him to be mean or argumentative, just that I wanted him to be more *dimensional*.

He was like being on a steady diet of chocolate. I love chocolate, but once in a while I'd like a baked potato.

He's so great I always feel as though I have to be on my best behavior, that any doubts I have about our relationship are viewed through my own insecurities.

Hell, basically I don't know *what* I want.

"No, I'm fine. Just go enjoy the Grand Canyon."

"I'll try to stay in touch, but cell service will probably be spotty once we get into the backcountry."

"Don't worry. I'll be fine. You be careful."

"I always am."

The jerk behind me blasted his horn at me because it took me more than a millisecond to move when the light turned green. I hit the gas pedal and my car lurched forward, reaching the speed limit of thirty-five miles an hour in no time.

While most of my attention was on Jane, a small part of my brain registered the fact that Patrick and I no longer ended our conversation—or our dates for that matter—with declarations of affection. I'm not the mushy "I love you, baby" type and he knows it. Maybe Becky was right. Maybe I stayed with Patrick not because he was theoretically perfect for me, sweet and kind, but because change is complicated and scary. Not to mention the fact that my taste in men generally sucks. Big time. Did I really want to reenter the dating scene? Could I? God, dating is so hard.

Step one is just finding a guy and that isn't always easy.

Step two is the whole getting-to-know-you ritual, which is total bullshit since everyone is always on their best behavior in the beginning. Step three is finding the flaws. That's the stage when the shield drops and you start to discover the little things that have the potential to make or break the relationship. Step four is accepting the flaws. Then you have to weigh the flaws against the benefits. It's not an art or some other intangible thing. It's simply weighing his pros and cons. Asking yourself if the positives cancel out the negatives. Step five is commitment.

I've never gotten beyond step four. In fact, Patrick is the first guy who's made it to step four. It took me a long time to find his flaw. It isn't a biggie. Maybe it isn't even a flaw. I'm just bored with the sex. Oh God! Maybe I'm my mother. Maybe I'm incapable of loving someone.

The mere thought that I was her clone was more troubling than the prospect of breaking up with Patrick. How screwed up am I?

I took the long way to Concierge Plus, opting to drive all the way to South Ocean Boulevard so I could ogle the beachfront mansions. Well, more like ogle their manicured, gated driveways and rooflines. Privacy was a big deal on the island, so most of the homes were guarded by six-foot hedges. They didn't want the little people like me to have a direct line of sight into their private oasis. Conversely, they often incorporated family crests in the center of the electric iron gates, so they might not want me to breach their privacy but they didn't mind openly proclaiming their status as residents.

Concierge Plus was on Clarke Avenue, just south of the Breakers Ocean Golf Course. The seven-thousand-square-foot, two-story building was a private home until it was converted to a commercial property in the mid-1900s. The original business occupants were architects, so they'd done some killer renovations to the Mediterranean-style house. I pulled into the horseshoe-shaped drive. Parking in my favorite spot beneath a live oak that created a canopy of shade on the pavers, I noted a fresh coat of white paint on the stucco.

I noted it for two reasons. It was the last thing on Liv's list of repairs from the past few hurricanes that had blown in from the Atlantic. And there was a big, dark sapphire-blue Bentley blocking the sign and walkway to Concierge Plus.

Okay, I was impressed. A Bentley Continental Flying Spur retailed for nearly two hundred thousand. I knew because I'd just had one appraised for the Lockwood estate I was handling. I'd made the personal sacrifice of driving the car to the appraiser myself. I'd taken the long way around then, too. Twice.

Depending on your perspective, I was either practicing due diligence in preserving a sizable asset of the estate or I was just a twenty-nine-year-old out on a joyride. "Joy" being the operative word. See, my mother has a Bentley but the only way she'd let me drive it was if both her legs fell off. I did make one unauthorized stop on the way back to work. I dropped in on a photographer acquaintance and had a digital picture taken. I made it the screen saver on my personal laptop.

The car, sculpture really, had all sorts of cool stuff. Aside from the incredibly soft, magnolia-colored leather interior with walnut accents, it had a push-button starter. No key needed. A single poke and the engine purred.

The Lockwoods were loaded and so was their car. That Bentley, like this one, had a combo DVD-GPS-radio-CD built into the front console. Not to mention a Bluetooth phone connection.

Liv drove a Mercedes. Jean-Claude had a Lexus. So this had to belong to the owners of Fantasy Dates. Sidestepping the car, I decided if Shaylyn drove a Bentley, she probably had a Rolex, too. Watch envy washed over me.

The first floor was a vast open space filled with the sweet fragrance from no fewer than a dozen large sprays of flowers. Classical music played softly from speakers deftly hidden in the ceiling. You felt more like you were walking into a spa than an event-planning business. That had been Liv's vision from the get-go. Concierge Plus was posh, which was why it enjoyed a great reputation with the Palm Beach elite.

Jean-Claude was at the opposite end of the room, near the double doors that opened out on a veranda overlooking a small man-made lake in the backyard. He was tall, thin, impeccably dressed, and easy on the eyes. Liv had lured him away from the Breakers Hotel. Smart move. Jean-Claude, with his thick French accent and elegant European mannerisms, had spent years perfecting his charm. The fact that he had light hair, blue eyes, and a cosmetically perfected but genuine smile didn't hurt.

"Welcome," he said, taking my hands in his as he kissed my cheeks.

His sexuality was ambiguous. He wasn't prissy but he wasn't football-watching masculine either. And he was discreet. I'd never seen him with a date. His desk was set off to one side, near the organized case of sample books covering everything from area caterers to fabric swatches. The only personal item was a framed, stylized black-and-white photograph of his parents.

"They're upstairs in Liv's office. May I get you something to drink?"

"A latte, please."

"Vanilla." He checked the sleek rectangular watch on his tanned wrist. "Over ice?"

I smiled. The man never missed a detail. During the summer, around noon, I liked switching to iced coffee. Even the barista at my favorite coffee shop wasn't that good.

My fingers slid along the polished wood banister as I climbed the marble steps to the second floor. About halfway up, I heard the muffled sound of conversation. As I reached the top, I could make out three distinct speakers—Liv, a man, and a woman.

I was intrigued by the whole situation and not completely sure how to handle it. I didn't know Zack and Shaylyn, but I still couldn't figure out why they'd been so quick to come to Jane's aid. Something about that seemed hinky to me. Unless they were just the do-gooder types.

Clearing my throat as I neared the door, I heard the conversation come to an instant halt.

Liv introduced me to the couple before I had both feet inside the office she'd decorated with soft cream fabrics. Like Liv, the room was feminine but not overtly girlie.

Zack Davis rose first, extending his hand, then stepping back slightly so Shaylyn could reach around and give my fingers a small squeeze. I was wrong about Shaylyn's watch—not a Rolex. A Cartier. A La Dona de Cartier, to be exact. Eighteen-karat pink gold, octagonal-set with round-cut diamonds.

She had hazel eyes, dark brown hair, and a killer black and white orchid dress I'd seen in the Neiman's catalog. She looked rich. Obviously the introduction service business was lucrative. Her pretty face got even prettier when she smiled. Her "So nice to meet you" seemed genuine enough. Perhaps I'd been too quick to judge.

Zack, on the other hand, was dark and brooding, not nearly as gregarious or people-oriented as his partner. He smiled too, though the effort didn't quite make it to his nearly-black eyes, making me wonder if helping Jane was Shaylyn's idea and he wasn't yet on board.

Ever the accommodating hostess, Liv had already placed a second high-back chair on her side of the desk. Jean-Claude delivered my latte along with refills of cucumber water for the others. I'm not a big fan of veggie water. Thirst-quenching? Yes. Contain any caffeine? No.

"Thank you for arranging to have Mr. Taggert represent Jane," I said, intentionally watching Zack's body language. He leaned back and away from me, which, according to Dr. Phil, indicates a passive-aggressive reaction to my compliment.

"We are happy to do it," Shaylyn said.

My curiosity bested my manners. "Even though she's a total stranger accused of killing one of your clients?"

"Finley!" Liv whispered through clenched teeth.

Shaylyn's burnished-berry-shaded lips never slipped their smile. "She isn't a stranger. No matter the circumstances, Jane was also one of our clients. I met with her so she could complete our questionnaire." Lifting a slim black briefcase into her lap, she pulled a folder from inside and passed it to us.

Flipping through the pages, I was astounded by the thoroughness of the thing. In addition to a photograph and the information provided in Jane's distinctive handwriting, Fantasy Dates had run a complete financial background check. "Did you do one of these for Paolo Martinez?"

"Of course," Zack answered.

His accent was pronounced but unfamiliar. It was a little bit New Jersey, a little bit French. But I couldn't pin it down. I added that to my list of suspicions about the couple.

"Do you have it with you?"

Shaylyn offered me an apologetic look. "Our business records are confidential."

I explained the attorney-client confidentiality thing to them. "So I'm prohibited from sharing that information with anyone. Even the police. Any information you share that can help Jane will be kept totally confidential by us as well."

"All right, then," Shaylyn relented.

"But!"

Zack's protest was silenced instantly when Shaylyn placed her perfectly manicured hand over his. "I'll have Paolo's profile messengered over to Mr. Taggert."

"Could you also send it to Becky Jameson?"

Zack's frown deepened. "If they're co-counsel, then—"

"It won't be a problem." Again Shaylyn's word was law. It was obvious who had the bigger gonads in their relationship.

That was another thing I noticed. Sensed, actually. I thought they were more than business partners. There's a vibe you get from a couple. I'd bet my last dollar that the two of them shared more than business interests.

Speaking of my last dollar. "It was nice meeting you. And again, thank you for your help." I stood, dismissing them with a handshake and a gentle reminder that I wanted the dossier on Paolo sent to Becky within the hour.

"Want to tell me why you were so abrupt with them?" Liv asked as soon as the echo of the front door closing reverberated up to the second floor.

"There's something not right about them."

"There's something not right about *you*. They're paying Taggert."

"Good for them. I need you to pay for a plane ticket. Kinda."

Liv groaned. "Finley, what are you planning?"

"A trip to Charleston. My cards are maxed."

"But you aren't supposed to—"

"The minute she was denied bail, Jane was moved from a holding cell at the jail. Do you want her stuck in the detention center with real criminals?"

"Of course not."

"Then I need to find out what happened."

"Shouldn't Liam do that?"

"He can't."

"Why not?"

"He has a thing," I said, nudging her with my hip in order to access the computer on the credenza behind her desk. "I'm not asking you to *pay* pay for the ticket. I'll use some of the money Patrick and Sam lent me. Oh, will you keep the cashier's check in your safe? I don't want to keep walking around with the thing in my purse."

I went to a discount travel site and found a flight that would work. It wasn't cheap. A last-minute booking apparently meant I'd be paying by the foot. "Seven-fifty-two for a freaking two-hour-and-ten-minute flight."

"Go ahead," Liv said, grabbing her purse and handing me her gold American Express card.

I filled in all the required information. I was cutting it close. The departing flight left in ninety minutes and I'd opted to stay overnight just in case. I added a moderate hotel to my itinerary. The early morning return would give me just enough time to swing by my place, change, and be at my desk by ten at the latest.

I gave Liv her card and my mother's cashier's check, and tried to pay her for the ticket.

"Hold on to the cash. You might need it."

"Thanks."

Liv's fax machine chirped, then began to spew pages. It was from Becky. She'd done a Westlaw search and come up with general information on the earlier case against Jane. Most importantly, I now had the names of the prosecutor and defense attorney on the case. That, with the case number, gave me a place to start.

I printed out the confirmation. I was on my way to South Carolina and if Vain Dane found out, I'd be on my way to the unemployment line as well.

Sometimes it really is all about the shoes.

Eight

There are a lot of things to like about Palm Beach International Airport. Starbucks, wi-fi, and it's relatively small, so no mad dashes to the gates at the far end of the concourse.

I get and respect the TSA folks, even when they made me toss my last tube of Chanel Tickled Pink lip gloss in the "prohibited items" bin. It didn't stop there either; I also had to cough up a travel-sized tube of toothpaste; the 15-ounce sample of Lulu Guinness perfume I carried for emergencies; and my half-finished frappuccino. Though reluctant, I was totally cooperative, better safe than sorry. Except that "safe" was going to cost me at least fifty bucks to replace. Fifty-five dollars and seventy-eight cents if I counted the coffee.

With another twenty minutes before my flight was scheduled to board, I pulled my laptop from my tote and waited as it powered up. Most of my fellow passengers were lined up— cattle style—near the uniformed ticket taker. Me? I don't have a problem being the last one on the plane. Someone has to, might as well be me. Besides, I was flying coach, so the wide, comfy seats overlooking the tarmac were twice the size of those inside the cabin.

I logged in to my e-mail, skipping the nonessential ones since I was hoping Becky had received, scanned, and attached the Paolo dossier to an e-mail in the time it had taken me to run by my place to pack an overnight bag and gather my electronics.

Nothing from Becky but I did have several alerts from eBay letting me know some of my favorite sellers had new items listed. Though my ready cash was dangerously low, a balance-replenishing paycheck would be direct-deposited on Friday.

Three of the alerts announced newly listed parts for my build-it-from-scratch Rolex project. Screen name PilotWife had seven new dresses up for bid. PilotWife was one of my absolute fave sellers and finding her had been fate. Not for the obvious reason, though there was a certain irony to doing business with some faceless woman from the Northeast who'd chosen a screen identity that closely mirrored my status. Well, not exactly closely, but that didn't matter. We were the same size and shared a passion for all things pink and pilots.

I'd been hunting for a gift for Patrick's last birthday and since his apartment is aviation-themed, I'd used "pilot" in the search criteria. Up popped listings from PilotWife.

Though we'd never met outside the anonymity of cyberspace, I'd created a whole history for the woman based on her selling habits. She must have had an aversion to dry cleaning that bordered on a phobia. All the clothing she sold was deeply discounted and worn once, maybe twice. She sold a lot of clothes, too. Everything from daytime casual to couture, hand-beaded evening gowns. Whoever she was, she had major bucks and obviously wasn't doing the eBay thing for profit. So I envisioned her as some sort of lonely woman, married to an older man who entertained often and/or regularly attended ritzy functions and fancy luncheons. I put her age between thirty and thirty-five since she followed trends but never submitted to them. Totally trendy was an area of fashion reserved for the twenty-one-to-twenty-four crowd. Or as I wax nostalgic—TPBY. The Perfect Body Years.

The final boarding call put an end to my eBay surf-by, so I shut down my computer, tucked it away, and headed toward the gate agent, bar-coded pass in hand.

"Have a nice flight, Ms. Tanner," she offered as she scanned the code and my name popped up on the screen just above her scanning device.

Shifting the tote higher on my shoulder, I thanked her and made my way down the incline of the gangway. The still air in the tunnellike corridor magnified the sounds of planes taking off and landing and the warning beeps as various service vehicles went from gate to gate.

A statuesque brunette flight attendant guided me to my seat. I don't think she wanted to help me so much as get me buckled in for takeoff.

One of the few advantages to being short is not needing a lot of legroom. I had a middle seat, which seemed to piss off the heavy guy on the aisle. He decided to punish me for my last-minute arrival by leaning his legs to one side instead of unhooking the seat belt extender and allowing me to take my seat. Selfish prick.

It took some doing, but I managed to gracefully climb over him and, swear to God, my tote slipping and smashing into his jaw really was an accident. A satisfying accident. I apologized, took my phone out of my tote, then shoved the weaponlike bag under the seat in front of me.

The woman in the window seat was already sleeping, snoring softly with her blue-gray hair resting against the window.

One of the flight attendants ran down the list of safety features while the other two stood in the aisle making hand gestures and demonstrating the correct use of the oxygen mask. I like the absurd part about my seat cushion doubling as a flotation device. I mean, I've never heard of anyone whose life was spared because of the buoyant qualities of their seat cushion. Then there's the whole lecture about the use of cell phones. One time I asked Patrick how something anyone can buy at their local Wal-Mart could screw up the navigational equipment of a commercial aircraft. Big mistake. He went into a long monologue about the electrical sensitivity of avionics.

The flight landed fifteen minutes early. The Charleston airport was a lot like PBI. It was small, so my bag was already on the luggage carousel by the time I reached baggage claim.

Looping the straps of my tote through the handle of the compact, rolling suitcase, I made my way to the rental car counter. As I waited in line, I thought about my last visit to Charleston. It was four years ago, to attend the wedding of someone I'd never met.

I couldn't remember if my mother had just filed for divorce from husband number three, or filed for death benefits for husband number four. Not that it mattered. Whatever the reason, I'd been called into duty as her escort since taking a date to the wedding a week after instituting divorce proceedings or burying a husband was bad form. Some people, like me, considered attending a wedding so soon after death or divorce bad form, but my mother would crawl off her deathbed before she'd renege on an RSVP.

So I ended up tagging along to watch the nuptials of the daughter of one of my mother's DAR friends. It started out okay; I mean the setting was lovely—a restored plantation on Kiawah Island built in 1739. The "I do's" were quick. It went downhill from there.

On the plus side, I must not have looked my age because most of my mother's acquaintances assumed I was Lisa. They would enthusiastically congratulate me on my budding medical career. Ever one to save face, my mother's reply was, "Oh no, this is my older daughter, she works for one of the most prestigious firms in Palm Beach. Estates and trusts."

Conveniently and intentionally, she'd leave off the part about me working as a paralegal, giving her friends the mistaken impression that I was a lawyer. Between introductions, she'd whisper something in my ear about hating the fact that my lack of a decent profession was an incredible burden to her and the sole reason she was forced to lie to her friends.

Me? I was on a first name basis with the bartender before the seven-tiered cake was cut.

The flight home was even worse. As a captive audience—though I did give some thought to asking the flight crew to move me into the cargo hold—I got to listen to the same refrain about how I was wasting my life and my potential. Unlike my sister, who wasn't afraid of a challenge, wanted to make something of herself, was faster than a speeding bullet, and could leap tall buildings in a single bound.

I'd toyed with the idea of going to law school, going so far as to take the LSATs. But once I found out that lawyers, on average, put in seventy hours a week, I lost interest. It isn't that I wasn't willing to work hard, I just want balance. I want a life.

Being a paralegal allows me that, and specializing in estates and trusts has the added bonus of autonomy. Under the guise of filing something in probate court, I was free to take two-hour lunches, shop, do errands, or anything else. So long as I met my deadlines, no one at Dane-Lieberman seemed to notice. Except Margaret.

On the way to the garage to pick up the rental Liv had arranged over the Internet, I turned on my cell. Becky had left three voice mails as well as a clipped text message that read **Call me NOW!**

Not wanting to go through Margaret, I hit the speed-dial number for Becky's cell and said, "Hi."

"About time," Becky grumbled. "I've spoken with Taggert and he said you need to go to the courthouse first. It closes in forty minutes and you need transcripts or anything else you can get your hands on."

"Okay."

"Track down the prosecutor and then the arresting officer."

"What about Jane's attorney?"

"He or she can't talk to you without Jane's permission and she isn't giving it to me. At least not yet."

"I wonder why?"

"That's what you need to find out. Knowing Jane, she's protecting someone. Call me with updates, okay?"

"You got it." I presented my contract to the rental car attendant. "Hang on a sec."

He leered at me and said, "It's the green subcompact in spot 44."

"Thanks." Not for the leer; the guy looked like he was maybe eighteen, tops. Returning my attention to Becky, I asked, "What about the Paolo stuff?"

"E-mailed it to you a few minutes ago. Move fast, you've got to be back here in the morning."

"I know." She hung up, leaving me with the to-do list and a sense of amazement. Becky was nothing if not efficient.

In record time, I headed east on 526, then south on 17, eventually working my way through the maze of one-way streets. The biggest obstacle was avoiding the horse-drawn carriages and tourist trolleys that enjoyed the right-of-way. In addition to being a college town, Charleston was a tourist mecca, even if the temperature hovered around a hundred with humidity levels to match.

The pleasant scent of night jasmine was sometimes overpowered by the stench of horse manure and sweat seeping in through the air-conditioning vents. I stayed focused on finding Court House Square, thanks to the map marked by the leerer at the rental counter. Another plus to Charleston was the fact that all things relating to the legal system were centrally located in a quarter-block area off Broad Street.

The feelings of uselessness I'd been getting since Jane had appeared at my door, bloody and babbling, were fading.

In fact, I was experiencing a bit of a rush. My adrenaline was pumping. Being a woman on a mission beat the hell out of being an ineffective friend.

Touches of the city's historic past were everywhere. Particularly the lack of parking spaces. Hitching posts still dotted the sidewalks, but it took me three trips around the block before a spot opened up.

Once I was inside the building and oriented, I went down to the records office and hurriedly filled out a request using the case number from the dismissal. The clerk was not at all happy as she glared at the triplicate form and then me. "This case is ten years old." She spoke with a slow, cultured Southern accent.

"Yes, it is," I said in my nicest voice. "I'll be paying the expedited fee for the copies."

She glanced at the clock, then reluctantly went in search of the file. She moved slower than she spoke.

Ten minutes after the posted close of business, she returned with a small stack of pages stapled in the upper left-hand corner. Licking her thumb, she counted the pages and said, "Sixteen pages at two dollars a page. Thirty-two dollars. Plus fifteen for an expedited request." She went to an antiquated adding machine and ran the total.

When she turned around, I had the forty-seven dollars waiting on top of the counter. Gathering up the transcripts, I said, "Thank you so much."

Taking the stone steps two at a time while reading the listing page of the transcripts was no easy feat. The prosecutor was a guy named Ned Franks and I'd remembered his name from the lobby directory.

Please let him be in his office.

Winded from the three-story climb, I weaved through the hallway, going door to door until I found his name stenciled on the frosted glass. I knocked once, then a second time, turning the worn brass knob in the process.

If he had a secretary or receptionist, she wasn't at her

desk, so I had no choice but to go for the second door, ignoring the PRIVATE sign clearly posted at eye level.

"Mr. Franks?" I asked as I boldly went inside without bothering to knock.

A man I put somewhere in his mid-fifties sat with his feet up on his desk, legs crossed at the ankles. The soles of his shoes were scuffed and worn. The top button at the collar of his white shirt was undone and the knot of his red-and-blue-speckled tie was loosened. His hair was a shock of white, prematurely so, I decided. Either that or he had great genes that kept his skin virtually wrinkle-free.

Though obviously startled by my sudden and unannounced presence, he handled the intrusion like a true Southern gentleman. Placing his feet on the floor, he straightened his tie and asked, "May I help you?"

"Yes, sir," I said, dumping my heavy tote into one chair and sitting in the other. I handed him the thin file fresh from the records office. "I'm Finley Tanner. I work for the firm of Dane, Lieberman and Zarnowski in Palm Beach. I'm doing some background on a client."

He didn't seem surprised by my request. Or that I'd barged into his office. It was almost as if he'd been expecting me. Which was silly. No one outside the Free Jane Team knew I was in South Carolina.

"You prosecuted Jane Spencer in 1997. I have a copy of the indictment but the victim's name has been redacted."

"The victim was a minor."

Mild irritation gnawed at my insides. "It's been ten years. He or she isn't a minor anymore."

He returned the copies to me. "Sorry, Ms. Tanner, but I can't help you."

"Can't or won't?"

"Both." He stood up and I sensed I was being dismissed.

"Both Florida and South Carolina have reciprocal discovery rules. Plus, the full faith and credit clause of the U.S. Constitution requires you to cooperate."

"Which I will be happy to do when and if I'm ordered to by a court of competent jurisdiction. Now, if there's nothing else?"

My spine stiffened as I rose and collected my things. "Yes, could you give me directions to the Detective Bureau for the Charleston Police Department?"

"Three blocks west, one block north. Gray three-story building."

My enthusiasm waned. Franks had been a total waste of time, and time was one commodity I couldn't afford to diddle away. I stopped by the rental car and tossed my jacket in the backseat. I was perspiring from the stagnant heat even though the sun was starting to dip toward the horizon.

Two blocks later, I decided discarding my jacket had been a stupid move. Large black mosquitoes were feasting on my bare arms and buzzing around my ears. Uselessly, I attempted to defend myself by swatting, but it was pointless. They were out for blood and I was completely outnumbered, leaving me no option but to cross to the sunny side of the street. Better to bake in the sun than be eaten in the shade.

Judging by the worn gray linoleum floor, the police station hadn't been remodeled in the last four or five decades. Phones rang seemingly unnoticed. The walls were painted a depressing shade of pale blue, dotted by several patches of stark-white plaster. Fans aided the air-conditioning, circulating odors ranging from antibacterial cleaner and bacon to the law enforcement staple of old, bitter coffee.

Still, it was better than my last visit to a police station. At least this time I wasn't in my jammies handcuffed to a prostitute.

When I finally got the attention of the uniformed woman behind the reception desk, I asked for Detective Colton Langston.

Barely glancing in my direction, she said, "Captain Langston is third watch."

"Which means?"

"He's on from eleven to seven. You'll have to speak to one of the other detectives."

Just great. "No, I need to see him personally."

"Give me your name, contact information, and a case reference. I'll leave him a message."

"I'll come back."

O for two. I called Becky on my way back to the car and gave her my nonupdate. Her voice sounded as dejected as I felt. Fatigue was starting to set in, so I decided to check in to my hotel for the nearly five-hour wait until the detective would report for duty.

I pulled into the first fast food place I spotted. I stopped at the drive-through of the Burger King, planning on ordering a salad. Instead I drove off with a Whopper Junior, large fries, and a gallon-sized Coke.

Backtracking on Route 17 while I ate my high-fat, high-carb, really, really good burger and fries, I found the Beachside Inn. Inn was a generous way to describe a two-story converted motel. My subcompact was the only car in the lot, swallowed by large pickups and conversion vans.

The owner checked me in, a creepy little guy with cigar breath and a potbelly. My room was a dank place with a snagged polyester bedspread and a matching green lamp shade with a small slit in the fabric.

The bathroom was small, with some disgusting blackish brown gunk growing on the caulking around the tub. One of those strong, chemical-smelling bricks of whatever hung inside the toilet bowl. Brackish water stained the toilet and the sink. I wanted to go running and screaming to the closest five-star hotel, but that wasn't in the budget.

Lining the bedspread that I was sure contained all sorts of body fluids with towels, I pulled out my laptop and rolled my eyes when I discovered the only Internet access was dial-up. With tax and a surcharge, it would add another twenty bucks to my night's stay at Hotel Hell. Slipping off my shoes, I then connected the provided phone cord to my laptop and waited. And waited. And waited.

The machine estimated it would take eleven minutes to download the e-mail attachment from Becky. Going to my suitcase, I retrieved the single-serving-sized box of Lucky Charms, munching on the marshmallow moons, stars, clovers, and hearts and washing them down with my Coke. The sugar rush chased away my fatigue, but the download was still in progress.

My mind wandered to Patrick. I suspected he was at some remote campsite near the Grand Canyon, laughing with his buddies as they sat around a campfire. I never thought I'd envy a tent and a sleeping bag, but that was before I checked into the Beachside Inn. Patrick was having fun. That was good.

Then I thought about Liam. My brain conjured a vivid image of him boffing Ashley. That was bad.

Shaking my head, I raked my fingers through my hair. Luckily my laptop dinged, the file was downloaded, and Liam was forgotten. Or at least pushed back into the deep recesses of my mind.

The first page was a photograph of Paolo. No wonder Jane had jumped his bones on the first date. He looked a little like Enrique Iglesias or a younger version of Antonio Banderas. Like Jane's dossier, Fantasy Dates had taken great care in compiling information on him. I whistled when I hit the page listing his personal assets. The guy was only thirty and had already amassed a seven-figure minifortune as a day trader.

It was easy to see why Zack and Shaylyn had paired him with Jane. They shared a lot of interests: sailing, jogging, working out, and other—in my opinion—pointless physical activities. Paolo was a huge Peter Sellers fan, as was Jane.

Unlike Jane's file, Fantasy Dates had run a criminal background check on Paolo. He had a couple of traffic tickets but that was it. He was a regular on the Palm Beach charity event circuit and according to his "wish list" he eventually wanted to get married and have a family. If the right woman came along.

The right woman. "That is so guy code for commitment-phobic," I scoffed.

I read the file a second time, then a third, but nothing jumped out at me. I tried to Google Paolo, but the dial-up connection kept tossing me off-line. Eventually I surrendered and shut down.

By ten, I was back on the road heading into Charleston. I stopped in a Quickie-Mart for a cup of coffee. It wasn't until I was back in the rental that I realized the coffee was laced with chicory. It was a coffee abomination but it was all I had, so I sucked it up.

Detective Langston arrived five minutes after I'd given my name to the desk sergeant and sat down in the visitors' section. His appearance saved me from the torture of thumbing through another ancient copy of *American Hunter,* and Lord knew, I'd learned as much about taxidermy as I could stand.

Langston looked like a cop. He had chiseled, weathered features and a perpetual frown curving his slightly chapped lips. I think he was wearing Old Spice, but I couldn't be sure if it was the cologne or the deodorant form.

He showed me into his office. It was a messy, cluttered place with files stacked haphazardly on every available space. I almost wept with pure joy when he offered me some coffee. I needed something to rid my mouth of the lingering, bitter aftertaste of chicory.

He returned with two steaming mugs, both handles gripped in one beefy hand. "So, Ms. Tanner, you're here about the Spencer girl?"

I blinked.

He shrugged. "Franks called and said you might drop by." Langston leaned against the edge of his desk, sipping coffee as he sized me up. "What is it you want to know?"

"Everything. Unless the D.A. said—"

"I don't like Franks. Never did."

I felt the tension drain from my body. "So what happened? I know it was a long time ago, but anything you remember would be helpful."

His expression softened. "Hard case to forget. It isn't every day you respond to a scene where a shoe was the weapon of choice."

"A shoe?"

"Yep."

"I was under the impression someone was stabbed. Are you saying Jane kicked—"

"No. She stabbed him with a three-inch spike heel. Caught him right in the jugular."

I was stunned. "Why?"

"You aren't from around here, so let me back up."

"Thanks."

"The Spencer girl shared an apartment with Molly Bishop. They were both students at the College of Charleston. Molly had a younger boyfriend, I think he was seventeen, something like that."

I was taking notes furiously.

"Molly and this boyfriend went to a rave and, depending on who you believe, were slipped or bought some Ecstasy. Well, turned out the crap was laced with LSD.

"So she takes him back to her place. They're high and decide to have sex. At some point, Molly starts hallucinating from the drugs and starts screaming and clawing at the boyfriend. The Spencer girl came home from her part-time job hostessing at a restaurant, hears the screaming, and thought Molly was being attacked."

"So she stabbed him with her shoe?"

"It was dark. Molly was out of control. I thought then and I still think that the Spencer girl was reacting to what she thought was an attempted rape."

"Then why all the secrecy?"

"Even though the boy nearly died, Molly's family wanted it to go away quietly."

"Why?"

"Because it was Molly Bishop."

"Sorry, that doesn't mean anything to me."

"Daughter of Senator Ray Bishop. He campaigned and won the election by promising to do everything possible to rid the city of drugs. How would it look if it got out that his kid was scoring X at raves? She had already been arrested twice for drug possession and gone to rehab instead of jail."

"Why wouldn't Franks tell me any of this?"

"He's still pissed that Senator Bishop went over his head and arranged for the charges to be dismissed. Again. He'd tried to prosecute her twice before, but the senator always stepped in and quietly managed to get his kid into a program. Franks knew Molly Bishop and Spencer were friends and I think what he really wanted was to use Spencer's arrest to get to Molly. Probably figured Molly would admit to violating the terms of her plea agreement if he got her on the stand and she had to admit to being high that night. Instead, the charges were dropped against Spencer and Molly went back to rehab. Must have worked—she was never in trouble again. At least not in Charleston."

"Do you know where I can find her?"

"Moved out of state right after the stabbing. Last I heard, the senator retired so he and his wife could move closer to Molly."

I thanked the detective profusely and practically danced out of the police station. Now it made sense. Jane didn't tell anyone about her prior arrest because that would mean slinging mud at Molly Bishop. That was Jane—loyal to a fault.

Though it was well after midnight, I was just about to call Becky when my phone rang.

"Finley Tanner, brilliant investigator."

"Liam McGarrity. Have you lost your goddamned mind?"

*A lateral move at work means you're screwed,
just in a different position.*

Nine

I wasn't sure if I was disappointed or thrilled when Liam wasn't at the airport to greet me/spank me when I arrived in West Palm. It was eight-fifteen. Maybe he wasn't a morning person. Or maybe he'd gotten all the hostility out of his system by berating me until well after midnight.

One thing was for certain—contrary to my proclamation the previous evening, he did not consider me a brilliant investigator. He thought my actions were careless, reckless, blah, blah, blah and carried the very real potential of costing me my job. Whatever.

I'd spent a good part of the flight figuring out a way to get him to reimburse me for the cell minutes his lecture had drained from my plan.

Dragging, I got my suitcase and wheeled it to the long-term lot. I could have gone straight to the office, but I needed a shower. A real shower. I wanted to wash off any residual cooties from the nasty motel.

I'd spoken with Becky during my predawn drive to the Charleston airport, filling her in on the details of Jane's prior charge on the aggravated-assault-by-stiletto incident. She seemed buoyed by the information and promised to arrange a lunch meeting with Taggert to discuss the next move. Hopefully it was something that would get Jane out of jail as soon as possible.

I rushed into my apartment, stripping off my clothing as I headed for the shower. My phone rang but I ignored it. Standing under the hot spray of water, I started thinking about the whole Patrick Situation. Okay. I didn't *start* thinking about it. The Patrick Situation was an ongoing mental debate that I'd been having with myself for the past few months. I'm not normally so man-obsessed, but this decision would be a major life-turning point. I don't want to screw up. Again.

I also didn't want to hurt Patrick. He'd been nothing but good to me. My ongoing mental rehearsal of dumping him still wasn't quite gelling. And the alternative—not breaking up with him—made me uncomfortably aware that *not* taking action would mean that I was prepared to settle.

Then again, believing that there was some theoretical Prince Charming out there that I'd miss if I stayed with Patrick was also kinda stupid. There are no Prince Charmings. Just frogs. The key is finding the one that won't give you too many warts. And avoiding the poisonous ones that can potentially kill you. The major flaw in my thinking is that the really dangerous frogs also happen to be the most visually appealing ones. Nature can be so cruel.

Screw it—all of this self-examination was giving me a headache, when I needed to focus on the Jane issue.

Besides, Patrick, I assumed, would be out of cell range for most of the next two weeks. Plenty of time to confront my demons later.

Except that when I emerged from the shower, the Queen of all Demons had left me a curt message.

"I'm calling to thank you for mailing back the documents promptly. I'm assuming there wasn't a problem with the check I sent. Of course, I can only assume since you didn't see fit to contact me regarding my generosity. Perhaps at Sunday brunch, if you have the time and inclination, you might consider properly acknowledging the loan." The message ended with a loud bang as my mother slammed her receiver back on its cradle.

Guilt dart! Direct hit.

"Flowers," I decided as I hurriedly dressed in a lime-green blouse and the lime and fuchsia Lilly Pulitzer print skirt I'd snagged really cheap because some careless shopper had broken the zipper. An easy and invisible fix. Not even the most discerning eye would know I was wearing damaged goods.

Yes, flowers would do it. *Public* flowers were even better. I made a mental note to pick up two dozen Monticello roses on Saturday. I'd take them to brunch and present them to her in full view of the Willoughby crowd. Yep, excellent plan. My mother craved the attention of an audience, so she'd love it. I'd be redeemed. The world could return to revolving on an axis that didn't center on my mother's mortification by my most recent fall from her good graces.

I really, really did appreciate her coming through for me and I wanted her to know it. An e-card would have been cheaper and easier. Except that she doesn't own a computer and hates all things computer-generated. She won't open a Christmas card unless her name and address are handwritten, preferably professionally calligraphed, on the envelope.

Freshly dressed, coiffed, and reinvigorated by a pot of coffee, I slipped on my favorite pair of pink wedges and transferred the necessities from my tote to my purse. The Paolo information was still stored in my in-box, so I could pull it up once I got to my desk.

It was 9:47 when my car screeched to a halt in the Dane-Lieberman parking lot. Me being tardy wasn't an uncommon occurrence, but as always, it earned me a disapproving, narrow-eyed glare from the surly receptionist. Maudlin Margaret scribbled something on a piece of paper as I walked past her. She took great pride in keeping a running list of my infractions—a list that magically found its way into Dane's manicured hands just in time for my annual review.

Becky was waiting in my office. Her brow knitted together in a frown as she made a production out of clicking her fingernail on the face of her watch. "You're late."

"Who are you? Mini Margaret?" I asked as I tucked my purse into my desk drawer, flipped on my coffeepot, and powered up my computer.

"You look tired."

"I am."

"But you did good work," Becky said. "Hopefully it's enough to convince Judge Faulkner to reconsider bail."

I sighed deeply as I fell into my vented leather chair. "It better be. I'm just sorry I didn't have the time to find Molly Bishop. Since Jane covered Bishop's butt in college, maybe she'll repay the favor." As soon as my computer booted, I Googled Molly Bishop. There were one million seven hundred thirty-something possible hits. Either I had to narrow the search parameters, or this was going to take a while.

Becky helped herself to coffee, then started out the door. "I got you reassigned to my department, so you have to meet with Ellen at ten-fifteen."

Checking my watch, a quick wave of panic washed over me. "Why?"

Becky's head tilted to one side and she tucked a tendril of auburn hair behind her ear. "Officially?"

"Yeah."

"She's now your direct supervisor. Think of it as . . ." She paused as her finger tapped against her chin, amusement flickering in her eyes. "Contracts boot camp."

I closed my eyes briefly and grimaced. "Be still my beating heart. Can I take a pass on the meeting and just go straight to sticking a pencil in my eye right here and now?"

Becky smiled. "No."

"Is there an unofficial reason for the meeting?"

"Yes. She's going to threaten to fire you if you so much as put your toe over the line for Jane."

I was confused. "So why is she helping us by hiring Liam and getting me reassigned?"

"She's helping us. That's all that matters," Becky said. "It did take some serious begging on my part, though. If it makes you feel any better, it isn't just about you. I got a strong lecture as well. But, with some exceptional negotiating on my part, she got with the program."

I didn't want to think about the specifics of any negotiations with Lieberman. The woman didn't negotiate so much as wear you down until you surrendered, then thanked her for the privilege of experiencing total defeat.

As soon as Becky left, I had just enough time to scarf down a small bag of peanut M&M's for breakfast before heading up to the executive suite on the top floor.

Stepping off the elevator, I offered a uneasy smile to the executive assistant seated behind the polished wood, semi-circle desk. The top floor was laid out like a wagon wheel. She was at the center of the spokes. Normally, I snake around her to get to Dane's office. This time I turned to the right and began a slow walk toward Ellen Lieberman's lair.

The faint scent of a citrusy air freshener surrounded me. I could only hope my antiperspirant lived up to the claims on the side of the container. Vain Dane irritates me. Lieberman flat-out intimidates me.

I've never quite understood why some women work really hard to reach the top, opening the door to success, then take such pleasure in slamming it behind them so no other woman can best their achievement. Almost like life is a competition and only one person with ovaries is allowed into the finals.

Lieberman is a finalist. She's driven and demanding and generally harsh on support staff and particularly hard on me. She doesn't get why I'm not more motivated; why I don't live up to my potential. When she starts in on me, it's as if she's channeling my mother. Save that my mother dresses better while doing it.

I knocked and waited until she called for me to enter. Shifting the pad I'd brought along—mostly as a prop—from my left hand to my right, I turned the knob.

Ellen looked up, her expression blank, her wild, curly mop of gray-streaked red hair gathered in a messy up-do. She didn't stand, just flicked one finger in the direction of a chair. "Morning, Finley."

"Good morning. How are you?"

"Fine," she said as she scrawled her distinctive signature across the bottom of a letter and then set it off to the side, tending to another. "You?"

"Great." This was starting to feel like an employer-employee version of a bad blind date. Awkward, forced, and probably useless.

Nervously, my eyes darted around the room. It was very gender-neutral, very Ellen. Two walls were floor-to-ceiling bookcases, filled with neatly organized law volumes and their supplements. Behind the desk, she had a window, though any outside light was muted by a pleated fabric shade. Ellen was a partner but she wasn't the managing partner, nor was she the senior partner. Which is why her view wasn't spectacular waterfront à la Vain Dane. But her office wasn't ego-centric like his either. In fact, very few items of a personal nature were visible beyond the requisite diplomas. Other than a small, black stone, primitive-looking statue—*please, Lord, don't let it be some sort of fertility god*—and a thing that looked like petrified wood with abstract carvings and faded paint, the room was pretty sterile.

No color. Beige on beige. By the way, not the least bit complimentary to pale, beige Ellen. As I sat waiting for her full attention, I marveled at her flawless, if pasty, skin tone. Unlike most natural redheads, she didn't have a single freckle. I knew for a fact she didn't wear makeup. She'd said as much, declaring it unnecessary and claiming it wasn't natural. Necessary was in the eye of the beholder. As for natural, I'd been tempted to tell her "natural" didn't always connote good. After all, arsenic is natural. She also shunned perfume and shaving her legs. Meaning the Ellen definition of natural boiled down to musky and hairy.

After what felt like the better part of a year had passed, Ellen's faded green eyes lifted in my direction. The sound of her snapping the cover on her fountain pen reverberated in the silence like a gunshot.

I'd given the fountain pen thing a try. Bad idea. Ink leeched out of the sucker, coating the inside of my, at the time, favorite Juicy Couture purse with a thick layer of black goo.

Lacing her fingers, she rested them against the brown leather blotter on her desktop. "We need to review a few things."

"Okay." Reluctantly taking my seat, I suddenly realized I'd brought a pad, but no pen.

As if reading my mind, Ellen pulled open a drawer and handed me a Bic. "So there's no misunderstanding, this reassignment doesn't in any way relieve you of your other duties to this firm. What's the status on your open cases?"

"The inventory on the Lockwood estate is finished. I just need to walk it over to the clerk of court. I'm waiting on an appraisal for the jewelry in the Benoit estate. The initial accounting is due on Zander. The Evans estate should clear probate this week. Just waiting on the final order from the court."

"While I'm your supervising attorney, you'll abide by my rules."

"Of course." Like I had a choice.

"You will be at your desk by eight each morning."

I swallowed the groan bubbling in my throat and nodded. Then I made a note on my pad to buy more coffee. To be here at eight I'd have to seriously consider mainlining the stuff. Or maybe an IV?

"I have several mergers in varying stages of negotiation. Your job, basically, will include things like annotating and amending contracts and any addendums, researching and writing memorandums on relevant case law and statutes, and basically doing whatever or going wherever I tell you."

My brain was already going numb. "I can do that."

One of Ellen's untended brows arched. "Can you?"

"Sure." Whether or not I wanted to was a whole different thing.

"Tell me the legal difference between 'shall' and 'may' as it relates to contracts."

Was she actually giving me a freaking pop quiz? "Excuse me?"

"Shall and may," she repeated, her gaze level and penetrating.

My heart thudded in my ears as I reached back, trying to recall everything I'd learned in the one and only contracts class I'd taken a decade ago. "*Shall* compels one or both parties to perform pursuant to the terms of the contract. Failure to perform constitutes a breach, voiding part or all of the agreement and/or creating grounds for legal action against the defaulting party."

Ellen's face remained expressionless. Not a good sign. Crap. She should have been impressed as hell. I was. My definition was dead-on and I knew it.

"May?"

"*May* defines an option or suggestion relevant to the consideration rendered by one or both of the parties to an agreement." I was on a serious roll. We spent the better part of the next thirty minutes with Ellen tossing terms at me and running various scenarios. By the time she was done grilling me on the party of the first part versus the party of the second part, well, I was partied out.

Then she surprised me by smiling as her bony shoulders relaxed against the seat back. Not that it was easy to see the outline of her body; she had a penchant for wearing veganish, commune-style tent dresses. Guess she thought they worked with her functional, gladiator-style sandals. If you ask me, it borders on criminal to wrap a size 2 body in a sports bra and a muumuu.

It had been too long since my last hit of caffeine. I was jonesing but Ellen didn't do coffee. She was an herbal tea kind of girl. What a silly contradiction—real tea has caffeine; herbal tea is, well, it's just colored, sometimes perfumed hot water.

"Did you enjoy Charleston?"

I stiffened. "Excuse me?"

Ellen made some sort of guttural noise, a cross between a scoff and a groan. "Don't confuse me with Victor," she cautioned. "I know all about your long lunches and clandestine shopping trips. I also know that you went to Charleston yesterday. What did you find out?"

Becky? My nearest and dearest friend ratted me out? How much did that suck? I told her everything I learned, wondering why she was so curious.

"You're meeting with Mr. Taggert at lunchtime?"

I nodded. "I was thinking he could file a motion to reconsider based on the new information."

"It should work," Ellen said. "Which is why I insisted Becky remove herself from any official affiliation with the case. She'll take on the role of an adviser only. This firm does not handle criminal cases, nor do we appreciate being associated with, well, with salacious cases."

So, I'm thinking now is not a good time to mention the subpoena Quinn served me. *That* trial was going to be a real sideshow. "With all due respect, Ellen, Jane needs her."

"No, Jane needs a criminal attorney and the support of her friends and family."

"She doesn't have any family."

Ellen's lips pinched together for a second. She was losing patience with me, but I was pretty nettled by her from-a-distance micromanagement of Jane's case.

"Still," Ellen began, scooting her chair back and rising to her full height of five-eleven, "the two of you need to be discreet. Particularly you. Becky can continue a passive involve-ment, preserving privilege, but not as co-counsel at the trial table. You will maintain a much less conspicuous place in all this."

Nettled went past really annoyed and straight to majorly pissed. My blood pressure was climbing with each passing nanosecond. "I won't turn my back on Jane. You can fire me if you want."

Ellen shook her head. "What I want is for you to go back to school and earn a law degree. You'd be much more valu-able to the firm as an attorney. We could bill your time ac-cordingly. Barring furthering your education, I want you to do your job, not just go through the motions."

That stung. Because it was basically true. Not the educa-tion part. The part about going through the motions. I'm a paralegal on autopilot. I like it that way. The thought that I'd have to be at my desk by freaking daybreak simply rein-forced my resolve. I didn't want a seventy-hour-a-week job. Forty hours was just fine. Thirty-eight? Even better.

Rising slowly and wearing a forced smile, I said, "I think you'll find my work more than satisfactory. If there's nothing else?"

"Your work is always satisfactory. That's the problem. With your brains, it could be exemplary. But yes, there is one other thing."

I waited, half expecting her to tell me I also had to wash the windows. It was almost enough to make me long for Vain Dane. At least he ignored me. Well, mostly he did. I could fly under his radar. Unless Margaret tattled like a snotty child. Then I got screwed.

"You will be at your desk on time."

Yeah, we covered that. "Yes, I will."

Ellen sat down, tucking the yards of fabric under her in-visible rear end. Pivoting, I walked toward the door, more than ready to leave.

"Finley?"

I stopped but in the smallest little display of defiance, I didn't turn around. "Yes?"

"You need to be on time."

Jeez! Beat that dead horse, why don't you? "I will."

"Good, because I expect you to have your work done before lunch. All of it. My assignments and your pending estate matters."

Had I missed something? I spun back and faced Ellen. She was back to signing things with her fancy tortoiseshell pen. "What do you want me to do with the other part of my day?"

"I've already told Victor that while you're on loan to me, you'll be spending your afternoons in Broward County."

"That's a long drive and I—"

"I didn't say you were going to be in Broward County. Just that I'd told Victor that's where you'd be. Details, Finley. Pay attention to the details."

"I'm not following you."

"If your work is completed, you could have your afternoons free."

I felt like dancing in place. "I can work on Jane's case?"

She held up one hand, then sliced into me with her stare. "So long as you stay out of the newspapers and out of trouble, I don't want to know what you do."

"Thank you. That's really very nice of you." There had to be a catch. Ellen Lieberman wasn't the warm fuzzy type.

"I'm not being nice, Finley, I'm being practical. Only an idiot would think you'd stay on the sidelines, so I'm willing to give you some leeway. But—"

Why was there always a *but*?

"This firm represents clients who will not take kindly to having reporters camped outside these offices because you've done something public and self-aggrandizing. They made that very clear to Victor after you got involved in that whole Marcus Hall thing."

"Where I was instrumental in unmasking the real killer."

"Listen to yourself," Ellen said, then blew out a frustrated breath. "You're not a superhero. You put yourself in physical danger and this firm's reputation in jeopardy. As for exposing the killer, we both know that was more luck than determination. Let's not forget that you defied a specific directive from the senior partner to back off. The only reason I'm paying Liam McGarrity to babysit you is I'm not convinced you learned anything from that experience."

Wrong. I learned to fear large dogs.

"I'm giving you some room here, Finley," Ellen said. "Yank too hard on the rope and I'll hang you with it. You and Becky."

"You and Becky," I muttered in a pretty unflattering imitation of Ellen's voice a few minutes later when I was tucked inside the safety of the elevator. I didn't think Ellen would actually fire Becky. I knew for certain that she'd kick me to the curb without working up so much as a bead of sweat. Great. Now I felt the weight of Becky's job security dangling off me.

Once I was back in my office with a mug of coffee poured, I called Liv. I knew she'd been to visit Jane and I wanted an update. Well, I also wanted to vent.

"Hi," I said when Liv answered her cell phone. "How's Jane?"

"She looks horrible. She's scared and she's really, really pissed at you."

"There's a lot of that going around." I raked my fingers through my hair, then checked the ends. I needed a trim. I could control the condition of my hair, but I had this sense of dread pooling in the pit of my stomach about every other aspect of my life. "Why is Jane mad?"

"She didn't want that thing with Molly Bishop to become public and now she's afraid Taggert will use it to get her out of jail."

I couldn't believe what I was hearing. "Of course he'll use it. Once Faulkner has all the facts, he'll have to grant bail."

"Jane doesn't want that."

"She doesn't want bail? She's definitely not thinking straight. Incarceration has obviously short-circuited her brain."

"She sounded lucid," Liv insisted. "I think there's more to the Bishop thing than we know. Some reason she doesn't want to talk about it."

"I'm on it. By the way, who's your contact at the limo company?"

"Harold Something from Drive Right Limousine Service. Why?"

"Was he the one who drove Jane and Paolo Saturday night?"

"No. He's the owner. I don't know who drove the limo. I only order the type of car, not a specific driver. Unless the client asks me to make a specific request. Want me to call him?"

I didn't have anything pressing on my plate and I could tell by the slight fading in and out of Liv's voice that she was on the road. "No, I'll do it. What's his number?" I scribbled it on a small pink Post-it as Liv recited it from memory. "Thanks. I'll talk to him and I'll see what I can dig up on Molly Bishop."

"No need."

I nearly dropped the phone when I heard the familiar, deep, and way, *way* too appealing voice from my doorway. Liam stood there, one broad shoulder brushing against the frame. His black T-shirt was faded, as were his jeans. On anyone else, the ensemble would have looked ratty. On Liam, it was full-on sexy as hell. As was his slightly crooked smile and those eyes of his. Mostly blue, they had just enough gray to make them look as dangerous as an approaching thunderstorm.

I love thunderstorms.

He sauntered—yes, that was the only way to describe his utterly masculine walk—into the room, a small folder tucked under one arm. The scent of his soap swirled around the room and threatened to overwhelm my senses. Or addle my brain. Being a whisper away from an honest to God swoon wasn't in my comfort zone.

He tossed the folder on my desk, then grabbed up my still steaming mug of coffee and helped himself.

Me? I was just struggling to get my pulse to stop racing. So much for not being man-obsessed. In my defense, only a corpse could be immune to Liam. Who doesn't appreciate walking, talking tall, dark, and handsome?

"I'll call you back," I said into the receiver before placing it on its cradle. Luckily my voice didn't betray me. At least I hoped not.

As I watched him drain the coffee from my mug, my equilibrium returned. No one gets between me and my coffee. "No, really. I don't mind at all. Help yourself."

Nonplussed by my tone, he nodded toward the file. The action caused a single lock of dark hair to fall forward against his forehead. Liam was a holdout. His hair was devoid of any product. While I'm normally attracted to more polished types, Liam's casual style had my heart thumping against my ribs.

Ignoring my inappropriate urge to stand, walk around the desk, and plant myself in his lap, I snatched up the file. Inside I discovered gory, disgusting crime scene photographs. "Ewww!" I glared at Liam as I slapped the folder closed and let it fall to my desktop. "A little warning would have been nice."

"You went to Charleston to play investigator. Pictures like those are part of the job."

Dry, ordinary, boring contracts were suddenly sounding better and better. Stubborn pride kicked in, and as much as I didn't relish the idea, I reached for the folder and opened it again. I wanted to hurl.

It was a vivid, color image of a pillow. A huge blood pool obscured all but the corner hem of the once-white case. In the lower right-hand corner was a small yellow sticker. *Charleston Police Department,* I read, followed by the date and what I presumed was a case number.

Continuing on, the pictures showed more blood on the bedroom wall; a second blood-drenched pillow; bloody towels on the carpet; then photographs of a younger Jane. A couple were limited to crimson smudges on her hands. Then finally, a booking photo.

The last few were of a small woman being loaded into an ambulance, an IV inserted in the crook of her arm. Her bloody arm. The caption told me it was Molly Bishop. Lastly, there were copies of police reports that I skimmed just to give my body a chance to purge the bile lodged in my throat.

"Thanks for the show-and-tell," I said to Liam as I took a second mug out from the cabinet of my credenza and poured myself a full cup and drizzled the last mouthful into the one he had expropriated. "And the point is?"

"No void."

Our eyes met. "Meaning?"

Moving my/his cup off to the side, Liam opened the folder and ran the tip of his forefinger around the image of the pillow. "There shouldn't be any blood here. Not if it happened the way Jane and Molly said in their sworn statements to the cops. There should be some sort of ghost impression because Molly's head, and probably her shoulders, would have prevented the blood from soaking the pillow."

"I'm still in the dark here."

"There's a news flash," he teased, amusement shining in his eyes.

"You don't get to make fun of me in my own office."

"Sure I do," he returned easily. "Anyway, according to the story Jane and her spoiled little rich girl roommate told the police, Molly was lying beneath the victim when Jane, um, shoed him."

"Shod."

"Whatever. You want to play Grammar Fairy or hear the facts?"

His irritation was kinda sexy. I wanted to play a quick game of escaped prisoner and the warden's wife. *No. Stop!* "Go on."

"Molly then stated she rolled him to the other side of the bed while Jane put pressure on the stab wound until the paramedics arrived seven minutes later."

"What did the victim say?"

"Too high to remember any real details."

"So what are you saying?"

He shrugged and I struggled not to notice the fact that his muscular chest and shoulders strained the soft fabric of his shirt. Tried. And failed.

"The evidence doesn't support the story."

Excitement rumbled though my entire system. "You're saying Jane didn't attack the victim."

"If Jane was the aggressor, then she'd have cast-off blood spatter on her clothes and her body. Puncture the jugular and you get a gusher."

"Thanks for that disgusting tidbit."

He flipped through the photographs, tapping on the close-up of Jane taken at the crime scene. "No spatter." He sifted through again, placing the one of Molly on the stretcher next to the one of Jane. "That's spatter on Molly's arm. And there's no blood in her hair or on her face. The evidence doesn't match the story they told."

"This is great." I felt like leaping up and kissing him. Well, I pretty much wanted to do that anyway. Not an option. "It means Jane didn't do anything wrong. Faulkner will have to grant bail."

He took in a deep breath, letting it out slowly. "It isn't great and you shouldn't say anything to Taggert."

"But this proves Jane—"

"Has a history of giving false statements to the police and willingly participated in a conspiracy. If the cops or the prosecutor gets wind of this . . ."

He didn't need to finish the sentence. I got it.

"What are you doing?" he asked as I scrambled to my feet, grabbing my purse in the process.

"I'm going to see Jane."

He stayed seated. "While you're there, you might want to ask her who she's pissed off."

"Why?"

"Someone here in West Palm sent the information about Jane's prior arrest to Brent. Plain brown envelope left on the floor of the lobby with nothing but Brent's name typed on the front."

"Jane does not have enemies."

As I started past him, Liam closed his large, warm fingers around my wrist. An electrified tingle shot right through me. *Wow. Zing. Shit!*

He stood, letting his hand slip away in the process. "I hate to break it to you, Finley, but she has at least one."

*Secrets are like dirty books—you stick them in the
back of a drawer and hope no one will ever find them.*

Ten

"The minute you get out of jail, I'm going to kill you
myself," I told Jane as she sat shackled to the seat
across the table from me. My hands balled into tight fists,
forcing my nails to dig painfully into my palms.

Protocol, specifically being the employee-agent of Jane's
legal adviser, allowed me to meet with her in one of the
counsel rooms at the detention center a few blocks from my
office. The place smelled stale and dank. And it was noisy.
Buzzers went off incessantly as people entered and exited
every door and hallway in the facility. Loud, boisterous conversations filtered in from the holding areas and exercise
yard. More distant, muted bass voices wafted over from the
men's side of the building.

Jane had the decency to cast her eyes down. Even the top
of her head looked guilty.

"Well?"

She shook her head sadly, slowly. Normally, her dark brown
hair was impeccably styled. Now it hung limply to her shoulders, parted haphazardly off to one side. When she looked at

me, I read all sorts of emotion in her dark eyes. Anger. Fear. Apology. Frustration. All diluted by the tears threatening to spill over her mascara-free lower lids. "Liam's right," she finally admitted. "I did lie to the cops."

I knew that. What I wanted to do was reach over, grab her by her orange-clad shoulders, shake her, and demand she help me help her. I wasn't digging into her past for fun. I was doing it to get her butt out of this hellhole. I was scared for her. Really, *really* scared. And scared that no matter how much I wanted it, none of us would be able to gather enough information to help her, and she'd end up in here for life. Or death. I shuddered. "Why?"

With her hands secured, Jane crossed one over the other in order to shove some of the dark brown hair back off her forehead. She broke eye contact and shrugged.

My simmering temper returned to a rolling boil. "I'll track down Molly Bishop and grill her like a cheese sandwich if I have to."

"You won't find her." Jane was pretty defiant for someone facing up to three months in jail pretrial.

"Oh yes, I will. If you won't talk to me, I guarantee you, by the time Liam and I get finished with her, *she* will."

"No, she won't."

"Well, then." I slammed my fist on the warped tabletop. "I'll leak what I've got to the press and they'll—"

Jane tried to jump to her feet, but ended up snagged by her chains and accomplishing nothing more than scraping the metal chair against the floor and frustrating herself. "Do not do that," she said through gritted teeth. "Okay, I'll tell you about the deal."

"Don't lie," I warned.

"I'm sorry about that," she said earnestly. "You and Liv and Becky deserved better. I should have been honest with all of you. Stupidly, I thought it was easier to pretend that chapter in my life was ancient history."

Most of the initial tension drained from the room. "I'm

sure it would have been had it not been for this whole Paolo thing. So spill, and don't leave out anything."

"Molly was a great roommate and a dear friend. It never mattered to her that I was the scholarship student and she was, well, pretty much the richest girl on campus. She told me all about her life: winter breaks in the Alps, Paris in the springtime, and summers spent sailing the globe. I told her about life in the trailer park.

"By the age of twenty, she was a master at playing her parents."

I could relate to that. While I wasn't yet a master, I'd had more than a few successes against the force greater than myself—my mother.

"Molly wasn't a bad person, she just had bad habits."

"Drugs?"

Jane nodded. "Drugs, alcohol, sex. She was pretty wild and liked to party. Looking back I believe, subconsciously at least, she was desperate for some real attention from her parents. Negative or positive."

"Molly and the guy impaled with the shoe?" I prompted. The plain white face of the large clock mounted above the door told me I had about twenty minutes until I was due to hook up with Becky and Taggert. Twenty minutes to get all I could out of Jane to help in her defense.

"His name was Michael Fry and he was a lot like Molly. Great home, great parents, too much disposable income. Aside from the drugs and alcohol abuse, he also had anger management issues. He liked to hit her."

My stomach seized. "Sounds like a real winner."

"Molly could pick 'em," Jane agreed, her shoulders slumping forward. "I'm not saying she was a saint, far from it. Molly liked to live on the edge. Her parents were decent, clueless people. All Molly had to do was say she was sorry, bat her mink lashes in their direction, and they flew into action.

"There was no way they'd let their precious daughter have her reputation besmirched."

"The detective in Charleston said she was on probation."

Jane nodded. "Only because Mommy and Daddy couldn't get back from China in time to get the DUI charges swept under the rug."

"Okay, fine. I understand covering up a DUI, but Jesus, Jane! She stabbed a guy with her *shoe*. Why the hell would you claim to do something so freakishly insane? Don't look at me like that. Liam showed me the crime scene photos. You couldn't possibly have shoed the guy." I pointed out every inconsistency Liam had shown me in the crime scene photographs. "The question remains. Why *did* you cover for Molly?"

"Money." The word sounded like a curse as it passed Jane's lips. "Even with my scholarships and part-time jobs, I was nearly twenty thousand dollars in debt by the end of my junior year. When I admitted my guilt, Senator Bishop paid off my loans and covered my last year's expenses."

"What about Michael What's-His-Face? Weren't you afraid he'd remember what really happened and—"

Fervently, Jane shook her head. "No way. Neither the Bishops nor the Frys wanted to risk the fallout. Michael had already gotten an appointment to the Naval Academy. They had a vested interest in making sure their son's record remained unblemished."

"So everyone let Molly continue down her self-destructive path?"

"One of the conditions I placed on accepting responsibility and the money was that Molly be placed in a residential treatment center."

"I've got to talk to her," I said, rummaging around my purse for a piece of paper and a pen.

"You can't."

I didn't even try to hide my frustration as I met and held Jane's gaze. "Your loyalty is commendable. Stupid and against your own self-interest, but commendable. I can't say anything to Taggert or Becky because they'd be forced to disclose the information to the state attorney. But I want to talk to her, make sure she hasn't grown a conscience in the last ten years. The last thing we need is her popping out of the woodwork and spilling her guts to the authorities."

"You can't."

"Jane. Don't be an ass. Someone here in West Palm tipped Brent off on the Charleston incident. What if they know the whole story?"

"Not possible. Aside from the Bishops, the Frys, me, and now you, no one knows the truth."

"Liam knows."

"Whatever. Isn't he banned from telling anyone because he kind of works for me?"

"Technically. Maybe." Nearly out of time, I rose. "Sorry, but I'm meeting with Taggert and Becky at Bacio's so I've got to go. Since you're not being all that forthcoming, I'll just Google Molly Bishop and find her myself."

"No. You won't."

I was taken aback by the unequivocal delivery of her statement. "You know I will. Given some time, I can find anyone."

"We have a 'no Googling our friends rule,' " she reminded me.

Actually, that rule had been my idea. I didn't have anything to hide, I just thought the computer made it too easy to find information. Friends shouldn't Google other friends. It feels too much like a high-tech version of rifling through someone else's panty drawer or medicine cabinet. "Doesn't apply. Molly Bishop isn't my friend."

"She also isn't alive. She OD'd about five years ago."

"Freaking hell." As much as I wanted to stay and grill Jane for more details, I just didn't have the time. Bacio's was on South Rosemary and I practically had to jog in the sweltering early afternoon heat just to reach the restaurant a mere ten minutes late.

My blond hair was slightly damp. Perspiration trickled down my back and into my cleavage, so I spritzed myself with perfume before scanning the room for Becky and Taggert.

Weaving my way through chairs and the strong, pungent smell of garlic and red sauce, I realized Becky and Taggert were seated at a table for six. Weird. Bacio's was almost always filled to capacity during lunch. They needed every available seat, so I didn't get why they'd donated a six-top when a quad would easily have accommodated the three of us.

Graciously, Taggert lifted out of his chair when I reached the table. He smiled politely, but the action never made it all the way to his bleached gray eyes. A tall server with a half apron sporting the red, white, and green colors of the Italian flag tied around his slender hips held out my chair.

I placed my purse off to the side, then put the napkin in my lap as I greeted Becky and the decrepit attorney. "Jane sends her regards."

"You went to see her?" Taggert asked.

He sounded slightly miffed. Maybe he was one of those proprietary types who insisted on being kept in the loop at all times.

"Yes."

"And?" he prompted.

I shrugged and diverted my eyes to watch the waiter fill my water glass. "We need to get her out of jail."

"Faulkner has already made his ruling."

Becky and I exchanged surprised glances. "Before he had all the information."

Taggert shook his head, the thick shock of white hair immobilized by some sort of industrial hair spray. "I've seen the arrest reports and read the statements. Ms. Spencer was involved in a prior stabbing. It will be almost impossible to overcome the state attorney's assertions that she is a threat to the community. Add to that Ms. Spencer's . . . reluctance to discuss the event, my hands are tied."

"Well, untie them." Legend or not, I didn't like Taggert. He came off like a doddering old quitter. "You could file a Motion in Limine. The charges were dismissed as unfounded. A fact Brent failed to mention to the court. They have no bearing on the current charge. Better yet," I continued as I accepted a menu from the server, "Jane really, really doesn't want to relive the event." *Or be placed in a position to commit perjury again.* "You could try an ex parte meeting with the judge to explain the circumstances."

Taggert's cheeks turned a fairly bright shade of red. "And where did you get your law degree?"

It was my turn to blush.

"I got mine at Emory," Becky cut in, saving me from leaping over the table and shoeing the old coot. "Finley's right. Either of those options has a decent shot at getting Jane released on bail."

"Please excuse my bluntness, Ms. Jameson, but your practice is limited to contracts and mergers. Criminal law is my milieu. I think I'm in the best position to determine what is and isn't in the best interests of my client."

"So, what *is* your plan?" I asked.

"Evidence. Judges like evidence. I'm considering hiring an investigator to find and interview everyone who had contact with Ms. Spencer and Mr. Martinez on the night of the murder."

"We've got that covered."

Now, I would have thought Taggert would be grateful. After all, our initiative saved him from having to get off his butt and actually do something proactive. My annoyance with the old geezer began to chafe. He didn't look grateful, he looked irritated.

"If and when I require your assistance, Ms. Tanner, I will ask for it. Until then, stay out of my case."

"She's covered," Becky said. "As an employee of my firm, she's bound by the same privilege as the rest of us. Including our investigator, Liam McGarrity."

"Ex-cop Liam McGarrity?" Taggert asked.

"Yes," I said, sounding a lot like Tammy Wynette's 1969 ditty about standing by your man. Judging by the curious arch of Becky's eyebrows, my defense of Liam hadn't gone unnoticed. Except by Taggert.

"Ms. Jameson was—"

"Becky," she interrupted, probably not for the first time.

From his seat across from mine, Taggert conceded. "*Becky* was telling me that she will not be acting as co-counsel but rather in an advisory capacity only."

"As it pertains to this case," Becky said. "I still have an executed agreement with Jane to represent her in all matters other than this criminal charge, so privilege is preserved."

For a split second, I wanted to say, "Take that!" then stick my tongue out to punctuate my childish urge. But I knew it wouldn't serve any purpose other than to make me look like a fool.

The tension at the table was palpable. It didn't last long. Drawn by the sound of someone coming up behind me, I turned, expecting the server. Instead I found myself looking up into the smiling face of Fantasy Dates owner Shaylyn Kidwell. On further examination, I realized she wasn't smiling, just suffering the aftereffects of recent collagen injections. Her lips were so plump she looked a little like a trout.

Zack Davis was right on her heels, looking dark and dapper. As a couple, they were quintessential Palm Beach. Tanned, toned, and impeccably dressed.

Taggert stood and greeted them with more gusto than he'd shown me. Then again, I had a sneaking suspicion I wasn't at the top of his Christmas card list.

Their arrival took me by surprise and judging from Becky's discreet, wide-eyed look, she hadn't known Shaylyn and Zack should be in this strategy session either.

"Glad you could make it," Taggert said as the couple took seats on his side of the table. We were reminiscent of the Sharks and the Jets. It was very *West Side Story*.

"We want to do everything we can to help Jane," Shaylyn insisted as she smoothed her perfectly styled dark hair. A huge—we're talking double digits—teardrop diamond ring acted like a laser pointer. Its reflection climbed the wall, then zigged and zagged across the ceiling.

"May I ask why?" Ignoring Becky's elbow jab to my ribs, I divided my attention between Taggert, Shaylyn, and Zack. "Other than preserving your business reputation, what's in it for you?"

Shaylyn's expression remained calm, cool, and collected. Too much so, if you ask me. People almost always have an agenda or some sort of self-interest. Altruism flies in the face of basic human nature. Unless you're a nun or a Peace Corps volunteer. I couldn't see Shaylyn in either role.

"We believe Jane is not guilty." Shaylyn said. "Don't you?"

"Yes. But I've known Jane a long time. You haven't."

"True. Paolo's murder was a terrible thing. I, Zack and I both, want to see justice done. Liv convinced us Jane could not possibly be responsible. And yes, protecting my, our, business interests was a consideration. Do you have a problem with that?"

Yes. No. Maybe.

"If you do," Shaylyn continued, her hazel eyes glinting, "then feel free to make your own arrangements for Jane's defense and we'll gladly step aside."

Becky went from poking to pinching. "None of us wants that," she said. "Finley and I are just very upset that Jane's bail was denied."

Shaylyn reached across and patted Becky's hand. Her nails shone with a fresh coat of OPI True Red polish. "Understandably so."

Like a Disney android, Zack did little more than order a bottle of trendy red wine.

Taggert ate an entire platter of pasta, which pretty much explained the genesis of the bulge at his waist. Shaylyn went with the fish. Zack ordered a steak while Becky and I contented ourselves with salad. Occasionally, the conversation drifted to Jane's plight. Taggert got around the client confidentiality thing by only speaking in the hypothetical.

I was fuming. He didn't once mention possibilities I'd suggested. Just limited himself to vague references about considering the options. My faith in him was almost nil by the time the check arrived. Shaylyn slid the check over to a less-than-enthusiastic Silent Zack.

It wasn't until we'd started to leave the restaurant that Shaylyn offered, almost as an afterthought, that they'd received a subpoena duces tecum from Brent.

"What do we do?" she asked Taggert.

"You have to comply or appear before the judge to show good cause why you shouldn't be compelled to turn over your business records. You don't have good cause."

"Send copies to my firm as well," Becky said. She turned to Taggert and asked, "You don't have a problem with that, do you?"

He looked like he wanted to say yes, but his thin lips said, "No."

"Great. We'll expect them first thing in the morning."

That lingering, distracting creepy feeling followed me back to the office. I knew I should tell Becky about the whole Molly Bishop thing, but didn't want to get her in trouble. She was an officer of the court. She could be disbarred for failing to disclose pertinent information. This was one of those times when being a paralegal really came in handy. If anyone found out about Jane's perjurious statements in the Charleston incident, and that was a big if, I could plead ignorance and hopefully shield Becky from any repercussions.

Still, it felt horrible to lie to my dearest friend. Speaking of which . . . I grabbed her hand as we turned down North

Olive Street. "Why'd you tell Ellen about my overnight trip to South Carolina?"

"I didn't."

"Then who?"

"Liam."

"I hate him."

"Do not."

"Do too."

"Keep telling yourself that," Becky said. "I can hear your toes curling at the mere sound of his name."

Curling and flexing. "You're wrong."

She tossed me a sidelong glance. "I know you, Finley. Admit it, you want him."

"I do not want him."

"No," Becky said as she shrugged out of my hold. "Let's clarify, you don't want *Patrick*, you're just too much of a chickenshit to admit it."

"That's really harsh."

"That's *really* true. Now's the perfect time for you to take the easy way out. Just send Patrick a text message telling him to kiss off. Or be pithy, like . . . Absence makes the heart go wander."

It was my turn to jab an elbow. "I can't do that."

"Why? Are your fingers broken? Mouth glued shut?"

"I can't hurt him like that." Luckily, we'd reached the front door to Dane-Lieberman. "It would be mean."

Becky leaned in to whisper against my ear, "Meaner than boffing him while pretending he's Liam?"

"I have never done that." *Dreams don't count, do they?* "Update. I don't hate Liam. I hate you."

I marched directly to the elevator, leaving Becky and her too-close-to-the-truth taunts to pick up messages from Margaret.

I had hoped to find comfort and solace in my office. Instead I found several files stacked in the center of my desk with Ellen-o-grams taped to each one. "So much for the whole 'your afternoons are your own' deal."

Bleary-eyed, I managed to read through the first file. It had more addendums than the U.S. Constitution, plus blueprints and all sorts of zoning stuff that kept me reaching for my legal dictionary. At this rate, I'd be at it until the age of forty. Assuming I didn't kill myself before then. Big assumption, I decided as I finished the memo and hit the key sending it to the printer.

Just like a kid in kindergarten, I needed a reward for my efforts. Something tangible to acknowledge that I'd completed one of the eleven files Ellen had unceremoniously dumped on my desk. All the really good tangibles were on eBay. At least the ones I could afford. Well, could afford after Friday.

Logging on, I was bummed to see that PilotWife's dress auction had climbed out of my price range. I detoured over to Rolexville, scouring the new listings for a part I could add to my coveted build-it-yourself project. Sighing, I read the detailed description for a diamond bezel. Not in the cards, though. First I had to build my fantasy watch; then I could think about embellishments.

I placed a bid on a link for the band, then clicked a few other items to place them in my "watch list." I'm an eBay professional; I know better than to bid too early. It just jacks the price up. Bid too late and you risk a last-minute grab by some lurker.

Not that I didn't trust Jane. I did. Just not as much as I had before I'd found out about her secret past. Going over to the Google search page, I started to type in her name, then felt a swell of guilt. No, Googling a friend is bad form.

I sat for a minute, contemplating my next move. Liam wasn't my friend, so that made him fair Google game. I'd typed L-I-A-M-M-C-G when my phone rang.

"Finley Tanner."

"Hi. It's Liam."

Like the proverbial kid with her hand in the cookie jar, I hit the backspace key until I'd erased the portion of his name. Silly, since he couldn't see me, but it just felt wrong to be cyber-snooping when the snoopee was on the line.

"Bad time?" he asked.

"No, just . . . No. What's up?"

"I've got preliminary results back on the champagne bottle and the glasses from the limo."

"And?"

"Traces of Rohypnol."

"GHB?" I asked. "The date rape stuff?"

"Yep."

"That's great! So the killer spiked their drinks, then followed them inside Jane's apartment."

"Or," Liam began in that deep, sultry, about-to-rain-on-my-parade voice of his, "Paolo did it to loosen Jane up. Or Jane did it to loosen Paolo up. Or they mutually agreed to give it a try. No way to know until the fingerprints come back. Assuming there are any prints."

I wanted to scream. "Just once, it would be great if you could call with good news. You know, something nice that would boost my spirits?"

"You want your spirits boosted?"

"It would be nice."

"Okay. You've got great legs."

I did. And they damn near buckled.

Fear will either motivate you or make you incontinent.

Eleven

Being mired in the minutiae of a merger between two software companies was enough to make me long for the days of the Pony Express. Technology was advancing faster than laws and statutes, so I really had to hunt to find any remotely relevant stuff for Ellen. This new assignment sucked.

Still, being in my office at 7:10 PM sucked more.

Knowing Jane was about to spend her second night in captivity sucked the most. I'd read the latest motion Taggert filed with the court. The one where he didn't bother asking that it be expedited. Plus, the decrepit son of a bitch had practically glossed over the fact that all the Charleston charges had been dropped. He'd opted instead to focus on Jane's ties to the community. Big whoop when she was facing trial for freaking murder.

"Asshole," I muttered as I climbed to the very top of the ladder—the part that had DANGER! DO NOT STAND ON TOP STEP! marked on a pristine neon yellow sticker. I was exercising caution—I'd kicked my wedges off and was balancing on tiptoe as I reached for some tome on congressional oversight as it related to the FCC's role in reference to shareware in the technology marketplace. With any luck, said tome would fall off the shelf and hit me on the head, causing actual unconsciousness. Maybe then I could go home.

But only for eleven hours, give or take. The 8:00 AM rule was in effect. Heaven forbid I renege on my deal with Ellen. I thought she might be testing me. Dumping all these files in my lap after she'd said my afternoons were my own was so Ellen-esque. She was trying to break me—and while I was nearing the precipice of insanity, I wasn't quite there yet. I was going to get through all of the files if it took me all night. I could do it. I only had one case left. I had determination. Most importantly, I had coffee.

It took some doing, but I finally managed to wiggle the rarely used book from the shelf. Then allowed it to fall to the floor of the firm's law library with a loud, reverberating thud. No one heard it. I was alone. No Maudlin Margaret. No Vain Dane. No Estrogenless Ellen. Just me until the custodial staff showed up. They arrived sight unseen in the middle of the night like some antibacterial version of the tooth fairy.

Struggling under the weight of the heavy volume and two others I'd already culled from the shelves, I slipped on my shoes and went to the elevator. I jabbed the DOWN arrow with my elbow, finally getting it to light on the third try.

The sound of grinding gears was magnified in the now silent building as the elevator arrived, then deposited me one floor below the library.

It took me more than an hour to review the information and draft a memo. A sense of satisfaction embraced me as I affixed the last memo to the last file and added it to Mount Mergers on the corner of my desk. I toyed with the idea of taking them to Ellen's office and leaving them outside her door. Her office was surely locked and frankly, the payoff wasn't worth the effort required to hand-deliver everything to the executive floor.

Pressing the heels of my palms into my tired, burning eyes, I took a deep breath, then lugged the reference books out to the reception area and placed them in the "Return to Library" bin.

I was tired but under the influence of a caffeine buzz, so I went back to my office. I have a decent aftermarket laptop I keep at home, but it's a dinosaur compared to my Dane-Lieberman machine with enhanced DSL.

Logging on to eBay, I was irritated to see all of Pilot-Wife's auctions had ended. I dashed off a quick e-mail to her, telling her I'd been tied up—handcuffed, actually, but she didn't need to know that—and asking her to let me know if any of the sales fell through. I amended the message, asking if she might have something else she was willing to sell. Lisa's wedding was still a few months away and I needed a rehearsal dinner outfit. Hitting SEND, my message was routed through eBay. I would have preferred to grovel directly, but that isn't how it works, so I had to hope the woman checked in regularly and would get back to me.

As I typed in the URL for Google, I noticed my voice mail light was blinking on the phone beside my monitor. I used the eraser end of my pencil to hit the speaker option, then keyed in my access code.

"Where are you?" Liv's tone was a blend of annoyance and mild panic. "I went to see Jane. She's putting up a good front. Did you talk to Harold at Drive Right? Call me. Bye."

Damn. I'd left a message for the owner but hadn't heard back. I scribbled a note to try him again as the voice mail began playing the next missed call.

"I saw your light on as I was leaving the office." Ellen Lieberman's voice was tinged with amusement.

"Glad you think this is funny," I said, glaring at the telephone.

"Details, Finley. Details. Have a nice evening."
Beep.

"What the hell does that mean?" I wondered. "I've been working my butt off for hours on details."

Taking a deep breath, I raked my fingers through my hair, then twisted it into a knot and secured it with one of the black binder clips from the top drawer of my desk.

"Hi, Fin," the next message began. Patrick's voice was muffled. He sounded like he was whispering, probably because he was in some gully, hundreds of miles from the closest cell tower. "Just wanted to see how you're doing and check in on Jane."

I heard a high-pitched squeal in the background. Not being a nature freak, I didn't know what kind of wild animal made that noise. Didn't want to know either.

"I'll call you when I can. Take care."

Beep.

The next message was short and to the point. "Harold from Drive Right returning your call. Sorry I missed you."

Beep.

The last message was from Becky's secretary. The Fantasy Dates files had been delivered by Taggert the Inept. The efficient woman had already made copies and sent them through interoffice mail.

Beep. "End of messages."

Since the files weren't in my in-box, or anywhere else obvious, I called Becky's cell. My call went directly to voice mail.

Scooting my chair back, I got up and went out to the center cubicles. I didn't rate an administrative assistant of my own. Instead, I shared the dozen or so support staff who occupied the cubicles across from the elevators. After a bit of searching, I found a white cardboard box on the floor next to the desk of one of the summer interns. On the top of the box, my name was clearly printed in bold, black Sharpie. The box next to the word *urgent* was checked.

Summer Intern C—they never stayed long enough for me

to learn their names—obviously had her own definition of urgent. Lifting the box, I was a little surprised that it was so light. Fantasy Dates was successful, so I'd expected literally dozens of files. Hearing the rattling and shifting as I walked back to my office, I knew the box was less than half full.

When I opened it, I knew why. Bright red hanging file folders dangled from metal T-hooks clipped over the lip of the box. Small plastic tabs were affixed to the top of each folder, precisely spaced and staggered in groups of six so each name was clearly visible. Sorta creepy to think Perfect Paralegal Mary Beth had a doppelganger out there.

Many of the names I recognized instantly, starting with the very first file. Jace Andrews was a totally hot real estate broker. I'd seen him at a couple of DAR events over the years. And now that I thought about it, he attended those things as his mother's escort. Tough to troll for dates with your mommy in tow.

Matthew Gibson was another familiar name, though I was a little surprised to find he had a Fantasy Dates membership. The *Palm Beach Post* has been running regular updates on his upcoming nuptials to Kresley Pierpont, infamous Palm Beach party girl. And the sole heir to the Pierpont all natural, all organic, no taste cereal fortune.

The impending Kresley-Matthew marriage was a blending of old and new. The Gibsons were old money, the Pierponts were, by Palm Beach standards, new. Their cereal fortune was born only after the health craze of the 1960s, whereas the Gibson fortune predated the signing of the Declaration of Independence. And, if I was remembering my trashy tabloid information correctly, Kresley was worth a fortune. Matthew was worth a few million.

Reaching into Matthew's file, I found nothing but a CD. Doing a cursory check, I found all the files were paperless. Not a problem for me. I could only hope Taggert had a competent secretary. If not, he'd never be able to look at the information on the clients, making it unlikely he'd develop leads on an alternate suspect. He didn't impress me as a computer guy. Okay, he didn't impress me period.

I wished Quinn was representing Jane. I wished he hadn't served me with a subpoena. Mostly I wished I wouldn't have to tell Ellen or Vain Dane, but that wasn't an option. It was, however, something I'd put off as long as possible.

Flipping through roughly fifty names, I smiled when I hit the letter P. Kresley Pierpont also had a membership. Funny, the newspapers hadn't ever mentioned that she'd found her one true love through an expensive introduction service. If I remembered correctly, the engagement announcement implied the couple had met in St. Barts. I guess that's more romantic and socially acceptable than admitting the two of them paid a combined total of ten grand for a suitable hookup.

I had a choice to make. Slip the CDs in my computer or pack it in for the night. If I thought staying in my office would get Jane out of jail, I'd gladly pull an all-nighter. Sadly, it wouldn't, so I put the top back on the box and scooted it off to one corner. Like me, it would be there ready and waiting in—I checked my watch—ten hours and seventeen minutes.

I had my purse in my hand and my finger on the light switch when I decided to try Limo Service Harold again. Drive Right was on my way home.

"Hello?"

"Hi, this is Finley Tanner. May I speak to Harold, please?"

"This is."

Finally, something that felt like success. "I'm trying to track down the man who drove Paolo Martinez and Jane Spencer last Saturday."

"Billy?" he said, clearly annoyed. "You and me both. I talked to him this morning after I got your call. Then he's a no-show tonight."

"Is he sick?"

"Who the hell knows? He's not answering his phone."

"Maybe I could give him a call?" I suggested. "May I have his home number?"

"I don't give out personal information on my drivers."

My shoulders slumped. "How about his full name?"

I heard the guy sigh deeply. "What the hell? Serves him right for screwing me over. I'm paying his replacement time and a half, so sure."

A few seconds later, I had William "Billy" Arthur's name and home address in my hands. Going back to my computer, I did a quick MapQuest on the Acreage address, then hit PRINT.

Map in hand, I left the building. The last few slivers of pink and gold from the disappearing sun painted the evening sky. In spite of the hour, the temperature hadn't dropped much. It was still in the eighties.

I got on 95 heading north, then took the Blue Heron exit. PGA Boulevard might have been more direct, but it didn't have a drive-through Dunkin' Donuts on the right-hand corner just off the exit ramp. Armed with a tall iced vanilla latte, I headed west.

The Acreage is one of the few remaining rural communities in the county. At least for now. The name is a relic from the days when Palm Beach County was the underpopulated escape from the urban sprawl creeping up from the south. The Acreage was just that—unnamed acres of undeveloped land. But in South Florida, home to the newlyweds and nearly deads, land was at a premium and the Acreage was shrinking fast.

Billy Arthur's house was at the end of a dirt lane. Okay, so "house" was a bit of a stretch. The hairs at the back of my neck tingled as my car bounced over the uneven, pitted roadway. His tiny, dilapidated, desperately-in-need-of-repair house was set about a hundred yards back from the main street.

And it was dark. Really dark. Maybe this wasn't a great idea, I decided as I parked behind a silver sedan with a caved-in bumper and a sheet of plastic duct-taped into the back window. I smelled rotting vegetation and swamp milkweed as I stepped out of my car. Judging by the overgrown plants and the knee-high grass, Billy didn't have a lawn service.

Intentionally, I left the headlights on. I didn't want to skulk around in the dark. I could feel the pounding of my heart thudding in my ears, and it dawned on me that I was having a serious blond moment. What if Billy was the killer?

"Forget this," I muttered, turning to head back to my car.

I didn't get far. Slamming into a solid chest and rock-hard muscle, I did the only logical thing. I screamed like a girl.

Several dogs howled as strong fingers dug into my arms. Flattening my palms against his chest, I was about to push when I smelled the familiar scent of Liam's soap.

Tilting my head back, I glared up to see his cocky, amused half smile illuminated by my headlights. "You scared the crap out of me." I shrugged out of his hold, scraping the back of my sandal on a hunk of cement at the edge of the drive. Balancing on one foot, I yanked off my shoe and inspected the damage. My nearly new wedges had an ugly gouge that ran the entire height of the heel. "Damn it! These are ruined."

Liam just shrugged. "I'm sure you have more than one pair of pink shoes. In fact, you probably have dozens."

I did, but these were my favorites. "What are you doing here?" I glanced around him, not seeing his piss-poor excuse for a car. "How did you get here?"

Hooking his thumb toward the street, he said, "Parked up on the road and walked."

"Why?"

"It's my job."

"To scare me half to death *and* ruin my shoes?"

"Sorry I scared you, and get over the whole shoe thing. I followed you here."

"Why?"

"It's my j—"

"Job," I cut in, imitating his tone and inflection. "To stalk me?"

He laughed. That annoyed me. Technically, the fact that I liked the deep, masculine sound was what really annoyed me, but so what?

"I wasn't stalking you. Lieberman doesn't want you getting into any trouble, remember?"

"Yeah." After slipping my shoe on, I kicked a small pebble with my toe. "She also said my afternoons were my own."

"Excuse me?"

"Forget it. For the record, I wasn't getting into trouble. I came here to interview the limo driver."

His head tilted to one side and he gave me a quick but pointed stare. "The one with six arrests and three convictions? That driver?"

I shivered and then did my best to convey confidence I didn't possess. "Obviously I didn't know he had a criminal record. Any of those arrests include a knife or a penis?"

"All domestic disturbance stuff. You were about to knock on the door of a guy who gets his kicks smacking women around. Not your smartest move. You should have called me."

"I didn't want to run the risk of disturbing you in the middle of a *thing*."

"If I'm in the middle of something, I'll let you know. Now, are we going to knock on the door of the obviously empty house, or just stand here?"

Great, both options made me look inept. "His boss said he called in sick, so he could be home."

He waved his arm in the general direction of the house. "Lead on, Nancy Drew."

Grabbing hold of a neglected iron railing, which jiggled like it might give way, I decided I was better off navigating the five nicked cement steps on my own. Liam was right on my heels, so close that I could feel the warmth of his breath against the back of my neck. It was so distracting that I considered yanking off the clip and using my hair as a shield against my inappropriate awareness of him.

Balling my hand into a fist, I rapped twice on the door. The sound echoed but garnered no response. I tried again. Nothing.

Liam reached around me, his biceps just brushing my bare arm. The contact was slight but enough to send a zing through me. That irritated me almost as much as Billy not being home.

Using the heel of his hand, Liam pounded on the door with enough force to make the thing rattle on its hinges. A second later, he reached for the knob and turned. It opened.

"We're breaking and entering?"

"Nope. Just entering," he said as he moved in front of me.

The inside of the house smelled like a locker room, dank and sweaty. Liam turned on a small table lamp, flooding the room with harsh light from the shadeless bulb.

Sam would have gone running and screaming if he'd walked in here. Billy wasn't much on decorating. The front room had an old, torn Barcalounger, an end table with the naked lamp, and a circa 1956 TV tray. The floor was tiled, though the grout was black, probably some sort of toxic mold. Most of it was covered by a very worn, braided oval rug.

"Circle the one that doesn't belong," I said as I took in the flat-screen plasma television mounted on the wall next to two photographs of a man smiling as he held dead fish from hooks.

Liam went over and ran a finger along the top ridge of the television. "It's new. No dust."

We went into the kitchen. Dirty dishes and food-caked pots and pans covered the counter and half of the ancient dinette set. I shook when I saw several cockroaches feasting on the filth. "Seen enough," I said, backing out of the room.

The only other room was a bedroom. One bed, an empty twelve-pack of generic beer, two condom wrappers—either Billy hired a prostitute or he was practicing safe masturbation—and at least a dozen more roaches shared the unkempt space with a neatly pressed uniform hanging on the door frame to the adjoining bath. I let Liam take the bathroom. I was busy making sure no bug made it within ten feet of me.

"No Billy," he said.

"So now what?"

"Jupiter Marina."

"Because?"

He pointed at the photographs on our way out of the house. "Billy's a fisherman. I noticed scratches on the sedan's bumper."

I had to hurry to keep up with his long strides. "How do you get Jupiter Marina from a scratched car and pictures of a guy holding fish?"

"You can see the Jupiter lighthouse in the pictures and the scratch on the bumper is right where you'd attach a trailer hitch."

Color me impressed. "I'll follow you."

"No, we need to talk. Toss me your keys."

"About what?"

"I got the fingerprint results back."

"And?"

"Three sets. Paolo, Billy, and Jane."

"So Billy had to be the one who put the GHB in the champagne."

"Or Paolo. Or—"

"Don't say it," I warned. "Jane wouldn't drug a guy."

"Did you ask her?"

I glared at him. "I didn't have to. She drinks carrot juice and works out. She won't even take an aspirin. There's no way she'd put GHB in her system."

"Not even to get a guy to—"

"Have you seen Jane?" I asked, not bothering to keep my simmering anger in check. "She's pretty. She doesn't need to drug a guy to get laid."

"But she joined a dating service."

I clutched my keys so hard it felt as if they'd pierce my skin at any moment. "To meet an interesting guy. Huge difference, McGarrity."

He shrugged. "Fine."

"Fine? That's it?"

"Sure. You know her, I don't."

The ready-for-a-fight adrenaline stopped pumping through my system. "Okay, then. Is there anything else we need to talk about?"

"Nope."

"Then I'll follow you."

"Fine."

"Fine."

Liam made me insane. Other than the fact that he was gorgeous, he didn't meet any of my criteria. A few years ago, in an attempt to keep from falling into the same lousy man choices that had plagued me from the get-go, I'd made a list. Patrick possessed most of the qualities on my list. Liam, none. I reminded myself of that every minute of the fifteen-mile drive to the marina.

We were about a half mile from our destination when we had to yield to several fire trucks racing north on A1A. I saw the red-orange glow up ahead and followed Liam as he pulled over, went about a quarter mile, then parked on the shoulder of the road.

The sirens were silent but the red and white lights from the fire trucks swirled on the pavement as we walked toward the marina's parking lot. There was an acrid smell in the air, causing me to lift my hand to cup my nose and mouth.

At the far end of one pier, a small boat was engulfed in flames. The hose from a marine rescue boat sent a steady arch of water cascading on the fire. The dockmaster and other people scrambled to move boats away from the burning shell.

"What's that smell? Diesel fuel?"

"Yes," Liam said. "And burned flesh."

I swallowed bile. "That's disgusting."

"No, that's probably Billy."

Whenever someone tells you it's not the gift but the thought that counts, you're about to get a lousy gift.

Twelve

Billy was dead. Though fried to a crisp, dental records confirmed his identity. That meant Liam was right. A frequent occurrence that was grating on my last nerve. Then again, it was seven-twenty in the morning and I was heading out the door. Squinting against the blinding light from the way-too-cheery sun, I juggled my briefcase and travel mug as I poked the button on my key ring, disengaging the alarm on my car.

According to Kevin and Virginia on the *Wild 95.5 Morning Show*, today would be hot as hell. Still, it was nothing like the hell Jane must be going through. My chest squeezed knowing my friend was entering her third day in captivity.

I'd called Liv and Becky to give them an update on the marina fire and to work out a visitation schedule. Jane needed support and I needed some answers. Well, not answers so much as confirmation. I wanted to hear from her lips that she didn't know anything about the GHB. The charges in Charleston and hearing the Molly Bishop saga had caught me off guard. I just needed reassurance that Jane didn't have anything else tucked away that might surface and bite her in the ass.

Especially not if someone was spoon-feeding that information to the assistant state attorney.

By the time I reached Dane-Lieberman, I'd added to my mental list of Things That Didn't Add Up.

As I walked into the empty reception area, I couldn't help but feel a small burst of smug superiority. For the first time in my seven years at the firm, I'd beaten Margaret through the door.

I had Ellen's files finished and ready for delivery. I am Finley Tanner, Paralegal Extraordinaire, hear me roar. It was enough to make me feel as if I should don a cape, but it wouldn't go with my ensemble. Said ensemble gave me an added boost of confidence. New clothes have that effect on me. My aqua skirt was from Dillard's midsummer clearance sale. Seventy-five percent off, plus the additional ten percent because I'd bought it on Senior Discount Tuesday, thanks to the elderly woman I'd convinced to add my purchase to hers. Though my poplin blouse was simple and tailored, it was lightweight enough to withstand the sweltering July heat.

A few of the brownnosing interns were already at their desks, glancing wide-eyed as I stepped off the elevator. I waved and smiled as if me arriving at the crack of dawn was nothing out of the ordinary. Thanks to a hefty amount of concealer, the dark circles under my sleep-deprived eyes were erased.

Usually, the first thing I notice when I go to my office is the scent of mango air freshener. Not today. Not when Ellen Lieberman was sitting in my chair leisurely flipping through one of the memos I'd diligently prepared.

"Good morning."

She smiled. Not a friendly, glad-to-see-ya smile. It was more like a Cheshire Cat thing. The metaphor worked since she was wearing a lose-fitting tabby-striped dress. "You were busy last night."

"Yes. You left me the files and—"

"Details, Finley." Standing, she sighed heavily.

"Yeah, I got your message." Don't have a clue what it means, but I got it. "I think you'll be satisfied when you review my work."

"I'm sure I will be. I just don't understand why you stayed last night to get them done."

I blinked. "Because you left them for me. You were very clear on the fact that you expected me to have all work you assigned completed promptly."

"Is that all I said?" she asked as she came around my desk and placed the file she'd been skimming on top of the others.

"Be here at eight. It's"—I checked my Kuber watch—"five till."

"You missed an important detail."

Not if the detail is you being a real pain in my ass. That one's coming across loud and clear. "I'm sorry. Refresh my memory."

"I said I expected all work finished by lunchtime if you wanted your afternoons free."

"It is finished. I made sure I didn't leave here until every i was dotted and every t was crossed."

"That's the detail you missed. I dropped the files off yesterday. I didn't change the deadline, so there wasn't any reason for you to stay last night."

"Would have been nice if you'd mentioned that."

Ellen shrugged. "I did; you obviously weren't paying attention." She headed toward the door. "You're a salaried employee, so the extra hours you put in were a donation."

The muscles in my shoulders knotted as I checked my anger. "Apparently." Maybe she'd remember that fact when it was time to dole out bonuses. Probably not.

"On the plus side, you're ahead of schedule."

My mood brightened. "So I can leave early?"

She shook her head. "No. You mentioned estate work that still needs attention and a couple of motions you need to draft." She pointed at my desk. "I left you some suggestions."

"On?"

"Becky showed me a copy of what Taggert filed with the court. The weak argument won't sway Judge Faulkner. You can do better. Write a new motion, have Becky do the cover letter, and messenger it over to his office."

"Taggert isn't very effective."

"Quinn would have been a better choice," she reminded me.

"Yes, well, that didn't work out."

"I know. I spoke with him yesterday afternoon."

"Did he tell you he served me with a subpoena?"

"Of course. Making me look pretty foolish since *you* failed to mention it."

I dropped my eyes to the floor, pretending great interest in the color variegations of the looped Berber carpet. "So putting the files on my desk was punishment?"

She patted my shoulder. "Think of it more like penance. And, Finley?"

"Yes."

"Stay away from limo drivers and fires. Got it?"

"Yes."

Gathering up the files, Ellen left, reminding me again that even though I was more than current on my workload, I was Dane-Lieberman's property until the stroke of noon. So be it. After starting a pot of coffee to brew, I read Ellen's notes regarding bail. I was miffed at being manipulated, but that evaporated when I saw the case law she'd provided.

She might be a pain in my ass, but the woman was a brilliant lawyer.

Wiggling the mouse to bring my computer out of hibernation, I quickly logged in to the Westlaw database and printed off the relevant information. I really wanted to dive right in, but I had to prioritize. There was a lot to read but I didn't dare incur the wrath of Ellen a second time by ignoring my primary job responsibilities. So I spent most of the next hour updating the status on my four open estates.

Having all my proverbial ducks in a row before nine felt strange. Not in a completely bad way either. Yes, I was sleep-deprived. Yes, I'd had to rush around to get out the door. But there was a small part of me that felt a little exhilarated knowing that when push came to shove, I could get the job done. And on time. Who knew! Of course a large part of me resented the push and the shove.

Contracts done, estates done, now it was time to focus solely on Jane. My chest squeezed as a mental picture of her wearing a jumpsuit while sliding a tray along the jail chow line played like a slow-motion video. Instantly, I felt guilty for being so whiny about my morning when hers was way, way worse.

Becky roamed in a few minutes after Ellen left. She un-screwed the bottle of water in her hand as she practically col-lapsed in the seat opposite my desk. "Never pegged you for the suck-up type, Little Miss Turn It In Early."

"Believe me, it was an unintentional suck-up."

"I figured as much. Jane says hi."

"You saw her?"

Becky nodded. "Went by this morning. I drove up to Stu-art and got her an almond croissant from Mr. Bread."

"That was nice. She loves those. How'd you get pastry past security?"

Becky gave a wicked little grin. "New corrections officer. Young and easily distracted by breasts." She flicked open the top button of her coral blouse, revealing just a hint of lacy bra. "While he was busy ogling my Victoria's Secret cleav-age, the contraband croissants tucked inside my briefcase sailed right past him."

"Literal tit for tat. Good plan."

She rebuttoned her blouse. "Anything for Jane."

Leaning back, I rubbed the cap of my pen along my lower lip. "Speaking of anything, what gives with Lieberman? Why is she being so . . . helpful?"

Becky diverted her gaze. "She can be helpful."

"Since when? Wait a minute! What did you do?"

"Nothing."

"Becky?"

She uncrossed and recrossed her legs. "I gave up some vacation time. No biggie."

"How much?"

"Not much."

"How much?" I asked more forcefully.

"Three."

"You had to donate vacation time for an introduction to Quinn? One that turned out to be a total bust? Or is three days of vacation the price she's charging to let you act as Jane's legal adviser?"

"Neither. It isn't three days, either."

"Three *weeks*?"

"Yes."

"That sucks. You already put in like a million hours a year. Now you'll only have one week away from here."

"It's no big deal," Becky insisted. "You drew the shortest straw. You're financially obligated to the Wicked Witch."

I winced. "I still haven't cashed the check."

"Right, but doesn't interest start to accrue from the day she made the loan?"

There was that. "I'll worry about that later."

"Watch it. Your 'later' is filling up. How long do you think you can keep your mother debt and boyfriend dismissal on the back burner? Unless you've already figured out how to dump Patrick. Have you?"

My jaw tensed. "I haven't even decided breaking up is what I want."

"Bullshit. You've chosen not to make a change. There's a big difference."

"You spent the morning flashing your boobs at a rookie corrections officer and you're giving me dating advice?"

Becky twirled a tendril of auburn hair around her index finger. "I didn't flash boob, I flashed bra. It wasn't for me, it was for Jane. A purely altruistic action on my part."

"Ha!"

"Think about it," she said, changing the subject. "He's out there communing with nature, walking among the pine trees, and you're not pining for him. That should tell you something."

"It does. It tells me you don't know anything about the Grand Canyon. No pine trees."

"Whatever. The thing between the two of you has run its course. Besides, it's a freaky relationship."

As much as I tried, I couldn't muster indignation or irritation. "It isn't freaky. He's good to me."

"Really? Is that why he's off traipsing through the woods when one of your closest friends is in jail?"

"He would have stayed if I'd asked. I didn't. Patrick respects my space."

One of Becky's perfectly shaped brows arched. "Love means never having to ask your boyfriend to stick around while you're being questioned by the police."

"I should write that down. Maybe Mary Beth could cross-stitch it on a pillow for me. Speaking of Mary Beth . . ."

"We weren't," Becky said. "You just want to change the subject."

"That too," I mumbled as I scooted my chair over and retrieved the Fantasy Dates box. Removing the lid, I pushed it around my desk. "It shouldn't take me long to go through their membership list," I said as I watched Becky pull a shiny gold CD from one of the files. "The stuff they sent is majorly organized."

"Mary Beth didn't do this?"

"Scary, huh?"

"They say everyone has a twin. Guess that's true," Becky said. "So, what's on these things?"

"Hand me one."

Once she did, I slipped it in the drive and waited approximately a sixth of a second before an error sound dinged and a box popped up on my screen. "Password-protected," I read aloud. Irritation came easily as I ejected and reinserted the disc, hoping for a different outcome. My hopes were dashed. "This blows."

"Can't you call Shaylyn or What's-His-Name and ask for the password?"

"I'll have to."

"How can I help?"

"This isn't a two-person job. But . . ." I paused and organized everything I'd amassed on reconsideration of bail. "I'll read through this stuff and do a draft for you. Give me about an hour?"

"I can do it."

I shook my head. "Ellen told me to handle it. I know she's looking over your shoulder, so let's do it her way."

Taking one last sip and screwing the top back on her water bottle, Becky wished me luck and left.

My estimate of how long it would take me to do the draft was off by roughly double. It was almost eleven by the time I sent two draft motions to Becky via interoffice mail. The first was for a motion in limine, requiring Faulkner to ignore anything having to do with the Charleston charges and base his decision solely on the Paolo crime. The second was a motion for an ex parte hearing. I didn't think that one had a chance; judges don't like it when the defense makes an argument outside the presence of the prosecutor. Even if it failed, at least the judge would know that Assistant State Attorney Brent was using information fed from an unnamed, unidentified outside source. Judges don't like anonymous any more than they like clandestine motions.

I made a note to have Liam try to find the source. He seemed to have contacts out the wazoo. If we could find the source, we could find Jane's enemy. It stood to reason that the enemy was the one who'd killed Paolo and framed Jane for the crime. I tried his cell phone but it went to voice mail.

The batteries could be dead.

He could still be at the marina. Billy's death was a little too convenient to be a coincidence, but we had to wait for the arson squad to do their thing.

Or Liam could be doing his "thing" with Ashley.

"I hate men," I grumbled as I dialed Liv. Jean-Claude informed me she was out meeting a client to go over wedding reception details and was stopping by the bank before returning to the office. He suggested I try her cell. I would, but not right away. A—If she was getting grief from clients, I didn't want to interrupt her with Jane business. B—The bank visit was crucial. If Faulkner granted bail, we needed money to pay a bondsman.

Reinserting the Jace Andrews disc into my computer, I made a few attempts at passwords. I tried fantasy, dates, client, and rich. Frustrated, I caved and called Shaylyn.

"Hello, you've reached Fantasy Dates, the premiere introduction service in Palm Beach. We're sorry we missed your call but if you leave your—" I hung up on Shaylyn's chipper greeting without leaving a message.

I didn't relish the idea of calling Taggert, but I needed the password.

"Clark Taggert's office."

My feminism slipped for a second; I hadn't expected doddering Taggert to have a male secretary. I wouldn't have pegged him as the equal opportunity type. "Hello. This is Finley Tanner from Dane-Lieberman."

"Yes, Ms. Tanner. How may I help you?"

"I got the box your office sent over but all the information is password-protected."

"Yes, ma'am."

"Well, it makes them kind of useless if I can't access them. Did Ms. Kidwell or Mr. Davis provide the password?"

"I don't know. Would you like me to check?"

No, I just called to pass the time. "That would be great. Thanks."

I cradled the receiver between my chin and shoulder as I listened to a full orchestra version of "Mack the Knife." The brass instrument heavy rendition didn't do the song justice. Not that I'm a raging Bobby Darin fan or anything, but one of the few gifts my mother had given me was a broad exposure to music.

"Sorry," the male secretary said as he returned to the line. "I can't find anything and Mr. Taggert isn't in the office right now. Would you like me to have him call you when he returns?"

"When will that be?"

"I'm not sure."

"Could he be at the jail with Jane Spencer?"

"I don't know, ma'am. He hasn't checked in and there's nothing written in his calendar for this morning."

I had a vision of Taggert roaming the streets of West Palm in a dementia-induced fugue. The vision got worse because for some reason, my mind had dressed him in a bright red Speedo. "I'll try him later. Thank you." *For nothing.*

No Liv, no Taggert, no Liam, no Shaylyn, no Zack, no password, no access. Serious amounts of frustration.

I was out of options. Well, not exactly out of them so much as completely lacking in patience. What I had was a state-of-the-art tech department a mere telephone extension away. I was pretty sure our geek squad could crack the code a lot faster than I could track down any of the principals.

While they were doing that, I would try some alternative methods. Moving the box closer to me, I opened a new document and began making a list of the names from the tidy tabs labeling each hanging folder.

They were alphabetical and color-coded by gender. The men's names were printed in blue ink, the women's in dark magenta. It wasn't until I'd typed Renee Sabato and Jane Spencer that I noticed a slight flaw in the otherwise perfectly configured system. Someone had skipped a slot, leaving a gaping space between the letters S and W. I derived some small measure of pleasure from the minor mistake. Perfection is daunting.

With the list complete, I lugged the box to the tech guys and sweet-talked my way into making the password encryption their top priority. Manipulating the techies wasn't much of a challenge. The closest most of them had ever been to a woman was the digital versions in video games. They were a nice enough group, just socially stymied with thumbs callused from years spent cyber-battling aliens in alternate universes.

When I returned to my office, I refilled my coffee mug, not really caring that hours of sitting in the carafe had turned it bitter.

I might not have passwords, but I had Google. And Lucky Charms. Separating the cereal parts from the marshmallows, I started searching.

Molly Bishop was my first target. According to the South Carolina Department of Vital Records and confirmed by an obituary, she was dead. I was glad Jane hadn't lied about that but annoyed because by checking, I had to admit to myself that my faith in my friend had been shaken just a little.

There wasn't anything I could find that even remotely linked the Charleston thing with Paolo's murder. Molly's drug abuse predated her friendship with Jane and as far as I could tell, there wasn't anything that would make the Bishop family suddenly go psycho and frame Jane. Senator Bishop was retired and other than a few public appearances, he and his wife were quietly fading into their golden years. A recent photograph of the couple cinched it. I just couldn't see the dignified-looking senator and his proper, staid wife lobbing off Paolo's penis.

Along that vein, I decided not to work in alphabetical order just yet. Better to start by seeing what I could find on the dickless victim. After refreshing my memory by reread-ing the file stored in my in-box, I surfed the Net for anything else that might be relevant.

Lots of fluff pieces from various area newspapers and local magazines, but virtually nothing of substance. The one interview I did find was two years old. It was a congratula-tory profile of Paolo, mainly focusing on his brave journey via inner tube from Cuba. His entire family perished in the crossing, leaving eleven-year-old Paolo all alone in the world. From that humble beginning, he'd mastered the world of fi-nance, making his first million before the age of twenty-five.

I stared at his picture for several minutes. "Maybe one of your fellow floatees had it in for you."

Flipping through my office directory, I grabbed the phone and called the paralegal who handled immigration cases for the firm.

"Estella Chavez."

"This is Finley in estates and trusts."

"Hi, Finley, what can I do for you?" she asked in heavily accented English.

Estella had only been at Dane-Lieberman for a few months. She was twenty-two, fresh out of college, and hope-fully doesn't know that firm policy requires me to submit a written request for out-of-department information. "I need the INS file on Paolo Martinez." Doing the math in my head, I added, "DOB March 31, 1978. Immigrated sometime be-tween 1989 and 1991."

I heard her fingernails clicking against her keyboard; then she asked, "M-A-R-T-I-N-E-Z?"

"Yes. Middle name Diego, if that helps."

"Are you sure?"

"Yeah." The little hairs on the back of my neck prickled. "Why?"

"Martinez is a pretty common name. It's like a Spanish version of Smith. But no Paolos in that time frame."

"Can you check 1978 to date?"

"Sure."

I drummed my nails on my desk, staring at Paolo's handsome face as I listened to Estella breathe in my ear.

"No Paolo Diego Martinez entered the country, at least not legally. Are you sure he's documented?"

Switching back to the Fantasy Dates file, I found his Social Security number. Virtually impossible to get one of those without proper documentation. "Yeah. Can you tell me how many eleven-year-old Cuban males entered the country between 1989 and 1991?"

"One hundred and three. Eighty-seven right here in Florida."

"Would you mind sending me those names?"

"Not a problem. Anything else?"

"Maybe. I'll get back to you. Thanks."

There were several possible explanations for Paolo's failure to appear on the immigration registry. Maybe he lied. The whole difficult and dangerous escape from the tyranny and oppression of Cuba made for good copy and was damned heroic. Much more heroic than, say, walking in from Mexico, Guatemala, or any number of South or Central American countries. Grabbing a flight from the Dominican Republic or Colombia or anywhere else just didn't have the same ring to it. Unfair and a tad racist, but very ingrained in the fabric of Florida's immigrant community.

I sent Estella an e-mail, asking her to broaden her search for any Paolo from any country. Just to be safe, I widened the search years just in case Paolo was older or younger than his profile indicated. I didn't know where he was from, but I knew one thing. The inner tube story was bullshit.

So much for Fantasy Dates doing thorough background checks. I could understand why they hadn't bothered with a criminal check on Jane, because Liv had vouched for her. The fact that they'd missed Paolo's faux past had alarms sounding in my head.

When Ellen told me I could use my afternoons to discreetly work on Jane's case, I'm pretty sure she didn't mean I could use the Dane-Lieberman account to run Paolo's Social Security number. But, since she hadn't specifically prohibited me from doing so, I filled out the form and faxed it to the credit bureau I used primarily to find any forgotten bank accounts, liens, or other financial abnormalities before closing probate.

Discouragement started to set in. The tech guys were still working on the CDs. The credit report would take at least a day, and Liv, Shaylyn, and Taggert were still AWOL.

On the plus side, I had the client names. On the minus side, there's no section in the Yellow Pages for rich people, so I couldn't even make calls.

Except for Jace Andrews. He had a real estate business. It was worth a try.

"Good afternoon, Prestige Properties."

"Finley Tanner from Dane-Lieberman calling for Mr. Andrews."

"He's with a client, Ms. Tanner. Would you like to speak to one of our other agents?"

Jesus, Mary, and Joseph. I should have sent out a memo to have the people I wanted to talk to stay at their desks until contacted. "No, thank you. It's a personal matter. Would you ask Mr. Andrews to call me at his earliest convenience?" I rattled off my cell number.

I started going through the alphabetical list I'd made earlier and suffered failure after failure. No wonder these people couldn't get dates—they were impossible to reach.

I needed a new approach. A creative one.

My Internet surfing yielded a few possibilities. A handful

of the dating service clients had jobs. Well, businesses. They weren't exactly the nine-to-five types. Payton McComber was a jewelry designer with a swanky shop on Worth Avenue. For Jane I would make the trek across the bridge.

Okay, so I'd make the trek for no reason, but that was beside the point. At least I had someplace to start. In addition to Payton's shop, Prestige Properties' main office was on the island. As were two of the three restaurants whose major investor was some guy named Harrison Hadley.

Before I ventured over to the land of the wealthy, I needed to stop by and visit Jane.

Her days in jail were taking their toll.

"You okay?" I asked as soon as the guard left us alone in the small counsel room. I passed Jane the can of Coke I'd gotten from the vending machine on my way in.

She thanked me, then asked, "Any word on bail?"

"Becky and I are on it. Tell me about Paolo's accent."

Jane seemed taken aback by my question. "His accent?"

"Yes, was it more like Ricky Ricardo or Andy Garcia?"

"Neither. He didn't have an accent."

"Okay, so not a pronounced one?" I asked.

"No. As in he didn't have one."

"Did he tell you anything about himself?"

"Not really. A lot of that night is fuzzy, but he seemed more interested in me. Or rather my investment preferences."

"Makes sense. You're both in finance."

Jane adjusted the collar of her ill-fitting orange jumpsuit. "I guess. I think he was just being polite."

"Why?"

"His questions were . . . amateurish. Mutual funds, T-bills, really basic stuff."

"Maybe he was more focused on getting the GHB in you?"

Jane raked her fingers through her hair. "That doesn't make sense. Almost from the get-go, he had to know I was interested. He was a gorgeous, healthy, virile guy and Lord knows I was ready to end my dry spell."

"You didn't tell him that, did you?"

"I *might* have mentioned it had been a while since my last relationship. I mean, it wasn't like I greeted him at the door by saying, 'Hi, how are ya? I'm Jane and I haven't had sex since the Clinton administration.' "

I held up one hand. "Okay, sorry. Did Becky tell you about the limo driver?"

"Yes."

"If Paolo didn't slip you the GHB, then it had to be the limo guy. Remember anything about him?"

She shook her head. "He opened the door and he closed the door." She drew her lower lip between her teeth. "Am I going to get out of here soon?"

I reached across the table and squeezed her cuffed hands. "We're doing everything possible. Promise."

We were both on the verge of tears but I was determined not to cry. Drawing my hands back, I caught the edge of the nearly full can, knocking it on its side and spraying myself with soda. "Damn it!" My blouse and skirt were splattered beyond repair. Worse, my loud curse alerted the guard, who came zipping into the room.

"Everything okay in here?"

"Peachy," I said as I surveyed the damage. Looking at Jane, I said, "I'm sorry, but I've got to change before I go over the bridge."

"It's okay. Becky said she'd come by after work. Liv, too."

I wanted to give her a hug, but the strict "no contact" rule prevented me from offering anything more reassuring than a weak smile before leaving.

Backtracking to my condo to change was going to eat nearly an hour out of my schedule. It would be close to four by the time I reached Worth Avenue. Still, plenty of time to ambush Payton, if she was at her shop. If not, I'd try Jace Andrews, then finish with Harrison Hadley. Businesses closed at five but Hadley's restaurants would be open for dinner.

I spied the flower box and the courier envelope propped against my door even before I cut the engine on my BMW. The flowers were probably from Patrick. The courier envelope was signature Mom. It was like being kissed and slapped at the same time.

Gathering the box and the envelope, I unlocked my door and went inside. I knew the flowers would make me happy, so I decided I'd save them to salve whatever injury awaited me as I tore the perforated strip of the envelope.

Inside the stiff cardboard, I found a second sealed card with my full name scrolled on the monogrammed and lightly scented lilac stationery. The note was short and to the point:

> Due to your recent activities, I'm going out of town for a few days. I have moved our brunch reservation to Saturday. Kindly be on time.

"I'm not feeling the love," I muttered as I glanced at the calendar hanging on my fridge. Not that it mattered. Even if I had plans, canceling wasn't an option. Mainly, I did want to thank her for the loan, but also, bailing on my mother was never a good idea.

With the change in plans, I needed to make sure the florist had the roses ready for me to pick up by ten instead of three as I'd originally ordered. That would give me plenty of time to make it to Stuart, public apology bouquet in hand.

I gently pulled on the pretty pink ribbon securing the flower box. On top of the crisply pleated tissue paper was a knife. A big knife. Weird. Moving the knife to the counter, I unfolded the tissue and froze.

It took a full second for my mind to process what I was seeing. Once it did, I couldn't turn away fast enough. Grabbing up the phone, my fingers trembled as I pressed the numbers while fighting waves of nausea.

"McGarrity."

"Liam, I have a penis."

*The 50-50-90 rule: Anytime you have a 50-50 chance
of getting something right, there's a 90
percent probability it will turn out wrong.*

Thirteen

"**A**ny idea why someone would send Paolo's di-*part* to you?"

I was standing by my patio door, arms folded, glaring at Liam. I couldn't get the image of poor dead Paolo's shriveled, *severed* penis out of my mind. "Of course not." It hadn't even *looked* like a penis. Not any penis I'd ever been acquainted with anyway. It looked like an old person's . . . dead finger. I felt kind of sick to my stomach at the thought of someone—who?—chopping off the poor guy's equipment.

I felt a lot sicker seeing it. That was an image I'd never get out of my head.

I had a right to be not only grossed out, but scared as hell that the killer had seen fit to mail me not only Paolo's part, but the knife as well. The one the cops had been searching for high and low since Jane's arrest.

Rubbing a hand across the nerves jumping in my stomach, I tried to hide any vulnerability in front of stoic, monosyllabic Liam—but the words just popped out. "What should I do?"

"Gotta turn it in to the cops. The knife, too."

Dread settled in my stomach. "I touched the knife."

"Not too swift."

"I was expecting flowers, not . . . that."

Liam raked his fingers through his thick, dark hair. "You gotta call them. I had to turn over the champagne bottle and the glasses to the cops."

My eyes widened. "What?"

He shrugged, the action causing his broad shoulders to strain against his silk and rayon blend surfer shirt. The print had faded to a color very close to the gray-blue hue of his eyes. Giving myself a mental bitch slap, I focused back in on the situation. How inappropriate was it to notice details about Liam when I had Poor Dead Paolo's penis lying in state in a box on my kitchen counter?

"The cops knew I took evidence from the limo and demanded I turn everything over. Didn't have a choice. Neither do you."

Squeezing my eyes shut, I fought the sting of tears. I hadn't exactly ingratiated myself to Detectives Graves and Steadman. There was no way of predicting exactly how they'd react to me being in possession of Paolo's privates. I just knew it wouldn't be good.

Even with my eyes closed, I sensed Liam had crossed the room. I felt the heat from his body and smelled the soothing scent of woodsy soap. Gently, he pulled me against him, my cheek resting against the solid hardness of his chest.

My folded arms were sandwiched between our bodies. The even, rhythmic beating of his heart calmed away the threat of tears. Crisis averted. It should have ended there. All I had to do was step sideways, step back; hell, step in any direction that would allow me to escape from the circle of his arms.

Indulging in a pity hug that could potentially lead to really great, really hot pity sex was a bad, bad idea. But the tip of his finger was making little circles in the center of my back.

Liam's touch acted like a huge eraser on my already compromised judgment.

Don't do it! the smart girl voice in my head warned. But that warning was obliterated by the bad girl voice screaming, *What the hell are you waiting for? Go for it! You want it. You know you do.*

My breath hitched as I slowly lifted my chin, until I felt the warmth of his minty breath against my face. His mouth, mere inches above my own, was a thin, straight line. His eyes shone as they roamed over my features, finally settling on my slightly parted lips.

As I unfolded my arms and planted my hands at his trim waist, his palms ran over my bare arms until his fingers entwined in my hair. His pupils dilated as the pad of his thumb traced the line of my jaw, then slowly explored my lower lip.

Gently at first, then with more pressure. It was just a touch but felt more exciting than a heated, passionate kiss. My stomach wasn't filled with dread anymore; it was burning. Every nerve in my body tingled as fire spread from the inside out.

If my conflicting voices of reason were still talking, I couldn't hear them over the sound of my pulse throbbing in my ears. This was one of those moments. Those magical, thrilling moments that make you want to tear his clothes off. And your clothes. And fast. Really fast.

Sliding my hand between us, I began to unbutton my blouse. I was three buttons into it when Liam took a step back. A giant step. Hell, a freaking leap.

"What are you doing?" he asked.

I pinched the seams of my top closed. "I thought we were going to . . ." I felt my cheeks flame.

"It doesn't work that way," he said in his normally steady voice. "You're not ready for sex."

Not ready? Was he nuts? I passed ready five seconds after he looked at me with those smoldering eyes. I was eager. I was needy. If that isn't ready, then what is?

That was then. Moment over. Now I'm just humiliated and furious. "What are you? My eighth grade health teacher?" I snapped.

He held up his hands, palms facing me. "Don't be pissy. I'm just a guy with rules. Unlike your usually absent pilot."

"What's that supposed to mean?"

"Sorry," he said, though his tone negated the apology. "That one you have to figure out for yourself."

Ellen Lieberman's mantra suddenly played in my head. *Details, Finley. Details.* Tilting my head, I glowered at him. "For your information, I figured it out months ago. The first time I saw you and Ashley together."

He seemed to be fighting a smile. He lost the battle. "Not that it's any of your business, but Ash and I have an arrangement going, and history."

I didn't want to hear this. Stiffening my spine, I walked toward my bedroom wearing my wounded pride like a ball and chain. And with my back turned, I hastily did up my blouse.

"Running and hiding?"

Hell yes! "Of course not." I didn't turn around. "I'm going to change my clothes, then call the police. You can leave."

I didn't hear him cross the room, but suddenly his fingers closed around my upper arm before I made it to the door. "Look, I'm sorry about what just happened. You looked like you were about to get all weepy so I thought a distraction might help."

"That wasn't distraction, McGarrity. It was a lame-ass attempt at seduction."

He leaned close to my ear and said, "Wrong. If and when I seduce you, you'll know it and it won't be lame. You change, I'll call the cops."

Shrugging free of his gentle grasp, I went into my bedroom, then closed and locked the door. "Dumb, dumb, dumb," I grumbled as I hastily found a suitable pair of khaki capris, a rust-colored cami, and a sheer, mocha floral over-lay top.

I had a great pair of new ballet flats that would have complemented my outfit, but instead I opted for Cole Haan slides. The three-and-three-quarters-inch stacked heels gave me height and I doubted Steadman, Graves, or Liam would notice the imperfection in the braided leather that had slashed the price down into my affordable zone. If it wasn't for factory damage, I'd be looking at a closetful of rubber flip-flops from Walgreens.

Deciding between a simple gold chain, no accessories at all, or a chunky beaded choker ate up another ten minutes. Okay, so I knew I wasn't going to put on anything but thin hoop earrings about five seconds after opening my jewelry drawer. The rest of the nine minutes fifty-nine seconds was just me stalling. I couldn't stay in my room forever, especially not once I heard someone knocking on my front door.

Less than an hour ago, I was on my way to Worth Avenue. Thanks to the soda spill, I'm now going to spend God knows how long explaining how and why I came into possession of the missing body part.

Emerging from my room, I really, really wanted to be mad at Liam but I couldn't. Not when I smelled fresh coffee. Caffeine always trumps annoyance. While he got the door, I grabbed a mug. It would have been polite of me to offer the detectives coffee, but as far as I knew, there were no hard and fast social rules when it came to severed penis delivery.

Shivering as I walked past the now closed box, I mustered a smile as Liam let the two detectives in. "Detectives."

Like a guided missile, Steadman went directly to the box, snapped some latex gloves over her hands, and removed the lid. Graves opened his small memo pad, retrieved the nubby little pencil, and fixed his chocolate-colored eyes on me.

"What time was the box allegedly delivered?"

Allegedly is not a good word. In fact, it's a bad word. Particularly when said by an officer of the law who already thinks you're complicit in a crime.

"I wasn't home, so I don't know." I leaned against the arm of my sofa, sipping coffee as my attention darted between Graves, Steadman, and Liam.

"Where were you today?"

"Work, then I went to see Jane."

Steadman bagged and tagged the knife and the penis, then tried to fit the flower box into a large brown bag. Liam watched her every move. I did my best to pretend it wasn't happening.

I mean, I don't even like to open a package of chicken, so the gory body part thing was grossing me out. I wondered how many scrubbings of bleach it would take before I'd be comfortable using my counter again. I didn't think I could count that high. Probably be easier just to move.

Easier but impossible. My bank account couldn't handle first and last months' rent and a deposit. Nor were movers a realistic option and I didn't really see myself as the do-it-yourself U-Haul type. I decided that I could use my kitchen only if I cordoned off the penis-tainted area in some way. A large plant strategically placed. Or a statue of some sort. Or—

"Miss Tanner?"

Graves's stern voice reeled me back to reality. "Sorry. What?"

"Did the Spencer woman have the knife and the . . ."

"Penis."

"Right," Graves agreed with discomfort. "Did she bring them with her?"

He might be uncomfortable, but I was eyelashes deep in a rising pool of fury. "Of course not."

"Ed?"

Liam called him Ed. Ed? As in they were friends? Traitor.

"Sorry," Graves said, looking at Liam and shrugging his bulging shoulders. "You know the drill."

"Hello?" I raised my hand. "I don't. What drill?"

"Please put the coffee cup on the table, stand up, and put your hands behind your back."

"What for?"

"Finley Tanner, you're under arrest for aiding and abetting in the murder of Paolo Martinez. You have the right to remain silent. Anything you say can and will be . . ."

I tuned out everything except the metallic click of the handcuffs.

For the second time in a week, I found myself in the police station. More specifically, in the holding cell. More of a cage, actually, with hard metal benches and hard-core roommates. Of the half dozen or so women, two were there on domestic charges. One had the beginnings of a black eye and she was sobbing softly. She looked more like a victim than a perpetrator if you asked me. But no one was asking me, so I kept my lips zipped.

There were three pacers, too. They were human versions of NASCAR—perpetual motion, left turns only as they stalked the inside of the fourteen-by-fourteen-foot cell. Given their jerky movements, shaky hands, bad skin, and worse teeth, I suspected they were meth-heads.

Talk about a "circle the one that doesn't belong" moment. Except that I was the worst offender of the lot. Chargewise, that is. The brawling babes would be held for twenty-four hours, Florida's definition of a cooling-off period. As for the meth-heads, some public defender would have them out in no time. Especially since they were afternoon tweakers. That meant hard-core addiction. Drugs might be a huge blight on society, but arresting the addicts was little more than a means to an end. Give up your dealer and get out of jail.

Me? My fate was a complete unknown. I'd used my allotted call to phone Becky. Her sage legal advice consisted of two words—Oh! and Shit!

A few minutes before seven, a parade of stumpy guards came in, each balancing trays of food. Okay, so food was a stretch. One by one we were given paper plates and plastic sleeves containing a cheap, thin napkin and a spork. That was the good part.

The meal was vile. Two slices of stale white bread topped a rancid-smelling, ice-cream-shaped blob of . . . tuna salad? Maybe chicken salad? Couldn't tell. A few limp carrot sticks, a small carton of lukewarm two percent milk, and some green Jell-O rounded out the offering.

"Coffee?" I asked. Okay, so it bordered on a plea more than a question.

Stumpy Guard Number One shook her nearly shaven head. "Sorry, honey. Can't serve anything that might be used as a weapon. Enjoy your dinner."

I've had bad coffee. But coffee used as a weapon? Who knew? The mixture of cheap, stale perfume and strong, fishy mayonnaise killed my appetite. That, and the reality of my predicament.

Arraignment was starting to sound good. At least then I had a chance of being transferred to the same building housing Jane. A friend would be nice. Freedom would be better.

"You gonna eat that?" the unscathed brawler asked, pointing to the tray I'd set on the bench beside me.

"Help yourself."

She scarfed the entire meal in just over a minute. She was quite adept with a spork, telling me this probably wasn't her first incarceration. Napkin use was a different matter. Apparently she preferred wiping her chapped lips on the back of her hand, then smearing . . . *whatever* on the front of her stained, way-too-tight-for-her-body-type T-shirt. The crowning moment was the loud, foul-smelling belch she let loose.

Now I really wanted to cry. Or in the alternative, slit my wrists. Tough to do when you have only a flimsy spork at your disposal.

A while after the trays were collected, a bailiff came in holding a clipboard. He pulled a pen from where he'd tucked it behind his ear and called out, "Tanner, Finley A!"

I jumped to my feet—feet, I might add, which were covered by a pair of paper forensic booties. Some brain trust had decided that heels also represented a clear and present danger, so my shoes had been confiscated during the booking process.

"Step forward, turn around, and place your hands on the ledge."

It was a dual-purpose ledge. The same scuffed metal slot was used to deliver and collect food trays and it was the first stop on the road out of the holding cell.

Again I suffered the pinch of handcuffs shackling my wrists and winced as he clicked them as tight as possible.

"Clear!" he called to someone; then a piercing buzzer went off; then the cage door clicked as the lock released. "You ladies step back. Tanner, you're with me."

For a split second, I considered offering to bear his children if he'd march me out to the parking lot. Then I looked at him. He could file an additional charge of bribery against me; plus, I couldn't get drunk enough to do him. He was medium height and had one of those "I'm in my third trimester" beer bellies. I suspected he spent his off-duty hours planted in front of a television in a grubby T-shirt eating chips from a bag on his chest. He wasn't all bad. If you Photoshopped out the second and third chins, his face could be okay. He had decent eyes. And a tight grip on my arm.

"Where are we going?"

"Night court."

Thank You, God. "My shoes?"

"You'll get them back once we get upstairs."

Because the city of West Palm Beach had gotten some

wild hair about preserving the original 1916 courthouse in the renovation and construction of its state-of-the-art replacement, a breezeway connected the old and the new.

A public breezeway. Lined with reporters. The bailiff commanded his way through the crowd while I was blinded by bright white camera flashes and trapped in the tractor beams of videographers.

They were screaming at me. "Finley, where exactly did you keep the evidence?"

"Finley, was Dane-Lieberman aware of your role in the murder?"

"Finley, if you aren't involved, why didn't you turn over the evidence sooner?"

And my personal favorite, "Finley, what is your relationship to Jane Spencer? Are you lovers?"

I couldn't decide which would horrify my mother more— that I stood accused of complicity in Paolo's murder, or that a reporter had just announced I was a lesbian. Neither was true nor substantiated, but that wouldn't matter. Not to her. And not, judging by her glare, to the property clerk who handed me my shoes when we reached Faulkner's courtroom. I didn't know if she was homophobic, but it was a safe assumption that she was criminal-phobic.

My body was a tight ball of tension as the bailiff opened the side door to the courtroom. I expected to see Becky at the counsel table. Feared it might be Taggert. Stunned when I saw it was Ellen.

As the bailiff escorted me to the table, I saw Becky and Liv seated next to Liam in the gallery full of reporters. My girlfriends offered diminished attempts at smiles. Liam was, well, Liam. He was relaxed, with one elbow resting atop the chair adjacent to him. For all intents and purposes, he seemed at ease, like he was at a Marlins game. I had neither the time nor the inclination to delve into his body language. Not when I was facing the very real possibility of going to jail. And the legendary wrath of Ellen Lieberman.

Still handcuffed, I was positioned next to Ellen. Her anger felt palpable as she slapped her brown leather backpack on the table. It doubled as an unattractive purse and a briefcase.

"I owe Victor fifty bucks," she said curtly as she pulled a thin folder from the center compartment. "He told me you'd screw up before the end of the week. Obviously my faith in you was misplaced."

Ow. Warranted, but a direct hit. "I appreciate you coming." Which, God only knows, I did. "But *why* did you?"

"PR, mostly."

I didn't like the sound of that. "PR?"

"Yep."

"I don't understand."

"Oh, you will," she said.

Her tone only added to my swelling anxiety.

Faulkner's arrival was announced along with a command for everyone to rise.

The judge looked more pissed than usual. Why wouldn't he? Normally the newbie judges sat night court, but since this was a matter directly connected to Jane's case, Faulkner must have been called in.

Glancing across the narrow aisle, I noted Allison Brent was present on behalf of the state. All the heavy hitters were teed up and ready to swing. Unfortunately, I was the one with the target painted squarely on her forehead.

The clerk of court instructed the gallery attendees to sit. Then the case was called. There is something scary hearing your name in a sentence that begins, "State of Florida versus . . ."

"Ellen Lieberman, counsel for the defendant."

"Ms. Lieberman," Faulkner acknowledged, obviously surprised.

Made sense, Ellen hadn't been involved in a criminal proceeding since her admission to the bar. Even I didn't know why she was there.

"You're waiving the reading of the charges, I assume?" Faulkner asked.

Ellen nodded her head. "Yes, Your Honor. Defense moves for an immediate dismissal of all charges based on insufficient evidence."

Brent leaned forward, her fingertips tented on the table top. "Your Honor, defense isn't seriously suggesting any insuffiency given that the victim's penis and one of the weapons used in the commission of this heinous crime were found in the possession of the defendant, is she?"

Ellen pulled several neatly and individually stapled papers from her folder. "Defense offers six sworn statements from neighbors of the defendant stating they witnessed the delivery of the box containing the evidence as well as affidavits from myself and Victor Dane attesting to the fact that Ms. Tanner was in her office at the time specified by the witnesses."

."The medical examiner placed the time of death at approximately two AM on Sunday. The police were not notified until six AM, giving Ms. Tanner plenty of time to assist Ms. Spencer in tampering with and/or concealing evidence," Brent argued.

"Based on the sworn statements of the eyewitness, we identified and verified the company hired to make the delivery. Accordingly, we were able to obtain an additional affidavit from the employee working the register of the courier service, who clearly recalls the date and time the package was dropped off as well as the gender and a general description of the person who shipped the items to Ms. Tanner."

The clerk delivered the stack of affidavits to the judge. The courtroom sat in hushed silence as he read them. You could hear the proverbial pin drop. Or more likely, the thudding of my racing heart against my ribs.

When he was finished, he passed them on to the prosecutor. Angrily, she flipped through them. A deep stain seeped up from her neck, finally painting her cheeks a bright red. I expected steam would shoot from her ears at any moment.

"Ms. Brent?" the judge prompted, seeming none too pleased.

The pendulum was swinging my way, taking some of my apprehension along with it.

"The state requests this matter be held over until it has an opportunity to review this information and interview the witnesses."

"The defense opposes any such request," Ellen said. "The state has failed to establish a prima facie case and the suspect nature of the probable cause is a clear violation of my client's Fourth Amendment rights."

The judge raised his gavel, allowing it to linger, along with my fate, in midair. "In light of Ms. Lieberman's compelling arguments, I'm dismissing this matter without prejudice, Ms. Brent. You are free to refile charges following a complete and thorough investigation."

Legalese meaning I was free to go but Brent was equally free to come after me at any time. At least until the real killer was found.

Immediately, the bailiff removed my handcuffs, and I was so relieved I started to hug Ellen. She reared back and gave me a silent warning. Right, not the touchy-feely type.

Didn't matter. Becky and Liv rushed me, leaning over the railing to embrace me.

"I'm so relieved," Liv said, her violet eyes moist. "Let's get you home."

Ellen parked herself next to us. "She has some forms to fill out first."

"We'll wait for you out front," Becky promised.

Ellen pointed a finger at Liv. "You can wait out front." She turned to Becky. "You and I need to talk."

I looked up in time to see Liam about to exit the courtroom. He winked and flashed an incredibly sexy grin, then disappeared. All things considered, it was probably just as well. I didn't need any distractions.

I had to find out who killed Paolo. It was that or spend every moment wondering when the police would haul me off again. Not to mention Jane's uncertain future. The only way we could put this behind us was to find out what really happened in Jane's apartment. With the knife. In the bedroom. Without the penis.

Okay, so I was giddy enough to be playing a silly version of Clue in my head while the police had me sign things in triplicate just to reclaim my purse. So what? I'd earned it. I'd also earned a martini. Or two.

If it was practical to skip in stacked heels, that's how I'd have left the courthouse. I breathed in the fresh, slightly salty scent of the ocean breeze and happily welcomed the warmth of the night air. Becky and Liv were across North Dixie Highway, standing on the sidewalk next to the parking complex.

The temperature dropped about thirty degrees when I found Ellen waiting for me. She was leaning sideways to accommodate the weight of her backpack. A bright white envelope was in her left hand. Oh, and she looked pissed.

I didn't care. She could ream me, lecture me, whatever. Nothing she could say or do was going to ruin this moment for me.

"Thank you," I said again, truly grateful for what she'd done inside the courthouse.

"Here," she said, holding the sealed envelope out in my general direction.

Okay, so maybe she could ruin my moment of jubilee. "What's this?"

"Your termination letter. Thirty days' severance pay and a prorated amount for the sixteen hours of vacation time you didn't use."

My eyes practically bulged out of their sockets. "Excuse me?"

"You're fired."

"You defended me and now you're firing me?"

"You were warned, Finley. You missed another important detail, by the way."

Screw you and your details. "Really?"

"Yes. I wasn't defending you, I was defending the reputation of the firm. I'm done and now so are you."

Budget: noun. Latin word meaning you're out of cash and your credit cards are maxed out.

Fourteen

It was day two of lime-green and pale-pink-striped cotton drawstring pants, and a white baby T. My hair was in a ponytail. My arms were crossed behind my head. I was lying on the floor, staring at the circular motion of the ceiling fan with my feet resting atop one of two boxes representing the sum total of the last seven years of my professional life. "I'm fired."

"I'm suspended," Becky sighed from her prone position on my sofa.

Liv was in the kitchen, making herself an omelet. "I've got to make sure the bounce house is inflated and the little princess arrives in her glass carriage by two."

"At least you're busy," Becky said as she unwrapped another Hershey's Kiss. My coffee table was littered with small silver foil balls. "Ellen keeps sending me work at home but not enough to fill up a whole day."

One empty, family-sized box of Lucky Charms was lying next to me. No amount of protein, sugar, or caffeine had managed to jump-start us out of our group funk. "At least you're still getting paid."

"There is that," Becky agreed. "Think positively, Finley. They could decide to rehire you once all this goes away."

"Maybe," I agreed, though I wasn't exactly bubbling over with hope.

"You could work for me," Liv suggested as she joined us. She pushed some of the scrunched-up wrappers off to a corner of the table, then scooted one of my armchairs closer.

Unlike me, who was dressed dangerously like a bag lady, Becky was at least presentable in jeans and a casual shirt. Liv was decked out in a periwinkle print Diane von Furstenberg wrap dress and flawlessly made-up.

"Doing what?"

"Party stuff."

"Busywork?" Not that I was above typing menus, faxing proposals, or anything else. The severance pay wasn't going to last very long. I just didn't think working for a friend was a great idea. Case in point, I was directly responsible for Becky's two-week suspension.

"You can light a fire under Taggert," Becky said. "We need to get Jane out of jail."

"I saw her last night." Liv pushed the plate away, leaving more than half her omelet untouched. "The motion Taggert filed was supposed to be heard today, but he faxed over a request for a postponement. Why would he do that?"

"He's an ass," I answered. He was more than an ass, but I figured, A—they both knew that, and B—The more I thought about the doddering old coot, the more afraid I became that Jane would end up in jail forever. Or worse. I shuddered. "Maybe we should hire Ellen. She was totally prepared when I went before Judge Faulkner."

"That was your hot P.I.'s doing, not Ellen," Becky said.

That got my full attention. I sat up. "What?"

"Liam got all those affidavits and tracked down the delivery service. Just showed up and dropped them in Ellen's lap."

"Why didn't he say anything?"

Becky finished chewing her zillionth chocolate Kiss. "I'm supposed to be a mind reader? Not that I'd be opposed to getting into his head. Or his pants."

"He really is hot," Liv said. "Seriously hot. So hot that I would happily go—"

"Point taken," I interrupted. I didn't know where her "go" was going and I didn't want to know. "We need to do something."

Becky tossed a foil ball at me. It missed. "You need to stop moping and take a shower. We need to be proactive. We need a plan."

"I'm going to take a shower in a few minutes. That's the start of a plan." I turned and gave Becky a "screw you" look. "I'm unemployed, under a cloud of suspicion, and yet I've maintained my positive outlook on life."

"Bullshit," Becky scoffed. "So I got you a little gift."

"Since the penis thing, I've developed gift phobia."

"Bullshit times two. You'll like this, promise."

"What is it?"

"The Fantasy Dates files. They should be here any minute along with the discs from the geekazoids."

"Did they crack the password encryption?"

"Yep, worked day and night. Well, unless one of them found a date to inflate."

Liv laughed, caught herself, and donned a chastising frown. "That's harsh."

"You haven't seen our techies," I said. "They're talented, but not exactly chick magnets. They tend to spend more time with *Halo 2* than humanoid women."

"It would help if I could talk to Zack and Shaylyn," I told Liv. "Any idea why they aren't returning my calls?"

She shook her head. "Fantasy Dates has gotten a lot of bad press. I suspect they might have slipped out of town to get away from the reporters. They aren't returning my calls either."

About an hour later, Liv went off to supervise the Pretty Princess party and Becky went back to her place to work. Me? I dragged myself into the bathroom and started the shower.

As the room filled with steam, I glanced disgustedly at the pile of dry cleaning that had long ago outgrown its wicker bin. I was looking at a minimum of two hundred dollars, and that was only if I drove all the way up to Hobe Sound and used the budget cleaner at the corner of Route 1 and Cove Road. My laundry situation wasn't much better. Five, possibly six loads were stuffed into the hamper. I added chores to my list of things to do later, stripped, and stepped under the stream of hot water.

Worth Avenue was one of my eventual destinations, so I dressed the part. The trendy, spendy chic shopping district on the island didn't welcome casually attired mortals. Tourists who wandered in with cameras hanging around their necks were treated much like invading aliens. If I had a hope of getting Payton or Jace or the Hadley guy to talk to me, I had to at least look the part.

Inland temperatures lingered in the mid-nineties, but Palm Beach ran five to ten degrees cooler thanks to the onshore breeze off the Atlantic. With any luck, I wouldn't melt in the ivory and black wrap dress. A pair of Steve Madden peekaboo-toe fabric and rope wedges dangled from my fingers when I heard a knock at my door.

Finger-fluffing my not-quite-dry-yet hair, I checked the peephole, then slipped the dead bolt out of the locked position. I recognized the man and the box he had tucked beneath one beefy arm. Opening the door, I was slapped in the face with a rush of hot air, thick with the scent of Darin's inexpensive cologne. "Hi, Darin."

"Finley," he said pleasantly as he held out the Fantasy Dates box. "Courtesy of Ms. Spencer. I thought you got canned?"

I imagined Margaret taking great pleasure in placing a banner smack in the middle of the firm's lobby announcing my untimely and sudden departure. She and her file room flunkies were probably dancing around like the Munchkins after Dorothy's house fell on the Wicked Witch of the East.

I smiled at my firm's—correction, *former* firm's—messenger. *Ah!* "Just finishing up a few things. Thanks."

"Take it easy," he called, jogging back to the Dane-Lieberman-leased SUV he'd left idling in the parking lot.

Dropping my shoes near the door after shoving it closed with my toe, I carried the box to the sofa and set it down. Retrieving my laptop from my bedroom, I set myself up in the living room. Normally I work at the counter, perched on one of the mismatched bar stools, but I'd sprayed half a bottle of Clorox Hard Surface cleaner and was letting it sit. I planned on repeating the process later. That should kill any creepies and cooties left by box-o-severed-penis.

While my agonizingly slow computer booted, I finished drying my hair and applied my makeup. I actually felt better. I was still unemployed, but at least I now looked good doing it.

Rummaging under the bathroom sink, I grabbed the box of tampons and pulled out the special one. It wasn't really a tampon, it was a cost-effective version of a safe-deposit box. I kept the diamond stud earrings Patrick had given me on our one-year anniversary inside one of the empty plastic applicators. I figured it was a good hiding place, unless I happened to be robbed by the first menstruating thief in recorded history.

They were a half carat each, appropriate daytime bling for a jaunt across the bridge. As I was going back to the living room, I happened to glance at the gift bag on my dresser. Liam's cryptic comment about Patrick and me played in my mind. Going over to the bag, I peeled back the tissue and peeked inside at the Christmas ornament. "How does Liam know you're gone a lot?" I asked the Brazilian beach girl as if the blown glass thing was some sort of surrogate Patrick. "He was probably just being snotty," I decided as I refolded the tissue and pinched the gold foil sticker back in place.

Running the pad of my finger over the sticker, I felt the faint embossing of a letter. No, two. No, three. Three letters too indistinct for me to decipher. "Screw you, Liam," I grumbled, setting aside the gift and refusing to allow his sibyline cynicism to get to me.

Well, trying to at least. What made him think he knew anything about my relationship? So what if Patrick was gone a lot? I liked that. Maybe too much.

Crap.

Everything about Liam was wrong. He was aloof and arrogant, not to mention he was still Ashley's plaything. Yep. He didn't have a single redeeming quality. Except that he made my blood sing.

Damn.

"Enough!" I said, physically shaking myself, hoping that would help. It did.

Turning my attention to the box, I discovered one of the techies had written me a brief note. *Password: Snowy Owl.*

Strange password. I didn't really care so long as it opened the CDs. It did.

"Hello, Jace," I said as I began digesting the actual life and secret longings of the real estate magnate. He was a nice-looking man. Forty with dark hair and sexy dimples. No wonder he'd made a fortune in sales. With a smile like that, I'd sign on the bottom line and thank him for the privilege. He was hot, he was rich, so why the hell did he need an introduction service?

The doughnut theory skipped through my mind. Said theory supports the reality that when it comes to dating, men are lazy. They might crave a meal from a great restaurant across town, but instead of putting forth the effort to go there, they grab the closest doughnut. Apparently, Jace was a doughnut dater.

I scrolled through the information, pretty standard stuff. The main thing of value was his home address and telephone number. I made a note. Next came his likes and dislikes, blah, blah, blah. On page three, it finally got interesting. Fantasy Dates had hooked him up with three different women in the past six months. Barbie Baker, Alexandria "Lexi" Haig and Alisa Williams. "For five grand, I'd expect more," I said as I continued to tap the Down arrow on the keyboard.

The last few pages were invoices. In addition to the membership fee and the actual costs associated with each date, he'd also been paying something coded as "Special Assessment." Whatever it was, it had better be special; the monthly payments were two thousand dollars each. I made another note. I needed to ask Shaylyn and Zack about the fee. Assuming they returned one of my twenty or so urgent messages some time before I started collecting Social Security.

Snapping my fingers, I grabbed my cell from its charging base and called Estella Chavez. After accepting her condolences on my "unfortunate termination," I asked her to see if the information on Paolo's Social Security number had come back from the credit bureau. She agreed and promised to call me back in a few minutes.

Lucky for me, Barbie Baker was alphabetically next in the Fantasy Dates filing system. Thirty-one-year-old divorcée. According to her credit report, her former husband was some sort of businessman from the Midwest who was paying her seven hundred grand a year in alimony. That was on top of the thirty-million-dollar oceanfront mansion she'd gotten in the settlement. Not bad considering she'd only been married to the guy for three years. Hell, for that kind of pension, I'd consider moving to St. Louis to see if the guy was interested in a second short-term money-hemorrhaging marriage.

If I didn't clear my friend and my name and find another job, being the potential next Mrs. Baker might have to be an option. "When did I become my mother's clone?"

The one glaring difference between the Barbie Baker CD and the Jace Andrews one was Barbie had stopped paying the special assessment. But she'd gotten a lot more bang— no pun intended—for her buck. She'd averaged a date every two weeks until about three months ago. Some were repeats; apparently she was quite fond of Jace and—Ding. Ding. Ding. She'd been out with Paolo three times. Maybe significant, maybe not. Worth noting.

By the time I'd worked my way up to the letter *G*, I had a stiff neck and eyestrain. Two things kept me going. I was waiting around for Estella to call me back, and I started to see a pattern.

Well, kinda. Special Assessment clients were paying the additional monthly fee, and almost all were actively dating. In fact—I paused, loading and ejecting CD after CD—they were doing much better than the average Fantasy Dates client. The two-grand assessment was starting to look like a date bribe. I made a list of their names. Harrison Hadley, Matthew Gibson, Kresley Pierpont—they stood out—Payton McComber, and Renee Sabato.

I didn't know anything about Hadley, McComber, and Sabato, but Matthew Gibson and Kresley Pierpont were weeks away from a multimillion-dollar wedding.

"So, why are you still paying a dating service?" I asked the photograph of Matthew.

Needless to say, the two-dimensional photograph didn't answer. But my phone rang. The caller ID readout told me it was Fantasy Dates. I grumbled a whispered "About freaking time" before flipping it open and saying, "Hello."

Nothing.

"Hello?" I said louder. Cell phones were convenient but not always reliable. Now was *so* not the time for a dropped call. "Hello? Shaylyn? Zack?"

Nothing.

I disconnected, then immediately hit the REDIAL button and listened as the phone rang six times, and then went to voice mail. "C'mon," I bitched, then tried again. Same result.

Poised, I was ready to try again when Estella called. "Hi."

"Sorry it took so long," she said, sounding slightly out of breath.

"Are you okay?"

"Yeah. Just a little out of breath from the stairs."

Stairs? Who took stairs when a perfectly good elevator was a button poke away? Energetic twenty-two-year-olds still blissfully operating under the assumption that their thighs would forever be cellulite-free. "Did the report come back?"

"Kind of."

"Meaning?"

"That social number does belong to a Paolo Diego Martinez, DOB March 31, 1978."

"But?"

"But he isn't an immigrant from Cuba."

"From where?"

"Dayton."

"Ohio?"

"Yes. There's more."

I ran my fingernail along my bottom lip, my interest piqued. "Go ahead."

"I thought you said this was some rich guy."

"He isn't?"

"There's got to be at least fifty creditors listed here. Visa, MasterCard, Discover, American Express, they all want a piece of this guy. Plus, he's defaulted on three car loans. Has a pending foreclosure *and* a criminal record."

"For what?"

"Doesn't say on here. Just that from 1998 to 2001, several creditors listed his residence as . . . House of Corrections in Jessup, Maryland."

"Thanks," I said, still scribbling notes on my pad as I closed the phone. So, either there were two Paolos with the same middle name and date of birth, or I had uncovered my very first tangible clue as to why someone would want to kill him.

Frustrated, I went to the kitchen and heated my now-cold coffee in the microwave. I was running out of ideas but not suspicions. Armed with caffeine, I went back to my computer.

Taking the Paolo CD and slipping it in the slot on my laptop, I quickly went to the criminal background page. According to the records, Fantasy Dates had requested and received the document nearly a year ago. No arrests, no convictions. "No way."

That left me three options. A—They'd never run a background check. B—The company they used dropped the ball, honestly or otherwise. Or C—Shaylyn and/or Zack and/or someone else had doctored the records.

My computer skills aren't great, but I'm not a total lost cause either. Closing out the file, I ran a directory check on the CD. There weren't any hidden files, no backups, nothing that inspired any new theories. It stood to reason that I wasn't finding anything because there wasn't anything to find. If the information wasn't on the CD, maybe I needed to try a back door.

I Googled Paolo again, this time using his full name and narrowing the search to the state of Maryland. I found a two-inch police blotter mention from the *Evening Capital*. In early '98, Paolo Diego Martinez was arrested on grand larceny charges. Not a lot of help. Just that grand larceny was a felony and usually applied to theft of property over a state-defined limit. Registering for access to the archives, I searched for anything else. No luck. Now I needed a side door.

I went to Westlaw and attempted to log in.

"User name and password invalid. What?" I retyped the information. Same error screen. "Margaret," I sighed, knowing with absolute certainty that she'd been the one to gleefully take the steps necessary to revoke my privileges.

I called Becky. "I'm locked out of—"

"Dane-Lieberman accounts. Yeah, me, too. I've already called and was told that my remote access would be restored after my suspension period."

I told her about Paolo's sordid past. "So how do we get stuff?"

"How much money is left in the Jane fund?"

"Almost all of it. I used most of Sam's five hundred on the Charleston trip. We still have Patrick's four thousand and the cashier's check from my mother, why?"

"We need a professional. I'm cut off, you're cut off, Paolo's cut off. Sorry, not funny. Point being, we need someone who knows how to dig up the dirt."

Only one name came to mind. "Liam?"

"Do I call him, or do you want to do it?"

I definitely wanted to do it with him, but I knew we were talking about two different things. My cell call waiting beeped. "I've got incoming, you'll have to do it."

"Chickenshit."

"Bye." I clicked over to the waiting call. "Hello?"

No response. I held the phone out and read the display. Fantasy Dates. "Damn." I pressed the microphone part close to my mouth. "If you can hear me, your freaking line is screwed up! Hello? Hello? Okay, I'll just pretend you can hear me. This whole phone situation is messed up. I'm leaving in a few minutes, so I'll swing by your office. I hope that's not a problem."

"No. You're the problem."

The tiny hairs on my arms stood on end at the barely-above-a-whisper, gender-neutral voice. "I can hardly hear you. Is this Zack or Shaylyn? Who am I talking to?"

"Me. I'm the person who'll kill you if you don't back off."

It's hard to stare down fear with your eyes closed.

Fifteen

Driving over to Fantasy Dates after the chilling phone call wasn't my brightest idea ever. Sharing my plan with Liv resulted in a stern lecture about recklessness and sage advice regarding the police. "Let them handle it," she'd pleaded.

Yeah, right. Like that was an option. Detectives Graves and Steadman were already convinced I was a conspirator, so they'd blow me off and/or haul me in to give yet another statement they didn't even pretend to believe. I'd spent enough time this week at the police station, so pass, thanks.

Becky was more adamant than Liv; she just shared her opinion in more colorful terms. Well, term, actually. Starting with "asshole"; then as the conversation progressed, adjectives were added—moronic asshole, incredible asshole, blah, blah, blah. She kept insisting I wait until she could track down Liam.

Not a great alternative. It was tantamount to admitting I needed a man to protect me.

Nor a practical one, as it turned out. While I'd been telling her my reasons for not wanting him there, she'd used her house phone to dial him up, listening to me vent through her cell. He was in the middle of doing one of his famous "things," and he'd "call her back when he was finished." I wasn't going to wait around for him, not when Jane was in jail and Taggert wasn't doing much to change that fact.

How could Liam have my back if he was busy giving Ashley his front? It wasn't like I needed him. After all, it was broad daylight. Fantasy Dates was open to the public, right on South Ocean, so what could go wrong?

Yes, Zack and Shaylyn gave me the willies, but so long as I was careful, I would be fine. I wouldn't go inside, just talk to them from the entrance, so I remained in full view of all passersby.

As I was reaching for the doorknob, my laptop dinged, alerting me of a new message. Going back to the computer, I discovered an e-mail from PilotWife.

> Hi WantItNow (my lacking in creativity but dead honest screen name): Happy to do business with you again. Have an event Saturday night. Willing to sell worn-once shoes and possibly dress as well. I'll get you a photo ASAP.

"Excellent," I said, then typed a quick Looking forward to it! reply.

Summoning as much nerve as possible, given the situation, I headed out the door armed with addresses for the Special Assessment clients and my only weapon—a cell phone. As an added safety measure, I went upstairs and knocked on Sam's door. Just my luck, he wasn't home. I could hear Butch and Sundance meowing inside. Sam worshipped his cats to the point of obsession, so I knew he wouldn't be gone long. Rummaging in my Betseyville hobo bag—the one with the slight tear on the front pocket I'd snagged for a cool sixty bucks—I got a pen and a receipt from my last trip to Publix. It was dated nearly two weeks ago. No wonder all I had in my fridge was coffee cream and a jar of mustard on the verge of making a suicide pact from the loneliness of it all. I scribbled him a quick list of places I planned to be and people I planned to see. Just in case.

No, I couldn't think like that. Item number one on my list when I confronted Zack and Shaylyn was to inform them that I'd made a point of letting three people—four if you counted Liam, and I wasn't—privy to my agenda. If they so much as pondered doing me physical harm, they'd be instant suspects.

I dismissed all the rest of my misgivings—basically being tortured, stabbed, and/or mutilated—by plastering the mental image of Jane in her orange jumpsuit in my brain. Freeing her was my only concern. I could take care of myself.

In no time, I'd negotiated my way down to Okeechobee, turned left, then headed over to the bridge. As soon as I reached the valet stand on Worth Avenue, the air temperature fell. The mean personal net worth skyrocketed. And the valet attendant was sporting a five-hundred-dollar stainless steel Seiko watch on his tanned wrist. Maybe I should add parking attendant to my list of new career possibilities.

Walking down the swankiest street in Palm Beach, one eye automatically peeled for celebrities, I admired some of the latest fashion trends. Actually, I ogled. I couldn't help it. Self-consciously, I held the damaged part of my purse against my body. These people were experts. They'd spot damaged goods in a heartbeat.

The Fantasy Dates files were inside a crisp new accordion file. I checked my reflection in the plate-glass window of Angela Moore, needing affirmation to build my confidence before I made the turn onto South Ocean. My stomach was clenched, and smelling the heavy vapor trails, no matter how expensive, left in the wakes of the passing idle rich wasn't helping.

I was maybe a half block from my target when I looked to

the right and checked out Exquisitely Yours. It was almost enough to make me want to drool. In the real world, Exquisitely Yours would have been a hair and nail salon. Here on the island, it was home to colorists, aestheticians, hair extension specialists, makeup artists, and massage therapists. Their select clientele was treated to relaxing reflexology while another attendant used the magic of restorative Restelyne to lift even the most miniscule wrinkle. Pampering didn't come cheap. Even if I saved for a year—like that was going to happen—I'd never be able to swing the fifteen hundred it cost just to add a half dozen sun-kissed highlights. But going there was on my to-do list. I just hoped if/when I made it I wasn't too freaking old to give a damn what I looked like.

Hearing my cell ring, I politely stepped to the right of the sidewalk, next to one of the tiled, elegant ground-level minifountains. On my first trip to Worth Avenue, the tiled fountains had left me puzzled. The water barely trickled from antique faucets, collecting in small, inset basins at select intervals along the walkway. Too low for drinking, and I just couldn't picture the crème de la crème stopping for impromptu foot baths. It wasn't until I'd stepped out of my windowshopping-only visit to Cartier that their purpose became clear. They weren't human fountains, they were upscale doggie dishes—a gift/service provided by the town for those who simply couldn't shop without Fifi in tow.

I knew the drill. My mother had recently acquired that particular affectation when she'd bought a teacup Yorkie from a breeder in Chicago. She's called it Diva, much more practical than the yappy little dog's overly long, pretentious title. It's something like Dame Maria Anna Sophia Cecelia Kalogeropoulos, Duchess of Singer Island. My mother found the name incredibly clever and befitting the prestigious lineage of the three-pound dog. I was pretty sure only elitist opera junkies would recognize the full birth name of opera great Maria Callas and get it—an opinion I didn't share with my mother. It would only have annoyed her and God knew I could do that simply by taking a breath. My only choice? Try not to cringe when my mother thinks nothing of dragging the dog along to anywhere, anytime. I had no doubt that Diva was with my mother now. More than I knew, my mother hadn't disclosed the exact location of her getaway from Finley's latest escapade retreat.

Hopefully, the flowers I'd ordered for our brunch tomorrow would buy me some forgiveness. "Hope" being the operative word.

Flipping open my phone, I read the text message. It was odd. Not the words themselves:

> Fin: Heard you were having troubles.
> Cutting trip short. See you Sunday.
> Patrick.

My first thought was it was sweet, and I started to reply. Then I got to wondering . . . if he could get a text message out of the wilderness, why not just call me? And where was he getting his information? I was positive the *Palm Beach Post* didn't deliver to the Grand Canyon. My arrest and the subsequent dismissal of the charges were hardly national news. Jane's arrest had been mentioned once on the networks, or rather, the crime itself. Okay, one part of the crime. The part that got cut off.

As I was putting my phone away, I heard a familiar voice behind me. Turning, I saw young, giggly Kresley Pierpont stepping out of Exquisitely Yours. I'd giggle too if I had her money and her body. Oh, and her hair. The woman had great hair. It was long, thick, and so shiny it practically glowed in the midday sunshine.

Taking a fortifying breath, I took the two steps necessary to reach her. Almost instantly, a gigantic man in khaki slacks and a Ralph Lauren shirt cut me off. Even in heels, my blue eyes fell roughly at the base of his sternum. Tilting my head back, I offered him my brightest smile. Private Security Guy was totally unimpressed by me.

"Kresley?" I called around him. Not that I had a choice—the size 0 heiress was completely obscured by her paid protector. "I'm Finley Tanner from . . ." Now was not the time to admit I was unemployed. "Dane-Lieberman."

"Move along, ma'am," the guard warned as he lifted his sunglasses, silently emphasizing his suggestion with slitted eyes.

Jane in a jumpsuit. Time to play hardball. "It's in reference to Jane Spencer?"

The guard stood his post.

"And your, um, connection to Fantasy Dates?"

A dainty hand sporting a blinding diamond closed around a portion of Private Security Guy's solid bicep. "Give us a minute, will you, George?"

Kresley Pierpont looked much younger than her twenty-seven years. She was tall, a leggy, narrow-shouldered, trim kind of tall that made her little more than a walking hanger for the Versace turquoise-white-and-black sleeveless dress she wore. The front closure was laced, trussing her—there is no way those puppies are real—breasts in a deep, cleavage-revealing V.

When the guard stepped away, I noted she was wearing the tangerine, cyclamen, mimosa, vanilla, and sandalwood with just a hint of vanilla signature blend of *D&G Feminine*. The perfume cost like a gazillion dollars an ounce.

She gave me a once-over and though she didn't say as much, I got the feeling I'd ended up on the short end of her assessment. She did smile, even if it was one of those "I've got a Harry Winston diamond and you don't" smiles.

"Yes?"

I extended my hand as she removed her Gucci sunglasses. In the process of the handshake, she maneuvered me around so that I was facing into the sun.

It took me a few seconds to process the flash of apprehension and annoyance in her bright blue eyes. No doubt she wasn't thrilled that I'd ambushed her in the middle of the sidewalk, calling out the name of her dating service.

"I'm sorry to bother you," I said. It wasn't an exaggeration. I read the papers. This woman had enough stalker problems that she sure didn't need me adding to the litany of her troubles. My eyes started to tear from the harsh sun, so I was happy to lower my gaze to pull her file from my folder. In a very soft voice, I asked, "Can you tell me why you're still using the services of Fantasy Dates, considering you're about to marry Matthew Gibson?"

The glasses dropped, as did any pretense of a smile. Kresley donned the pissy-pouty look often plastered on glossy magazines and/or trashy tabloids.

"Am I?" she asked, voice flat.

Taking the invoice out, I passed it to her. "According to the records my firm received, you—"

"I thought Clark Taggert was representing the woman who killed what's-his-name."

Small alarm bells sounded in my head. I knew from the files that Kresley knew exactly who Paolo was. "He is, but Ms. Jameson from Dane-Lieberman is also active in the case." Nice evasive answer if I did say so myself. "If we could get back to you for a moment?" Why did I think everything in Kresley's world was about her?

"Sure," she said, testing her freshly painted, bright red nail polish in the sunlight.

"Why is your membership still active?"

She shrugged. "An oversight. I'll mention it to my business manager."

My business manager was whoever was standing at the teller's window when I went to the bank. "What about this charge?" I pointed to the Special Assessment column on her invoice.

"Oh, that?"

For the first time I heard a hitch in Kresley's voice. Panic? Irritation? Not sure.

"Yes. Would you mind telling me what it's for?"

She gave a dismissive little wave with her hands. Her emerald-cut engagement ring weighed down the motion of her left hand. "Some sort of charity fund thing. Zack and Shaylyn are very philanthropic. I think any donations go to one of those help-dying-kids foundations."

Her compassion for her fellow child fell decidedly short of sincere. I'm guessing she and Matthew won't be starting a family any time soon.

Kresley gave a subtle nod to her security guy. Promptly, he opened the back passenger's door to a late-model, blue Mercedes sedan. The color was almost a perfect match to the pale blonde's eyes.

"If there's nothing else?" she asked.

My theory is she didn't give a flying fig if I still had more questions. She was done with me. In a flash, she slipped inside the car, then disappeared behind the tinted privacy windows.

I watched as she was driven away, knowing full well I was just dragging my heels. I'm not a complete wuss, but I wasn't exactly relishing the idea of confronting Zack and Shaylyn. Though Kresley had adequately explained away the Special Assessment and it was completely plausible that maintaining her membership was nothing more than a clerical error on the part of her manager, there was still the matter of the threatening call.

It wasn't like they could deny it. I had the caller ID log to prove the creepy, genderless call had come from their office. What I didn't get was why they'd be threatening me. I hadn't had a lot of successes uncovering who was framing Jane. Nor did I have anything more than a gut feeling that there was something hinky about the introduction service.

All I'd really accomplished was to incur the wrath of the

police department; lose my job; accept money from my mother; oh, and get arrested. Not exactly a stellar track record.

Knowing that didn't seem to ease the swelling knot of apprehension in the pit of my belly as I strode toward the office of Fantasy Dates.

The business was located in one of the newer buildings on Worth Avenue. It was typical Florida architecture—single story, tropical colors, and Spanish influences. Set back about ten feet from the road, the driveway had been expanded to accommodate two vehicles. I recognized the only one parked there. It was the same dark sapphire Bentley I'd seen at Liv's office a few days earlier.

My initial apprehension was leaning more toward scared shitless the closer I got to the matching fountains flanking the manicured walkway. The bubbling water was drowned out by the sound of my heart thudding in my ears.

Maybe I should have called the police. Maybe I should have waited for Liam. Maybe I should just turn around and go home.

"No," I said, my voice barely above a whisper. "You can do this. You might not want to, but you can. You have to. Think of Jane."

Jane. Jane. Jane . . . Jimmy?

I blinked, not trusting my eyes. However, there was no denying it. Deep pry marks gouged the wood near the brass door latch. Yep. Someone had jimmied the lock. Glancing over my shoulder, I made sure there was a steady stream of people strolling the sidewalk. There was.

Now, a smart woman would call for help and wait until said help arrived. Only *this* woman had a friend in jail, so "smart" went flying out the proverbial window. Stepping back so I was even with the trunk of the Bentley, I called Liv and told her what I'd found.

"Call the police."

"Their car is here," I said as I walked around and placed my palm on the hood. "The engine's cold."

"I don't care if the engine is a block of ice," Liv virtually screamed. "Get away from there. For all you know there could be a burglar inside."

"Or Zack and Shaylyn are in there, maybe tied up and in need of assistance."

"Another reason you need to call the cops and get the hell out of there."

"Just stay on the line with me," I said as I fished into my purse and pulled out a tissue.

"Finley?"

"Shush. I'm just going to take a quick peek."

"This is not a good idea," Liv warned.

I heard a scratching sound and guessed Liv had covered the mouthpiece. "I know what you're doing. Please don't tell Jean-Claude to call the police," I asked. "What if Zack and Shaylyn really are in trouble? Plus, maybe there are clues or something else that could get Jane out of jail?"

"Or maybe you've lost your mind. Please, Finley—"

"Just hang on," I said as I used my toe to push the front door open. "Hello?" I called, hearing my own voice echo through the house. Wanting both hands free, I propped my folder against a planter to the right of the door. "Zack? Shaylyn? It's Finley. I've got the police on the line!"

"Liar."

"Shush!" I repeated harshly. "I'm putting you on speaker so you can hear everything but you have to be quiet." Pressing the sleek button on my phone, I tucked it into the side pocket of my purse and took an initial, tentative step over the threshold.

Because of the open floor plan, I could see almost every nook and cranny. The place had been trashed. All four chairs had been sliced open, the cushion fibers spilling out like white puffy clouds against the shredded fabric. The sofas had suffered the same fate, though they'd been tipped and cut and the buttery leather peeled back to expose the wooden frames.

To the right of me, I saw an elegant desk and surmised the

papers strewn around had come from there. The drawers of twin lateral files were askew, left partially open.

Though my hands were trembling, I was careful to wrap the tissue around my fingertips as I cautiously ventured farther into the room. The smell of something sickly sweet hung thickly in the warming air.

I'd intentionally left the front door wide open. The heat from outside was taking the chill off the overly air-conditioned room.

"Holy crap," I mumbled.

"Finley?" I heard Liv's distant voice coming from my cell phone. "Finley, are you okay? Finley?"

Holding the phone near my mouth, I said, "Yeah. I'm here. I'm fine. No sign of Zack or Shaylyn, but someone did a real number on this place."

Stepping over one of the sofa cushions, I found a few pages tossed over by a small counter. Four stools lay on their side and a few shards of glass glinted against the terra-cotta-tiled floor. Automatically, I glanced at the window above the small sink in the kitchenette. It was intact. Examining one of the larger pieces, I noted it was too thin for a drinking glass. A carafe, maybe?

"I'm calling the police. *Now!*"

"Hang on. Give me a minute," I told Liv, placing the phone on the floor.

Ignoring her protests, I carefully picked up one of the pages. My heart stilled when I read the name typed on the top of the first page. Spencer, Jane.

It was her questionnaire. The same one I'd read from the electronic version supplied to Taggert by Zack and Shaylyn. Only now I paid specific attention to the section marked *references*. My name and telephone numbers were listed on the second line.

I gathered the dozen or so other pages as well as the folder with Jane's name on the label. There was another difference between the actual file I now held in my hand and the one provided by Fantasy Dates. A copy of Jane's criminal record, faxed from an 843 area code.

Excitedly, I picked up the phone and said, "I think I know who's been spoon-feeding the prosecutor information on Jane while pretending to help." Anger simmered in my veins as I shared my discovery with Liv. "I knew there was something weird about those two."

"You think they killed Paolo and framed Jane?"

"Yes," I said without hesitation. "Except . . ." I scanned the automatically generated date and time stamp on the fax. "Except they didn't get this information until about an hour before Jane went in front of Judge Faulkner for the first time. Which means they couldn't have known about her past troubles when they framed her for Paolo's murder."

"Is that important?"

"Maybe. Paolo and Jane's date was arranged three weeks ago. If they were going to use her as a patsy, why wait until after the date to find out if she had any skeletons in her closet?"

"Finley, I think you should get out of there. What if Shaylyn and Zack come back?"

"You're right. I'll call the cops from outside."

I was still crouched on the ground when I felt a hard metal object tap my shoulder. I turned just enough for my eyes to focus on the barrel of a gun.

Everyone makes mistakes; the key is not getting caught making the really stupid ones.

Sixteen

In a feeble attempt to get away, and suffering from a sudden jolt of holy-shit-that's-a-gun adrenaline, I stumbled, toppled over, and smacked my head on the rock-hard tile.

Palpable fear had my heart racing. Through the head-trauma stars strobing in my field of vision, I expected to see Zack or possibly Shaylyn sneering down at me. I braced myself, terrified, as I imagined how much it would hurt to get shot. I've never been shot, but I'm thinking it can't be good.

Instead of bad guys aiming guns, it was Liam wielding the weapon. Amusement glinted in his eyes as he casually scratched the side of his five o'clock shadow with his trigger finger.

"You son of a bitch!" I hoisted myself off the floor, grabbing up my cell and the file pages and adjusting the strap on my purse in the process. My dignity was still on the floor, seeping into the grout. Couldn't pick that up with a spoon.

"Finley? I hear Liam? Thank God he's there with you. Finley, tell him how much we—" Hearing the not-so-muffled sound of Liv babbling over the speaker, I disconnected the open line.

I hated the fact that I had to tilt my head back in order to make eye contact. Almost as much as I hated the tingle in my stomach every time I looked into those incredible eyes of his. "You scared me."

"Good to know something does," he said, tucking the gun into the back waistband of his jeans. After a quick scan of the room, he let out a low whistle. "Your handiwork?"

My spine went rigid. "Of course not. It was trashed when I got here."

"You should have waited outside."

He shook his head slowly, causing a few strands of dark hair to fall against his forehead. My fingers twitched from the inappropriate desire to reach up and smooth them back into place. The last time I'd twitched in his presence, I'd made a total ass of myself. My cheeks warmed just thinking about the whole "boy, did I misread the signals, stripping off my clothes" incident.

"Well, I didn't," I replied, hearing almost childish defiance in my own voice. "I did, however, take a thorough and cautious look around. There's no one here."

"Put that in the sheer dumb luck pile."

Ya think? Already did that.

"Liv's assistant called me. Becky called me. Five times. When they told me you were on your way here to . . . *investigate*, I didn't believe it."

I glared at him. "*Someone* has to investigate." *It's not like you're doing it.* "If not, Jane spends a second weekend in jail. I can't sit idly by and do nothing."

"Right. So what? You dropped a hundred points of IQ and waltzed blindly in here? That's your plan to get your friend out of jail?"

Okay, when he said it like that, I sounded like a complete moron. "Someone was crank calling me from here and I wanted to know who."

"Crank calls or threatening calls?"

"Is there a difference?"

"Huge one."

"Not calls, plural. Okay, calls, plural, but the first ones were hang-ups, so they don't count. Call. One threatening call," I said, as if that made me sound less incompetent. "Something I've done has hit a nerve with Zack and/or Shaylyn. I was going to confront them about it."

His expression darkened and what I guessed was anger flashed in his eyes for just a second. "Then what?"

"Then what *what*?"

He pointed at the items clutched in my hands. "Here's a free lesson from Interview 101. Don't confront people. What if they were here, Finley? Or if whoever trashed this place was still inside? Assuming you did react quickly—and I'm being generous here—you couldn't run worth shit in those high heels, and most attackers don't stand there while you calmly dial nine-one-one."

"Whatever. So this wasn't my finest hour," I acknowledged defensively. "But that doesn't change the fact that Taggert isn't doing anything, so Jane is *languishing* in jail."

"No, it doesn't."

"Not only is time an issue, but so is money. Jane's stuff is mostly investments. It takes time to liquidate those kinds of assets. Liv's partner is still contemplating allowing her to pull funds out of the business and I've already milked my friends and my mother." I felt my muscles tense. Brunch was less than twenty-four hours away. Let the groveling begin. "Bottom line? I'm it. I have the time and—"

"That was pretty cold of Dane-Lieberman to can you."

I shrugged. "In a manner of speaking, they canned you, too. I'm sure Ellen called you on her way home from the courthouse to let you know your services were no longer needed."

"She did."

I felt frustrated tears sting the back of my eyes. "I'm also sure I don't know what I'm doing. But at least I'm trying. I'm not a big whoop-de-do P.I., but I am finding clues."

"This isn't a board game, Finley. Clues are for amateurs. What you want is facts. Oh, and not getting yourself hurt in the process would probably be a good plan."

"Well, I'm out of options."

He cursed under his breath. "No, you aren't. I'll help you."

"For a reduced fee? Pass, thanks." I was still pissed at him for that one.

"If you promise to behave, I'll make this one a freebie."

I smiled, relief flooding every amateur sleuth cell in my body. I couldn't help myself. Much as I wanted to think I could find the answers on my own, I did have certain limitations. "Great, so where do we start?"

"Not we. Me."

Vehemently, I shook my head. "This may be a pro bono case, but technically I'm the client. I'm not going to sit in my apartment waiting on you. Not when you have 'things' every hour on the hour."

Now he was the one smiling. Annoying bastard. I narrowed my eyes. "Did I say something amusing?"

"Yeah, but we can talk about that another time. Right now we bring each other up to speed."

He listened patiently as I told him about the password and the fact that I hadn't found anything to explain "Snowy Owl." Then there was the whole Special Assessment angle. Excitedly, I handed him the Jane file and pointed out the odd timing on the criminal background check weeks after the Paolo date had been arranged.

"So," I began once my self-esteem moved back in, "now all we have to do is figure out how Zack and/or Shaylyn killed Paolo and why they framed Jane before they knew about the Charleston case."

"You skipped a step."

"No. I've been making notes." I dug them out of my purse

and handed them to him. "I know the names of all the Special Assessment clients and—"

"Not that step," he said. "The proof step. This is a good start, but it's all conjecture. Until we have motive or, better yet, tangible evidence, we can't assume Zack and Shaylyn are the killers."

"They have to be. The only common thread is this dating service."

"Maybe. Maybe not."

He was starting to irritate me again. *Free. Free. He's working for free.* "You have a better suspect in mind?"

"Maybe. Ma—"

"Got it. So what's the next move?"

"You go home and I do my job?"

"Not gonna happen."

"Didn't think so." He raked his fingers through his hair, then swung his arm in an arc. "What's all this?"

"Papers."

"About . . . ?"

"I didn't get the chance to look at anything but Jane's file. Thanks to that thing you did with the gun on my shoulder. Was that really necessary?"

"No."

I walked toward the desk, righting a side chair and depositing my purse on the sliced cushion. "So why'd you do it?"

"Because I could."

Loved his deep, sexy voice. Hated his wiseass answer.

Liam and I spent the better part of an hour splitting our time between reconstructing the office and making frequent checks out the window to make sure we wouldn't get caught. I was good at organization and not so good at recon. Every time I went to the window, my chest constricted. Eventually, I tossed my pride aside and asked him to be lookout.

"I'm not finding anything really out of the ordinary," I admitted. "Hang on," I said, excitement building as my eyes scanned the "referred by" sections of the Special Assessment clients. "Matthew Gibson joined two years ago. Just after Fantasy Dates opened. He referred Kresley Pierpont."

"She's got a hefty trust fund. Think he did that just to hook up with her?"

Touching the pad of my index finger to my tongue, I quickly flipped through the other applications. "If he did, it backfired. At least in the beginning. Kresley's first few dates were with some guy named Cameron Wells."

"Is he paying the bonus fees?"

I shook my head. "Nope. And he dropped his membership after only five dates with Kresley. Which just happens to coincide with Kresley's first date with Paolo."

"Now we're getting someplace," Liam said, moving to stand behind me. His hands rested on the back of my chair and I felt his warm breath against my ear as he leaned in to read over my shoulder.

My heart thumped against my ribcage and I started hating myself for pseudo-cheating on Patrick. My conscience was bothering me, but then again, so was the scent of Liam's soap. I willed myself to stay focused on the pages in front of me.

"Doesn't look like Paolo held her interest very long," Liam said. "Only two dates. The last one was eighteen months ago."

I told Liam all about Paolo's real identity. Born in Dayton, several years in prison on larceny charges, and the fact that his whole Palm Beach life was fiction. And despite all of that, he'd passed Fantasy Dates' supposedly stellar scrutiny. "What if she found out he was a fraud?"

"Not likely."

My gut was telling me this was important, so I didn't let it go. "Why not? The Kresley Pierponts of the world don't like slumming or being conned."

"They're also too spoiled to wait a year and a half to do something about it."

"Good point."

"If she somehow found out Paolo was a felon, she probably would have sued Fantasy Dates right out of business. She didn't. She kept dating."

"Until she met Matthew Gibson. They got exclusive fast. Maybe he found out Paolo was a felon and killed him to avenge the wrong done to his bride-to-be."

"That would make perfect sense . . . *if* this was Regency England," Liam joked. "Does this whole introduction service thing work on referral, or what?"

I missed the heat of his body as he moved to sit on the edge of the now tidy desk. He was flipping through the pages I'd deemed unimportant and set aside.

"From what I could cobble together, when the business first opened, Shaylyn and Zack held small, intimate parties on rented yachts or VIP rooms at various hot spots."

"Feeling out the rich and dateless?"

"Yes. But now they operate almost exclusively on a referral basis. There are a lot of referrals from Kresley Pierpont, and I thought I was on to something, but it didn't pan out. Paolo had just as many, as did some woman named Barbie Baker."

One of his dark brows arched. "Quietly settled, profitable-divorce Barbie Baker?"

I never would have guessed him for the gossip column type. "How'd you know?"

"P.I.s have our own Yahoo group."

"Really?"

He grinned. Lopsided and sexy as all hell. "No. Ashley mentioned it. She subscribes to a lot of fanzines and keeps up with that sort of junk."

Why do I think that's not the only thing Ashley keeps up?
"What do you remember about the ex–Mrs. Baker?"

"Not much. I don't get very interested in things like that."

"I should Google her," I said, reaching for the sleek silver laptop on the floor next to the desk. It took some doing to re-connect the cables, but I finally got it up and running.

"We're obliterating any usable prints, you know that, right?"

"I won't tell if you don't," I mumbled as I read the error message on the machine. Prying the back of the machine open with a nail file I'd found in the top desk drawer, I in-stantly understood why the computer wasn't cooperating. "Someone took the hard drive."

Liam looked up from the stack of papers he'd been leisurely reading. "So we're looking for a computer novice."

I met his gaze. "How can you know that?"

"A computer geek would wipe the hard drive and leave it in place. Which also makes it less likely that Shaylyn and Zack are our killers."

"Because?"

He fanned me with the pages. "This whole operation is computerized. One of them has technical knowledge. Plus, it's their computer. If it had something damning inside, why not take it with them? Or just dump it?"

"Where do you think they are? No one's heard from them in forever."

"Taggert might know."

I blinked, then felt some of my enthusiasm rekindle. "Good thinking. He's a friend of theirs, so it only stands to reason he might have some information."

Using his thumb and forefinger, Liam slipped a neatly stapled, two-page document from the unimportant pile. "He's more than a friend," he said, sliding the document across the desk. "Taggert was their attorney of record on the lease for this place."

Flipping to the second page, I easily found his signature boldly scrolled and dated on the indicated lines. "I made a stack of vendor invoices," I told Liam. "See them anywhere?"

"Got 'em." He handed them to me.

Bypassing various and sundry items like electric bills, water bills, and office supply orders, I hit gold. Well, more like silver or bronze. "These are invoices from Clark Taggert for legal services rendered, marked *Paid in full.*"

"We've already established he's their lawyer."

"But"—I shuffled papers around until I found a bank statement—"no payments are listed as sent to Taggert. That has to be significant."

"Or it could just mean they have more than one operating account and they paid Taggert from another account. Or they just cashed checks and paid him in cash for some other reason."

A pattern was developing. My enthusiasm morphed into vexation. "Do you enjoy taking every one of my ideas and peeing on them?"

"Sometimes."

The man was as honest as he was irritating. "I need to go home where I have a real computer."

"First we have to wipe down every surface. If not, when we call the cops, both our fingerprints will pop in a matter of hours. I'm going to take you to meet some friends of mine. Then you go home."

Friends? What the hell did that mean? It could be step one in integrating me into his life or . . . it could mean we were meeting Ashley at the Blue Martini. Not a pleasant thought. "Wait, no. I have to see Jace Andrews, Payton McComber, and maybe Harrison Hadley."

He gave me a quizzical look but lifted his chin in a challenge. "We're doing that why?"

"Fantasy Date clients. They all have offices here on the island and I want to interview them now. Your friends will have to wait until after that. I have to go to my place. I need a functioning computer so I can pry into the lives of Barbie Baker, Cameron Wells, and all the other clients. Zack and . . ."

Liam lifted the hem of his shirt and started wiping every

surface. My throat constricted as I took in his deeply tanned, perfectly sculpted abs. Normally, I'm not fond of the whole boxer-shorts-visible-above-the-waistband thing, but on Liam it worked. Correction, it worked on my libido. Really well. Knee-bucklingly well.

Even though he was standing in profile, I could see his grin. "When you're finished checking me out, you need to take a breath, finish your sentence, and start helping."

My cheeks weren't just flushed, they were roasting. "I was not checking you out." Technically not a lie. I was no longer checking him out. I had moved on. To a full-color fantasy of the two of us tangled in my sheets.

"Whatever. You were saying Zack and . . . ?"

It took three mental bitch slaps to pull me back to reality. "Um, I'll do deeper checks on Zack, Shaylyn, and Taggert, too. You may not think there's a connection, but I do. Someone password-protected all the files. Whoever trashed this place was obviously looking for something. I'm guessing the 'it' is someplace in the files, which explains why he took the hard drive."

"Or Zack and Shaylyn took it as a precaution to protect the privacy of their clientele," he said as he ran his shirt along the length of the U-shaped counter.

"Why is it so hard for you to accept that my instincts might have merit?"

I heard the crunch of glass and looked over to see Liam pulling his gun. "You checked this whole place when you got here?" he asked as he slowly rounded the counter, his gun parallel to his line of sight.

"Pretty much." Okay, so I didn't go into the kitchenette, but that was only because I'd been distracted by finding Jane's background check on the floor. Besides, it was totally open; I would have noticed someone lurking in the shadows.

"You must have done this room with your eyes closed."

"Wrong. I found a piece of a glass carafe. So if you've just discovered a broken coffeepot, don't bother patting yourself on the back."

The unmistakable sound of door hinges creaked and echoed off the high ceilings.

Leaning around the knee wall, I watched Liam lower his gun to his side before crouching down. The sickly sweet smell got stronger, as did the sense of panic tightening my muscles.

"You missed something."

"Like?"

"The blood spatter on the floor."

Honesty is the best policy unless the truth will get you arrested.

Seventeen

"We should have stayed," I told Liam for the umpteenth time as we left Fantasy Dates.

"Only if you wanted to spend the night being grilled by Steadman and Graves. By the way, they don't like you."

I glared up at him as I struggled to keep pace with his long strides. "I figured that out all on my own."

Activity on Worth Avenue was waning, as were my hopes of getting Jane released in time for the weekend. It was just a few minutes past four and I could see shop employees through their windows already dusting counters and straightening merchandise. Even though the posted business hours ran until six, cocktail hour started promptly at five. Time for the idle rich to man their battle stations. Hosts and hostesses were heading back to their stately homes to dress for the evening.

It's a very Palm Beach thing. There's some sort of gathering every evening. *If* you can make the guest lists. I'd been to a few events, but only as a crasher. Well, technically Liv snagged me an invite so it wasn't really crashing, but I'd never been included on my own merit. No matter how I came to be there, I enjoyed the up-close and personal view of their opulence.

"Here," I said suddenly, grabbing Liam's forearm. "Stop here."

"Payton's Place," he read from the sign above the small combination gallery and retail. "Distinctive Accessories. You jonesing for jewelry?"

"Don't be stupid. I want to talk to Payton McComber. She's a Special Assessment client."

Liam held the door open for me. As I passed, he whispered against my ear, "Make it quick. I've got a thing in West Palm in about an hour."

Thing. Always with the *thing*. "Feel free to go on your merry way." A vague chime sounded softly as I crossed the threshold.

The shop was painted stark white and smelled faintly of gardenia. The long, rectangular display cases running down either side of the room were filled with artistically displayed, one-of-a-kind jewelry. The center aisle was dotted with smaller, octagonal cases that rotated at a barely discernible speed and displayed smaller pieces. The ceiling was about fourteen feet high, leaving plenty of room to exhibit the artsy larger pieces. Along the back wall, various awards and accolades hung symmetrically, interspersed with photographs of the corresponding winning works. In addition to jewelry, Payton was a well-credentialed metal artist and quite adept at creating blown glass pieces as well.

I heard a door open and held my breath. I'd know Payton on sight. She was frequently in the news and quite popular with the island residents. Mostly because all her pieces were one of a kind. I'm told nothing irritates a rich woman like spending thousands on accessories only to arrive at a party to find some other—usually younger—woman sporting the same bauble.

It wasn't Payton. It was a small woman with closely cropped hair dyed a bright shade of purple. The hair and her funky clothing practically screamed *artist*. I've never understood why people who are capable of creating beauty often have a personal style that mimics an unsupervised toddler.

She smiled at me and extended her small hand. It was hard to get a firm grip given the fact that she had this silver thing that connected her thumb and index finger, creating a webbed effect. Perhaps Payton's winter collection would include a Peter Parker line. *Spider-man*–inspired jewelry, purple hair, and circa 1983 Cyndi Lauper–esque attire aside, she was a very pretty young woman.

"Hi, I'm Astrid. Welcome to Payton's Place. Are you looking for something specific today?"

"Yes. Payton McComber. Is she available?"

"She's in the studio out back and doesn't like to be disturbed. I'm sure I can help you find what you need."

"Okay," I said as I reached into my purse for a pen and something to write on. This time the lucky winner was a Starbucks Chai Tea postcard I'd been meaning to use. Hurriedly, I scribbled on the back, then folded it in thirds. "Please take this to Ms. McComber. We'll wait."

As soon as she was gone, Liam said, "You do snotty bitch really well."

Not sure whether it was a compliment or a criticism, I wasn't quite sure how to respond. "It's a gift."

Seemingly restless, he started prowling the cases. "If you ask me, a lot of this looks like the junk you can pick up in any dollar store."

"Add a few more zeros," I suggested, my eyes drawn to a really fabulous oval-cut, lime-green necklace and matching earrings. Being unemployed, I had to settle for admiring from a distance. Who was I kidding? Even employed I couldn't afford a Payton original unless I saved and scraped. Two S adjectives I've managed to avoid for almost thirty years.

Astrid returned, her face all scrunched in a confused frown.

"She's waiting for you in the studio." She pointed her webbed finger toward the back of the shop. "Right through there."

When Liam's palm flattened against the small of my back, I felt every centimeter of his large hand. I played it cool. Barely.

"What did you write on the note?"

"That we were here about her past due Special Assessment for Fantasy Dates. She didn't pay the fee last month."

"Smart."

"I thought so." Yes, I've been around long enough to know better than to let flattery melt my bones. Recognized the danger in it, knew better than to let it affect me, felt it happening anyway.

In order to get to the studio, we had to pass through a curtain of brightly colored glass beads. They jingled, then swayed back into place as we continued down a narrow but short corridor. Focusing on the orange glow from the EXIT sign above the door, I kept moving, though it was a struggle.

We passed a single room on our direct, lineal route to the studio. A room with a pot of coffee sending me telepathic "come hither" invitations. I knew I was back to normal when the desire for coffee overwhelmed the fleeting and fruitless desire for Liam to put his hand on me again. How sad is that? Would I really rather have coffee than a man?

My eyes stung as I stepped into a ray of harsh sunlight. Squinting, I lifted my hand to shield my vision. A few feet in front of me stood what looked like a detached garage. Well, if garages had chimneys billowing heat that created that watery mirage effect.

"Smell that?" Liam asked.

"Yeah. Smells like that stuff you use to refill a cigarette lighter. What is it?"

"It's a gas that evaporates quickly and is highly combustible."

I stopped like I'd hit a wall. "You think Payton is going to blow us up?"

Pushing me forward, Liam said in a low voice, "No, I was thinking about the limo driver's boat. Something ignited the gas cans on board."

"Should I be scared?" Like I wasn't already.

"Nope."

A single door with the word PRIVATE stenciled by a skilled hand stood ajar. I could hear the sound of metal banging against metal and a whistling noise as we approached.

"Miss McComber?" I called over the dissonance.

"Come in," she replied, though her voice was oddly muffled.

As soon as I went inside the studio, the reason was apparent. Payton was straddling a padded sawhorse, her face obscured by a welding mask. One hand held a ball-peen hammer, the other a small blowtorch streaming a blue-hot flame about three inches from the nozzle.

She put the hammer on the bench in front of her, then turned a small valve on the torch, and the flame disappeared with a poof. Other than the sounds of an oscillating fan and the buzz of the air conditioner, the place was eerily quiet.

Payton broke the spell. "You can tell Zack to do what he needs to do. I'm not paying him another penny."

I guess we're skipping the introduction part. "Excuse me?"

When she snatched off the mask and gloves, I found myself being glared at by a pair of hostile dark eyes. Her hair, though mussed, was an unnaturally brutal black, and worn in a severe ponytail that seemed to pull her eyes into an almond shape. Either that or she'd had a bad face-lift.

My gaze dropped to her neck. Yep, definitely had a face-lift. The sagging skin confirmed her neck was about ten years older than her face and her hands; well, add another five to that. After doing the math, I figured that regardless of the cosmetic surgery, she was somewhere in her early forties.

Like many face-liftees, she allowed her age-defying appearance to define her sense of style. Toss in the aforementioned weird artist elements, and the result was strange. Payton McComber looked a little like a biker chick. Worn chaps covered her thighs and she had on Harley-Davidson Dazzle leather fashion boots. Not the only fashion item and definitely not the only leather. Swinging one leg over the sawhorse, she stood up and, thanks to the three-inch heels, she was a good inch or more taller than Liam.

Payton was thin but very fit. Her arms were toned and her torso was trussed into some sort of leather vest with hand-blown beads dangling from the laces. Beneath the chaps, she had on denim shorts embellished with bugle beads. When she turned around and untied the chaps, I discovered the shorts had been cropped and cut into an ass-revealing thong.

I shot a quick glance over at Liam, who seemed completely impervious to being flashed. His attention was on inventorying the studio.

Payton planted her hands on her nonexistent hips, her eyes blazing in my direction. "You're the best he can do? A prissy Junior Leaguer? Well, you tell that north-of-the-border jerk-off that I'm not intimidated and I'm definitely through paying. I wasn't getting my money's worth. Besides, my . . . *tastes* aren't exactly a secret. Oh, and you can also tell him to take his DVD and his threats and stick them up his—"

I knew I didn't like that creep. "Zack threatened you?"

She shrugged, revealing a small portion of a tattoo on her right shoulder. I didn't get a very good look, but I'm pretty sure it was a snake.

"Tried to," Payton answered. "I was okay with the extra fees so long as I was getting what I paid for."

"Which was?" Liam asked.

She gave him a slow, deliberate smile. "I like games but I had a hard time finding playmates after I moved down here from New York."

It didn't take long for me to get that she wasn't talking about Yahtzee. "So how'd you hook up with Zack and Shaylyn?"

"They found me. Came into the studio. We got to talking and at the time, it seemed like a win-win situation. I got to meet people with similar . . . *interests* and they got to make some extra cash. Then, a few months ago, the maple-leaf–licking bastard sent me a home-burned DVD and a typed note threatening to go public with the original of it if I didn't pay an additional twenty grand."

"Someone taped you playing games?" Liam asked.

"Yeah. But I'm an artist. An established one. Having my sexual proclivities shared with the whole world would probably let me double my prices. Look at Mapplethorpe. Look at John Lennon and Yoko Ono's *Self-Portrait*. Sex and art sell. That's exactly what I told Paolo when he showed up here to collect."

"When exactly was that?" Liam asked.

"Late May, early June, maybe?" Payton's expression was guarded. "Wait. You're not thinking I had anything to do with Paolo's death, are you? I went out with him several times. He was an excellent playmate."

Eeewwwww.

"Didn't they already arrest some woman for it?"

As if it mattered, I said, "She's innocent."

"He was killed last weekend, right?"

I nodded.

"Sorry to disappoint you, but I was at the opening of a new exhibit at the World Erotic Art Museum in Miami from Friday until early Monday."

"Is there anyone who can verify that?" Liam asked.

"Several anyones," she said, followed by a sly laugh. "I was very popular at the after parties, if you get my meaning."

I got her meaning and a nasty visual as well.

"Do you still have the DVD?"

Payton was completely nonplussed by Liam's question. She walked over to a small cabinet next to some blank stacked canvases and reached inside. Then held up a shiny disc in a clear plastic sleeve. "Right here."

"Could we have it?"

"You can borrow it," Payton said.

"We won't make copies," I assured her.

She scoffed. "Copy away. I just want it back because I like watching it. It gets me off."

More eeewwwww.

"I need a shower," I grumbled shortly after leaving Payton's gallery. We both slipped on sunglasses as we walked east. "I want you to check her alibi."

"Why?"

His dismissive tone chafed. "Well, for starters, how many people under the age of forty remember that John and Yoko made a movie starring John's penis? Paolo died without his penis on. Some people might consider that suspicious. She had all sorts of knives in her studio. And motive."

"What motive would that be?"

"Gee," I said, tapping my finger to my chin. "Zack and Shaylyn were shaking her down?"

"I think Payton's the kind of woman who enjoys a good shake. We'll know more after we watch the DVD."

"Oh, goody. I can't wait to see Payton's sexcapades."

"Are you a prude or just pathetically loyal to the pilot?"

Given that I'd been, and still was, mentally cheating on my boyfriend, I was hardly in a position to take the moral high ground. No choice but to go with the tried and true nonanswer answer. "There's nothing pathetic about being loyal."

"There is if it's only one-sided."

His cryptic remark could only mean one of two things. Either Ashley had cheated on him or vice versa. The fact that they were still involved made it more likely that the latter was true.

"Stay out of my relationship with Patrick."

"I have."

The swiftness of his response stung. It shouldn't have, but it did. Which made no sense. Did I actually want him to want me just so I could have the satisfaction of saying no? Or did I just want Liam, period? Both scenarios fell firmly in the stupid column. Arriving at Prestige Properties saved me from having to work my way out of the maze of my guilty conscience.

The real estate office was upscale but basically no different than every other sales office. Well, except that the receptionist offered us everything from bottled water to champagne while we waited for Jace Andrews. Oh, and most of the listings being offered for sale ran upward of eight figures.

It took less than two minutes for the real estate broker to appear. Probably because I'd used the same ploy on him. Apparently a single mention of the Special Assessment was enough to get an audience with the owner.

The first thing I noticed was that he was way cuter in person than in the eight-by-ten photograph in his Fantasy Dates file. The second thing was that he was pissed.

With slitted brown eyes and a forced smile, he ushered us into his private office. It was very big, very masculine, and very neat. Lots of large, dark wood furniture with masculine printed fabrics in burgandies and navy blue.

"Take a seat," he said as he held his Hermès tie against his chest, while he sat behind a massive mahogany desk.

"We're here about the extra fees you've been paying," Liam said without preamble.

Jace's cheeks reddened as he glared angrily at the two of us. Liam's cell phone rang and he went out into the hallway. Though I knew he was only a shout away, I also knew someone—not Jane—had stabbed and mutilated Paolo. Maybe Jace, who I was now alone with.

With no other option, I picked up where Liam left off.

"We know about the Special Assessments you've been paying."

His eyes squeezed shut for a minute and he raked shaking fingers through his dark brown hair. "How much more?" he asked, his fury bubbling toward the surface.

"More what?"

"Money," he said, sliding open a drawer and pulling out one of those large, leather-bound business checkbooks. "Like I told Paolo, I'm willing to pay to keep this quiet. It isn't like I have a choice, now, is it?"

"Uh, no. I doubt your client base will increase when word gets out that you're an S&M freak."

His head shot up and the pen he'd just grabbed from the desk set froze in midair. He put the pen down and leaned back in his chair. "I don't know what you're talking about."

"A DVD of you *not* on your best behavior. Ring any bells?"

"No." He rose out of his chair. "I'm sure you can find your way out."

Whoa. What was I missing? "Paolo is dead."

"So I read. The door is that way," he suggested again.

"The woman who was arrested didn't kill him."

"Not my concern."

I didn't budge from my seat. In fact, I gripped the armrests so tightly he'd have to move the furniture to get me out of the room. "Wrong. I'm making it your concern. I know Fantasy Dates charged certain clients special fees for . . . for special requests. You just admitted you've been paying the Special Assessment."

"So you say. Repeat it and I'll deny it."

"To a judge?"

Jace Andrews looked like he'd enjoy nothing more than to wring my neck, administer CPR, then do it all over again.

"To support a local children's charity."

Same bullshit line Kresley had used earlier. "I've—" I

glanced toward Liam, who was still chatting away on the phone. "We've already got confirmation from one of the individuals being blackmailed by Fantasy Dates. We know about the S&M and we know about the DVDs."

He shook his head and snorted at me. "Then you don't know anything, Ms. Tanner. I've asked you to leave twice. Now I'm telling you to get out."

"We were just leaving," Liam said as he stepped back into the room and closed his fingers around my arm. "Sorry to have bothered you, Mr. Andrews."

"But!"

Liam's eyes bore into me. "Now," he insisted in a low growl.

We were barely out the front door when I practically screamed, "We have to go back in there! Press him, squeeze him, get him to crack."

"Get him to crack?" Liam repeated. "When did you start channeling Edward G. Robinson?"

His obvious amusement didn't sit well with me. "Confess. Whatever the hell you call it. When he thought Zack and Shaylyn sent us, he was all set to pay. Then when I mentioned S&M, he blew me off."

"We can come back later. He's not going anywhere."

"He was lying. Something you would have noticed if you hadn't had that phone glued to your ear like some teenager."

"Speaking of phones, yours is dead."

"What?" I reached into my purse only to see the LED display was, in fact, blank. "I can charge it in the car."

"Don't bother. Becky called me. Faulkner docketed the motion to reconsider bail for nine tomorrow morning."

"That's great!" My excitement was tempered as I did a mental calculation. If the hearing was over by ten, I could still hit the florist, pick up the roses, and be at Willoughby Country Club to meet my mother in Stuart with a few minutes to spare. "I hope Taggert is ready. My car's parked over there," I said once I realized we were walking in the wrong direction.

"We'll come back for it. I've got to get to The Lord's Table ASAP."

"We're going to a soup kitchen?"

"Yep. Now that you're unemployed, I thought it would be good for you to familiarize yourself with your dining options."

I slapped his rock-hard biceps. Definitely causing me more pain than him. "That was so not funny. Where are you really taking me?"

"The Lord's Table."

"Why?"

"We have to get there before Crazy Frank leaves."

"Please tell me Crazy Frank is another one of Fantasy Dates' clients?"

"Nope."

"Then who is he? And why do they call him crazy?"

"They call him crazy because he hears voices."

"So it's a derogatory term for a guy who's either psychotic or schizophrenic? And why is he more important than interviewing the Fantasy Dates people? They're the ones leading the perverted double lives."

"Lots of people lead double lives. Crazy Frank, on the other hand, is the guy who sent you Paolo's penis."

*I assume full responsibility for my actions, except the
ones that are someone else's fault.*

Eighteen

"Ever been to a soup kitchen?"

"Yes. As a matter of fact, I've done my civic duty
more than once." The quick slash of his grin told me he had
my number. I gave him an innocent look. "What? You think
I'm lying?"

"Nope. But I doubt it was your idea. Community service?"

Lucky guess. "I got a few speeding tickets, so it was either eight Saturdays of driver reeducation classes, six weekends of picking up litter on the side of I-95 wearing some
hideous yellow reflector jacket, or volunteer at a shelter for a
month."

The seat belt rubbed against my neck, forcing me to repo-
sition myself against the cracked leather upholstery. Unlike
my whisper-quiet BMW, Liam's vintage Mustang conducted
an entire concerto of assorted noises. The soloist in this case
was the muffler. It backfired often; a loud, pounding blast that
would have made John Philip Sousa proud.

The seat belt wasn't the only thing rubbing me the wrong
way. "Don't you think it's odd the way Payton and Jace didn't

ask us who we were? It was almost like they were expecting us or something."

He shrugged. "Your notes implied we were connected to the dating service. At any rate, Payton didn't strike me as a shrinking violet. I'm sure she liked talking about her kinky sex life."

"Jace was a hairsbreadth away from writing a check. Then I casually mentioned the whole S&M thing and he shut down. How weird is that? On one hand, I got the sense that he was a real tight-ass. But I'm also having trouble picturing him as the whip and leather type. I'm going to go back there and talk to him. He knows something and I'm going to find out what it is."

"Do you always act first and think second?" His tone was only half teasing.

"No. I'm battling a ticking clock here."

"Is that why you went into Fantasy Dates alone?"

I took a deep breath and exhaled slowly while I prayed for patience. As usual, God put me on hold. "In case you didn't notice," I reminded him, "it gave me time to search the office."

"Still no word from Zack or Shaylyn?"

I shook my head. "Liv is supposed to be hunting them down. I should call her later. Becky, too. I can't believe my damn phone is dead."

"Not Patrick?" he asked, one dark brow arched tauntingly.

There was no winning answer for that kind of question. If I said no, it sent the signal that our relationship was on the rocks. Maybe it was, maybe it wasn't. If I added Patrick to my call sheet as an afterthought, well, that just made me look like it *was* an afterthought. In reality, calling Patrick was a nonthought.

I cracked the window and gathered my hair to one side as warm, humid air swirled inside the car. At least that air was moving, which was more than I could say for the weak stream of exhaust-scented stuff spewing out of the air vents.

"Hot?"

Loaded question number two. Temperature-wise, yes. Libido-wise, hell yes. I couldn't control the weather, but I was in complete charge of my body's inappropriate desire for Liam. Besides, I had Jane to think about. What kind of friend lusts when another friend is in jail?

"Where is this place?" I asked, changing the subject.

"Off Forty-fifth."

I knew the area well. Strip malls, gas stations, fast food places, and most importantly, a Dunkin' Donuts drive-through. "Could we stop for some coffee?"

"You want coffee when it's ninety degrees?"

"Iced coffee."

Again I knew he was smiling without turning to look at him. Well, not smiling so much as smirking. "What sin did I commit now?"

"Oh, nothing. No one will mind when you walk into a soup kitchen carrying a grande whatever that costs more than most of these guys have in their collective pockets."

"So I'll skip the whipped cream as a show of solidarity." I tried not to heave a giant sigh. "I can leave it in the car while we talk to Crazy Frank. Okay?"

"Your call."

I glanced at his profile. "I think better with caffeine in my system."

"Then you must have been a few mugs short when you went inside Fantasy Dates. Especially when you knew someone had called you from there, threatening you. Not smart, Finley."

"So you've said." *Three times.* Add that to the ninety-nine times I'd said it to myself, and that was a hundred and two times stupid. I got it. "How much blood was in the kitchen?"

"Not a lot," he answered. "Someone got hit, but it wasn't fatal."

"How can you know that?"

"The blood spatter was oval. That's high-velocity spray, indicating the victim was in motion at the time the blow was struck."

Now I needed coffee and a barf bag. "In English, please."

Liam took the Forty-fifth Street exit, drove two blocks, then turned into the drive-through lane. His car belched another backfire, startling the elderly gentleman crossing the parking lot. Though it was Liam's car that caused the old guy to drop his newspaper, I was the one he glared at.

"You should get this heap fixed."

"Working on it." Liam shifted the car into park.

It didn't idle so much as it vibrated.

Releasing his seat belt, he turned and lifted his fist, swinging it at his own face in slow motion. "The natural reflex is to turn away from a punch. Like this," he said, demonstrating the move. "That sends the blood spraying in the direction the person was moving at the time of impact."

"What about the glass?"

"Could mean there was some sort of struggle, or it's completely unrelated. Until I know what happened, it's impossible to tell."

"Until *we* know," I corrected. "I'm thinking Zack punched Shaylyn, maybe after he called and threatened me."

"I thought you said you couldn't tell the gender of the person who called."

"I couldn't, but Shaylyn doesn't strike me—no pun intended—as the battering type. She's too . . . cultured. Zack, on the other hand, gives me some serious willies." I shivered.

"So how come they sprung for an attorney for Jane?"

I wondered the same thing. "Maybe they didn't want anyone to find out about their tawdry sideline? I've gone over their records a zillion times and I'm pretty sure the majority of their dealings were legitimate. The S&M perverts represent a small fraction of their business."

"S&M isn't illegal."

"It should be," I said. "If for no other reason than the fact that wearing leather in Florida in the summer is just wrong."

He flashed me a very sexy, slightly crooked smile that caused my stomach to flutter. "Not into the smell of leather and the crack of a whip?"

I vehemently shook my head. "No." Forget the whip. But the image of Liam stripped down and wearing nothing but black leather pants made my stomach dance and gave me a serious hot flash. "You seem to know a lot about it, though. Anything you'd like to share with the class?"

"I worked vice for a few years."

It was hard to reconcile the man next to me now in a police uniform. He didn't impress me as a rules and regulations kinda guy. Probably why he wasn't a cop anymore. "Why'd you leave the police force?"

Liam moved up another two spots in line and checked the Breitling Chronograph adorning his left wrist. "It was time."

"Why?"

Liam eased the car forward until he was even with the speaker. As he placed the order, he leaned to one side and pulled a worn wallet from the back pocket of his jeans.

At the same time, I was rummaging in my purse for my cash. He looked at my pathetically limp five-dollar bill and said, "It's on me."

"Thanks."

He reached across me and opened the glove box, retrieving an antiquated plastic cup holder that clipped into the small slot between the door and the window. He handed it over, then passed me my whipped-cream-free iced latte.

I left the cup holder in my lap, preferring to jab the straw in the drink and savor the much-missed taste of icy coffee. "You didn't answer my question," I reminded him after I'd drained nearly a third of the cup before we'd even exited the parking lot.

"No, I didn't."

"Is it some sort of state secret?"

"Nope. Just not something I talk about."

Well, he might as well just wave a red flag in front of my face. "You know I can Google you, right?"

"Yep. But you won't."

Wrong. I started to and now I definitely will. I added it to my mental list. I did have a strict rule against Googling friends, but Liam and I weren't friends. We were . . . oh, hell, I didn't know what we were. "You sound pretty sure. How come?"

"You didn't know about Jane's past."

"That's different. My friends and I have an agreement."

"You should rethink that agreement."

"Why?"

He shook his head and sighed heavily. "You'll figure it out eventually."

Okay, the whole Jane arrest thing had blown up in my face, but his cryptic remark puzzled me. Did he think Becky and Liv had secrets as well? And frankly, even if they did, I didn't see the relevance to Jane's case. I would have pressed him, but we'd reached our destination.

I knew from several profiles done over the years that the soup kitchen was the creation of lovely eighty-something Bea Gaitlin. Bea and her husband had made a, by Palm Beach standards, modest fortune. In the late 1950s, Bea and her husband had bought a large tract of land in Martin County, about twenty miles north. They opened an unassuming restaurant that developed a loyal following. Thirty years later, they began selling off parcels of property and Bea used some of the proceeds to start up the soup kitchen. Her philanthropy didn't stop there; she and her family sponsored everything from Little League teams to Red Cross relief efforts. Still, The Lord's Table remained her baby and she could often be found serving up plates in spite of her age.

The single-story, cinder block building was painted a bright salmon background color with a large mural of the

Disciples breaking bread as decoration. The hand-painted sign at the entrance to the small grass lot next to the building tilted heavily to one side. A leftover hurricane repair, no doubt.

Double doors were propped open with metal folding chairs, and the instant I stepped from the car, the scent of roasted turkey hung in the heavy air. Unfortunately, it was tempered by the smell of two or three dozen people milling around the entrance. A few shirtless men were at the far end of the parking lot, availing themselves of the open fresh-water shower.

I'm charitable. Almost all of my M&M's come from schoolchildren hawking fund-raisers in the front of the grocery store, and I'm really good about regularly culling my closet and donating my unloved cell phones to battered women's shelters. But looking at the people waiting patiently for what was probably their only decent meal of the day made me feel guilty.

I reminded myself that I was unemployed and carrying nearly as much debt as a small developing nation. Yet I still had a great place to live, beautiful clothes, and as much food as I wanted. I could take as many showers as I wanted, *whenever* I wanted. Looking at this mass of humanity waiting patiently for their one meal of the day made me realize just how damned lucky I was.

As we approached the building, Liam pulled a photo from his shirt pocket. I glanced over and realized it wasn't a photograph, it was the dual-view mug shot of a grungy-looking man with half-closed eyes, dirt-brown hair, and really bad teeth.

I got a couple of catcalls that were instantly silenced by a harsh glare from Liam. I needed to learn that look; it was damned effective.

The interior was set up like a school cafeteria, long metal tables with attached benches. There was very little conversation and a great deal of spoon-fisted food shoveling.

"Far table on the left-hand side," Liam said, leading the way.

I practically glued myself to his back as we weaved our way through the throng of people devouring sliced turkey, mushy green beans, and blobs of potatoes. Much of the meal was coated in a layer of thick beige gravy and topped with a single slice of white bread.

"Shit," Liam mumbled, then took off running.

Crazy Frank bolted toward the back door. He moved amazingly quickly for a guy wearing about seven layers of clothes. I, on the other hand, was quite limited by my trendy but impractical wedges.

Frank was maybe twenty feet into the field behind the building when Liam caught hold of his collar, yanking him to an abrupt halt. Another five feet and Crazy Frank would have ended up in the canal.

I wasn't thrilled with the idea of wading though calf-deep weeds, but it was the only available option. The two men tussled a bit, but Liam was larger, stronger, and not distracted by hallucinations about aliens.

"I'm not going to hurt you," Liam told the man as he placed him in a tight hold.

Crazy Frank earned his moniker, rambling for several minutes about Liam being sent from the outer galaxy to harvest his liver. Given the strong odor of liquor on Crazy Frank's breath, my guess was his liver was already long gone.

Liam eventually managed to quiet him by dangling a twenty-dollar bill in front of him. Crazy Frank made a grab for it, but Liam held it just out of reach. "Tell me about the package you mailed a couple of days ago."

"I didn't."

"Yes," Liam countered, again waving the money, "you did." Frank's eyes darted back and forth, following the movement of the bill like an animal hunting prey. "It was a long time ago."

"Think, Frank," Liam said.

"Please?" I asked.

At the sound of my voice, Frank jerked his head around and his chapped lips curved into a smile. He'd lost a couple of his front teeth since his last mug shot. Some of the longer, stringy strands of hair fell forward and caught in his food-crusted beard.

"The box, Frank?" Liam prompted. "Where'd you get it?"

"She gave it to me."

"Who was she?" Liam asked.

"Dunno."

Liam waved the bill again. "Where did you meet her?"

"She came to my place."

"You have a place?" I asked. My uncensored question earned me a nasty look from Liam.

"She was in the park?"

Crazy Frank nodded. "They were together but she gave me the money."

"A man and a woman?" Crazy Frank seemed confused by my question. I took the nonanswer as a yes. "Was she about this tall?" I asked, raising my hand to approximate Shaylyn's height. "Dark hair? Pretty?"

"I guess so."

I wanted to shake a more definitive answer out of him but decided abusing a homeless guy was bad form. "What about the man with her?"

"He was pretty, too."

"C'mon, Frank. You can do better than that," Liam said, loosening his grip but keeping hold of the guy's scruffy collar. "Tall, short, black, white?"

"Didn't get a good look. She just handed me the box and told me to take it across to the mail place."

"How did you know where to send the box?" Liam asked.

Crazy Frank ran his hand over his beard. "I copied it off the piece of paper she gave me."

"Do you still have it?" If he did, maybe there would be prints or something to prove Shaylyn was the killer.

"Had to give it back to her. Only way she'd give me the money. A fifty."

"Do you still have the money?" Liam and Frank looked at me like *I* was the crazy one. Granted, it was a silly question.

"What about the car?" Liam asked.

"Black, maybe blue," Frank answered after a long pause. "Dark."

"A Bentley?" I felt a surge of excitement. Shaylyn's sapphire luxury-mobile could be described as dark, especially by a guy who drank early and often. "Big car? Sleek?"

Crazy Frank shrugged. "Yeah, maybe."

Forget shaking him. I wanted to strangle him. "Maybe it was big, or maybe it was sleek?"

Liam pulled another twenty-dollar bill out of his pocket. "Give me something here, Frank."

The homeless guy's glazed eyes fixed on the cash. "It had a sticker."

"A bumper sticker?" I asked.

"On the front window. A circle," Frank said, his fingers itching to make a grab for the money. "Some words, an X, and a palm tree."

"Good job, Frank." Liam gave him the money and Crazy Frank dashed back toward the soup kitchen.

"Why did you let him go?" I asked. "We should take him to the police and make him tell them his story. It proves Jane didn't kill Paolo. She was in jail when Shaylyn paid Frank to send me the penis."

"In case you missed it, Frank didn't identify Shaylyn. He isn't a credible witness."

"But he's the only one we've got."

Liam pointed toward his car. "To what? There's no way to

verify his story. The cops could easily think Jane or you paid Frank to send the box after the fact just to throw them off track. We're going to need more than Frank's word to take to the cops."

"So the first thing we do is check out the sticker?" I was getting pretty good at this whole investigating thing. "The Bentley is parked at Fantasy Dates. But won't the police be there?"

"Not by the time we show up."

It was maybe a fifteen-minute drive. "Are we walking?"

"No. I've got to meet a friend first."

I could feel my heels sinking into the sandy soil as I hurried to keep pace with Liam. Along with ruining my practically new shoes, I was starting to hear the buzz of mosquitoes buzzing in my ears. I was actually looking forward to getting back to the Mustang.

"Who is this friend?"

"Trena."

He said the single name as if it should have been instantly recognizable. Like Cher or Madonna. "Who is Trena?"

"A tech at the ME's office. She likes me."

Bully for her. I slid into the passenger's seat, fanning the air around my face in an attempt to keep the insects from tagging along for the ride. As Liam got behind the wheel, his cell rang.

"McGarrity." After a brief pause, he passed the phone to me.

As I held it to my ear, I could smell the faint scent of his soap before it was obliterated by the stench of fumes as he started the engine. "Hello?"

"God, his voice is hot," Becky said, sighing heavily.

Imagine him in tight black leather pants. "You called to tell me that?"

"I called looking for you. Hearing his voice was just a bonus. Why didn't you charge your phone?"

"I haven't had a chance. I've been meeting Liam's . . . *friends*."

"And?"

I told her about Crazy Frank. "Now we're off to see someone named Trena from the ME's office."

"Why?"

"Apparently that's classified," I said. I didn't like his secrecy. I didn't like being overruled about taking Frank to the police. I didn't like not having my own phone. And I didn't like being in such close proximity to Liam. "How's Jane?"

"Holding up. Liv and I spent an hour with her."

"Any word from—"

"Still no Taggert. Still no Shaylyn. Still no Zack. Weird, huh?"

"What if Taggert doesn't show at the motion hearing in the morning?"

"He'd be an idiot to risk a contempt citation for failing to appear on his own motion."

"He is an idiot."

"Not a professional idiot," Becky countered. "I'll keep trying to get in touch with him. Call me when you're on your way home and I'll meet you there."

"Sounds good. Make sure Liv keeps looking for Zack and Shaylyn. She knows every waiter, bellman, driver, and concierge in Palm Beach County. They have to be hiding somewhere."

"Have fun with Liam. See ya later."

"Bye." I handed Liam his phone, ignoring the electric charge I felt when his fingers brushed my palm.

"I've got feelers out on them, too," he said. "We'll find them."

"Before or after they kill someone else?" *Like, um, me?*

"You don't know that they've killed anyone."

It was dark but I glared at him anyway. "Right. They're just misunderstood. It's a total coincidence that they had a kinky sex sideline to their business and that Paolo was part of it and then Paolo gets killed and his part gets removed.

"They knew every detail of Jane and Paolo's date. It's completely plausible that one or both of them committed the murder, then framed Jane. They knew my name and address from Jane's application, so all they had to do was find someone like Crazy Frank to deliver the box."

Liam rubbed his chin. "Why would they kill Paolo?"

"Because they're evil?"

"Possible. But there's almost always something that triggers a murder and I'm not seeing one here."

"Payton said she wouldn't pay the assessment anymore," I suggested.

"Which is motive to kill Payton, maybe. Not Paolo. I'm not feeling the Special Assessment thing as motive. A few grand is pocket change to the Kresley Pierponts and Jace Andrews of the world. Not enough to commit murder over."

"Maybe they killed him when he failed to get more money out of Payton. If Paolo was their muscle—*What*?"

He stopped laughing. "Their muscle? Now you're off on some Mafia tangent?"

"Excuse me." God, he was infuriating. "Paolo was— whatever the PC term for the guy who collects the blackmail money is—only he went to Payton and didn't collect so they killed him."

"If that's true, then killing Paolo wouldn't be a smart move," Liam said.

"Murder is supposed to be smart?"

"With this kind of preplanning? Yes. If Jane didn't do it, then someone put a lot of time and thought into this."

"Jane didn't do it."

"I agree."

"I thought you didn't care one way or the other."

"I don't. But I also don't know who trashed the Fantasy Dates office. Doesn't make sense for Zack or Shaylyn to do it and I doubt it's a coincidence."

"Someone was looking for something." I thought for a second. "A home-burned DVD?"

He gave a little shrug as he turned into the parking area behind a nondescript stucco building adjacent to St. Mary's Hospital.

I glanced around, seeing nothing but a half dozen dark vans parked along the chain-link fence surrounding the lot. "We're meeting Trena here?" I asked.

"In there," he said, pointing at the building.

"But that's—"

"The morgue."

The closer you get to the truth, the more people start lying to you.

Nineteen

Being a morgue virgin, I wasn't quite sure what to expect as I followed Liam through metal double doors, and past big toxic-waste warning signs printed in both English and Spanish. Cherry deodorizer tried—and failed—to cover the antiseptic smell that permeated the air. Several thankfully empty gurneys were pushed off to one side of the hallway.

Liam seemed completely at ease while I was replaying every graphic slasher flick I'd ever watched. The alarm on my creepy-meter was ringing loudly in my head. Intellectually I knew the corpses weren't going to rise and chase me until they caught me and tore me limb from limb, but my imagination was in overdrive. So much so that when a perky brunette poked her head out of one of the doorways, I jumped and made some girly yelping noise.

"Hi, Trena," Liam greeted. "How's everything?"

She smiled brightly and batted her big brown eyes up at Liam. It wasn't flirtatious. More of a brother-sister kinda thing than boyfriend-girlfriend.

"Hi," she said, leaning around Liam to offer me her hand. "I'm Trena."

"Finley."

"Nice to meet you."

Her handshake was quick and firm. Trena was dressed in Carolina-blue surgical scrubs and a large sweater that threatened to swallow her not-quite-five-foot frame. As she turned back into the room, the soles of her white leather tennis shoes squeaked against the tile floor.

We followed her through what looked a lot like a high school chemistry lab. Several microscopes lined the high Formica counter that ran along both sides of the room. Above and below the counter were cabinets and drawers all labeled in neat, black block printing.

As soon as we pushed through a second set of metal doors, the temperature dropped and I nearly did as well.

There were dead people all over the place. Okay, so maybe I was exaggerating a little. There were five sheet-covered outlines wearing toe tags. Worse still, they were on the stainless steel drain tables I'd only seen on various versions of *CSI*.

Trena went to the next to last table and yanked back the sheet. "Liam McGarrity, meet William Arthur."

Bile rose in my throat when I saw what was once a human being. "That's disgusting."

Trena shot me a sympathetic look. "First time?"

I brought my hand up to cover my nose and mouth and nodded.

"Want to wait in the hallway?" Liam asked.

Hell yes. "N-no. I'm fine."

Liam leaned closer to the corpse, near where a large Y incision dissected the torso. "So, did our limo driver blow himself up or did he have help?"

Taking a clipboard from a hook on the edge of the table, Trena licked the tip of her index finger, then flipped through the pages. "Died from impact injuries consistent with an explosion. Burns over a hundred percent of his body. Charring in the trachea and lungs."

"So, he was alive when the boat caught fire?"

Trena nodded. "In a matter of speaking. See this?" she asked as she pointed toward darker flecks of flesh barely attached to the underlying skeletal structure. "Analysis indicates high levels of gasoline in the tissue. Could have splashed on him during the explosion or could have been poured on him prebarbecue. Not enough tissue to make a definitive determination. Tox screen showed a blood alcohol level of point three."

"He wasn't drunk?" I asked.

"No. The alcohol looks like it was just the delivery system."

"For?" I prompted.

"GHB. There was still a high concentration of it in his stomach contents at autopsy."

I was *so* sorry I asked. And while unhappy about being unemployed, ecstatic that I didn't have *her* job.

Trena scanned the last page, then returned the clipboard to its place. "Someone slipped roofies in his Miller Lite. Or he slipped them to himself."

"Date masturbation?" I asked.

Trena laughed. "What can I tell you?" she asked as she covered the crispy corpse with the sheet. "Some people dose themselves with the stuff. I'm told there's a real euphoria in the first ten to thirty minutes. As far as your friend here, all I can tell you is that he had it in his system. How it got there is a whole different thing."

"No other injuries?" Liam asked.

"Minor bruising on the right cheekbone."

"Like he was punched?" I was thinking of the blood spatter on the floor at Fantasy Dates.

"There wasn't enough flesh left on the face to be certain."

I *really* needed to rethink the whole asking-questions part of this thing.

"But it is a possibility," Trena continued. "I can tell you that the death certificate is going to list this as suspicious, but there's not enough evidence to work with for the ME to classify it as a homicide."

"Thanks," Liam said.

"Not a prob."

We started to leave—good thing since my stomach was in full revolt—when Trena called, "You wanted to know about that Martinez guy, too, right?"

"Yeah. Anything other than . . . the obvious?"

Trena smiled at me. "Notice how freaked men get when it comes to genital mutilation?"

"It's a guy thing," I agreed.

Placing her palms on the edge of one of the empty autopsy tables, Trena hoisted her small frame up until she was comfortably seated with her legs crossed. Actually, I couldn't imagine being comfortable on something used to dissect people, but I'm picky that way.

"Two different knives used in the attack," Trena began as if she was composing a grocery list. "No signs of struggle. Blood alcohol level well within the legal limits. Negative for drugs."

"No GHB?" Liam asked.

She shook her head. "Not at the time of autopsy, but that stuff is stealthy. It leaves the system . . ." She paused to snap her fingers. "Like that. Only marks on the body were a leaf tattoo on his left shoulder and a small scrape with a rectangular bruise 11.2 by 9.2 centimeters at his temple."

Liam raked his fingers through his hair. "From?"

Trena shrugged her shoulders. "Got me. Bring me something sharp, small, and roughly one-half-inch rectangular and I'll tell you if it's what left the scratch and the bruise."

Several minutes later I was alone by the chain-link fence

sucking in deep gulps of air and doing my best not to puke all over my formerly favorite pair of shoes. Now I'd only associate them with the past few hours. Now they were shelter shoes or morgue shoes—whatever. Bottom line? They'd have to go the way of my jail jammies.

To his credit, Liam wasn't mocking me. To his discredit, he was leaning against the hood of his car, one foot propped on the chrome bumper, chatting on his cell phone while I was being tormented by skittish lizards and the memory of Fried Guy.

Patrick wouldn't do this to me. He wasn't the kind of man to leave me pseudo-lurching in the weeds. Then again, Patrick wasn't the kind of guy to go sneaking into a morgue after hours either.

No compare and contrast! I told myself. *Again.*

Reaching into my purse, I shoved aside Payton's porn DVD, found a mint, and popped it in my mouth hoping to relieve the acrid taste of death coating my tongue. It's amazing to think I've spent the last seven years as an estates and trusts paralegal and this is the first time I've ever been up close and personal with a body. Not so amazing, I decided as I pushed my hair off my face and tried to fan away some of the perspiration. My job is—*was* to deal with the aftermath of death. Not this.

"Finley?" Liam called. "Gotta go!"

"Let me choke down the last vestiges of stomach acid and I'll be right with you," I muttered as I walked back to the Mustang.

"You okay?"

I glared at him. "Just dandy, thanks."

"Why are you pissed at me?" he asked as we got into the car.

"You could have warned me. A heads-up. A little *something* would have been appreciated. I just wasn't prepared to see my first real life dead person."

"Real life dead person?"

I smiled in spite of my annoyance. "You know what I meant."

"Yeah. Anyway . . ." He paused to start the pitiful engine, then pointed the sputtering thing toward I-95. "I'll drop you off, then swing by Fantasy Dates to see if there's a sticker on the windshield of the Bentley."

"What should I do?"

"Go home."

"I can be useful," I argued.

"Life is all about perception, isn't it?"

"That was mean."

"You want to be useful?"

"Yes."

"Then go home and watch *Payton Does Palm Beach*."

"You get to revisit a crime scene and I have to watch homemade spank-me porn? How is that fair?"

He laughed, a low, sensual sound that reverberated through the interior of the car and resonated deep inside me. "One of us has to watch it and I have a thing."

My fists clenched when he said it. I wanted to take the DVD out of my purse and slap it against his forehead. Not because he'd said "thing," though that did annoy me. And not because he'd placed me in charge of porn viewing; I wasn't going to get the vapors or anything. No, I was just royally miffed because I figured he was probably on his way to hook up with the not-so-ex Mrs. McGarrity. Correction, I was miffed that I was miffed. There's something decidedly loathsome about lusting for a guy that is totally wrong for you in every way while you're in a relationship with someone who's totally right.

As a human being, I suck.

"You're quiet," he commented as we drove over the intracoastal waterway.

"I'm saving my energy for the 'Payton's Been a Bad, Bad Girl' film fest."

"If it's going to bother you to watch it, then—"

"It's not going to bother me," I insisted. "It's going to bore me."

"Not into watching, eh?"

"Not really, no. You?"

"Depends on who and what I'm watching."

"Why do you do that?"

"Do what?" he asked as he pulled the Mustang to the curb behind my BMW.

"Give me a simple answer to a simple question."

He checked his watch, unhooked his seat belt, reached across me, and opened my door. "Let's get you headed home."

Wait, did I miss something? I blinked, watching dumbfounded as he stepped out of his car and walked toward mine. Gathering up my purse, my keys, and my dignity, I managed to swallow my irritation. I couldn't demand explanations; from him, that was too . . . too *girlfriendish*.

Key at the ready, I clicked the disarm button. The taillights flashed amber and a loud chirp cut through the early-evening quiet.

Liam opened the door but lingered by the side of my car. His presence crowded my space, leaving me only two options. Number one: turn sideways so I could slip behind the wheel without any part of my body touching his. Number two: screw it all and take the half step that would press me firmly against him.

Heat surged through me. Granted, some if it was the humiliating memory of the last time I'd misread the signals and started unbuttoning my blouse. Most of it was pure, unadulterated curiosity. I was drawn to him in a self-destructive way. Kind of like when you know the iron is hot but you touch it anyway just to make sure.

However, I was not going to make an ass of myself a second time. Though my pulse was pounding in my ears and my hormones were positively riveted by his smoky blue-gray eyes, I took the high ground and went with option number one.

Almost.

Liam's hands closed on my waist and suddenly I found my back against the cold metal of my car and my front pressed against him. His feet were planted shoulder width apart, creating a comfortable cradle for me in the V of his thighs.

His warm, coffee-scented breath washed over my face as my mind tried to process the sudden onslaught of sensations. I didn't know where to focus first. Everything was coming at me at once—the smoldering, seductive look in his eyes. The hardness of his chest. The solidness of his thighs against mine.

I opened my mouth, hoping something pithy would magically come forth. Some quip that would diffuse the situation and prevent me from doing something really, *really* stupid.

Nada. I was witless, mute, and so incredibly hot I couldn't stand it. It was a libidinous version of rock-paper-scissors. Rock beats scissors, scissors beat paper, paper beats rock. Liam was paper. I was . . . toast.

Mixed metaphors aside, I was transfixed as I focused on his features. The muted glow cast by the streetlamp softened the sharp angles of his face. His fingers splayed slightly, but the deciding vote was cast when the pads of his thumbs started making slow, dizzying little circles just below my rib cage.

Lifting my hands, I tentatively bracketed his waist and waited. And waited. His mouth hovered no more than a whisper above mine.

"Well?"

The corners of Liam's lips curved into a smile. "Impatient?"

"You started this."

His fingers stilled but he didn't let me go.

"My mistake," he said; his voice was as steady as his gaze.

I, on the other hand, was a quivering blob. Weak in the knees. Had it been physically possible, I would have tossed his tall, dark, handsome, having-second-thoughts ass into the backseat of my car. To my credit and surprise, I actually managed to drape myself in a cloak of disinterest. "Then, we're done here?"

He shook his head. "Oh, we're definitely not done. But I have a—"

"Thing? Ashley waiting for you, is she?" No, no, *no!* Did I really just make a snarky, jealous reference to his ex? Despite my silent, fervent pleas, the ground did not open and swallow me whole.

Liam stepped back but his hands still gripped my waist. "You're hardly in a position to offer commentary. As soon as you clean up your own house, you're welcome to have an opinion."

My house? I shrugged out of his hold. "Want to tell me what that means?"

"I've been trying to tell you, Finley. Subtle doesn't work on you very well, does it?" Tossing his keys in the air, then catching them, he turned and started back to his car. "Just an FYI, I'm not meeting Ashley," he called over his shoulder. "I'm going back to Fantasy Dates, then to the mail place to watch the security footage again. That's how I found Crazy Frank. Now that I know what to look for, I'll see if a dark car is visible anywhere on the tape. Find the car, find the killer."

Twenty minutes later, my skin was still flushed. My nerve endings were still on fire and my conscience was . . . guilty.

Shit. Shit. Shit.

As I drove home, I knew I could intellectualize my way out of this. All I had to do was blame everything on the emotional roller coaster of the past week. Jane's arrest, my arrest, a death threat, a severed penis delivery, borrowing money from my mother, losing my job—any one of those things could justify why I wanted Liam.

It was time to face reality.

It was time to end my relationship with Patrick.

But first, I had to watch porn.

*The only thing worse than feeling like a fool is
actually being one.*

Twenty

"**P**ass the popcorn," Becky said, holding her hand out.
I gave her the bowl but my eyes remained fixed on the
television screen as I felt around on the coffee table for my
Diet Coke.

Our heads turned sideways in unison. "Is her nipple ring
attached to her dog collar?" Becky asked.

"Yes."

"That's going to leave a mark."

Payton was getting lashed by the guy in the Hannibal
Lecter mask again. There were thirty-six more minutes of
jumpy, poor-quality footage.

Face Mask Guy and Payton were moaning and groaning.
Conversely, Becky and I were groaning and cringing. Especially once the spanking and whipping and lashing moved
beyond stings and welts to the actual drawing of blood. To
make it worse, the camera often zoomed in for close-ups of
the wounds.

As soon as Payton started to unzip her playmate's full
leather bodysuit—using her teeth, no less—I reached for the

remote. "I'm going to fast-forward through the consummation."

"Please do," Becky said as she tossed a fluffy kernel of popcorn in her mouth. "This crap is enough to make me want to take a vow of celibacy."

"Thought you did that already." The joke earned me a quick jab in the ribs. "You're the one always complaining about your lack of a social life."

"My life. My right to complain," Becky said. "Besides, we have a—"

"What's that?" I asked, switching from fast forward to slow motion replay. I concentrated hard on the grainy video.

"A half-naked guy."

"No, on his shoulder." I got up, went to the television, and tapped my fingernail against the flat screen. "This. Is it a tattoo?"

"Or a mole. Or a birthmark," Becky suggested. "Hard to tell. Too bad we can't enhance the image."

I jumped up. "We can."

"What did you buy now?"

I shot her a nasty look. "I didn't buy anything. Sam has a new computer with all sorts of cool graphics programs." I was already dialing his number. "I'm sure it can do whatever."

Sam answered on the second ring. "Hello?"

"Hi. Can you bring your fancy new laptop down here?"

"Finley, I love you but I won't be an enabler."

"Um, huh?"

"Until you get another job, you really should curtail your online shopping addiction."

"I don't want it to shop," I told him. "I want it to watch sadomasochistic porn."

"Why didn't you say so? I'll be right down."

I'd barely had time to return the phone to its cradle when two things happened. Someone knocked at my door and my recharged cell phone began to ring and vibrate across the coffee table. "Grab that, would you?" I called to Becky as I went to look through the peephole.

It was Liv.

"Hi," she said. She had a white garment bag hooked over her shoulder.

Knowing Sam was on his way down, I left the door ajar and followed Liv as she lugged the bag over to the chair and heaved it off her shoulder. She rubbed the reddish indentation of the hangers on her palm; then her violet eyes widened and her brow furrowed questioningly as she noted the frozen image on my television screen. "Is that what I think it is?"

I nodded and quickly brought her up to speed. I finished at about the same time I heard Becky snap my cell phone closed.

"That was Liam. He said to tell you there is a sticker on the Bentley. It's from the Palm Beach Polo Club."

Scanning my memory, I vaguely recalled the few times my mother had insisted on dragging me along to see a match. The club's logo is circular, with crossed bamboo mallets, a palm tree in the center, and the club's name printed around the image. It fit Crazy Frank's description.

I'm not a fan of polo, though I do enjoy certain parts of the experience. Okay, one part. Seeing all the ladies of means dressed in their finest is akin to attending fashion week in New York. Not that I've been to fashion week, but it is on my list of things to do.

On the downside, polo takes forever; you're outside; it's broken into chukkers—a stupid name—and they have this ridiculous halftime tradition of stomping divots. Divot stomping requires spectators to wander all over the field replacing hunks of grass torn during the match. Some of the players join in, but for the most part, it's just overdressed people ruining overpriced shoes.

"That's great news. Does he want me to call him back?"

"No. He said to tell you it isn't great news. Man, does he have your number, or what?"

Ignoring her small barb, I asked, "Why isn't it great?"

"In addition to AWOL Zack and Shaylyn, he checked and several people on the Special Assessment list are members of the club. Jace Andrews, Barbie Baker, Matthew Gibson, Kresley Pierpont, and Renee Sabato."

Well, that took the air right out of my sails. It also didn't help that I was slightly perturbed that Liam didn't wait to speak directly to me. Silly, I know, but I was still suffering the aftereffects of his nonkiss kiss and the veiled remark about my inability to grasp subtlety and my need to clean my own house.

"Hello?" Liv waved a hand in front of my face. "What do you think? The periwinkle suit or the cream dress?" Grabbing the second outfit, she held them side by side.

"For?"

"Jane to wear to court in the morning. I figured something new would lift her spirits and give her confidence."

"Her spirits will be lifted enough if Taggert wins the motion to reconsider bail," Becky said. "The guy still hasn't returned any of my messages."

Liv and I exchanged worried glances. I pointed to the periwinkle suit. "She'll like that one."

"Okay."

As Liv was putting the outfits back inside the garment bag, Sam arrived, lugging his oversized laptop. "This thing is heavy," he said as he moved the popcorn and soda cans to one side and wiped the tabletop clean with a napkin before gingerly placing the laptop on the coffee table.

While he connected cables and got the thing up and running, I took the DVD out of my machine, then made a pot of coffee. I was running possibilities through my mind. Thanks to Payton's honesty, I knew the Special Assessments had nothing to do with charity. Thanks to her DVD, I knew they had everything to do with S&M. But Kresley had lied. And Jace had lied. Why?

Crazy Frank said a woman gave him the penis, so unless

Jace had a quick gender reassignment, he was an unlikely suspect. Kresley was a possibility, but given her net worth, it seemed highly unlikely that she'd have to resort to murder in order to avoid blackmail. Though I'd left a couple of messages for Barbie Baker, I hadn't heard back yet. I would make a point of tracking her down immediately after the dreaded brunch with my mother.

Again, though, I'd seen Barbie Baker's financials, and paying a little hush money wouldn't put a dent in her cash flow. Barring any new information, Zack and Shaylyn were the most obvious suspects.

"All cued up," Sam called.

I delivered coffee to everyone, then sat between Sam and Becky so I could see the image on his computer screen. "Can you zoom in on the red spot?"

With a few maneuvers of the wireless mouse, he boxed and segregated the area of interest and clicked a couple of times. A new window opened, revealing a mosaic of color blocks that looked more like abstract art than anything else.

"That doesn't help much."

"Give me a minute," Sam said, clicking more stuff on the toolbar.

The image on the seventeen-inch screen cleared, revealing a bright red maple leaf tattoo. A bad one. I instantly recalled Payton's assessment of Zack. *Maple-leaf-licking bastard.*

"That's ugly. And cheap," Becky said. "The veins in the leaf look more like a spiderweb."

Paolo was the one with the tattoo but Zack was the one Payton had slammed. The hairs on my neck tingled. I was missing something. "Can you go back to the DVD?"

"Sure. What are we looking for?"

"Zip through it to see if the guy ever takes off his mask."

No luck. We saw every inch of the guy *except* his face. "That was a waste of time," I grumbled, sipping the last of my coffee.

"Go back to the beginning," Becky said. About two minutes into the vile film, she yelled, "There!" and pointed to the nightstand. "Can you zoom in on that?"

Sam complied. "Pills?"

A white pill with what looked like five letters. Below the print was a circle with either the letter *Z* or the number 2 inside. "Can you make it any clearer?" I asked.

He shook his head. "Sorry."

"Let's Google it," Becky suggested.

"No. Absolutely not," Sam said vehemently. "Gay man with Patriot Act paranoia here. You want to Google illegal drugs? Do it on Finley's computer."

While Sam was packing up his computer, Becky went into the bedroom to retrieve mine. I was rummaging through the Fantasy Dates files, frantically looking for Payton's home phone number.

It was only when I heard her groggy voice that I realized it was after midnight. "I'm sorry to disturb you."

"Who is this?"

"Finley Tanner. We met this afternoon. You gave me your DVD?"

Payton perked right up. "How'd you like it?"

Disgusting. "Fascinating. I couldn't help but notice there were some pills on the nightstand."

"Paolo's idea. He claimed they would . . . enhance the experience."

"Do you know what he gave you?"

"I didn't ask."

Someone needed to tell this woman there was a difference between adventurous and stupid. "Did they enhance your experience?"

"No, not really. Well, a little."

"Can you be more specific?"

"That night is a little foggy. If it wasn't for the video, I'm not sure I'd remember much more than snippets."

"Did you always tape your . . . encounters?"

"No, and I didn't know Paolo was going to tape that night."

"It wasn't consensual?"

"No, but he didn't need to drug me, I wouldn't have cared. That was his first mistake. His second one was thinking I'd pay them off to keep it quiet."

"They?"

"Look, Paolo was fun and all that, but he wasn't the brightest guy on the planet. There's no way he dreamed up this scam on his own. He never said so, but I figured Zack and Shaylyn orchestrated the whole thing."

"Were Zack and Paolo . . . Did they . . ."

"As far as I know, Zack isn't a switch hitter, if that's what you're getting at. His loss, if you ask me. There's nothing more erotic than two—"

I wanted to stick my fingers in my ears and start chanting la-la-la-la. I already knew more about Payton's sex life than my own. Not an option, so I just said, "Thanks. Sorry I bothered you," and got off the phone as quickly as possible.

"I hate to bail, but I still have to swing by Jane's and get shoes and jewelry," Liv said. "Do you guys need me for Googling?"

"Go on." I gave her a hug. "We'll see you at the courthouse at eight-thirty."

"Hopefully, this will be the end of it," Liv said, her shoulders slumped forward.

"It will," Becky said.

I could only pray she was right. The fact that Taggert was nowhere to be found didn't exactly inspire confidence.

"She feels guilty," Becky said as soon as Liv left my apartment.

"She got Jane a membership at Fantasy Dates. I'd feel guilty, too."

"It wasn't her fault."

I agreed. "She'll get past it once Jane is out of jail. Do you really think Taggert will come through in the morning?"

Becky shrugged. "He's devoted his whole life to his profession. Never married or had a family. He may be slipping a little but he is a good lawyer."

"A good lawyer *hired* by Zack and Shaylyn. I think they killed Paolo. And the limo driver."

"But you said they didn't have the Charleston information on Jane until after Paolo was killed, right?"

"Yes. So help me here. If they're the killers—and everything points in that direction—why would they help the woman they framed for their crime?"

"That does seem like an oxymoron," Becky agreed. She got her purse, pulled out a slightly smashed Moon Pie, and unwrapped it.

"How can you eat those things?"

Becky laughed. "This from a woman addicted to Lucky Charms?"

"Let's Google."

Settling on the sofa with my laptop, I had no problem finding an image of a Rohypnol pill. It was an exact match to the ones on the bedside table in Payton's porn flick. "There was GHB in the champagne bottle and the glasses from the limo, and the limo driver had GHB in his system when he died. This can't be a coincidence."

"Maybe Paolo was planning on blackmailing Jane with a compromising DVD?"

"He had to know Jane was a scholarship member. She'd never be able to pay blackmail. Hell, it's been a week and Liv still can't get the various banks to liquidate Jane's investments. It makes no sense for Paolo to dose Jane so he could tape . . ."

"Finley?"

My mind was spinning. "Paolo wasn't filming. There was a third person in the room."

"And you know this how?"

"The camera moved."

Becky's green eyes grew wide. "Yes, it did."

"Zack? Shaylyn?"

"My money's on Zack," Becky said. "He's the creepier of the two. Google him."

I typed in his name and my excitement plummeted. "There are three million nine hundred ninety-some page hits. We need to narrow the search."

"What did Payton say about him?"

I typed in his name and added "maple leaf" to the search. Maybe three hundred fewer listings. "Davis is too common a name."

"Try adding Shaylyn's name."

I did. That cut the total down to just under four hundred thousand. Next I tried adding "maple leaf" and "snowy owl," the password from the Fantasy Dates file. "That made it worse. Now I have like a million tourist pages for Canadian vacations."

"Wait a minute," Becky said, taking the laptop.

I watched as she typed in Zack's name, Canada, and every variation on felon she could think of. "Well, well, well. Seems Zack did time in federal prison in Canada for fraud. I don't remember that being in any of the Fantasy Dates promotional brochures."

"Paolo did time, too," I reminded her. "Can you see if he's a multicountry criminal?"

In no time, Becky had a copy of an article up on the screen. "Zack and Paolo were codefendants in the fraud case."

"The spiderweb."

"What?"

I took back the laptop and searched for prison tattoos. "You noticed that Paolo's body art was bad, right? A spiderweb is a common prison gang tattoo in Canada. Most likely, he had the red leaf done to cover the spiderweb."

"What made you think of that?"

"The Discovery Channel did a thing on prison life."

"You need to get out more."

I set the laptop aside and went into the kitchen to refill my coffee mug. "Liam said the weirdest thing to me."

"He wants to jump your bones?"

"No."

"He doesn't want to jump your bones?" Becky's voice perked right up.

"No." Technically. "He said he's been trying to tell me something." I poured cream in the mug and didn't bother stirring. "Kinda like Ellen harping on me that I miss details."

"About the case?"

I shook my head. "No. He'd tell me if he knew something that could help Jane. It's personal, except that we aren't *personal*."

"Betcha could be if you blew Patrick off."

"I'll get around to it."

Becky jerked as if she'd been slapped. "Really?"

"Probably. Maybe."

"Why are you vacillating?"

"It's a big deal. I don't want to hurt him. He's been good to me."

"Too good, if you ask me."

"I didn't. Has Liam been coaching you? He never misses an opportunity to rag on my relationship."

"Maybe he knows something you don't?"

"How could he? He met Patrick one time. In passing."

"When?"

"When I was in the hospital after the Hall thing."

"You know, he was the one who tracked Patrick down."

"What?"

She shrugged. "I asked him to. I wasn't going to leave the hospital until I knew you were okay."

"What could he possibly know about Patrick that I don't know after all this time?"

"You could ask him," she suggested.

"I'd rather cut off my own tongue."

"We could Google."

I winced. "I am not going to do a computer search on my own boyfriend based on nothing but some snide remarks from a man who does nothing but make me crazy."

"You don't have to."

"Good."

"I will."

A decent, trusting person would have grabbed the laptop and steadfastly refused to invade the privacy of another. Apparently, I'm neither. "Well?"

"Lots of Nick Lachey Web sites. He's cute. I'd do him."

"Becky!"

"Sorry." I heard the tap of her fingernail as she scrolled through the listings. "There's some pilot association stuff."

I let go of the breath I didn't realize I'd been holding. My muscles relaxed, then tensed again when I thought about how Liam had manipulated me into participating—albeit passively—in violating the no-Googling rule. "There's nothing to find."

"Maybe not. Maybe—holy shit!"

"What?"

As she lifted her eyes to mine, Becky's expression registered complete and utter shock. "You're not going to like it. But it does explain a lot of things."

I remained planted about two feet away. "Like?"

"His trips."

"Are you telling me he isn't a pilot?"

"No."

"He's gay? Bi?"

She shook her head. "Worse."

"What's worse than finding out your boyfriend is cheating on you and is on the down low?"

"You're halfway there, Finley."

"What did you find? Is he running an Internet personal ad or something? Is he cheating on me?"

"Kind of."

"Cyber-cheating is cheating." So is intellectual cheating, but this wasn't about my transgressions.

"This isn't virtual. This is real."

"How real?"

"*Really* real."

"Tell me."

"According to Ancestry.com, he's married."

Betrayal is like wearing cheap shoes; you smile through the pain and hope no one notices.

Twenty-one

After the shock wore off, the anger set in. Becky offered to stay, but I wasn't exactly in the mood for company. I don't mind being shallow at times. Or being selfish occasionally. But I never wanted to be a poacher. Yet, thanks to Patrick's lies, I was exactly that. I was the other woman.

And if that wasn't bad enough, Liam knew it. Had known it for months. I added him to my list of men I hated as I continued tossing every gift Patrick had ever given me into white trash bags. Once I finished with the closet, I went to the dresser.

The first thing that caught my eye was the gift bag with the Christmas ornament inside. I ran my finger across the three letters on the foil sticker and felt like I'd swallowed the big stupid pill all over again. "NYC," I said. Not some fancy initials for an exotic store somewhere. "New York City."

Thanks to an in-depth search, I now knew cheating Patrick and his presumably innocent, genealogy-obsessed wife lived in Westchester. I wondered how many of the gifts he'd given me actually came from trips abroad and how many came from stores in the city. *Prick*.

At some point, I realized three things. A—I wasn't as mad at Patrick as much as I was mad at myself for being so stupid. B—I wasn't going to add to my stupid quotient by returning *all* the gifts. Hell no. I'd keep the Coach bag, the Prada shoes, and most of the jewelry. I felt perfectly justified. It was kind of like a fine for two freaking years of deception. My only regret was I wouldn't be seeing him for another thirty-six hours, so I felt cheated out of the opportunity to toss the reject gifts in his face. Or at his nuts. No, I didn't want any part of his nuts. His nuts were married. Briefly, I'd thought about calling his cell or sending him a text message. However, it was the middle of the night and I didn't want to run the risk of having his wife find out about me. Being the other woman was one thing. I sure as hell didn't want to add home-wrecker to my résumé. Even if I was just as much an innocent bystander as the wronged wife. Only wronged wife trumps wronged girlfriend every time.

C was a little harder to work through. I needed to get some sleep. Just a few hours so I wasn't brain-dead for Jane's hearing followed by the dreaded apology-slash-gratitude brunch with my mother. As soon as I finished surgically removing all traces of Patrick from my apartment, I laid down and managed to grab a couple of hours of fitful rest.

It showed, too. It took three doses of eyedrops to get the red out and two passes with concealer, foundation, and powder to cover the dark circles. Was I really going to let Patrick's deception mess with Jane's day of freedom? Hell no. Stomping thoughts of the assholejerkwadprickhead to my very deepest subconscious, I promised to dedicate the next few hours to Jane, and whatever it took, smiling through the pain.

The temperatures were predicted to top ninety again, so I paired a lime-and-turquoise-print skirt with a simple turquoise top and sweater. It was a little matchy-matchy for my taste but it was exactly the kind of ensemble my mother liked. Since I was about to spend twenty-five thousand of her dollars on bail for Jane, I figured it was the least I could do.

I poured the last of the coffee from the pot into my travel mug. I had to remember to pick up the roses before brunch. And I wrote the addresses and phone numbers for Barbie Baker, Renee Sabato, Harrison Hadley, and Matthew Gibson on a small piece of paper and tucked it inside my purse along with the Payton DVD. My afternoon would be devoted to visiting the rest of the Fantasy Date Special Assessment clients. I doubted Jace or Kresley would give me another shot, so it was time to press the others for information. Might as well do it alphabetically, so I'd start with Barbie Baker. If Ms. Baker wouldn't answer my calls, I'd make a point of dropping in on her.

My stomach was in a tight knot by the time I drove to the Palm Beach County Courthouse. I parked, looped my sweater over the slightly irregular handle on my Dooney & Burke bag, and stepped out into air that was already thick and hot.

Becky and Liv were waiting in the breezeway. One look at Liv's face and I knew Becky had blabbed. I shot the tattletale a "Thanks a lot" while Liv gave me a long, sympathetic hug.

"Are you okay?" she asked.

"I'm fine." I glanced around, refusing to acknowledge that I'd wasted the last two years of my life on a—"Today is about Jane. Please tell me that Taggert's inside." They both shook their heads. The knot in my stomach twisted. "So, what do we do?"

Becky glanced at her watch. "We still have twenty minutes."

"Have either of you seen Jane?" I asked.

"Yeah, we had a few minutes when I dropped off the clothes Liv brought."

"How is she?"

"Holding up."

"Has she heard from Taggert?"

"No," Liv said, obviously angry. "He can't just disappear off the face of the earth."

"A lot of that going around," Liam remarked as he joined us.

I kept my eyes fixed on the top button of his shirt, gritting my back teeth to stop the flooding of humiliation. I was furious that he hadn't told me about Patrick when he'd apparently found out four months ago—but I didn't dare get side-tracked.

"Shaylyn and Zack?" Becky asked.

"No one's seen them. A friend of mine pulled their DMV records. In addition to the Bentley, there's a black Lexus, a brown pickup, and a horse trailer registered to them or the business. There's also a boat title registered with the tax collector's office in Broward County. I'm working on finding out where they keep it docked."

"Can we use the DVD?" I asked, slipping the corner of the case out of my purse. "Wouldn't that and the fact that the limo driver was killed after Jane's arrest prove to the judge that Jane should be released?"

"I'm not counsel of record," Becky said. "Faulkner's a real stickler. I don't think he'll grant me leave to represent Jane without proper notification being given to Taggert."

I sighed heavily. "Just in case, did you bring my mother's check?"

Liv nodded. "It's in my purse. Along with what Patrick— oh, sorry."

I felt my cheeks burn. "We should get inside," I suggested.

"I talked to the detective in Charleston, again," Liam added.

Curiosity got the better of me, so I looked up and met his gaze. "Why?"

"It's been bothering me that Zack and Shaylyn would have set Jane up to take the fall if they didn't know about the Molly Bishop thing in Charleston."

"And?"

He glanced over at Liv. "When did you make the arrangements for the date?"

"Three and a half weeks ago."

He smiled. "Three weeks ago a woman contacted the criminal courts division and asked for a copy of Jane's arrest record."

"Tell me Shaylyn left her name," I practically pleaded.

"Said she was Taggert's secretary, only the fax number she used wasn't Taggert's."

"Fantasy Dates?"

He shook his head. "Nope. It was disconnected last week. Before then, it was one of seven lines listed to R. Sabato."

"Renee Sabato?"

"Who is she?" Liv asked.

"A Fantasy Dates client. I'm going to talk to her this afternoon."

"Not smart," Liam said. "Would you ladies mind going in and saving us a seat?" he asked as his fingers closed around my upper arm. "We'll just be a few minutes."

Becky and Liv waited for me to give a silent nod of approval before they left me alone with Liam. Turning, I planted my feet slightly apart and jerked my arm free of his hold. "How could you *not* tell me?"

"I'm telling you now."

"Your timing sucks."

"I just found out."

I blinked. "Exactly what are we talking about here?"

"Renee Sabato."

Oops. "What about her, specifically?"

"Don't you read the newspaper?"

"Yes."

"Three months ago a female torso washed up on the beach near her house. Ring any bells?"

I vaguely remembered the grisly story. No head, no hands, no way to identify the body. "Renee Sabato's dead?"

He shook his head. "No, she's alive and well."

"All the more reason for me to talk to her. I mean, I'm sorry a body part washed up on her beach, but she might know something that could help Jane."

"Let me handle this, Finley."

"You don't think I'm capable?"

"It's not about capable. It's about the fact that I carry a gun and you don't. For all you know, Renee Sabato is some lunatic killer."

"You think she killed someone, then tossed the body on her own beachfront?"

"It happens," Liam said. "I know you're really committed to solving this yourself, but at least let me check the woman out before you go barging blindly forward. Let me do my job."

"You didn't even want the job."

"So, I changed my mind."

"I'll think about it. Jane's hearing is about to start."

"Why are you pissed today?"

"Because my friend is still in jail and her attorney is a no-show?"

His eyes narrowed. "Nope. There's more to it than that. Jane was in jail last night when we—"

"Did nothing. Which is good," I said as I took a step backward. "Better than good. I have no interest in you or any other man for that matter. You're all pigs."

Slowly, the corners of his mouth curved into a sly grin. "Figured it out, did you?"

"No thanks to you." I crossed my arms. "How long have you known about Patrick being . . . being . . . ?"

"A while."

"So you amused yourself by keeping quiet?"

He lifted his hands, palms up. "It was none of my business."

"You're right. It still isn't."

"Not that I have to defend myself, but until a week ago, I thought you knew your boyfriend was married."

"What kind of person do you think I am?"

His grin broadened. "I try not to judge."

"I'm going inside."

"Finley?"

"Kiss off," I said, back straight and eyes focused on the security station ahead. "By the way, if you're so well-trained and well-informed, how come you didn't know Zack and Paolo spent time in a Canadian prison for fraud?"

"Where'd you hear that?"

I dropped my purse on the conveyer belt. "Read it on the Internet." I passed through the metal detector.

"You have to—"

Beep!

A large, burly, shaved-head security guard practically shoved Liam back through the detector. "Sir, you have to empty your pockets first."

"Finley," Liam said as he started emptying the contents of his pockets into a plastic container. "Hang on a minute." He tried to make it through the sensors again.

Beep!

He was muttering a curse when my purse slipped through the X-ray machine into my waiting hands.

"Finley!"

Beep!

"Sir, if you'll step this way?"

I didn't turn around as the security guard escorted him into the cordoned-off area. I did smile, though.

"Why isn't Liam sitting with us?" Liv asked in a whisper.

"He's radioactive."

"What?"

"Had a run-in with the metal detectors. Too bad they

don't use that paddle thing to do body cavity searches."
Becky was standing at the front of the gallery waiting for
Jane to emerge from the holding area.

"Taking your anger out on him?"

"You bet. If it has testicles, I hate it. Men are nothing but
a big-time suck. I think I'll get a dog. A *girl* dog."

"You don't like dogs."

"Okay, a fish."

"Did you call him?"

"Fish have telephones?"

"Patrick. Did you call Patrick?"

"No."

"Going to?"

"No. I've decided to handle it like an adult."

"Put everything in a box already, did you?"

"Trash bags."

Liv patted the back of my hand. "Very adult."

"Thank you."

Jane entered the courtroom looking so gaunt and terrified
that I wanted to cry. Her desperation was palpable and it got
worse when her dark eyes darted around the courtroom. It
didn't take long for her to realize that her attorney wasn't
present.

Becky started whispering to her, but whatever she was
saying didn't seem to be alleviating the panic.

"I hate Taggert, too," Liv said.

"Shame we can't put him in a trash bag."

"All rise," the bailiff announced.

Judge Faulkner took the bench, scowling when he saw the
vacant chair at the defense table.

It looked as if State Attorney Brent would do a happy
dance. "Your Honor, in light of the fact that defense counsel
isn't present, the state moves for an immediate ruling on the
motion."

My whole body tensed. I half expected the judge to agree,
bang his gavel, and head for the closest golf course.

"If I may?" Becky began as she stood. "Rebecca Jameson, Your Honor."

"Yes, Ms. Jameson?"

"Due to Mr. Taggert's absence, I would like to be named replacement counsel for the defendant."

"Are you prepared to proceed?" he asked.

"Yes, sir."

"The state objects," Brent said. "My office did not receive appropriate notice of Mr. Taggert's withdrawal from the case. As this is a Motion to Reconsider Bail, it would seem prudent to stay this matter until such time as appropriate notice is filed with both the court and the state attorney's office."

Faulkner didn't miss a beat. "I tend to agree."

"Your Honor," Becky argued, stepping past the swinging gate separating the gallery from the counsel tables. "Ms. Spencer should not be forced to remain in jail when, respectfully, the right to counsel is hers, not subject to the opinions of Ms. Brent. To dismiss the motion without argument would be tantamount to denying the defendant due process."

"It's Saturday, Ms. Jameson. You'd have a hard time finding an appellate court to accept your theory. However, in the interests of justice, I will continue this hearing until four PM, at which time I expect you to have Mr. Taggert or his duly executed Motion to Withdraw in hand. If you can't produce one of those things, call my clerk. Do not waste this court's time."

"Is that good?" Liv asked as we stood in deference to the judge's departure from the room.

"It means we have seven hours."

"To do what?"

After a huddle, it was decided that Liv would stay with Jane, who was on the verge of a total meltdown. Becky was going to write the motion and prepare her arguments, including getting subpoenas if necessary for Payton to appear in court to tell the judge about the DVDs and the whole kinky S&M side of Fantasy Dates.

Liam, over my strenuous objections, was going to see Renee Sabato, Harrison Hadley, and then find Taggert. Since I couldn't skip brunch, I was given the lesser assignments of seeing the widow Baker and Matthew Gibson. Everyone was dogging Zack and Shaylyn, though Becky reminded us that their suspicious absence might work in Jane's favor.

My first mistake happened about thirty minutes later. I'd forgotten to stop at the florist. If I turned around, I'd be late for brunch. I knew in Motherville that was a mortal sin, whereas showing up on time but empty-handed was more the venial variety.

Willoughby Country Club is a stunning, manicured estate community near historic Stuart. Historic being relative— pretty much anything built before 1929 was designated historic in Florida. I was granted entry by the guard, and then practically screeched into the parking lot.

The clubhouse was an expansive building with a large, open dining room and several smaller rooms reserved for private gatherings and card games. As soon as I walked through the frosted glass doors, I smelled the wonderful aromas from the five-star kitchen. My view was blocked by an enormous arrangement of Asiatic lilies and a small maître d's podium.

Of course none of that mattered; I didn't need a direct line of sight to know my mother would cast her eyes upon me with disapproval.

She did. The instant she watched me walk to the linen-draped table, I got *the look*. It was a subtle yet effective expression that all but announced her true feelings. I have no doubt that she loves me. She just doesn't like me very much. She wanted a different kind of daughter. I wanted a different kind of mother, so on that point, at least, we agree.

To anyone noticing, our air-kissed greeting was picture

perfect. My mother is a beautiful woman. She's tall and slender, and has perfectly styled hair the same dark hue as roasted chestnuts. The only feature we share is pale blue eyes.

Though she was smiling, I knew she was critiquing me as the waiter pulled out my chair and offered my napkin. I also knew I'd failed the litmus test du jour. Nothing new. Unless I could magically morph into my perfect younger sister Lisa, I was, as usual, subpar.

She reached across and patted the back of my hand. "I'm proud of you, Finley."

I glanced around suspiciously; I'd always wanted to know what the *Twilight Zone* looked like. Fidgeting in my seat, I cleared my throat and said, "Thank you."

"No, I mean it," my mother insisted as she did a little two-fingered motion to wave off the waiter. "Judging by your poorly applied makeup, you must have been up all night looking, I presume, for new employment."

I felt the other shoe drop squarely on top of my head. "I've been looking at various options." If you count being a morgue attendant chick, which, for the purposes of this brunch, I totally was.

"That's good to hear. I will admit that when your friend Jean—"

"Jane."

"Whatever. When she was not released, I assumed you would return my money. Interest did begin to accrue from the date I handed you the check."

Like I needed reminding. "And it will be repaid in full, as promised." And witnessed and notarized. Under the pretext of needing a sip of water, I pulled my hand away and reached for the glass. "I want to tell you again how much I appreciate your generosity."

"Not again, Finley. Again implies that you've thanked me before."

"A horrible oversight on my part for which I am truly sorry. We both know you raised me better."

"Yes, I . . ."

It was unusual for my mother to drift off midberating, but something behind me had grabbed her attention. I turned my head and saw a very dapper, silver-haired man standing by the maître d's station. Then I looked at my mother. She was smoothing her hair, adjusting her Chanel suit, and straightening the strand of pearls around her neck. In addition to Chanel, she had that predatory look in her eyes.

Realization dawned quickly. I should have known. Changing our mandatory brunch to Saturday had nothing to do with me. Switching from Iron Horse Country Club to Willoughby had nothing to do with me.

The coy little smile and the casual yet must-be-acknowledged wave in his direction left the man no option but to stop by our table.

"Cassidy! What a surprise," he said, grasping her hands in both of his.

Poor bastard, if he only knew.

"I didn't know you were a member here."

"I just joined," she said. "I've been looking for a new club for some time."

Liar. You've been looking for a new husband for some time.

"I think you'll like it here."

I think you'll need a prenup.

"Where are my manners?" my mother asked. "Truman Caldwell, I'd like to introduce you to my daughter Finley."

"How do you do?" *Or should I ask, "How is your wallet?"*

He offered me a genuinely warm smile. "Your daughter? I would have guessed your sister. Nice to meet you, Finley."

If that's really true, then don't go on Jeopardy.

"Can you join us?" my mother invited.

"I'm sorry, I'm meeting a friend for lunch. Perhaps next Saturday, if you two aren't busy?"

I bit down on the inside of my lip. I so wanted to say, "I'm unemployed, so yeah, next Saturday works for me," but I was already in Cassidy Presley Tanner, blah, blah, blah's doghouse. Taking a page from Liam's playbook, I said, "That's very sweet, Mr. Caldwell, but I've got a thing next Saturday."

"It's Dr. Caldwell," my mother inserted.

"Sorry."

"No need," he said, patting my shoulder. "And please call me Truman."

Oh, I have a feeling I'll be calling you Daddy in no time. "Thank you."

"I'll have to consult my schedule, of course," my mother practically purred. "But with some rearranging, I'm sure next Saturday will be fine. Say noonish?"

Say barfish?

Dr. Caldwell noticed a man seated at the other end of the dining room and held up his index finger. "My doubles partner is waiting. It was a pleasure to meet you, Finley, and, Cassidy, as always, I look forward to seeing you next week."

As if the whole thing hadn't been a well-executed mission, my mother lifted her menu and began to peruse the options. "The salmon here is supposed to be excellent."

"He seemed nice."

"Nice?" my mother repeated.

Based on her tone, she didn't approve of my choice of adjectives. "Pleasant? Affable? Gracious? Decent? Mom, he was here for like thirty seconds."

"You don't know who he is?"

Quickly and discreetly, I looked over at the doctor. "Sorry, no."

"He was named one of the top ten cardiologists in the United States. He consults at Johns Hopkins and St. Joseph's in Arizona, which, for your information, is ranked the best cardiac center in the country year after year. He's semiretired and was once in the running for surgeon general of the

United States. He is listed in *Who's Who* and comes from a prominent Massachusetts family. Quite an impressive pedigree, wouldn't you say?"

"Are you going to breed him or show him?" I wanted to grab the smart-ass remark and shove it back in my mouth, but too late. "Sorry."

"You always are," my mother commented, her tone icy. "Given your unstable employment situation, perhaps you should give more consideration to marriage. Patrick is good marriage material."

Gee, why don't we call his wife and confirm? "Yes, he is."

Her mood lightened. "So you're finally going to make a commitment?"

I bobbed my head and almost wept with joy when a Bloody Mary appeared in front of me. "I am very committed when it comes to Patrick." Technically, it wasn't a lie. I was totally committed to dumping his cheating ass the instant I saw him.

"I'm glad to hear that. Since you're not working, I could arrange a small dinner party. I wonder what night would be best for Truman? Is Patrick in town?"

"No. In fact, he's got a long trip ahead." *Straight to the bowels of hell.*

"That's a shame. Well, as soon as you have his schedule, call me and we'll work something out. I've got a few engagements coming up. Did you decide on the Templeton party? After all, it was generous of them to include you in their invitation to me."

Twenty-five thousand reasons to be nice. "Tell me again. What exactly are they celebrating?"

My mother frowned. Or at least tried to. Tough to accomplish with a gazillion ccs of Botox in your forehead. "It's their fortieth anniversary. You've met their daughter Trisha."

I was drawing a total blank. "I have?"

Our forced conversation was interrupted when the waiter

came for our order. I loved salmon, but the rebellious child in me ordered eggs Benedict.

"Trisha is your age. She's dating Devon Gibson."

"Matthew Gibson's older brother?"

This time my mother's smile was genuine. "Yes. Quite a catch, too. Had you been so inclined, you could have ingratiated yourself into that crowd. Then you wouldn't be in the position of having to beg me for money."

Ah, the famous mother kiss-me-while-you-slap-me moment. "I appreciate the loan, Mom. Really."

"Yes, well, I'll appreciate when it is repaid. It must be nice to be Leona Gibson, what with both her boys settling down and starting families of their own."

I took a generous sip of my Bloody Mary. "I don't see Kresley Pierpont starting a family any time soon."

"Of course she will. Children solidify a marriage."

"She's a little flaky."

"Apparently not. She's marrying one of the wealthiest young men in Palm Beach. Truman's been invited to the wedding."

"That'll come in handy if anyone suffers heart failure at the reception."

"Finley, you're—"

My mother blanched when my cell phone rang. I'd forgotten to put it on vibrate. "Sorry. Hello?"

"Miss Tanner?"

"Yes."

"This is Emma Killington, Mr. Gibson's personal assistant. He asked me to call and tell you he can see you at one."

I checked my watch. "That's a little over an hour from now. Can we make it later? Say one-thirty?"

"I'm sorry, ma'am, but that's his only opening for today."

"Then one o'clock it is. Thank you." My eggs arrived just as I closed my phone and scooted back my chair. "I'm sorry, Mom, but I've got to go."

Her recently lifted eyes grew wide. "But we haven't had

brunch. You can't leave without eating. It's both wasteful and rude."

"Sorry."

I knew before I reached my car that I'd have to pay dearly for walking out on my mother. With interest. But I needed to meet with Matthew Gibson more than I needed to please my mother.

Ignoring the posted speed limit, I raced down Cove Road toward the I-95 interchange. The area was in transition. New construction was slowly swallowing the multiacre home sites. There were only a few orange groves left. I was within a mile of the interstate when I heard a loud crack, then a pop; then my car lurched over on two wheels.

I didn't even have time to scream before my car went careening down a drainage ditch, then slammed into a pine tree.

All things happen for a reason, not necessarily a good one.

Twenty-two

By the time the paramedics had bandaged the small cut on my forehead, I'd given a semilucid statement to the sheriff's deputies, arranged for a tow truck, and had Jean-Claude bring me Liv's car. I'd missed my appointment with Matthew Gibson.

Oh, and it was only due to the miracle of a Tide pen that I was able to get the bloodstains off my shirt. They weren't major stains, more like drops. It wasn't the quantity as much as the placement. One was directly over my right nipple, making me look like a single-sided lactation machine.

Still, my pitiful appearance wasn't enough to get me past Matthew Gibson's personal assistant. Even after being summarily dismissed, when I remained perched at the edge of her desk, the matronly, efficient gray-head didn't relent.

"I am happy to reschedule," she suggested for the third time.

"There's a court hearing in less than three hours," I explained. "Mr. Gibson has information relevant to that hearing. If I could just have a phone number, something? Anything?"

"This is a legal matter?

"Yes."

"I'll see if the family's attorney is available. Wait here."

As soon as she disappeared down the long hallway of the waterfront offices of Gibson Investments, I slipped behind her desk and started reading Matthew's appointment calendar. The only thing I learned was that he was having lunch with Kresley. "Damn," I muttered. No restaurant.

I had better luck when I flipped through the Rolodex. I scored two telephone numbers for Matthew. I recognized one as his home number—that was on his Fantasy Dates application. My best guess was the other number was a cell.

Nervously, and with adrenaline rushing through my system, I glanced down the hallway, then decided to just go for it. My hand closed on the polished brass knob to Matthew's private office and to my astonishment, it was unlocked.

It was professionally decorated and neat as a pin. No papers on the large, cherry desk. Nothing but knickknacks on the shelves. The only piece of art was a huge, ornately framed oil painting of Kresley. So the rumors were true. Matthew's position in the family business was ornamental. Apparently he'd inherited the Gibson family looks but none of the brains.

Seeing a closet door, I further pressed my luck and gave the lever handle a try. It opened. And it wasn't a closet.

It was a shrine. The five-by-five-foot space was covered floor to ceiling with all things Kresley. Creepy. The vast collection of photos included candid shots as well as posed portraits. Interspersed with the images were news clippings dating as far back as three years. Well before Matthew and Kresley hooked up.

"What are you doing?"

I turned to find the personal assistant and a man I assumed was the family attorney glaring at me from the doorway.

Oh, shit. "I was looking for the ladies' room."

"That isn't it," the lawyer told me. "You're trespassing, Miss Tanner."

"Then, I should leave, right?"

"Not until you tell me what information you think Mr. Gibson has that is relevant to the Martinez murder."

I closed the door and hoped they couldn't see my heart pounding in my chest. "And you are?"

"Richard Helms. Mr. Gibson's attorney."

"I'm just conducting interviews with all the Fantasy Dates clients. Mr. Gibson is still a client."

"His membership was terminated."

"When?"

"Yesterday. After Ms. Pierpont informed Mr. Gibson that she had neglected to cancel her membership, I discovered Matthew had made the same oversight. It's been remedied."

How convenient. "That's all well and good, but I'd still like to speak with Mr. Gibson."

"That isn't going to happen."

I narrowed my eyes and glared at the man. He was buffed and polished and reminded me a little too much of Vain Dane. Another man on my hate list. "A woman has been falsely accused."

"That's for a jury to decide."

No way was I backing down, not when Jane's life as a free woman was at stake. "I just want to talk to him. What's the big deal?"

"The Gibson family values its reputation and standing in this community, Miss Tanner. Allowing Matthew to be dragged into a high-profile murder case would in no way serve the interests of the family."

"I think that ship sailed when Matthew joined a buy-a-date service."

He reached into his jacket pocket and pulled out a tri-folded document, handing it to me. "If you or anyone else mentions that in public, you'll face a contempt charge and a civil suit."

"You got an injunction?"

"Signed by Judge Faulkner about an hour ago. A copy is being messengered to Ms. Jameson and Mr. Taggert. Since there is no evidence that Mr. Gibson or his fiancée has any knowledge relevant to the murder, their names may not be used in any context. Now, security is waiting to escort you from the building."

Flanked by two uniformed private security guards, I was escorted to Liv's borrowed Mercedes. They remained in place until I drove out of the parking lot. I didn't know their names but added them to the Men I Hate list.

Pushing my sunglasses higher on the bridge of my nose, I brushed my fingers over the butterfly Band-Aid at my hairline. So far the only things I'd accomplished on this incredibly horrible day were pissing off my mother, pissing off the Gibson family attorney, and pissing off the dealer I'd leased my probably totaled car from. While it hadn't left me time to wallow in self-pity over Patrick the Prick, it still wasn't a stellar showing. The first two were my fault but I wasn't willing to accept blame for a tire blowout. The dealer could eat dirt and die. After we negotiated a replacement.

Hopefully, I'd have better luck with the widow Baker. I was bruised, tired, angry, frustrated, worried, hungry, and caffeine deprived. I was also very determined when I hit the buzzer on the call box outside Barbie Baker's estate.

"Yes, ma'am?"

Hearing the man's voice and realizing he'd identified me by gender, I glanced around until I spotted the video camera mounted just above the hedge line. "I'm here to see Mrs. Baker."

"She's unavailable."

Desperation breeds . . . creativity. Reaching onto the passenger's seat, I grabbed the Gibson Family Injunction and held it up for the camera. Now I just had to hope that Barbie Baker's security camera was no better than the ones employed by banks and convenience stores. "Process server," I lied. "Someone's got to sign for it."

I held my breath until the intricate iron gate began to swing open. Only in Palm Beach would anyone buy a process server driving a Mercedes convertible.

Driving up the long, curved driveway, I was impressed by the house. It was Tuscan-inspired, with lots of fountains and statues. And it sat on an acre of primo oceanfront. Barbie Baker divorced well.

A uniformed butler stood waiting in the courtyard. I might have gotten in the gate but it would take some doing to get past the formidable-looking butler. Lying wasn't going to get me anything, so I decided the truth was the only way to go. Kinda.

"You have a document for Mrs. Baker?"

"I really need to see Mrs. Baker."

The impeccably dressed, stout man was expressionless. "That isn't possible."

Time to break out the ultimate weapon—tears. It wasn't all that hard to muster the moisture. Just as the first tear was about to spill from my eye, I said, "I'm here on behalf of Jane Spencer. She's the woman who was falsely arrested for the murder of Paolo Martinez. I know he was a friend of Mrs. Baker's, so it's really, *really* important that I speak with her."

I saw a tiny crack in his stoic indifference as I brushed the dampness from my cheek.

"Miss. I can't help you."

"Yes," I insisted, "you can. Just five minutes of her time. That's all I'm asking."

"You don't seem to understand. I can't help you. Mrs. Baker isn't in residence."

"Where can I reach her?"

"I have no idea."

"C'mon. You have to have an emergency number or something, right?"

He shook his closely shaved head. "I expected her back two days ago."

"From?"

"Mrs. Baker went on a cruise around the world."

"When did she leave?"

"A little over three months ago."

Roughly the same time she stopped paying Fantasy Dates. "When was the last time you spoke to her?"

"Mrs. Baker always sends me on vacation when she travels for extended periods. She's quite considerate that way. So it would have been the day before she left for Greece."

Roughly the same time the torso washed up on Renee Sabato's beach. I hoped for the butler's sake that he had a good retirement plan. "Thanks."

Jogging back to the car, I dug into my purse for my cell phone, dialing as I started the engine and peeled out of the driveway. As I was waiting for the gate to open, Liam answered.

"McGarrity."

"I know who the torso is."

"How are you?"

"Did you hear what I said?"

"Yeah. I also heard you took a header into a tree."

How could he possibly know that? "Forget that. The torso has to be Barbie Baker. She's been missing for three months."

"No one reported it."

"She doesn't have any family. Well, unless you count the ex-husband who hates her. She was supposed to be on some extended cruise, so her disappearance would have gone unnoticed. So you were right. Renee Sabato probably did kill her and then tossed her into the surf. We should call the police."

"We could do that," Liam said. "Only we'd have to call

the police in Maine. Renee Sabato has been in Kittery, Maine, since April."

"For what?"

"She didn't say."

Deflated, I asked, "You spoke to her?"

"Yes. And about a dozen people who verified she hasn't left Kittery since opening her summer home."

"That's crappy news."

"I have good news, too."

"Really?"

"Zack and Shaylyn's boat is docked at Oak Harbour Marina in Juno Beach. I'm on my way there now."

"What should I do?"

"Put ice on your head."

I actually glanced around, expecting to see either Liam or a camera. How did the man know I'd hit my head? "I could go see Hadley."

"Been there. He's not talking."

"Taggert?"

"Not at his office, or his house or any of his known haunts."

"Maybe he's just not answering the door."

"It, um, fell down while I was knocking. Trust me, the guy isn't there. Go see Jane or help Becky. I'll call you as soon as I know something."

I've never been very good with authority, so Liam's suggestion that I go sit and twiddle my thumbs was easy to ignore. Instead, I headed north and found my way along the intracoastal to Oak Harbour.

I didn't know anything about the boat, no description, nothing. However, Liam's Mustang stuck out among the luxury sedans and top-of-the-line SUVs.

It was really hot and the strong stench of diesel had my

empty stomach churning the instant I started walking along the wooden pier. The marina wasn't that big and it was prime boating time, so there were only three boats tied to pilings on the dock closest to Liam's car.

A pelican perched on top of one of the wooden posts flapped its gigantic wings as I passed. Other than that, all I could hear was the lapping of small waves sloshing against the fiberglass hulls.

The first boat was a fishing vessel. I couldn't picture Zack or Shaylyn baiting a line, so I moved on. The second boat seemed more of a possibility. Hiking up my skirt, I climbed aboard and found every hatch latched tight.

The last one was a forty-two-foot sailboat. Or miniyacht. I'm not a boat person, but I know polished teak and custom touches when I see them. I can also read, "Snowy Owl." I'd found it.

Climbing aboard, not an easy task in a skirt and heels, I might add, I went around the giant wheel and was immediately hit by the stench of rotting something. Another reason I'm not a boat person—bait smells like, well, bait.

I looked at the closed hatch leading belowdecks. Liam's car was in the lot so it stood to reason that he was on board. I fanned away the foul-smelling air, more than a little reluctant to go down the two stairs. "Hello?" I called tentatively.

I heard some bumps and thumps; then the hatch flew open and Liam was glaring at me. "You don't listen well, do you?"

"Not really, no. Did you find them?"

He nodded.

"Are they talking?" I asked, my eyes watering as the smell intensified.

"No. But Taggert's here, too."

"That's great."

"Not really. They're all dead. Here." He tossed me the jar of Vicks VapoRub. "If you're coming down, you're going to need that."

I can do this, I kept repeating as I smeared menthol-scented gel beneath my nose. But absolutely nothing in my life could have prepared me for the scene awaiting me in the hull of the ship. Death and pestilence, times three. Zack and Shaylyn were seated at the small table on the port side. In the center of the table was a jewel case and a thin file. At first glance, they looked like a couple of schoolchildren with their heads resting on their desks. Until you saw the large puddle of dark blood pooled at their feet.

Though dead, Taggert was still moving. His body dangled from a makeshift noose with his feet no more than a couple of inches off the floor.

The cabin hosted more than corpses. Flies swarmed everywhere.

My stomach lurched. "What happened?"

Liam sidestepped the blood and motioned me closer. "There's a note."

I didn't move. "Can you just tell me about it?" *Quickly, before I hurl or pass out. Maybe both.*

"Basically, Taggert is confessing to having killed Paolo and these two. Claims Paolo, Zack, and Shaylyn were blackmailing him. The proof is on the DVD. Then I guess in a final act of selflessness, he hanged himself."

Relief washed over me. "Thank God. We can finally get Jane out of jail."

"Not necessarily," he said.

"They're dead. Taggert was so guilt-riddled that he confessed and committed suicide. We should call people. What are we waiting for?"

"We need to find the gun."

"What gun?"

"Zack and Shaylyn were shot. So where's the gun?"

My eyes flitted around the small cabin. No gun. "Taggert tossed it overboard before he hanged himself?"

"A stretch, but okay." Liam raked his fingers through his hair.

"Why does it matter?"

"If he killed Paolo so he wouldn't have to pay any more blackmail, drove over here to kill these two and himself with typed note in hand, how come he went to the bank and withdrew twenty grand?" Liam pulled a small white receipt from the dangling attorney's front pocket. "According to the time stamp, Taggert went to the bank three days ago. Which I'm betting is about how long these three have been dead."

"But that's not possible. I got the creepy call from Fantasy Dates yesterday."

"My point exactly."

"Okay, so what do—" My cell phone chimed. The caller ID read Martin County Government. "Hello?"

"Is this Finley Tanner?"

"Yes."

"This is Deputy Sheriff Ray Brown. I'm calling in reference to your accident."

"Thank you for your concern. The car's been taken to the dealership and they—"

"We just got a call from them, Ms. Tanner. Seems your accident wasn't an accident."

"The tire exploded," I insisted. There was no way the dealership was going to stick me on this one.

"Technically speaking, it did. Because it was shot."

My blood stilled in my veins. "Excuse me?" I depressed the speaker button so Liam could hear as well.

"Someone shot out your tire."

"Kresley or Matthew?" I asked Liam as we left the boat the way we found it.

"Kresley."

"Matthew," I countered. "You're forgetting Barbie Baker. I think all this started with her death. In her book, Dayle

Hinman says it's more likely for men to kill and dismember than women. The dismembering stuff is such a guy thing."

"It is, but you're forgetting Paolo. A guy doesn't cut off another guy's johnson. Except in bad wiseguy films."

"Maybe they did it together? A Bonnie and Clyde thing. Crazy Frank did say there were two people in the car." I checked my watch. We had just over an hour before court reconvened.

"Could have been Kresley's security guard. Anyway, I'll call the cops and let them know about the bodies. You need to see the sheriff in Martin County about the shooting."

"In an hour?" I asked. "No, I'll talk to them later. Matthew and Kresley first."

Liam grabbed me by the shoulders. Not hard but with enough pressure to get my attention. "You are done, Finley. Someone called and threatened you. Someone shot at your car. You want to end up like those people on the boat?"

I shook my head.

"I'm going to follow you to the courthouse and you're going to stay there. You'll wait there where it's safe. I'll go find Kresley."

"But—"

"No. This isn't a debate. Cooperate or so help me God, I'll take you home and tie you to a chair."

I opened my mouth, then, reading the determined set of his jaw and the way his eyes were narrowed, I thought better of it. "Fine."

"Fine."

Under the watchful and annoying eyes of Liam, I went inside the courthouse only long enough to find out from Liv which wedding planner Matthew and Kresley were using. I didn't have time to fill her in on all the details, so I just told her to call Becky and let her know Taggert was dead. If nothing else, maybe she could use that to buy some time with the judge.

I kept in the shadows of the building, checking both sides of the street for any sign of Liam. I didn't doubt for a minute that he'd actually tie me to a chair. Nor did I doubt that Jane was destined to spend another night in jail if I didn't do something.

Of course, I had no idea what that something was; hopefully it would come to me soon. Using the number I'd pilfered from Matthew's personal assistant, I was happy and terrified when he answered on the third ring.

"Hello, Mr. Gibson? This is Gretchen from Wedded Bliss. I'm Daphne's assistant."

"Yes?"

"If you and Ms. Pierpont aren't in the middle of anything, I have the, um, final sketches for the cake."

"You just missed Kresley. She's really making all these decisions, so—"

I heard the sounds of dishes, traffic, and muted conversation. A restaurant? "Gretchen said she needed the changes approved as soon as possible."

"Drop them off at my office. I'll make sure Kresley gets them when I see her later."

"I'm supposed to put them directly in your hand. Gretchen's orders. I can meet you anywhere." *So long as it's a public place with lots and lots of people.*

"Sorry. Listen, if it's that urgent, give Kresley a call on her cell."

"I would but I . . . I just spilled coffee on your file and I rubbed the ink and smeared the number and . . ." *Now I'm rambling.*

"I'm happy to give it to you."

"Thank you." *If I can't get to you, I'll settle for her. For now.*

"You know," he said, hesitation suddenly evident in his voice, "I don't think Kresley will want to be disturbed right now. She's meeting a man about a boat."

"Really?"

"Yes. She tried to keep it a secret but the broker called a little while ago and I happened to overhear a snippet of their conversation, so she had to tell me."

"Tell you what?"

"It's her wedding gift to me."

"That's very extravagant."

"Kresley is like that," he said.

He sounded so . . . normal. Well, wimpy, but normal. "She is, is she? Generous to a fault."

"Hummmmm."

He sighed heavily. "Trust me, she's nothing like she's portrayed in the tabloids. Kresley is kind and considerate. She never gets credit for the good things she does."

Keep talking. Maybe someone will say the name of the restaurant or I'll get some other clue to tell me where you are. "Hummmmmm."

"She does a lot for others. Most of it anonymously. She goes out of her way to keep that part of her life private."

"Really?" I inflected a tiny bit of doubt.

"Yes. Like the other day."

"When?"

"She read an article in the newspaper about a woman and it touched her so she sent the woman flowers."

My heart skipped a beat. "Did she use our florist, I hope?"

"No. That would have been showy. Kresley actually paid a homeless guy to—"

I cut him off. My fingers were trembling when I dialed Liam's cell.

"McGarrity."

The connection was horrible, a lot of static on the line. "You were right. It is Kresley."

"Yes. I know."

"Yeah, yeah, you're better at this than I am. You can gloat later and—"

"He won't be gloating," a woman interrupted. "In fact, he won't be breathing if you don't get here in the next fifteen minutes. Alone. No police. No discussion."

My heart stopped. "Kresley?"

"Fourteen minutes, fifty-nine seconds."

Click.

"Here? Where the hell is here? Think!"

Sometimes you have to squeeze big mistakes into small opportunities.

Twenty-three

I could barely drive over the bridge. It's difficult to see when your entire body is a shaking, sweating, heart-racing mass of fear. My best guess—and it was truly that—was to go to Kresley's oceanfront home. It was the only "here" that made any sense. Initially I'd thought maybe Liam had talked her into meeting him at the marina in Juno Beach, but if that were true, Kresley would know I was more than fifteen minutes away.

Or Kresley couldn't count and Liam's death would be on my conscience for all eternity. There was something really wrong about all this. He was the one with the gun. I'd dumped the contents of my purse during the short drive even though I knew I didn't have anything remotely weaponlike. Unless I could magically subdue Kresley by overlining her lips.

Probably not.

I drove around the block once, relieved and terrified when I spied Liam's Mustang in Kresley's driveway.

On the third pass, when I was about fifty yards from her address, I eased the Mercedes off on the shoulder. Every intelligent cell in my body was begging me to call the police. Someone. Anyone who might be able to help. Except that I couldn't risk getting Liam killed.

I have no idea why, but I shoved every useless thing back in my purse before I circled back to the delivery gate belonging to the house adjacent to Kresley's. I still had roughly seven minutes to come up with a plan. For now? I was winging it.

The first obstacle was to fit my body through the small space between the gate and the hedge. I managed that without much trouble, though I did catch my skirt on a branch and heard the fabric rip. Amazing that the sound registered, given that my heart was drumming in my ears.

I followed the hedge around to the back of the house, then down to where the tall sea grass met the sand. If Kresley was watching the beach, I was screwed and Liam was dead. The wispy grass provided little cover but it was the best I could do.

Kresley's soft pink house was two stories. Unfortunately for me, the first floor was mostly glass. Not exactly conducive for sneaking up undetected.

My heels were getting swallowed by the sand, so I simply abandoned them and pressed forward. The sun was burning my skin and it cast a bright reflection off the calm surface of the ocean. There was a large pool in the back surrounded by several tables and comfy-looking chaises. My heart palpitations got worse the closer I got to the house.

There was an umbrella in the center of one table, but unless jousting had come back into favor when I wasn't looking, no help there. I was out of options and almost out of time.

Going to the first set of sliding glass doors, I squinted and looked inside. It was an empty bedroom. Taking a deep breath, I yanked the handle and felt the door give. Fear amplified even the smallest noise. To me, it sounded more like I was opening a boxcar than a door.

Cool air rushed out as I rushed in. I had no way of knowing if Kresley had the kind of alarm system that beeped
whenever a door opened. Or if she was on the other side of
the door. Or if Liam was okay.

I still didn't have a plan. Hell, I barely had control over
my bladder. Hoisting my purse higher on my shoulder, I
soundlessly went to the closed door and pressed my ear
against the cool wood. I didn't hear anything, so I slowly
and carefully opened the door a crack and listened.

I could hear Liam's voice. Then Kresley's. It was clear but
hard to locate the source given the acoustics of the two-story
great room. My best estimation was that the voices were
coming from the front of the house.

Moving toward the sound of the voices, I kept my back
pressed against the wall.

". . . like she isn't coming."

"Told you," Liam replied. "We don't have that kind of relationship."

"It doesn't matter," Kresley said. "I found her earlier
today. I can find her again."

"What are you going to do, Kresley? Kill everyone in
Palm Beach County?"

"It wasn't my fault."

There was a small, well, *smaller* room just past the kitchen.
I was almost positive that was where Kresley was holding
Liam. Just to be sure, I crept close and used the highly pol-
ished wood floor as a mirror. Two of them. Liam was seated,
Kresley was pacing.

With incredible care, I reached into my purse and sent a
quick, pointed text message to Becky:

Kresley's house. Gun. Help. No sirens.

"Whose fault was it?" Liam asked.

"Paolo. If he hadn't killed that Baker woman, none of this
would have happened."

"Really?"

"He took it too far. She was into autoerotic asphyxiation."

"If Paolo killed her, how did you get involved?"

"I was there."

If Kresley was there while Barbie Baker was doing the nasty with Paolo, then it held to reason that she was the one who'd taped Payton.

"You could have turned him in," Liam said.

"And risk everything?" Kresley scoffed. "I used to be worried that Matthew would find out I was into voyeurism. Can you imagine how he'd feel if he knew about the murder? My trust fund is stretched a little thin. Marrying Matthew solves that issue for the rest of my life. I wasn't about to blow it by letting him find out that I was the one supplying Paolo with GHB just so I could watch him and whomever he happened to be screwing that day. It wouldn't go over well."

"Probably not." Liam's voice was unbelievably calm and matter-of-fact considering his situation. Fine. I was scared spitless enough for both of us.

"It was Paolo's brilliant idea to blackmail people with the DVDs."

"Zack and Shaylyn didn't know?"

"I think they suspected, but they were hardly in a position to do anything about it. I mean, they were arranging group sex for Renee Sabato. Jace Andrews has to dress like his mother just to get it up. Payton's into some seriously kinky stuff. Hadley has a thing for being tied up, and Taggert, he was the worst."

"You lost me. Taggert was part of this?"

"Why do you think Zack and Shaylyn had him defend that woman? They were terrified any investigation might uncover their slimy pimping. Then I gave him a little . . . incentive."

"What was Taggert into?"

"Men, preferably boys."

"And your incentive?"

"I made a tape of him with Paolo. I thought he'd lose it when I showed it to him."

"I'll bet he did. So you offered to sell him the DVD?"

"I needed some way to lure him to the boat." Kresley sighed. "Sorry about this, Liam, but your time is up. I have to look out for myself. Try not to take it personally. Get up."

Oh, crap. Nowhere to hide.

"Where are we going?"

I heard a chair scrape against the floor. *Shitshitshit.* I looked around frantically for a place to hide. My heartbeat was threatening to choke me. I felt as large and conspicuous as a flamingo on the frozen tundra. In two seconds she was going to walk right into me.

"Bathroom. It cuts down on the mess."

They were coming closer.

"Practical."

"A girl's gotta do what a girl's gotta do."

I knew Liam saw me pressed against the wall, but to his credit, he didn't so much as flinch. His hands were bound in front of him and the sunlight glinted off the barrel of the gun pressed between his shoulder blades.

Luckily for me, Kresley had her arms extended and her elbows locked. So, when I leapt forward and shoved her up and away from Liam, her head hit the door frame. Unfortunately, she managed to get off a shot before I landed on top of her.

I was rendered deaf by the noise and nauseated by the smell and taste of gunpowder. I was also unrelenting as I pummeled her with my purse.

It wasn't until I saw Liam's foot crunch down on her wrist that I realized she still had the gun in her hand. Back arched, I skittered away on my hands and feet, kinda like a crab moving along the sand.

I backed into something hard, looked up, and shrieked when I saw another gun. A very large one.

* * *

"To good friends," Becky said, raising her wineglass in one hand and hugging Jane with the other.

Liv and I leaned forward and joined in the celebratory clinking of the glasses.

"This has not been the best week of your life," I said as I pushed my nearly clean plate nearer the center of the table.

"I don't know how to thank all of you," Jane said for the fiftieth time since we'd met for a late Sunday lunch. She looked at me and smiled. "Even *I* was starting to think I'd killed Paolo."

"Thankfully, it's over," I added, absently rubbing my sore shoulder.

"Did you give your mother her check back?" Liv asked.

I nodded. Everyone was in such a good mood that I didn't want to spoil it by mentioning that due in large part to my abrupt departure from Willoughby Country Club, she fully expected me to pay her the interest on the money I didn't use for five days.

Becky grinned, then said, "I hear Kresley is throwing her bling-encrusted self on the mercy of the court. Her family is lining up a gaggle of shrinks who'll swear she was suffering from some sort of mental disease or defect causing her to kill four people."

"And almost two more," Liv added. "Don't forget Liam and our own resident ass-kicker, Finley."

"Did you seriously kick a SWAT guy in the balls?" Jane asked.

"I didn't know he was a SWAT guy," I defended. "All I saw was the gun. It was an honest mistake."

"Did his cheeks puff out and did he turn all green?" Liv asked. "Men are such wusses when it comes to their genitalia."

"Let's just drop it," I said, letting my fingertips touch the bandage on my forehead. "I hate to break this up, but I've got some, well, breaking up to do."

"Can we come watch?" Becky asked, a wicked glint in her eyes.

"No. Trust me, it isn't going to take that long."

On the way home, I was trying to get used to the rental car and wondering how long I could afford it. Apparently the insurance company doesn't have a code to use if a leased vehicle is totaled during an attempted homicide, so for now, I'm footing the bill. Which in turn meant I couldn't buy myself a congratulatory Rolex part, nor bid on the really, really cute Betsey Johnson dress PilotWife had offered to sell me. Okay, I probably could have done the deal with PilotWife, only that was another thing Patrick had ruined for me. I couldn't stand the idea of wearing something once owned— even at a great price—by the wife of a pilot.

I pulled the stripped-down sedan into the parking lot, miscalculated the sensitivity of the brakes, and rammed the front tires into the cement thing bolted into the blacktop. My head snapped back against the barely adjustable seat with a dull thud. "Ouch," I grumbled as I tossed off the seat belt.

I'd planned it so I'd have enough time to touch up my makeup. There's nothing more empowering than dumping a guy when you look your best. Learned that from my you-still-owe-the-interest mother.

I was about to put my key in the door when I heard the rumble of a tank. Turning around, I shielded my eyes and watched wide-eyed as Victor Dane maneuver his H3 Hummer into the lot. He parked—in two spaces.

As he got out and walked to me, she said, "Finley, how are you?"

"I'm fine." *Unemployed, but fine.*

"Can we step inside?"

"My apartment?" I asked. Not a strange question seeing as he'd never set foot in the place during my seven years at Dane-Lieberman.

He flashed his veneered smile and I just shrugged. It wasn't like he could hurt me. I don't think a person can be refired.

Once we were inside, the smell of his cologne filled the small foyer. He stayed near the door while I dropped my purse on the countertop. He stood there in three or four thousand dollars of casual wear curiously eyeing the two white garbage bags I had propped against the wall.

"Would you like some water?" I asked politely. What the hell was he doing here?

"No, I came by to offer you your job back."

Color me stunned. I met his level gaze with suspicion. Vain Dane did nothing out of the goodness of his atrophied heart. "Why?"

"The decision to let you go was . . . premature. A knee-jerk reaction, if you will."

"Ellen threatened to fire me three times, then she did. What part of that was knee-jerk?"

A faint red stain started creeping up his recently shaved neck. If it wasn't illegal, actionable, and really bad form, I think Vain Dane would have hit me. I saw that little vein at his temple throbbing, so I knew he was pissed. Only with me as a former employee, it wasn't my problem.

"Finley, I'm asking you to return. You're a valuable asset to the firm."

Crossing one foot over the other at the ankles, I rested my good shoulder against the wall. "When did that happen?"

"What?"

"When did I get so valuable?"

"You're bright and articulate. That makes you an asset."

My mind was racing. "Matthew Gibson?"

Vain Dane wore his guilt on his sleeve. "Yes, the Gibson family has been in contact with me. As have Renee Sabato and Jace Andrews."

Ah. I had a lightbulb moment. This was priceless. "They don't want their perversions aired in public?"

He shrugged. "You are, of course, free to speak to anyone you wish. I'm sure the press has been hounding you."

"A little." What the annoying reporters didn't know was

that with my mother as a, well, mother, I could dodge unwanted calls without working up a sweat.

"However, if you were to return to your job, the Canon
of Ethics would prevent you from discussing our clients with
the press."

Brilliant tactical maneuver. Really brilliant. "So, I get my
job back and you get several new high-profile clients?"

He nodded. "They all indicated they'd be open to moving
some of their business to Dane-Lieberman if you were with
the firm. In light of that, I've decided the best thing for
everyone would be for you to return to work."

No wonder people think lawyers are smarmy. Okay,
maybe not *all* lawyers. Becky was one of the good guys.

"Uh-huh. Sorry, I'm not comfortable with that."

"I don't think I heard you correctly. You're saying you
don't want your job back?"

I gave him a cool look. "I'm saying I don't want my old
job back at my old salary."

There were a few seconds when I thought Vain Dane's
product-immobilized hair would stick straight out while
steam shot from his nostrils. I had him by the balls and he
knew it. This was killing him. Slowly.

The faint stain darkened but his smile never slipped. "How
much?"

I wanted to be greedy, I really did. I considered thirty. But
I was a reasonable woman. "A twenty-five percent raise."

The smile slipped. "Twenty-f—You *just* got a ten percent
raise a few months ago."

"You're right," I said sweetly. The power trip was a hell of
a lot of fun. "It should have been fifteen."

I saw Patrick's car pull into the lot. Good warm-up to bargain with your not-so-ex-boss when your not-so-ex-married
boyfriend is in the vicinity. Hell, now I was on a roll. Line
'em up.

"Ten," Dane countered.

"Fifteen."

"Twelve."

"Sold." I shook his hand and practically shoved him out the door. "Thank you."

"Don't thank me," he said. Negotiations over, deal closed, no more pretense of a smile. "Thank Liam McGarrity. Our new clients approached him first and apparently he wouldn't agree to be discreet unless you got your job back."

I would have celebrated that bit of information if I hadn't been distracted by Patrick. He was carrying a cactus. A prick carrying pricks, hummmmm.

He and Vain Dane exchanged one of those I-vaguely-recollect-you nods. When Patrick was about a foot away from me, I held up one hand. I wanted to slap the fake concern off his face so much my fingers twitched.

"I brought you a present," he said, waggling the cactus.

"From your fabulous camping trip in the Grand Canyon?"

"Yes. Great news about Jane. But how are you?" He tilted his head and made a pathetically pouty face as he surveyed the small bruise on my forehead. "I should have been here for you. What can I do to make you feel better?"

"Throw yourself under a bus?"

"What?"

I grabbed the first bag and tossed it at him. Unprepared and still gripping his cactus, Patrick didn't react fast enough, so the bag hit him squarely in the chest. Air whooshed out of his lungs. "Fin? What the hell is wrong with you? What's all this stuff?"

I had the second bag at the ready. "Things you've given me over the last twenty-six months and eleven days. Things you said you picked up on your faux flights. Things like that stupid flipping cactus." I hefted the other bag at him.

"I'm confused."

"Well, I'm not." I stepped back, stared him in the eyes, and said, "No, Patrick, you're not confused, you're married."

I slammed the door so hard I could hear the glasses rattling in the cabinets.

"Fin?" he called through the door. "It isn't what you think."

"I think I know your wife's phone number!" I called back. "Go away or I'll call her and see if she wants a freaking cactus!"

I should have felt something. Remorse, grief, anger, guilt . . . something. Two hours had passed since I'd tossed Patrick and his gifts out of my life. Well, not all his gifts. I kept the good stuff. I'd been wronged, not lobotomized.

I was restless. I'd already called Becky, Jane, and Liv. Sam must have had his ear to the floor since he came down to congratulate me the minute Patrick had driven off into . . . wherever cheating husbands drive. I flipped through the television but nothing held my interest. Nothing on any of the movie channels either.

I could go to the grocery store. Grabbing my purse and the ugly green, rubbery key chain off the counter, I headed outside. The sun was setting, so the heat was no longer oppressive. A small breeze rustled the palm fronds, not enough to keep the mosquitoes from buzzing around my head.

I needed food.

I wanted Liam.

I turned right and headed east toward the ocean. The grocery store was to the west.

Liam and I had been nearly killed together, so it made perfect sense for me to want to be with him. Plus, I did owe him for getting me my job back.

I strained to read the street signs. Though I'd never been to Liam's house, I knew his address from the invoices he'd sent. I'd memorized it. That, in and of itself, said it all. Who was I kidding? This wasn't about bonding or thank-yous or anything other than pure, unadulterated lust. But, I justified as I eased off the gas while I tried to read the numbers printed on the mailboxes, we were consenting adults. We could have sex; I'd get it out of my system. Take a vow of celibacy for at least a year, then start looking for a guy who wouldn't play me like a cheap banjo.

I found the house. Okay, "house" was generous. "Shack" was probably a better description. What it lacked in ambience, it more than made up for in location. Liam's modest home sat right on the beach. And several lights were on. And the Mustang was in the driveway. Only the Mustang. So, unless Ashley biked it around town, he was in there. Alone.

I cut the engine and took a deep breath. Maybe this wasn't a good—too late! The front door opened. So did my mouth.

Liam stood there, shirtless. Tanned skin, rippling muscles, great hair. A heady combination.

I opened the car door and smiled at him. "Hi."

"Get lost in the dark?"

"I came to thank you." *So take your pants off.*

Stop it! Now.

"Really?"

"Yes. Thanks for getting me my job back."

He shrugged. Not that I really noticed. I was a little busy admiring the soft, dark hair on his chest. It tapered into a V, then disappeared into the waistband of his jeans. It was like a big directional arrow pointing the way to the fun house.

"Finley?"

"Sorry. You were saying?"

"Paolo's bruise?"

Paolo who? Oh, right. "Yes?"

"The rectangular one on his temple that Trena told us about?"

I nodded, afraid if I opened my mouth drool might dribble down my chin.

"It matched Kresley's engagement ring."

"Good to know."

"Want a beer?"

Among other things. "Sure."

The inside of his house was . . . interesting. "Work in progress?" I asked as I followed him past the saw table in the living room.

"Renovating," he said.

When he turned and reached into the fridge, I had to swallow the groan in my throat. That bronzed skin and those broad shoulders were impressive.

Liam twisted the tops off, tossing the caps into a garbage can off in the corner. When he handed me the bottle, our eyes locked briefly as his fingertips brushed against mine.

My pulse was pounding and a liquid desire was spreading to every cell of my body.

Tipping the longneck bottle, Liam never took his eyes off me. Then he put the bottle on the counter. "Why'd you really come here?"

Afraid my hands might tremble, I laced my fingers around the cold bottle. "To thank you."

He smiled, but not in a good way. "You did that outside."

"You invited me in."

"My mistake."

The words hit me like a slap. "What?"

He took the untouched beer away from me. "Go home."

"That's pretty rude."

Liam bracketed his hands on the counter behind him and practically cut me in two with his eyes. "No, Finley. It's honest."

This wasn't working out at all like I'd imagined. "You don't want company? Fine. I'm leaving."

Liam came up behind me, caught me around the waist, and pulled me against him. Using his free hand, he lifted my hair off my neck and placed hot, quick kisses from my shoulder to my earlobe. Then softly, his breath warm against my ear, he said, "Go. Home."

He let go and I turned, confused and addled by the rush of desire coursing though my system. "Did I miss something?"

"Yeah. A big something."

"Is it a secret or are you going to tell me?"

He breathed deeply, then exhaled slowly. "I don't do this."

"You don't do sex?"

His lips curved into a lazy, easy smile. "I'm fine with sex. But . . ." He paused, hooking his thumbs in the back pockets of his jeans. "I'm not the guy you screw 'cause you just got screwed over."

"I did not—"

He placed his finger to my lips. "Don't lie. You really suck at lying. Go home."

"Gladly." I moved as quickly as I could. In the dark. In three-inch heels. Over uneven terrain, trailing my dignity behind me.

"Finley?"

I refused to look at him. Instead, I jammed the key in the ignition and ground the engine to life. "What?"

"Do this again, and I will be that guy."

"You don't need to worry about that. I will never come back here." I heard him chuckle as I jerked the car into reverse.

"Wanna bet?" he taunted.

"No!" I called as I backed up. Hell no, I didn't want to bet. Not when I knew I'd lose.

*You're never out of money until your
credit cards are maxed out.*

One

If I could find a way to deep-fry chocolate, my life would be whole.

Or at least that's what I told myself as I parked my BMW in its regular spot in front of the law offices of Dane, Lieberman and Zarnowski. I often muse about food when I'm in a funk.

It was a beautiful, sunny April morning, making it really hard for me to get excited about going to work. Okay, so I rarely got excited about going to work regardless of the weather. Then again, who does? I grabbed my adorable new Chanel bag, and with a quick, surreptitious glance, checked to be sure I was holding the pale pink bowling bag correctly. I was, and tugged it onto my shoulder.

It would be freaking embarrassing if my coworkers noticed the big black smear of God-only-knew-what on the lambskin leather. The smear would out me. I'd bought the damaged purse at the outlet in Vero Beach. I would take my secret vice to my grave.

No one would ever know that I, Finley Anderson Tanner,

am a . . . *discount shopper.* And my other really huge fashion secret—I'm a tribute to Slightly Irregular. My wardrobe is a collection of the unloved cast-offs from the factory and/or the snagged and stained seconds discarded by the trendy stores, then sold at deep discounts. Thanks to the smudge, my new purse was marked down low enough to fit in my budget.

Well, that wasn't *exactly* true. I didn't have a budget so much as a propensity to carry just enough credit-card debt to force me to acknowledge that I have little if any shopping self-restraint.

Well, not just shopping. My excesses seem to be limitless, guided only by my overwhelming desire to have it *now.* *It* can be anything. Anything I can pay for in installments, that is. My favorite word is *preapproved.* I especially like it when it's stamped across a solicitation for yet another credit card.

So, that's how I morphed into a twenty-nine-year-old woman who doesn't technically own anything. My apartment is rented, my car is leased, and if we still had debtors' prisons, I'd be serving life without parole.

Which is the reason I'm dragging myself into work when I'd far prefer to be headed for the beach on this spectacular South Florida Monday. I'd much rather be lying in the sun, listening to tunes on my almost paid-off iPod, wearing my five-percent-down, custom-made, barely there, body-hugging bikini and matching sarong, ignoring all the warnings about the dangers of sun exposure in favor of a bronze, blonde-complexion-flattering tan. Debt sucks.

Especially for a person like me, who—of my own volition—has gone from moderate riches to heavily financed rags. The only high point of my week thus far has been finding a great deal on a solid screw-down crown on eBay for my build-it-from-parts Rolex project. Hey, everybody's gotta have a hobby. Over the past year, I've acquired the pink mother-of-pearl face and a sapphire crystal. I figure by the time I'm thirty-five, I should have enough parts to assemble the watch of my dreams.

For today, I'm dependent on my really cute Kuber to let me know that I'm more than twenty minutes late.

Stepping into the ornate lobby of the firm made my watch irrelevant. I was instantly given the evil smirk by Margaret Ford. As always, the fifty-five-year-old receptionist was stationed behind the crescent-shaped desk, pen poised, Bluetooth tucked into her right ear.

Margaret's crooked and overly thinned brows arched disapprovingly. "Nice to see you, Finley."

Liar, liar, pants on fire. I knew Margaret was the source of the unflattering nickname bestowed on me at the firm. It wasn't all that original, either. I think I was in elementary school the first time someone put my initials together and called me Fat. The only difference between then and now was that in elementary school, the kids called me Fat to my face. The receptionist and her pudgy posse didn't have that kind of nerve. I greeted her politely, then asked, "Any messages?"

She shuffled through the neat stack of pink notes, looking completely put out by my very reasonable request. Then again, Margaret always looked put out whenever she was forced to deal with me. With a less than subtle "*Humph*," she passed four messages and a thin folder across the polished mahogany desk. "Mr. Dane left this for you to review. The client will be here in"—she paused for effect—"twenty minutes."

Twenty minutes? Damn. Barely enough time for a decent couple of cups of coffee. Still, I smiled, thanked her, and collected the stuff before heading toward the elevator.

The Estates and Trusts Department of the firm occupied the entire second floor of a six-story building in West Palm Beach. Several secretaries—oops—administrative assistants were arranged in a cluster around various fax machines, laser printers, networked computers, and incessantly ringing telephones. None of them so much as looked up when I passed, exiting to the right and heading down the corridor toward my office.

Thanks to one of those plug-in things, my space smelled faintly of mango. I went about my usual morning ritual—flipping the light switch, opening the blinds to my stunning view of the parking lot below, turning on my coffeepot, then jiggling the cordless mouse to awaken my hibernating laptop.

I slipped my purse into the desk drawer and reached for the telephone. Maudlin Margaret took messages only from people who were too impatient or too incompetent to leave a voice mail.

"You've reached the desk of Finley Tanner. Today is Monday, April second. I'm in the office but unable to take your call right now. Please leave a message, and I'll get back to you as soon as possible. If you need immediate assistance, please press zero for the receptionist."

I checked my voice mailbox and scribbled the gist of the message from the court clerk regarding the D'Auria estate.

Being far too impatient to wait for the coffeemaker to finish, I filled my mug with coffee sludge before turning my attention to the file I'd brought up from Reception.

It was unusual for Victor Dane to assign a case to me. He was a civil trial attorney and I was an E&T paralegal, so rarely—thank God—did our paths cross. Victor is a total asshole. Worse even, an asshole with money, dyed hair, and a passion for man-toys. His latest toy is a black Hummer. *A freaking Hummer!* I shook my head at the thought. Who needs a Hummer in the flattest state in the country? The same guy who has his nails buffed and his teeth bleached at regular intervals, I suppose.

So, thanks to Vain Dane, I opened a new document on my computer and began entering the data before Stacy Evans arrived. I had gotten as far as the basic information off the death certificate before my intercom buzzed.

"Yes?"

"Mrs. Evans is here. Should I send her in?"

"Yes, thanks."

I stood and went toward the door to greet the grieving widow. It was something I'd grown pretty good at during the past seven years. Florida had a goodly amount of grieving widows, most of whom fell into two general categories. Real widows were normally over sixty and devastated by their loss. Faux widows ranged in age from mid-twenties to early forties and had dollar signs embossed on their pupils.

One look at Stacy Evans told me she was a real widow. Her slender shoulders were hunched forward, and her sunken green eyes were red and puffy. She looked frail and fragile.

After showing her into my office, I discreetly moved a box of tissues to within her reach. "I'm Finley," I began, bracing myself for the possibility of a crying jag. "I'm very sorry for your loss."

"Thank you," she responded in a flat voice. She clutched a large leather tote to her chest. Two thick manila folders peeked out from the bag.

"Would you like some coffee? Tea? Water?"

She shook her head. Mrs. Evans was a golfer. She had the brown, leathery skin, a no-frills haircut, and wore those horrible little socks with tiny golf tees rimming the ankles.

I'm going to hell. Here this woman was in the throes of despair and I'm ragging on her socks.

I pointed at the files she held, prompting, "Mr. Dane asked you to bring along your late husband's will?"

I took a sip of Kona macadamia nut coffee while she eased the folders from her tote. She placed them on my desk but seemed reluctant to completely surrender them to me. Instead, she placed her palms on top of them and met my eyes. "My husband didn't die."

I almost choked on my own spit. I had a copy of his death certificate. Marcus Evans was very dead. So dead, in fact, that he'd been cremated. Now I understood why Vain Dane had passed this woman off to me instead of meeting her himself. Weenie.

"Mrs. Evans," I said, donning my most compassionate expression, "perhaps you'd be more comfortable if we put this meeting off for a little while. There's no hurry, and it sounds as if you need—"

"He was murdered," she injected, her face suddenly animated. "Marc would never fall asleep behind the wheel of a car. And he most certainly wouldn't do it at nine in the morning."

"Accidents happen," I suggested gently. Bad idea. The woman across from me suddenly looked seriously pissed.

"Young lady," she began, her colorless lips pulled taut, "do not dismiss me. I may be old, but I'm not senile." She took in a deep breath and let it out slowly. "I tried to tell Victor my husband was murdered during our telephone conversation."

Victor? *Oh, crap.* It would have been nice for Vain Dane to tell me the woman was a personal friend. Time to backpedal. "Mrs. Evans, I'm sorry if I've upset you."

"My husband's murder upset me," she fired back. "You are just annoying me."

"I'm truly sorry." I sat back against my vented leather chair, folding my hands around my now tepid coffee mug as I bought some time. "Why don't we start from the beginning?"

"Marcus was murdered." She took a sheet of paper, neatly typed on both sides, from one of the files and slipped it across my desk, then remained as still as a statue while I scanned it. The official accident report. If there was something wrong, it sure as hell wasn't jumping off the page at me. I figured maybe I was just having a prolonged blonde moment, so I read it again. That seemed to please Mrs. Evans.

At nine-o-five on the morning of March twenty-seventh, Marcus Evans had driven his Cadillac off I-95, down an embankment, and landed—roof down—in a canal just south of

Jupiter. The official mechanism of death was drowning. The manner of death was accident.

Mrs. Evans wasn't senile so much as she was just plain wrong. Or maybe psycho? All I knew for sure was Vain Dane had handed her off to me. Which was just the kind of thing I should have expected.

"Have you spoken to the police?" I asked with due seriousness—due, that is, to my boss being a chickenshit, cowardly asshole for palming his psycho friend off onto me instead of handling it himself.

Eyes narrowed, Mrs. Evans pursed her lips. Apparently I wasn't the first person to ask. "They dismissed me." Waving one hand—the one sporting a five-carat, emerald-cut diamond—she deposited her bag in the second chair and leaned closer to me. "It had to be murder," she said, speaking in a conspiratorial tone.

In the library? With a wrench? By Professor Plum? "Was the car examined for mechanical defects?" *Have you been examined for psychological defects?*

Which wasn't really fair, I had to admit. The woman was *grieving.* I got that. But couldn't she have worked through that before coming to see me? It was hard trying to have a rational conversation with someone who wasn't in the here and now. I felt bad for her, but, really, she should be telling this story to the police— Oh yeah. They didn't believe her, either.

It took everything in me not to sigh. I folded my hands on my desk and gave her my I-am-hanging-on-your-every-word look that I'd perfected over the years. I was pretty good at it. I'd used it frequently during bad dates.

"Not by the police," she said flatly. "Something about the witness statements supporting their theory that it was an accident, and they claim that no further investigation is warranted. I had his car towed to Palm Beach Motor Specialists on Okeechobee Boulevard," she explained. "I need you to arrange for an expert to inspect it. Again. Marc took care of his car. Never missed a single service appointment. Someone tampered with something, maybe the brake lines. I don't know what, specifically, but something must have been done to the car, and I fully expect you to get to the bottom of it."

Stacy smoothed her hand over her functional yet expertly coiffed pale brown hair while I tried to think of the best course of action.

I read the determination in the set of her jaw that was mirrored in her narrowed eyes. I also reminded myself that she was a personal friend of the senior partner. Which meant my first priority was to appease the client. It didn't matter that my investigatory skills were pretty much limited to researching clear title to effect a transfer of real property. For two hundred dollars an hour, if she wanted me to do a Nancy Drew, so be it.

"I should make copies of what you have," I told her, watching the tension drain from her shoulders as I spoke. I pulled a retainer agreement from my desk drawer and passed it to her. I recited the high points of the agreement by rote. "This case may necessitate the hiring of a private investigator as an independent contractor," I explained, "any of those charges are considered separate from and not included in the hourly rates charged by Dane, Lieberman and Zarnowski."

"What about you?" she asked pointedly.

"Excuse me?"

"Well, why was I relegated to a paralegal? Shouldn't a real lawyer be handling a murder case?"

Yes, I thought, *a murder case would be handled by an attorney. The paranoid delusions of a grieving widow are, however, my cross to bear.* "I work under the direct supervision of an attorney," I told her as I started affixing "sign here" flags to the signature lines on several forms with a little more pressure than necessary. "Mr. Dane is and will continue to be personally involved."

"That's acceptable, then," she said after a brief pause. "I

expect regular updates on your progress. I'm taking my husband's ashes up to New Jersey this afternoon for the memorial service." She pulled another neatly typed sheet of paper from her tote. "These are all my contact numbers with the dates and times most convenient for you to reach me."

Paranoid, grief-stricken, and anal. Great combination.

"Do you have a cell phone or a pager?"

I was a little surprised. No one had ever asked me for that information. "I have voice mail," I offered. "I check my messages regularly—"

"I prefer a direct number," Mrs. Evans said in a way that pretty much said it wasn't so much a preference as a requirement.

Grabbing one of my business cards, I hated myself as I scribbled my cell number on the back. Something told me giving Stacy Evans unrestricted access to my life was something I would definitely live to regret.

By lunchtime that prophetic thought was fact. Stacy had called no fewer than three times. Once on the office line and twice on my cell. Now, as I walked slowly down Clematis Street, on my way to meet my friends Becky, Jane, and Olivia, my purse was vibrating incessantly. I checked the incoming number, recognized it as Stacy's, and refused to answer. She might be a close, personal friend of Vain Dane, but I wasn't her indentured servant. At least not between twelve-thirty and two. Which was my definition of the forty-five-minute lunch hour.

The best part about being a estates and trusts paralegal was the relative freedom. No one ever questioned my absences from the office, so long as I grabbed a few folders and mumbled something about filing things with a court clerk. No one seemed to notice that my "meetings" were almost always linked to mealtimes. Or if they did, they didn't say anything, which suited me just fine.

Downtown West Palm Beach was crowded, but that was about to change. Locals claim there are two seasons in Florida, summer and snowbird. Summer lasts from February through the first week of November. Snowbird season lasts roughly from Thanksgiving through Easter, defined mostly by caravans of RVs clogging I-95 as their occupants flee winter in search of a milder climate to wait out the snow melt.

For year-round residents like me, it means parking lots filled beyond capacity, long grocery-store lines, and forget trying to get a prescription filled. The pharmacy is apparently some sort of Mecca for the sixty-five-and-older crowd. Easter is late this year—two additional weeks of "Season" before they head back to their homes and families.

A horn blared, startling me. I ducked to avoid a low palm frond as I maneuvered past a white-haired woman and her walker. I know I should feel compassion. Respect my elders, yada, yada, yada. But, in my defense, whoever made those rules was never cut off on the highway by a ninety-year-old whose reflexes no longer included a glance in the rearview mirror before a lazy lane drift.

I allowed myself a subtle vanity check as I neared the corner at North Olive Street. Sushi Rok was a trendy, relatively new Asian/Japanese seafood place that catered to the business crowd. It was a good choice for lunch, since the tourists tended to avoid this place in favor of the more casual spots that welcomed shorts, T-shirts, and scrunchies.

Okay, I had to admit, while I loathed every second I spent in my gym, the results made it all worthwhile. Especially now that I was entering the danger zone, when my body started acting like a cereal-box disclaimer: some settling may occur during shipment.

Spring meant one thing to me—Lilly Pulitzer. I'd paired my seventy-percent-off-because-of-a-lipstick-smudge hibiscus pink cardigan tied around my shoulders with a—gulp—full-price patchwork dress in her signature citrus colors. Since the cotton spandex dress was both form-fitting and left my arms bare, I did have to give a little mental nod to my stump-necked personal trainer, Neal, who pushed me mercilessly. While I was giving silent praise, I also thought of my wonderful dry cleaner, who managed to turn the smudge into little more than a faint ghost near the jeweled neckline of the worsted cashmere sweater.

The ensemble, paired with my new purse and strappy sandals, was, I decided, really, really flattering. Lilly *is* the blond woman's best friend.

The restaurant was fairly crowded. A low buzz of overlapping conversation was punctuated by the clinking of glasses and tableware. Shoving my sunglasses up on my head, I scanned the tables for my friends. It took just a second for me to spot Olivia, casually waving her hand.

I weaved toward the table, checking out the men in the room on single-woman autopilot. Well, I wasn't completely single. And the pilot in my life is actually Patrick. Thinking of him should have made me happy, giddy . . . something. Something more than *comfortable*.

I sighed heavily as I joined Olivia and Becky. "Jane's late?" It was a rhetorical question. Jane was always late. Jane would die late. Olivia was on her BlackBerry, so I directed my greeting to Becky.

Becky sipped on peach iced tea. Her dark brown eyes were hidden behind orange-tinted glasses. Rebecca Jameson and I have been friends since college. She's a junior associate at the firm, a contracts specialist working under the watchful eyes of Ellen Lieberman, only female partner and all-around über-bitch.

I'm the one who convinced Becky to apply after she graduated with honors from Emory Law School. I'm also the one who suggested she focus on some area of the law other than contracts. Becky didn't heed my advice, which, it turns out, worked in her favor. For some unknown reason, Becky and Ellen actually work well together. As well as anyone can work with Ellen, who, incidentally, believes the road to success requires draining all estrogen from her being. Ellen Lieberman is all drab suits, Birkenstocks, and gray roots.

Becky was dressed in taupe slacks and a cotton blouse in her favorite shade of orangey red. "Nice top," I complimented.

"Thanks," she replied, twisting her long hair into a knot as the midday sun streamed in from the window at her back. "Coffee's on the way."

I smiled, grateful that my friends loved me enough to anticipate my continual need for caffeine.

Turning my attention to Olivia, who was slipping her latest and most favorite electronic toy into her purse, I said hello, then asked, "How is Garage Boy?"

Olivia's perfect mouth turned down at the corners. "He is not a boy."

"He lives in his parent's garage," I pointed out. "He's thirty-six. He doesn't have a job. He's—"

"An asshole," Becky finished unapologetically. "Geez, Liv, cut him loose and find a real man."

"Like you?" Olivia returned smoothly. "Your last date was when? Your high school prom?"

Becky smiled, since we all knew the assessment wasn't all that far off. "I'm building a career. There'll be plenty of time to find Mr. Right later."

"Later, huh?" Liv asked. "Like when you're alone in your apartment, about to hit fifty, watching reruns of *The Gilmore Girls,* while you devour an entire box of Moon Pies and are surrounded by sixteen cats?"

"Do not mock the Moon Pie," Becky cautioned as she glanced around the restaurant. "It's my comfort food."

"Ladies?" I interjected, knowing full well the constant barbs could go on indefinitely. Becky and Liv enjoyed teasing each other. Probably because they were polar opposites.

"That was an e-mail from Jane," Liv said. "She can't get away."

Becky and I both gave little groans, then immediately grabbed our menus. I was vacillating between the yellowfin tuna special and California rolls when the waiter arrived with my coffee.

"We're still waiting for the fourth?" he inquired. Predictably, he spoke predominantly to Olivia. It used to bother me, her getting all the male attention. Now I understand they can't help it. Olivia is just *that* pretty. Exceptionally pretty. She has exotic coloring and flawless features. At first glance, most people think her violet eyes are fake—those horrid contact lenses created in hues not known in nature. They're real, as are her high cheekbones, bowed lips, tapered neck, ample boobs, small waist— Hell, her whole five-seven, size-two body is just a thing to be envied.

"Actually, it will just be the three of us," Liv supplied. She batted her lashes. Flirting was as natural to her as breathing. "Could we have a few minutes?"

"Certainly, ladies," the waiter said. "I'll run and get you another cucumber water while you decide."

He was attractive enough to warrant my glancing over the top edge of my menu to assess his butt. "Too skinny," I murmured.

"Too short," Liv added.

"I'd do him," Becky announced.

"You've been celibate too long," I said with a sigh. "You'd do anyone." I looked up at my tablemates. "Thanks to your recent color change, Becky, we now look like we belong on *Petticoat Junction*."

Becky twirled a lock of her recently tinted red hair. "I'm Betty Jo. Wasn't she the red-haired one that ended up with the cute crop duster? Speaking of pilots, how is Patrick?"

I shrugged. "Fine. He's due back late tonight." Again I hated it that thinking about him did little to inspire my fantasies. On paper, he was *the* guy. The *one*. The man of my dreams. He was thirty-four, moderately tall, blond, blue-eyed, and a pilot. Perfect, right? His income potential is on target; he's intelligent, funny, and athletic; we like a lot of the same things—the beach, movies, restaurants, etc. Genetically, he's the ideal person to father my children. There's just no . . . magic.

I long ago abandoned fairy-tale *special,* but I'd like it a lot more if I felt my heart flutter when I opened the door. Or, the alternative, toe-curling sex. The sex was okay. Patrick was considerate enough to be . . . methodical. Methodical was satisfying, but it didn't exactly inspire passion. When I'm with Patrick, all the foreplay is accomplished in a determined, specific order. It's like sex has a preflight checklist that he has to complete before he can achieve lift-off.

I frowned and laid my menu on the table to await the return of the server.

Liv reached over and patted my hand. Twin chunky bracelets clunked against the tabletop. "Still no fireworks?"

I shook my head. "Not even a spark."

"It won't get any better," Becky commented. "In my experience, bad sex is not like good wine. It doesn't improve with time."

"When was the last time you had sex?" Liv asked. "Bad or otherwise?"

"I'm trying to remember," Becky drawled. "Let's see, it was on a sofa after my boyfriend's parents went to sleep. No, wait! That was *you.*"

"Tease me all you want, Betty Jo," Liv responded. "At least I'm not wedded to my work."

"Weddings *are* your work," I inserted. "Speaking of which, any good bridezilla stories to share?"

Liv is a much sought after wedding planner, with clients on both sides of the bridge.

I should explain that "the bridge" is the section of Okeechobee Road that crosses the Intracoastal Waterway, separating West Palm Beach from the super-rich, invitation-only world of Palm Beach. Old money, like the Posts, the Flaglers, and the Kennedys, mix reluctantly with the new-money residents.

New money is something of a misnomer, since nothing much in Florida predates 1924. Nothing but the family fortunes used to build some of the most incredible oceanfront mansions on the East Coast. Along with offering primo golf and deepwater slips for personal yachts, Palm Beach is an event haven.

Liv and her partner, Jean-Claude DuBois, had turned Concierge Plus from kid's party planners into *the* premiere wedding coordinators in the area. Now they were branching out into coordinating other things, like some of the elaborate balls that raised funds for a diverse list of charities.

Still, the wedding mishaps were my personal favorites. Probably because I derived some sort of childish, perverse comfort knowing that if I wasn't happily walking down an aisle, no one else was, either. Which makes no sense whatsoever, since I really don't have any burning desire to embrace hearth and home. Not yet.

Lunch was pretty uneventful. Good food, casual chit-chat, and a lot of laughs. I prepared to leave feeling recharged, ready to tackle the remainder of my day.

Becky and I waited with Liv until the valet brought her champagne-colored Mercedes convertible around to the front of the restaurant. Unlike me, Liv was making really great money, but, like me, she spent freely.

Becky was probably earning three times my salary, but her only vice was clothing, so she had more money in the bank than any of us.

As soon as Liv pulled away from the curb, Becky turned and said, "I heard Victor sent a case your way this morning."

"Yeah." I recounted my strange meeting to Becky before scrolling through the messages on my cell phone. Stacy Evans had called two more times during lunch. I glanced at the time on the screen. According to the schedule she'd given me, she was just about to board a plane for Newark. With any luck, she'd land a few minutes after I was done for the day.

"What does she expect you to do?"

More Mischief, Murder
& Mayhem in These
Kensington Mysteries